GRIPPED
part 4

GRIPPED PART 4
SMOKE & MIRRORS

Written by Stacy A. Padula
Edited by Elizabeth Harvey

Briley & Baxter Publications | Plymouth, Massachusetts

ISBN: 978-1735016825

Book Design: Amy Deyerle-Smith

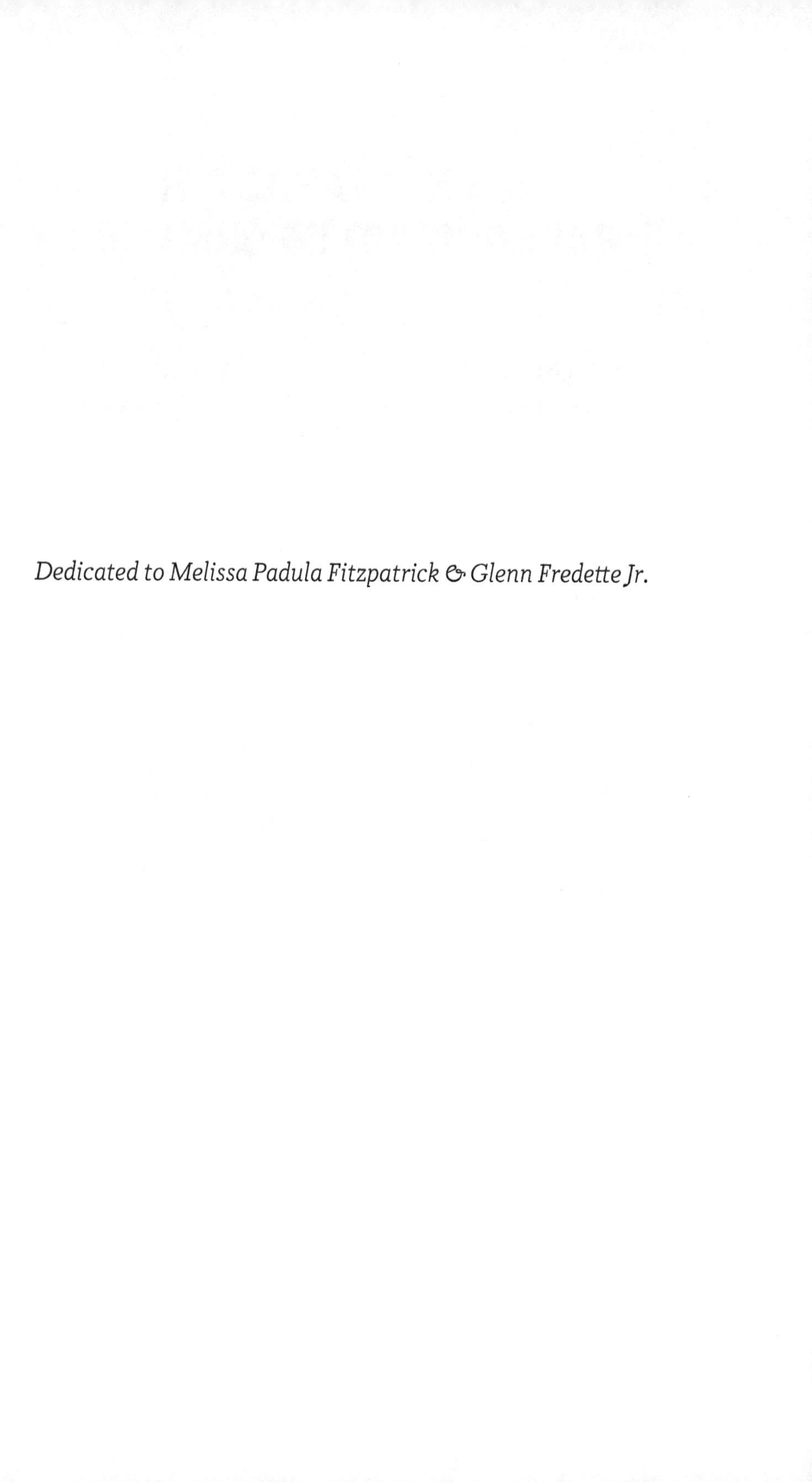

Dedicated to Melissa Padula Fitzpatrick & Glenn Fredette Jr.

MAIN CHARACTER BACKGROUND INFORMATION

Taylor Dunkin

Taylor was the quarterback for Northeastern University and ranked by ESPN as an NFL Top Prospect until he tore his ACL, MCL, and both menisci during a football game in September 2016. Taylor underwent two surgeries and fell into a deep depression, blaming himself for Northeastern's losing season. Taylor has been battling a painkiller addiction since his second surgery.

Marc Dunkin

Marc is Taylor's youngest brother and a senior at Montgomery Lake High School. He is committed to attend Boston College in the fall of 2018. In November of 2017, he found out that Taylor was selling drugs to Luke Davids—Marc's best friend—and that Luke was giving drugs to kids from their hometown. Marc has since set off to reverse the damage caused by Luke and Taylor.

Jordan Dunkin

Jordan is the middle Dunkin brother. He is a college sophomore, who plays football for the University of Notre Dame. Jordan was known for taking nothing seriously in high school; however, he has matured a lot in college. Marc and Jordan had a falling out during Jordan's senior year of high school over a girl they both liked—Michelle Taylor. Marc erroneously believes Jordan tried to date rape Michelle.

Chris Dunkin

Chris is the younger cousin of Marc, Jordan, and Taylor. He is a freshman at Montgomery Lake High School. His parents travel frequently for their business based in London, so Chris has grown up being very close with his older cousins, who frequently babysit him. Chris began partying at a very young age and experimented with many different drugs. After hitting his rock-bottom in April of 2017, he became a spiritual person and got sober a few months later.

Jason Davids

Jason was Chris's best friend for ten years until Chris got sober. Jason, like Chris, is a freshman at Montgomery Lake High. He is well known for his wit, humor, and charisma. He was in a long-term relationship with Cathy Kagelli until November of 2017. Jason has developed an addiction to Adderall, which he is prescribed, and a penchant for offsetting it with other pills and marijuana. His brother Luke has been supplying him with drugs since eighth grade.

Cathy Kagelli

Cathy is a freshman at Montgomery Lake High School, known for her beauty and intelligence. She dated Jason Davids until November of 2017 and has been seeing Marc Dunkin since December of 2017. Cathy has struggled with anxiety and depression since she and her identical twin sister, Chantal, had a falling out in 2016.

Chantal Kagelli

Chantal is Cathy's identical twin, also a freshman at Montgomery Lake High School. She is a kind hearted, devout Christian, known for her optimism. For a year and a half, she erroneously believed that Cathy pretended to be her and broke up with her middle-school boyfriend, Jon Anderson. She just found out that the breakup was a huge misunderstanding on Jon's part and that Cathy never backstabbed her.

PREFACE

To Readers Across America:

Each day, more and more young adults fall prey to substance abuse. As an educator who works mainly with high school students, I was moved to write a book series for teenagers that shares how it happens—how good kids become drug addicts, how downward spirals start, how harmless fun can quickly turn into a life-threatening addiction.

The story told in the series is raw and realistic. I did not censor much of the content, for I believe the truth is important and powerful. In our world in which twelve-year-old kids overdose in middle school bathrooms, it is time for authors to stop sugarcoating their content to appease schoolboards. I am aware that this book may be banned by public schools because of the harsh realities portrayed between its covers. However, I did not write any part of the *Gripped* book series in hopes of it being taught in English classrooms. The truth is far too controversial for that, even though the events depicted in *Gripped* happen daily across America.

The series portrays the story of Taylor Dunkin who was an acclaimed college athlete, seemingly destined for the NFL but sidelined by injury. His depression leads him to begin abusing his pain medication and eventually become a drug dealer to support his habit. He supplies drugs to high school students from his hometown, which leads to other characters becoming ensnared. The story shows how drug abuse can skew individuals' values and change their perspectives. It follows other characters such as Luke Davids, Cathy Kagelli, Chris Dunkin, and Jason Davids (also featured in my *Montgomery Lake High* book series) whose lives have been affected by Taylor's decisions. It shows the psychological, biological, and environmental reasons behind why people often begin experimenting with drugs and how slippery the slope can be. Most importantly, this book series educates readers on how people can pick up the pieces of their lives and recover from such a horrific epidemic.

I have written five other young adult novels that address teenage social issues. They comprise the *Montgomery Lake High* book series. Over the past eleven years, the books have frequently been on the Amazon top 100 best seller list for young adult books that address substance abuse. In the fall of 2017, four of the books were top 10 best sellers within the category. Considering the sharp rise in prescription drug overdoses and opiate abuse, I feel that the *Gripped* book series is needed now more than ever. Please join me in helping to protect the youth from opiate and benzodiazepine abuse by recommending Gripped to a teenager you know.

Sincerely,
Stacy A. Padula

SCENES FROM GRIPPED PART 3

March of 2018

UPSTAIRS IN TAYLOR'S BEDROOM, Marc handed his brother the black cell phone Detective Roth had given him. "What's this?" Taylor asked in confusion.

"At BC, I had the privilege of meeting Detective Roth of the BPD. He's a BC grad."

Taylor's throat instantly went dry.

"Evidently, they're investigating our family," Marc added.

"What?" Taylor asked, feeling immediately sick to his stomach.

"They think you're in danger," Marc replied and locked his eyes on Taylor. "He said they know you're clean and that you want 'out of the game.' They want to work out a deal with you to help you break away from your supplier."

Taylor widened his eyes. "What do you mean 'a deal'?"

Marc shrugged. "He said the less I know, the better, so I didn't ask many questions. The lead detective's number is in that phone. Detective Roth said you're likely being watched, so you can't use it in public or for any other calls. The point of my meeting today was to give me that phone so you could open a line of communication with the BPD. I bet they want your testimony."

"Donny would have me killed," Taylor said and shook his head. "I can't rat."

"I'm sure the cops have a plan."

"My supplier is connected to some *really* nasty people," Taylor stated with emphasis. "They wouldn't stop with me. If I ever ratted, they could come after you and Jordan, Mom and Dad. I'm stuck in this."

Marc's eyes widened. "So, that's why BC is cooperating with them," he muttered.

"The cops wouldn't discuss the details of the case with your coaches," Taylor assured him, "but if I were to stop selling drugs or to rat on my guy, you could be in danger."

"So, you still sell drugs?"

"I have to," Taylor replied honestly. "I got involved with the wrong people. I made them too much money. They're not going to let me off the hook unless I recruit someone else. I can't do that. I can't drag anyone else into this pitiful lifestyle."

"So, what's your plan?" Marc questioned him. "To sell drugs for the rest of your life?"

"I don't have a plan. I'm just praying for a miracle right now," Taylor admitted. "I know no way out of this."

"Well, maybe my meeting was an answer to your prayers," Marc said. "You should at least call and hear the guy out."

"I should get a lawyer," Taylor reasoned. "I don't want to say anything to incriminate myself."

"Wouldn't meeting with a lawyer look suspicious if you're being followed?"

Taylor let out a heavy breath and rested his head in his hands. "I should go home and talk to Dad. He'll know what to do. He has friends who are lawyers. Maybe one of them can meet me at our house."

"I never thought in a million years you would put our family in danger," Marc stated with a look of disbelief. "You were the favorite child, the perfect athlete, the straight-A student, the pinnacle of success. I cannot comprehend how a *pill* stole all that from you."

Taylor closed his eyes and let out a deep breath. "You and me, both," he said after opening his eyes. "It really is true what they say. You think that it will never happen to you, that you're just experimenting, and that you are strong enough to work and play hard. I had too much confidence in myself—false confidence, obviously. Everyone had built me up so much that I believed I was invincible. I had no idea what I was capable of doing. When you stormed out of my apartment months ago, I got a glimpse at who I had become. I thought I was a leader, but I was wrong. I no longer knew how to make Dad proud, and I couldn't stand it. Without football, I had no idea who

I was, and instead of trying to find myself, I copped out and got high."

"When did you stop?" Marc asked.

"I haven't had an opiate in my system since the last time I saw you."

"When you snorted Xanax and Percocet to sleep?"

Taylor nodded.

"You scared me that day. I thought you had snorted heroin."

Taylor winced. "I've never touched heroin."

Marc let out a sigh of relief. "That day, you said you ran out of OCs, but I saw that you had a bunch of Percocet left. It's basically the same thing. What stopped you from snorting it?"

"When I ran out of OCs and started going through withdrawal, I realized I was addicted, and it scared me."

"You didn't know?" Marc asked.

Taylor shook his head. "Dude, drugs mess with your mind. I knew I had screwed up at school and ruined some of my relationships, but I had no idea I was physically dependent on anything."

"So, you stayed clean after I saw you?"

Taylor nodded.

"You suffered through days and days of withdrawal pains without going to rehab?"

"Weeks," Taylor admitted.

"What motivated you to do that?"

"Football and you," Taylor replied without a second thought.

Marc raised his eyebrows and peered at his brother in a perplexed manner. "What did I do?"

"You left."

Marc lowered his eyebrows. "Yeah, probably when you needed your family the most," he muttered.

"You did the right thing," Taylor assured him. "Losing our relationship is what I needed; it motivated me to face my problems."

"Are you still with Julie?" Marc asked.

Taylor shook his head. "She tried to be there for me, but I pushed her away. She didn't know I was dealing, and I felt like a scumbag for hiding it from her."

"That's too bad. Our whole family loves her."

"I do, too. She thought I was just depressed about not playing. She knows the truth now. After we broke up, she found out everything," Taylor explained. "There's no chance for us."

"I've seen drugs ruin a lot of relationships lately."

"Speaking of that... The last time you visited me, you mentioned that Luke was giving Jason pills. Is that still happening?" Taylor asked.

Marc shook his head. "Jay's fine," he replied. "He went through a short-lived phase with some stuff, but Chris helped him realize there was a better way to deal with pain."

Taylor sighed with relief. "Glad to hear. Chris seems to be doing great."

"Chris is doing awesome."

"Okay, I have to ask. What are you doing with Jason's ex-girlfriend?" Taylor questioned him. "She's what? A freshman?"

Marc took a deep breath. "Yeah, but she's old for her grade. She'll be sixteen in July," he replied.

"Marc, you're going off to college in less than six months," Taylor said matter-of-factly. "You're going to enter BC dating a sophomore in high school?"

Marc rolled his eyes. "I'll worry about that when the time comes. We're not boyfriend and girlfriend; we're just seeing each other. Although, I don't usually focus so much of my attention on one girl."

"So why her?"

"We get along great, and she hasn't pressured me to 'commit' to her... Plus, I want to keep her away from Jason because he got her into drugs."

"Is she clean?" Taylor asked.

Marc shrugged. "I honestly don't know."

"You've spent all this time with her, and you can't tell if she does drugs?"

Marc shook his head. "The only thing she's ever done around me is drink, but according to Chris, her drug of choice was Xanax. He said it changed her personality so much that Jason thought she had turned into a narcissist. I don't think he realized it was a side effect of the pills he was giving her."

"Do you feel like you're dating a narcissist?"

"No, but narcissists don't show their ugly side until they have people wrapped around their fingers."

"True."

"She's a hard one to crack," Marc admitted. "After a few months, I still can't tell if she actually likes me or if she just likes having my attention."

"Do you like her? Or are you with her to keep her from getting back together with Jason?"

"Both," Marc replied. "I'm trying to undo the damage Luke caused."

"According to Luke, he and Cathy spend a lot of time together," Taylor remarked. "He could still be giving her drugs. He still buys drugs from me, Marc."

Marc sighed. "I know, but I can't question him about it without admitting I know you're his dealer. I don't want that getting around Montgomery. No one knows Luke gets his stuff from you."

"Chris knows," Taylor retorted. "Other people must know."

Marc shook his head. "None of my friends know you sell to Luke. Very few people even know Luke deals. Matt thinks he just buys coke and molly off someone in Montgomery. Luke's done a good job at keeping things hush-hush."

"Well, that makes me feel a little better," Taylor admitted. "You didn't slander me, even though we were in a fight?"

"What good would that have done?" Marc asked rhetorically.

***

Cathy locked her green eyes on Marc's muscular body as he and Taylor entered the living room. She could not help but wonder what had been said during their private conversation in Taylor's bedroom. The dynamic between the brothers appeared to have improved since they went upstairs. This made Cathy happy, but she feared telling Marc about her previous visit to Taylor's condo with Luke would cause a problem. Nevertheless, for the sake of her own mental health, she had resolved to be honest with Marc. The idea of creating space between Marc and herself by withholding such information turned her stomach. She could not bear the thought of losing him, and this brought the realization that she might actually be falling in love with him.

"How's the game?" Marc asked while glancing from Cathy to the television.

"Scoreless," Cathy replied, hoping they would head to TD Garden soon.

"Glad we haven't missed any goals," Marc commented. "You ready to leave?"

Cathy nodded.

"All right. T? See you Sunday?" Marc questioned his brother. His words and warm tone took Cathy by surprise.

"Most likely," Taylor replied.

Marc gave Taylor a thumbs up sign and then nodded for Cathy to follow him to the door. After saying goodbye to Taylor, Cathy followed Marc down Broadway Street until they reached his truck. She was debating over telling him about her afternoon visit with Taylor on the way to TD Garden or after the game. Assuming the news would upset him, she decided confiding in him afterward would be better.

***

As Marc led Cathy toward section 324 of TD Garden, he felt happier than he had all year. Taylor was clean, and that meant more to him than he could possibly express in words. For over a year, Taylor had been the first person on Marc's mind when he woke up and the last person on his mind when he fell asleep. Although Marc knew Taylor was in a terrible predicament with his supplier and the police, he felt a remarkable sense of relief knowing he would not have to worry about his brother overdosing any longer. Marc had just spoken with *the real Taylor*. The driven and levelheaded leader Marc grew up admiring had been resurrected.

Marc's feelings of anger toward Taylor for selling drugs had dissolved. Taylor was not that person anymore; that person had been crucified through weeks and weeks of withdrawal pains. Was Taylor temporarily trapped in a rough situation and forced to sell drugs to stay alive? Yes. But was he happily selling drugs to teenagers? No.

For over a year, Marc had feared he would never have a conversation with *the real Taylor* ever again. Seeing him sober, alert, and motivated was the best sight in the world. Marc hoped he would join their family on Easter. Even more, he hoped Taylor would move back home. He felt certain that with his father's and the detectives' help, Taylor would be able to safely break free from his supplier.

"I love these seats!" Cathy exclaimed, stealing Marc away from his thoughts as they entered their row in the balcony. "Perfectly centered behind the Jumbotron—you never even have to turn your head to follow the puck. I'm so glad Luke was able to get us his family's season tickets."

Marc laughed. "For the balcony, they're great—and we didn't miss a goal." He placed his hand on Cathy's back as they made way to their seats.

Cathy turned and smiled at him before sitting down. Her green eyes sparkled, and she appeared far less anxious than she had earlier in the day.

"You look *very* happy," Marc commented as he sat down beside her.

"I am," Cathy remarked. "I miss coming to games."

"Oh, right. I'm sure Jay brought you a lot."

"A few times a year," Cathy replied. "But tonight, I'm happy to be here with you."

Marc smiled and put his arm around her. Then he pulled her close to his chest and kissed the top of her head. "I hope they win for you."

Cathy lifted her head and looked up at him adoringly. "I hope they win for both of us."

A few minutes later, Marc and Cathy were standing up in their seats, cheering to the Bruins goal song. At that moment, Marc felt more optimistic than he had in a long time.

CHAPTER 1

March of 2018

TAYLOR DUNKIN STOOD IN his tidy bedroom, staring at himself in the mirror that hung above his dresser. "You know what you need to do," he said aloud and then took a deep breath. He dropped his blue eyes to a framed picture of himself and his ex-girlfriend Julie that sat on his dresser. It had been taken during the summer of 2016—before he blew out his knee, snorted a painkiller, or broke Julie's tender heart. Picking up the photo and admiring the sparkle in her eyes, he wondered where she was at the moment, who she was with, and if there was any chance that she could still love him.

After carefully setting the picture down and glancing to his left, Taylor picked up another framed photograph and smiled. The snapshot of his immediate family had been taken five years prior, after Taylor and Jordan's high school football team won the Super Bowl. Taylor had one arm hooked around his youngest brother Marc's neck, and his other arm was holding a trophy high in the air. Jordan was pointing at the trophy with a cocky smirk on his fifteen-year-old face, and their parents were proudly gloating on either side of Taylor. He smiled again before setting the picture frame down on his bureau, filled with hope that he and his brothers would become close again.

Taking a deep breath, he sat down on his bed and rested his head in his hands. "Just do it, T," he commanded himself. Lifting his head, he let out a heavy breath and then made his way over to his nightstand, which held his drug supply. He retrieved his big green box of drugs and opened its lid. Sifting through the contents, he estimated there was approximately $4,000 worth of his supplier's product left to sell, which equated to a street value of roughly $10,000. He set the box down on the bed and let out another heavy breath. Looking up at the ceiling, he shook his head in disbelief that his life had become so complicated. It felt as though he was trapped in a nightmare. After regaining his composure, he pulled his cell phone out of his pocket to call his father.

"Hey, T. How'd things go with Marc?" his dad greeted him.

"Good—good enough for me to come home for Easter," Taylor replied, knowing he could not mention anything about the police investigation over the phone, although he desperately needed his father's advice.

"You have no idea how happy that makes me. Mom will be thrilled."

"I was actually thinking of coming home tonight if that's okay?"

"You don't need to ask. You'll always have a room here."

"Thanks. It's just been a while," Taylor said in a regretful tone. "Do you want me to pick up Jordan to save you a trip into the city?"

"Oh, that would be great. He'll be pumped to see you. He's landing at 10:10 on JetBlue."

"Awesome. I can't wait to see him."

"Mom and I will wait up for you guys. We'll have food ready."

"That sounds great. I'll shoot him a text and let him know to look out for my Jeep."

"I'll leave him a voicemail, too. Oh, man. I'm so glad you and Marc talked."

"Yeah, I don't think he believed I was clean until he saw me," Taylor remarked. "He seemed happy when he left."

"I'm sure. He missed you. You're his favorite person. Going four months without talking to you couldn't have been easy."

"I hurt him—a lot."

"T, that wasn't you. That was the painkillers. As long as you keep drugs in your past, your relationship with Marc will fix itself."

Taylor glanced at the green box beside him that was filled with coke, molly, Adderall, marijuana, and acid. "I hope so."

"You boys spent countless hours at Al-anon, yet you and Marc both seem to have a hard time understanding grace."

Taylor sighed. "I'm trying. It's just hard to forgive myself for hurting so many people. There were a lot of kids from Montgomery affected by my poor decisions—even some of Marc's and Chris's friends. They're so young."

"It was their decision to use the drugs—just like it was *your* decision to abuse your meds."

"I know," Taylor admitted begrudgingly. "I just can't believe I did what I did. It feels like someone else was in control of my mind and body for a solid year. I can't even wrap my head around how I let that happen."

Taylor heard his father let out a heavy breath on the other end of the line. "*Drugs* were in control of your mind and body. I've told you this before; the devil uses drugs and alcohol to trap people in his grip, and then he condemns them for it. It's all part of the spiritual battle being fought over your soul. If you learn to depend on God, He'll help you win the war."

"I hope I can learn how to do that because I need all the help I can get."

"It's good you're coming home. The longer you stay, the more I can help you."

"Thanks," Taylor said, feeling a sharp pang of guilt as he glanced again at his box of drugs. "Well... I should go pack, and I have to run a few errands before I head to the airport, but I'll see you around eleven."

"Can't wait."

"Bye, Dad," Taylor said distractedly and ended the call. He glanced again at the green box beside him and then rested his head in his hands. His palms were sweating, and his heart was pounding heavily against his muscular chest. He felt more anxious than he ever had before a big game, and he desperately wanted to suppress his emotions so he could think clearly. Although his primary care doctor had prescribed him Xanax to help him sleep, he had not taken it in months because he feared it could cause him to relapse. That night was no exception.

He lifted his blonde head-of-hair out of his sweaty hands and stood up. While walking over to the safe in his closet, he felt like cinder blocks were attached to his legs. Kneeling before the safe, he entered the code 0-3-2-7, chosen for March 27th—the day of his and Julie's first date. Two days prior would have been their two-year anniversary. In November, his deep love for her and hatred for himself had moved him to end their relationship because he believed she deserved more than he could offer. Shortly after, he realized he was addicted to painkillers and somehow found the will to get sober. Nevertheless, trying to reconcile with Julie was out of the question until he could free himself from the violent crime ring he had ignorantly joined.

Opening the safe, Taylor locked his blue eyes on his handgun, wondering if he would be safer armed or if that would intensify the problem. Reaching past the gun, he retrieved two envelopes: a white one filled with money for his supplier (forty percent of his recent sales) and a yellow one filled with his own share of the profits. Between the two envelopes, he had roughly

$1,000, which was all he had to show for three and a half months of drug dealing. On numerous occasions, he had easily sold $1,000 worth of coke in one night. His supplier, Donny Bilotti, was going to find Taylor's level of production completely unacceptable.

Taking a deep breath, he reached further into his safe and pulled out another yellow envelope with $2,400 in it—money he had set aside for his April rent that was due to his landlord on Monday. Sitting back, he eyed the cash before him, trying to focus on what his gut was telling him to do. The problem was he no longer trusted himself or his instincts, so he questioned everything he perceived. His heart was beating so loudly that he feared he was on the verge of a panic attack. Leaving the money spread out on the floor, he hustled downstairs to his living room and retrieved his dab pen, which was filled with a blend of CBD and THC oil. He eyed it apprehensively, fearful of what would happen to him if he hit it and fearful of what would happen if he didn't.

Marijuana was legal in Massachusetts but so was alcohol. Getting drunk would ruin his four months of sobriety, so getting high would too, right? He feared that weed would cloud his judgment and weaken his will, which could cause him to relapse. He did not want to do anything to threaten his sobriety because it was the only thing that made him feel remotely proud. He also needed a clear head for the difficult task ahead of him. Anxiety or not, he couldn't allow himself to get high.

After setting the dab pen back inside its box, he leaned back on his couch and placed both of his hands over his throbbing heart. He took a few deep breaths and tried to find the nerve to do what needed to be done. An image of a gun barrel pointing at his forehead flashed into his mind, followed by another vision of himself tied up in chains with burns and cuts all over his body. With that thought, he rushed over to the sink in his kitchen, afraid that he might vomit. After splashing cold water on his face, he slumped onto the cold tile floor and buried his head in his hands. The combination of trepidation and self-loathing that overcame him caused tears to well up inside his eyes, plunge down his cheeks, and drip from his chiseled jaw into his sweat-coated hands. He knew every step he took from that point on would be pivotal for his survival.

CHAPTER 2

With a two-hour layover, Jordan Dunkin was sitting by the gate for his flight to Boston in Newark Liberty International Airport. He had opted to dive into some of his coursework for his Christian ethics class, while sipping on a Vanilla Bean Frappuccino. Jordan had signed up for the course to fulfill a core requirement, never imagining he would find the curriculum very interesting. However, he had quickly realized there was an immense amount of wisdom in what was being taught.

Prior to taking the course, Jordan was trying his best to become a better Catholic than he had been in high school. He wanted his family, coaches, and professors to take him seriously. After earning a starting spot on Notre Dame's football team and having a winning season, Jordan began to believe God was blessing him for the positive changes he was making to his lifestyle. When he ran into Michelle Taylor over Christmas break, she expressed interest in keeping in touch, which he took as a sign he was on the right path. His Christian ethics class gave him and Michelle a lot to discuss because she was a devout Christian with a sound understanding of the Bible. She had a knack for explaining things in a way that made sense to Jordan, and he found himself growing more and more interested in not only Michelle, but also the things of God. He finally desired to have the type of relationship with Christ that his father had been talking about for years.

Jordan noticed that the more deeply he dove into the curriculum, the more his perspective on life was changing. One year prior, he never would have passed up on a spring break trip to the Caribbean to go home. Now, he was excited to spend a week in Montgomery with his family. He specifically wanted to uncover what was going on in his older brother Taylor's life. Taylor, who had once been Jordan's greatest role model, had been struggling with a painkiller addiction for over a year. Although Jordan was doing everything in his power to avoid following his older brother's footsteps, he respected the leader Taylor had once been and hoped that person still existed somewhere inside of him.

It had been like a dream to attend Montgomery Lake High as Taylor Dunkin's younger brother. Taylor had paved the way for Jordan to have great success on the football field without much effort. Making varsity as a freshman was unheard of, but Taylor made it happen for Jordan. Of course, as Captain, Taylor trained Jordan harder than anyone else on the team, making sure he was an effective receiver. Taylor and Jordan grew up playing catch together in their backyard, so the connection they shared on the field was unprecedented. As a freshman, Jordan became the number one targeted receiver, and MLH had an undefeated season. The opportunity that Taylor gave Jordan to shine led to numerous recruiters contacting him—albeit illegally—well before his junior year of high school.

It honestly felt wrong to attend Notre Dame without Taylor. It was the university Taylor had chosen over Vanderbilt, Auburn, USC, 'Bama, BC, Northeastern, Clemson, The U, and Penn. At the time, Taylor and Jordan had dreamed of playing on the same team again, and that had motivated Jordan to focus in school. When Taylor lost his chance with Notre Dame—due to an arrest after a supposed senior-prank-gone-wrong—Jordan assumed Taylor would, at the very least, try to transfer there in the future. He never expected Taylor to settle for playing on an unranked team. When Taylor opted not to transfer as a sophomore, Jordan grew concerned about his brother's mental health.

It became apparent that losing his chance to play for a ranked team had taken some wind out of Taylor's sails. His arrest had been unfortunate because it was completely out of character for Taylor to participate in any sort of prank. The news had completely shocked Jordan, who had always considered his older brother a bit uptight. Moreover, it shook the bottoms off their parents and teachers. Jordan honestly believed that if Taylor had never been arrested, his current situation would have been very different. He assumed the resulting failure and embarrassment Taylor felt was what drove him to begin experimenting with recreational drugs in college. While most people blamed Taylor's painkiller addiction on his knee injury, Jordan believed Taylor's 2013 senior-prank-gone-wrong was the root cause.

Jordan's cell phone vibrated on his lap, pulling his attention away from his ethics book. He smiled when he saw a text from Michelle on the screen. Sliding her message open, he read:

Michelle: *When do you land in Boston? I'm in the Seaport now with my friends. You won't believe it, but I ran into Taylor at Northeastern today.*

Jordan: *I hope you're still pulling for ND after your tour today!*

Michelle: *For sure!!*

Jordan: ☺ *I land around 10. My parents are picking me up. Otherwise I would take an Uber and meet you in the Seaport. How did Taylor look?*

Michelle: *Oh bummer... are we still good for tomorrow? Taylor looked and sounded great.*

Jordan: *We are most definitely good for tomorrow. I'm going to head into the city to visit T in the morning and then I'm all yours.*

Michelle: ☺ *Will you text me after you land in Boston safely?*

Jordan: *Sure thing*

Michelle: *Praying you have a safe flight!*

Jordan: *Thanks. Have fun tonight!*

Jordan smiled as he set his phone down on his lap. He felt incredibly blessed to have Michelle back in his life. She had first caught his eye when he was a junior and she was a freshman in high school. Of course, at the time, he had been too immature to appreciate her inherent goodness or purity. In fact, during his senior year, he had foolishly told his younger brother Marc that he planned to take Michelle's virginity, which was most likely why Marc erroneously believed Jordan had slipped something into Michelle's drink at a party. While home for spring break, Jordan hoped to set the record straight with Marc. The secret of what really happened that night had been concealed for over two years, and it was time for the truth to be told.

CHAPTER 3

Michelle Taylor pulled her long brown hair into a tight ponytail, allowing a few wispy pieces to frame her makeup-less face. She wiped beads of sweat off the back of her neck with a soft towel that the bathroom attendant had handed her and then tossed the dirty cloth into the bamboo hamper, which looked like it belonged in a day spa. After smiling at the attendant, she sat down on a white leather bench to wait for her friends to finish using the facilities. Although they were patrons at the most upscale, eighteen-plus nightclub in Boston, the atmosphere made Michelle feel grimy.

Girls rocking perfect curls and fake eyelashes were hustling in and out of the bathroom. While some of their outfits were shockingly revealing, others were perfectly appropriate for the scene. Michelle, on the other hand, appeared quite out of place. Earlier that day, she had toured a couple of local colleges with her friend Katie McKnight. Michelle's high-waisted, pinstripe dress pants, white long-sleeved blouse, and high-heeled boots were perfect for meeting with admissions counselors. For dancing inside a steamy, overcrowded nightclub? Not so much.

Michelle locked her eyes on her friends Missy Kent and Laurelle Mahoney as they came out of a stall together, laughing and giddily holding each other's hands like small children. Missy's platinum blonde hair was styled in a braided updo centered perfectly on top of her head. Her baby-blue lace top, which matched the color of her eyes, had been purchased in the lingerie section of Victoria's Secret; together with her high-waisted, tight, white skirt and white platform heels, Missy was a gorgeous spectacle. Laurelle, revealing much less skin, had a bohemian flair to her style. Her pink and white lace dress was sheer in the sleeves and across the stomach. It flowed loosely down to her knees, about three inches above the top of her leather cowboy boots. Wherever Missy and Laurelle went, their contagious laughter, bright smiles, and childlike pep captivated everyone's attention.

As Missy and Laurelle skipped over to the sinks, a stall door opened to reveal Michelle's best friend, Day Angeletti. Michelle assumed Day felt just as out of place as she did. Wearing a sleeveless, black blouse, an argyle skirt, nylons, and heeled pumps, Day was likely less drenched in sweat than Michelle but just as morally conflicted. Observing the overwhelmed expression on Day's face, Michelle assumed the atmosphere of the club was stirring up memories Day would have rather forgotten.

Michelle stood up from her seat to join her friends by the sinks. Laurelle was repeatedly filling the palm of her hand with water and pouring it on the back of hers and Missy's necks. Every time the water landed on Missy's skin, she would close her eyes and say how good it felt.

"Laurelle, you're getting water all over me!" Day exclaimed in an annoyed tone after water splashed onto her shirt for the third time.

Laurelle laughed. "It's raining!" she cried and flung her hands up in the air, causing water droplets to fall on top of Day's head.

"Tell Katie I'm going to find John," Day huffed before abruptly exiting the bathroom.

Michelle glanced towards the stalls, wondering why Katie was taking so long. "Katie?" she called out loudly.

"Sorry!" Katie cried and immediately swung her stall door open. With her phone to her ear, she raised one finger to Michelle. "Missy put you guys on the guest list," Katie spoke into her phone, "so you shouldn't have to wait in line... No, I'm in the bathroom so I can hear you... Text me when you get here, and I'll let you know where we are... See you soon!" She hung up the phone and looked at Michelle apologetically. "Sorry. That was Ally," she said. "Matt's looking for parking. Robby's with them."

"Oh, good. Day's at her wits end with them," she whispered and gestured towards Missy and Laurelle. "She'll be glad to see Ally."

"Day thought we were all coming here for a fancy dinner," Katie said while washing her hands. "She didn't know this place turns into a club after eight."

"I had no idea either. We should have checked online instead of trusting Luke with the plans," Michelle stated dryly.

Katie peered at her reflection and chuckled. "Shell, we look like we're going on job interviews."

Michelle latched onto Katie's arm and laughed. "Can you imagine if Jordan came *here* from the airport to see me? He'd question everything he thinks he knows about me."

Katie playfully nudged Michelle. "The Jordan Dunkin I remember would be the master of this space."

"He's *not* who everyone thinks he is."

Katie widened her eyes. "Sounds like you're in love."

"There's more to him than just football and partying—"

"—Girls! Lots of girls!" Katie interjected.

Michelle rolled her eyes.

Katie peered at her in an amused manner. "You know he's probably been with, like, a hundred girls, right?"

"No, he hasn't!" Michelle exclaimed.

Katie laughed.

"Don't forget that he's kept our secret for over two years," Michelle retorted.

Katie smiled. "I know. I'm just playing."

"At the expense of people thinking he tried to date rape me," Michelle added.

Katie leaned back against the sink and crossed her arms. "I can't believe Marc *still* thinks that."

"Jordan could have told him the truth, but he stayed quiet to protect our friend. He's a good kid."

"It's not just about *her*," Katie said matter-of-factly. "It's about *you*. He kept silent because you asked him to."

Michelle groaned. "Marc and Jordan's relationship is suffering over something that never even happened."

Katie gazed at Michelle thoughtfully. "You're going to tell Marc the truth, aren't you?"

Michelle placed her hands on the sink, put her head down, and slowly nodded.

Katie stared at Michelle's reflection in the mirror. "You know what could happen, right?"

Michelle lifted her head and looked at Katie's reflection before turning around to face her. "Marc won't tell anyone," she insisted.

"Maybe you should wait until college decisions come out?" Katie suggested.

Michelle sighed. "Jordan's been the scapegoat for two and a half years, Katie. Marc will barely speak to him. I have to set things straight while he's home for spring break."

"We told Marc that Jordan was trying to take care of you. Marc doesn't want to believe it because he's still in love with you."

Michelle shook her head. "We're best friends. That's it."

Katie rolled her eyes. "You're going to have a big choice to make on May first."

"I have to get into Notre Dame and BC before I can make that decision," Michelle retorted.

"Are you or are you not third in our class?" Katie questioned her facetiously.

Michelle laughed. "Stop."

"With a 34 ACT?" Katie continued.

Michelle could feel her cheeks turning red.

"Oh, and three 700+ subject tests!" Katie exclaimed.

"Oh my gosh, we are such nerds!" Michelle cried and began to laugh, realizing again how out of place she and Katie were inside the club. "Who hides in the bathroom at a nightclub to discuss class rank and test scores?"

Katie chuckled. "Stop being so humble! You're going to get into both of those schools and have a huge decision to make."

Michelle glanced over at Missy and Laurelle, who were sitting together on a nearby chair. Missy was perched on Laurelle's lap with her arms around Laurelle's neck. They appeared to be in a deep conversation.

"We should go find everyone else," Michelle suggested, deliberately shifting the conversation away from Marc and Jordan.

"If we can get them to leave the bathroom," Katie remarked dryly before walking over to the girls.

"Hi!" Missy cried as soon as she noticed Katie and Michelle. "Do you guys want to sit down?"

"We want to find Day and the boys," Michelle replied.

"Oh, they're fine," Laurelle assumed and waved off Michelle.

Katie laughed. "Well, we didn't come here for the bathroom. There are places to sit in the club, too."

Missy sighed. "Just tell Luke we'll be out in a few minutes. It's fine. He won't care."

Wondering if it was a good idea to leave Missy and Laurelle unattended, Michelle made eye contact with Katie. Katie looked amused by the girls' altered states of mind.

"Enjoy the bathroom, you weirdos!" Katie cried sarcastically. "I can't wait to see what your boyfriends are up to."

"Pat's not my boyfriend!" Laurelle insisted.

"He is *so* your boyfriend," Katie teased her. "In fact, you guys will be the next ones to get engaged."

Laurelle laughed. "When two people can be with anyone else they want but choose to keep seeing each other, that's beautiful. That's our style. No commitment, just choosing each other over and over again."

"You guys are so in love," Missy sang.

"There's a chance he could—"

"—We're going to find everyone else," Katie interrupted Laurelle and tugged on Michelle's arm.

"Come find us soon!" Michelle called back to the girls as Katie pulled her towards the exit.

"They're going to sit in that chair and talk about Pat and Luke for *hours*," Katie whispered to Michelle.

Michelle opened the bathroom door and paused. "They'd rather talk about them than hang out with them?"

Katie playfully pushed Michelle through the doorway. "It only makes sense to people on molly."

"Is that what they took?" Michelle asked while gazing at the crowded dance floor, where at least 300 bodies were bumping and grinding to EDM.

"Oh, yeah," Katie replied assuredly. "I could tell by their pupils."

"Do you see anyone?" Michelle asked.

"No. I'll text Day," Katie said and pulled out her phone. "Oh, Ally texted me that they're here, over to the right of the stage."

"I dread walking through that crowd—all that body heat and sweat," Michelle groaned. "I am, like, sweltering."

"Do you want to go outside?" Katie asked. "I'm totally fine with that."

"Maybe just for a second," Michelle agreed. She could feel numerous pairs of eyes on her, and without any of her guy friends by her side, she felt vulnerable. "Actually, I'd rather find Matt, Robby, or John," she admitted.

"I don't want to fight our way through that dance floor," Katie admitted. "I'll text Robby to meet us by the bathrooms."

During the few minutes it took for Robby to find his way to the girls, Michelle and Katie were approached by three different groups of college kids. When one boy would not stop leaning closely into Michelle, Katie cried out, "Do you know who her boyfriend is?"

"Is he here?" the kid responded.

"Jordan Dunkin. Does that name mean anything to you?" Katie asked and crossed her arms.

The kid squinted at Katie in thought. "Is he related to Taylor Dunkin?"

Michelle's heart began to pound. She was not Jordan's girlfriend, and she hoped it would not get back to him that Katie had made that claim.

Katie looked startled to hear Taylor's name come out of the boy's mouth. "How do you know *Taylor*?" she asked.

The boy looked surprised by her question. "Everyone in this club knows Taylor."

"He's got the pure stuff," one of the other guys said.

"But we haven't seen him here in months," another kid chimed in.

"Do you have his number?" the boy closest to Michelle asked in an excited manner.

Katie and Michelle shot each other confused looks.

"I think we're talking about two different people," Michelle replied. "We thought you meant my friend's brother."

"Northeastern football player?" one of the kids asked.

Michelle felt a lump form in her throat. Were these guys implying that Taylor was a drug dealer? Jordan and Marc had told her about Taylor's struggle with painkillers after his surgery, but the idea of Taylor dealing drugs was foreign to her.

"Must be a different person," Katie responded and inconspicuously nudged Michelle. "The Taylor we know isn't in college."

"Hey, girls," Robby greeted them as he stepped into their circle. Robby was dressed nicely in a button-up shirt and khakis, but his attire was far different from the metrosexual-hipster look that the majority of the guys were rocking. Michelle assumed Robby had known as little about the venue as her.

Katie threw her arms around Robby and kissed him on the cheek. Thankfully, the group of guys who had been huddled around them walked away without another word. Michelle was a bit stunned by the conversation that had transpired. As out of place as she looked inside the club, she believed she was meant to be there to hear the rumor about Taylor. She wanted to find out if Jordan or Marc knew anything about Taylor dealing drugs. She could not picture Taylor doing such a thing. In Montgomery, he was highly regarded as a role model, and even though he was no longer playing football, people considered him a living legend.

CHAPTER 4

Chantal Kagelli's green eyes widened as Jason Davids' name appeared across the screen of her cell phone. Jason had dated her identical twin sister, Cathy, from seventh grade until the beginning of their freshman year. In November, they had a tumultuous breakup, but since then, Jason had significantly matured and had ironically become one of Chantal's closest friends.

While taking a deep breath, Chantal answered the phone, knowing whatever else Jason planned to share about Cathy would likely upset her. Nevertheless, it was important to uncover why her twin's personality had changed so drastically.

"Hi, Jay," Chantal greeted him.

"Hey. Is now a good time to talk?"

"Yeah. Cathy isn't home."

"I just told Jon what I told you earlier. Don't be surprised if you hear from him. I think he's pretty upset."

"Well, he's probably mad at himself for assuming the voicemail was from me in the first place. Our breakup wasn't your fault."

"I hope he sees it that way."

"I'll point it out to him. So... you wanted to tell me about the drugs that caused Cathy's downward spiral?"

"I caused Cathy's downward spiral."

"Jay, whatever she did was her choice."

"I was in a dark place," Jason admitted. "I put your sister through hell."

"It looked like she put *you* through hell."

"I lashed out at her. I blamed her for things she never did. I said every hurtful thing I could think of when we broke up."

"Well, she must have done something to make you break up with her. I know you loved her."

"I still love her."

"Still? But she's not the person you fell in love with anymore."

"Maybe not, but don't you want her back? Don't you miss her?"

"Of course, I do."

"Then help me," Jason pleaded. "Help me remind her of who she is."

Chantal sighed. "Tell me the rest of the story."

"Brace yourself," Jason warned her. "It might be hard to hear."

The Boston Bruins had a two-to-one lead over the Tampa Bay Lightning going into the third period. Cathy Kagelli's green eyes were darting back and forth, closely following the puck, as fans sitting around her inside TD Garden jeered and cheered. Every few minutes, Marc Dunkin would lean in close to her and either rub her back, take hold of her hand, or playfully nudge her. Marc's attention, along with the excitement of the game, was a great distraction from her ex-boyfriend Jason Davids' letter, which was still tucked inside Cathy's front pocket. Although she'd had an eventful day, Jason's words had repeatedly popped into her mind.

"You're a true fan," Marc commented and tugged on Cathy's hat in a flirtatious manner.

Cathy smiled. "I like to think so. I wish MLH had a girls hockey team."

"Would you play?" Marc asked.

"I've never worn a pair of hockey skates, but I'd try," Cathy replied with a short laugh.

"Luke said you kick ass on skis, so I bet you'd be a good skater."

"Luke just likes to ski with me because I'm not afraid to play in the glades."

"If *he* says you're good, then you're good."

Cathy smiled. "Luke's a sick athlete for a pretty boy who gets manicures with his girlfriend every weekend."

Marc chuckled. "But do you think he deserves to be Captain as a junior?"

Cathy tore her eyes off the ice and glanced at Marc. "Don't you?"

"Being captain of the hockey team, dating Missy, driving the nicest car in the school parking lot, and throwing parties are all means to an end for Luke," Marc replied.

Cathy cocked her head to the side, wondering what Marc was implying about their mutual best friend. "Are you mad at him about something?" she asked. Had Taylor told Marc about her and Luke's afternoon visit to his apartment?

Marc let out a heavy breath. "I didn't mean for it to sound like that. Let's just watch the game."

Cathy eyed Marc apprehensively. "Okay," she agreed and turned back towards the ice. "Remind me to tell you something later about Luke and Taylor," she added nonchalantly.

"Luke and *Taylor*?" Marc questioned her.

Cathy nodded without glancing away from the ice.

◑ ◑ ◑

Inside the nightclub, Michelle, Katie, and Robby stood near the bathrooms, taking in the scene. The strobe lights and the emotion-raising EDM beats could even make sober people feel a bit high.

"You had no idea this was a club, did you?" Katie asked while turning to Robby.

Robby smirked. "What gave it away? The skinny jeans I left at home or the ten pumps of cologne I forgot to put on?"

As Katie and Michelle laughed at Robby's typical sarcasm, someone tapped on Michelle's shoulder. She turned around to see Missy and Laurelle, who had finally vacated the bathroom.

"Oh, hey, you two," Robby greeted them. "Luke and Pat were looking for you."

"Hi!" Missy cried and threw herself at Robby. "It's so good to see you! You're so handsome, Robby Rosetti!"

Robby laughed.

"Make room for me!" Laurelle exclaimed and wrapped her arms around the other side of him.

"You two are incredible," Robby remarked and squeezed his arms tightly around them, "but you should go find your boyfriends."

"He's not—"

"—I know," Robby interrupted Laurelle, "but he's looking for you."

Missy and Laurelle set Robby free from their embrace and grabbed each other's hands.

"I think they're on the dance floor. Matt, Ally, Day, and John are over there," Robby added and pointed towards the DJ booth.

"Thanks!" Missy cried and dashed off with Laurelle.

"So... Luke got caught up dancing with some sorority girls," Robby said once Missy was out of sight.

Katie laughed. "She'll have no problem stealing him away. I think the competition turns her on."

"Matt's slightly pissed that Luke didn't tell him we were going to an upscale rave," Robby stated in an amused manner.

"When is Matt not pissed at Luke?" Katie joked.

After pushing past countless bodies, Michelle, Katie, and Robby found Matt and John, standing near the edge of the dance floor.

"Ally and Day," Matt said while pointing across the way. "Do you see them?"

Michelle peered through the sea of ravers until she saw her friends in the midst of the crowded dance floor. The one thing all her best friends had in common was their love for dancing. Ally was, by far, the best dancer in the group, so Michelle was unsurprised that she was enjoying the music.

"You want to leave, but Ally wants to stay, right?" Katie questioned Matt.

"Um, it's not really my, uh, vibe, but we're already here, so she might as well enjoy herself," Matt replied. "I wish I took my parents' Bruins tickets."

"They're up two to one," John stated after glancing at his phone.

"Marc went," Matt said. "He must have known what Luke was walking us into."

"Where *is* Luke?" Robby asked.

"Probably giving Pat a back rub," Matt replied facetiously. "They're rolling face."

"That's why Missy and Laurelle stayed in the bathroom for a half hour," Katie said. "They were cuddling on a chair, having a deep conversation about Pat and Laurelle's non-relationship."

"We need to all vote for Pat and Laurelle to be 'Class Couple.' It'll be the best page in the yearbook," Matt stated in a jovial manner.

Robby, John, Katie, and Michelle burst into laughter.

"You and Day are going to win, but you should waive it so that can happen," Matt said jokingly to John.

John laughed. "They'd secretly love it."

Michelle wiped sweat off the back of her neck with the palm of her hand. "Does anyone want to go outside for a minute?" she asked.

"I'm roasting in this sweater," Matt admitted, "but I told Ally I'd stay right here."

"Katie?" Michelle asked.

"Yeah, if Robby will come with us," Katie replied. "I don't feel like getting bombarded by random guys. You're a freaking magnet for them."

Michelle blushed.

"Let's go," Robby said and nodded for the girls to follow him. "They're letting people out the door by the bar. There's no line to come back in."

CHAPTER 5

After peeling his six-foot-two-inch body off the kitchen floor and returning upstairs, Taylor placed his supplier's money inside the box of drugs. He closed the lid, picked up the box, threw his backpack over his right shoulder, and walked downstairs to the kitchen. His own cell phone was in his pocket, but the detective's burner phone was in his backpack, along with his clothes for the weekend. Before leaving the apartment, he left a note on the kitchen counter that said, "Meet Don Bilotti @ Brigham Pizza / Pick up Jordan - JetBlue 10:10." Leaving a paper trail was imperative in case things went south.

After putting on his Patriots hat, leather snow boots, and North Face jacket, Taylor locked up the apartment and headed outside to his black Jeep Grand Cherokee. Upon climbing inside the SUV, he placed the green box on the passenger's seat, dropped his backpack to the floor, and started the engine. His heart pounded heavily while he waited for the navigation system to load. He knew how to get to Brigham Pizza, but he needed to leave as much of a trail as he could in case he went "missing" after his meeting with Donny. He also turned on the setting in his iPhone that allowed his location to be tracked.

Once the Jeep's navigation system loaded, Taylor typed in the address. The drive was calculated to take fifteen minutes with an ETA of 9:02. If all went well, he assumed he would have no trouble getting to the airport by 10:10. Therefore, he texted Jordan, *Hey bro. Guess what? I'm picking your ass up and bringing you home. Text me when you get your luggage and look for my Jeep. So glad you decided to come home for spring break.*

After sending the text, Taylor was stricken with fear that he would never make it to the airport and never see his brother again, which prompted him to write a second text: *I can't wait to tell you to your face how proud I am of you little bro. See you soon.*

While letting out a heavy breath, Taylor opened up a message to Marc: *Hey man. Thanks for coming by and convincing me to come home for Easter. I'm actually coming home tonight so I can spend a few days in Montgomery. Grabbing J at the airport around 10. Hope the Bs pull off a W for you. It was great to see you and hear about your plans for BC. I'm so proud of you. Thanks again.*

After setting his phone down in his cupholder, Taylor glanced at the green box. If Donny accepted the drugs back, they would be distributed to other dealers and bought by brothers, sisters, fathers, mothers, sons, and daughters.

Taylor closed his eyes and sighed. "Too many people have already been hurt," he said aloud and shot his blue eyes wide open. He slammed his hands down on the steering wheel and shook his head.

Without another thought, he shut off the engine, grabbed the box and his cell phone, and headed back inside his apartment. Still wearing his jacket and boots, he marched into the first-floor bathroom and knelt down in front of the toilet. He swallowed deeply as he opened the green box and picked up a large bag of cocaine. After tearing open the seal, he poured it into the toilet, followed by every single tab of acid, capsule of molly, and caplet of Adderall. Then he opened the small bags of cocaine and emptied them into the toilet bowl. He held his breath and flushed the toilet.

A feeling of relief washed over Taylor as the stream of drugs disappeared and fresh water began filling the bowl. He glanced down at his remaining stash: about a dozen bags of marijuana, each holding one ounce. Legally, he could possess ten ounces without getting in trouble, so he needed to flush at least two bags, but was keeping any of it a smart idea? "I'm sure Jordan would want some of this," Taylor reasoned. "Ugh, do I even want to condone that?"

Taylor sighed and flushed two bags worth of marijuana down the toilet. He felt relieved, knowing if his condo got raided, he could no longer get in trouble for possession. *You could easily sell the rest of this to your friends and make $3,000,* he thought. *Weed is not going to ruin anyone's relationships. It will just help people sleep at night.* Even though his words were logical, something inside of him was urging him to empty every bag into the toilet to be free, once and for all, from drug dealing. He shook his head and sighed. If he truly wanted a fresh start, he needed to flush it, so that is exactly what he did.

He stood up and stared blankly into the toilet as the last bud of marijuana disappeared. "$10,000 literally down the drain in minutes," he remarked. "That was a bold move," he added. At that moment, he realized being free of the burden to sell those drugs meant a lot more to him than $10,000.

After pulling his phone out of his pocket, he saw that it was almost nine o'clock. "Crap," he muttered. Two minutes later, Taylor was armed with his handgun and on his way to Store More in Dorchester, where he had roughly $25,000 locked in a strongbox. Getting his license to carry once he moved off-campus was one of the best things Taylor's father ever made him do. At the time, Taylor had never imagined that he would carry around large quantities of cash, but because of Northeastern's proximity to some of Roxbury's most crime-ridden projects, Mr. Dunkin had insisted that Taylor be able to protect himself. Thankfully, he had never been forced to pull his gun on anyone, but that evening, he was in far more danger than usual.

CHAPTER 6

MICHELLE AND KATIE FOLLOWED Robby outside to a roped-off patio on the side of the building. The frigid air jolted Michelle's entire body, but she was just happy not to feel faint. Groups of kids in their late teens and early twenties were huddled near heaters spaced sporadically throughout the area. Some were Juuling; others were smoking; a few looked like they were on the verge of passing out. Couches and lounge chairs were centered around glass-encased fire pits. Aside from the large vape clouds and faint smell of cigarette smoke, the outside ambience was quite nice.

"Is that Luke?" Katie asked and pointed towards one of the fire pits.

Michelle glanced over to see Luke sitting on a couch with a blonde, who was wearing a tight black dress and rubbing Luke's shoulders. His eyes were closed, but he was wearing a wide grin.

"Oh, $@#%!" Robby exclaimed and then started laughing. "I guess Missy never found him. He's so effed up."

Katie rushed over to the couch. "Luke Davids!" she shouted. "What are you doing?"

The girl rubbing Luke's shoulders paused and looked up at Katie. Luke slowly opened his eyes.

"Katie!" Luke exclaimed excitedly. "Where's Robby? Where have you guys been? Come hang out."

Katie scoffed. "Where's your girlfriend, and who's this?" she asked and nodded towards the girl in the black dress.

"This is Jess," Luke replied while patting the girl's hand. "She's going to come hang out in Montgomery with us this weekend."

"Hi!" Jess greeted Katie in a friendly manner. "I can get up if you want to sit here."

Katie waived off Jess and motioned for Michelle and Robby to come over to them. Michelle had feared that Luke getting a massage from a random girl could cause a fight if Missy came outside, but then she remembered Luke and Missy were both on molly; nothing was going to anger either one of them.

"Shells! Rosetti!" Luke cried once Michelle and Robby came into view. "Isn't it awesome out here? I love this fire. It's the perfect night for this. I'm so glad you guys are here."

"Um, yeah, it's really nice," Michelle said flatly. "Where's Missy?"

Luke shrugged. "I wish she was here. I don't know where she went."

"Where's Pat?" Katie asked.

Luke looked confused. "Hmm... he was out here, but then..." He turned towards Jess. "Then we started talking about concerts in Boston this summer... and I totally have no idea where he went."

"I don't know," Jess said with a shrug. "He could be with my friends."

"We can find Missy and tell her you're out here," Robby offered.

"Pat probably found Laurelle," Katie assumed.

Luke widened his eyes and nodded. "Oh, yeah. That's definitely where he went. He *loves* Laurelle. Do you guys want to sit down? It's nice and cozy."

"I'm good," Michelle replied, trying not to laugh at Luke's childlike enthusiasm. "I need to cool off away from the fire."

"It's way nicer out here than in there," Luke said. "Robby, do you have a Juul? Mine got checked with my coat."

Robby reached into his pocket and handed Luke his vape.

"Vaping feels so much better when you're rolling," Luke remarked before taking a draw off the Juul. "I don't even like it when I'm straight," he admitted after exhaling and handing the vape back to Robby.

Robby took a small draw off it before offering it to Katie.

"What flavor?" Katie asked.

"Mint," Robby replied.

"Oh, uh-uh. No thanks," Katie said. "I only like the fruit kind."

"Shell?" Robby offered.

Michelle shook her head. Vaping was an epidemic at MLH. No one seemed worried about getting addicted to nicotine; no one seemed concerned about the unknown consequences. Friends of Michelle who had never smoked a cigarette, now vaped on a regular basis. Not knowing the long-term effects of vaping was enough to scare Michelle away from trying it, but most of her friends—even the straightedge ones—thought it was harmless.

Robby took one more draw off the Juul before tucking it back inside his pocket. Then he turned to Katie and Michelle and asked, "Do you guys want to go find Missy?"

Michelle glanced at Luke, who was chewing on a bottle cap and leaning closely into the girl he had called Jess. "We should at least tell Missy where he is," Michelle replied.

After saying bye to Luke, Michelle followed Katie and Robby inside and over to where Matt and John were still standing. Ally and Day were in sight, but Michelle did not see Missy, Laurelle, or Pat anywhere. The club seemed even more crowded than before and, consequently, ten degrees hotter.

"So, Pat and Laurelle left to go 'talk' in the car," Matt informed them in an amused tone.

Robby laughed. "Class Couple 2018."

"They always do that!" Katie cried. "When they're together, it's like no one else exists."

"If they left, then where's Missy?" Michelle asked.

"She must be with Luke," Matt assumed. "We haven't seen her."

Michelle shook her head. "She is *not* with Luke. Luke's outside with some girl he just met."

Matt scoffed. "What? Seriously?"

"Oh, yeah. Evidently, she's coming to hang out with him in Montgomery this weekend," Robby replied.

Matt let out a heavy breath. "Wait here. Watch the girls. I'll be right back," he stated in a frustrated manner and then rushed off towards the exit.

"No one has seen Missy?" Michelle questioned John.

John shook his head.

"I can text her," Katie offered.

"I'll text Laurelle to see if she knows anything," Michelle said while pulling her phone out of her pocketbook. "I doubt Laurelle and Pat left her alone."

"She's probably just dancing," Katie assumed. "It's Missy. I wouldn't worry too much."

"Let's do a lap around the dance floor to see if she's there," Michelle suggested to Katie. "She's probably up on a platform, knowing her."

Katie nodded. "Do you want to wait here?" she asked, turning to Robby.

"Whatever you want," Robby replied with a shrug.

"Come with us," Michelle urged him, thankful that he was so protective of Katie.

Michelle did not like walking around clubs, concerts, or even parties without one of her close guy friends in sight. She was a magnet for guys; Katie had not been exaggerating. A lot of girls would consider her lucky, but Michelle felt differently. She had been regarded as "the hottest girl at MLH" since she entered high school, which was a nice compliment, but at the same time, it made her question the motive of every male who tried to befriend her.

When anyone expressed interest in Michelle, she never knew if they viewed her as a "conquest" or if they truly liked her. She believed there was much more to people than their physical appearance or reputation, and she wanted a boyfriend who valued her mind and heart more than her face or body. Therefore, she wore little makeup, dressed modestly, and prayed for God to shut the door on every guy that was not meant to be in her life. Having Marc as her best friend was a huge blessing because she felt safe with him, and he looked out for her in every situation. However, he had hardly been around since he began seeing Cathy in December. Truthfully, Michelle found it strange that Marc was spending so much time away from his friends to be with her. She also found it odd that Luke and Cathy were best friends, considering that Luke's younger brother was Cathy's ex. Marc was yet to refer to Cathy as his girlfriend, but it was clear she had become his main love interest. Michelle could not tell if she was slightly jealous that Marc was giving another girl more attention than her or if her intuition was telling her there was more to the situation than meets the eye.

Nevertheless, she had an uneasy feeling about their relationship. Marc was someone who loved Michelle for her heart and mind; he was one of "the good guys," who deserved someone who could love him back wholeheartedly. The only reason Michelle broke up with him in eighth grade was because she thought if they stayed together for years and years before getting married, they would end up sleeping together. Maintaining her virginity was incredibly important to her, and she believed if Marc was the one God designed for her, then they would get back together someday. She assumed Marc would date other girls throughout high school, but she felt nothing would come between them in the long run if they were truly meant to be. Jordan was what she never expected.

Once labeled "the hottest guy at MLH," Jordan was a magnet for girls, so he and Michelle could relate on that front. During the two years they were in high school together, Michelle had witnessed girls go to great lengths to get his attention. Of course, Michelle had always been attracted to Jordan—his looks rivaled those of a famous movie star—but she never knew the depth of his character until he chose keeping a promise to her over saving his reputation. He graduated from MLH in the eyes of many as "a four-star football recruit, who was the captain of the football and wrestling teams, the Homecoming King, and the one who tried to date rape a young virgin." It pained Michelle that keeping her secret had tarnished his reputation in Montgomery, where his older brother was a sacred cow.

After the party at which Jordan supposedly tried to date rape her, Michelle realized how much her and Jordan's friendship bothered Marc, and since he was her best friend, she opted to stop hanging out with Jordan. Ultimately, she regretted that decision because cutting ties with Jordan made people believe he had, in fact, wronged her.

Over Christmas vacation, which was when Marc started spending most of his free time with Cathy, Michelle ran into Jordan and his cousin Chris at her church's Christmas concert. Jordan was only home for a couple of days because of Notre Dame's upcoming bowl game, so they were unable to make plans, but she gave him the green light to contact her. If Marc had moved on to Cathy, Michelle had no reason to feel bad about rekindling her friendship with Jordan. Moreover, she ran into Jordan at *church*, which she believed was a sign from God that she and Jordan were on similar paths. This was confirmed when their phone calls quickly turned into deep discussions about faith, redemption, and spirituality. Prior to seeing Jordan in church, Michelle had no idea he had any interest in religion, despite the fact that he attended Notre Dame. Evidently, the culture and curriculum at the university, along with his father's and Chris's testimonies, had piqued Jordan's interest.

While Michelle did not know if she was meant to become romantically involved with Jordan, she knew for certain she was meant to clear his name. Only four people knew what really happened to Michelle at the party. Expanding that number to five seemed like a risk worth taking if it would repair Jordan and Marc's relationship. However, Michelle knew the potential backlash was immense, considering that the truth could taint more than one person's reputation and possibly make headlines.

CHAPTER 7

WHILE DRIVING TO DORCHESTER, Taylor frequently glanced in his rearview mirror, trying to decipher if anyone was tailing him. The Boston Police had been investigating him for months without him ever noticing. That was quite a wakeup call. He realized that he needed to pay much more attention to his surroundings when he was in public. Having a propensity to get lost in his own thoughts, Taylor knew this would be a challenge. What he loved so much about football was that it forced him to focus on the present moment and get out of his own head for a few hours.

As he steered his Jeep through the Store More parking lot, he was relieved to count ten other vehicles at the facility. His unit was fairly close to the security station, which had its pros and cons. That night, however, it was comforting. After parking his Jeep in front of his small unit, he took his gun out of his glove compartment and tucked it into his jacket pocket. He glanced in all of the mirrors before climbing out of the vehicle. Convinced that no one had followed him, he locked his Jeep and slipped inside his storage unit, carefully locking the door behind him. His heart pounded as he slid open the drawer in his old bureau where he kept his strongbox. It was perfectly in place, as he had left it. He felt an enormous sense of relief when he unlocked the box and saw the bands of cash inside. He needed to buy himself time.

If Donny pressured him to sell another batch of drugs, he reasoned that he could flush them all and use his savings to pay for them. That way there,

Donny would not suspect that Taylor wanted out of the game. Taylor knew he was the weak link, so he needed to do everything in his power to convince Donny that he wasn't. $25,000 meant he could "sell" five more batches of drugs before running into financial peril. He hoped he would be able to find a way out of the crime ring before going through all of his savings because he wanted to pay towards his college tuition. However, staying off Donny's rat radar was priority number one. With the money in his storage unit, $3,400 in his safe, $2,000 in a safety deposit box, and roughly $4,500 in his bank account, Taylor reasoned he could register for three summer courses without putting himself in danger, but his parents might have to pay for the rest. Once again, Taylor found himself ten steps ahead of reality in his mind when he needed to focus solely on the difficult task at hand.

After locking the strongbox and securing the money he needed to pay Donny inside his inner-jacket pocket, Taylor warily exited the storage unit. He glanced in every direction before locking the door. By the time he got back on the highway, it was already 9:25. His navigation said he would arrive at the pizza shop in ten minutes. He had never before sat on the same box of drugs for longer than a month, which was why he assumed Donny would be wary of his commitment to the job. Drop-offs typically only took a couple of minutes, but Taylor expected an interrogation that night. If he was going to cooperate with the police, then he could not give Donny any reason to suspect he wanted out of the game.

When Taylor parked his Jeep a block away from Brigham Pizza, he sat in thought before shutting off the engine. Donny would likely have men guarding both doors to the backroom where they were planning to meet. They always patted down everyone who entered, checking for weapons and wires. That was standard procedure. Although Taylor knew he could be in danger, he decided that locking his gun in his glove compartment would be a wise choice. He could not let on that anything felt out of the ordinary, and he could not seem nervous. Pulling out his cell phone, he decided to send his location to Jordan along with a message: *Hey bro. Sorry I might be a few minutes late. Heading to the airport soon from Brigham Pizza. Text me when your plane lands.* Then, while taking a deep breath, Taylor exited his Jeep and began his two-minute walk.

As he neared the pizza shop, his heartbeat grew louder. Although he thought he had a good plan in place, he felt more nervous than he had anticipated. Thankfully, it was only fifteen degrees out, so his palms and forehead were not sweating like they had been earlier, and he hoped he looked more at ease than he felt. As he approached Brigham Pizza, he saw one of Donny's other guys, a middle-aged man whom everyone called Cappy, standing out front and smoking a cigarette.

"Hey, T!" Cappy called out in a friendly manner. "You heading in to see Donny?" he asked and nodded toward the door. He seemed genuinely surprised to see Taylor—or perhaps just surprised to see him sober.

Can he tell I'm sober? Taylor wondered. *Did the other guys even know I was into Oxy? Is it safer to pretend I'm still using?* "Hey, Cappy," Taylor greeted him casually. "Yeah, I told him I'd swing by."

"Good to see you, man. It's been a bit."

Taylor nodded. "Yeah. It has."

"Are you in a rush? Do you want a smoke?" he asked and held up his pack of cigarettes.

Taylor was certainly in a rush, but for Jordan's protection, he did not want any of Bilotti's men to know Jordan was flying into Boston for the week. Their crime ring was filled with heavy gamblers, and they all followed college football closely enough to know a lot about Jordan. Taylor cleared his throat. "No big rush," he said and took a cigarette and a lighter from Cappy.

Ugh, smoking. Taylor hated smoking. In fact, he had never smoked a cigarette until he started dealing for Bilotti. He had forgotten that almost every time he made a drop-off someone had expected him to smoke a butt and shoot the breeze for a few minutes. Taylor had gone along with it just to blend in with their culture, but he dreaded it immensely.

After taking a few drags off the cigarette, while Cappy talked nonsense about a fight everyone was putting money on, Taylor felt himself start to relax a bit. When he went to AA with his dad, he had heard a staggering statistic that over eighty percent of people in recovery were smokers. Since smoking multiple times with Bilotti's crew had done nothing but gross Taylor out, he had found that statistic quite baffling. It seemed illogical to go from one addiction to another—especially a cancer-causing one. However, at that particular moment, he viewed anything that could help him relax as an asset. Appearing at ease in front of Donny would be imperative.

Realizing he was once again lost in his own thoughts, Taylor jolted his attention onto Cappy's elaborate theory about why the fight would only go six rounds. "Well, I'll keep that in mind if my friends and I decide to bet on it," Taylor said with a smile. He took one last drag of the cigarette and then stomped it out under his boot. "I better get in there and see the boss," he added while nodding towards the door.

Cappy patted Taylor on the back and led him inside. The pizza shop was mainly filled with college kids, who were likely grabbing something quick to eat before heading out for "thirsty Thursday." Thursdays had always been big nights out for Taylor and his friends because football games often tied up their weekends. Glancing around at the unfamiliar faces, he longed for simpler days.

"That's Taylor Dunkin," he heard a female voice say as he made his way toward the back of the shop where Donny's office was located.

"The football star?" another female voice asked.

Taylor fought off all temptation to turn around to see who was talking about him. He needed to take care of business and get to the airport.

"The girls around here still love you, huh?" Cappy joked as they neared the backroom.

Taylor laughed. "I don't know why."

Cappy knocked twice on the door to Donny's office, which prompted Stevie, one of Donny's more muscular men, to open the door. As soon as Cappy and Taylor entered the room, they were frisked for weapons and scanned for bugs.

"Hi, guys. Give Stevie your phones and take a seat," Donny said.

Taylor cocked his head to the side. That was a first. He pulled his iPhone out of his pocket and handed it to Stevie without hesitation. A few seconds later, Stevie left the room.

"Cell phones, man," Donny remarked offhandedly while Taylor and Cappy sat down, "they're always listening. I tell my wife I want to see a movie; the next time I google something on my phone, an ad for that movie pops up. It's freaky."

Taylor eyed Donny warily. Phones certainly seemed eerily intuitive lately, but asking Taylor to hand over his phone instead of just turning it off was a cause for concern.

"Make sure your phones are off when you meet with customers," Donny added.

"All right," Cappy said. "Everything okay?"

"I'm just trying to tighten up the ship."

"Do you think the cops are onto something?" Cappy inquired.

"I always assume that. T, you missed some stuff."

Taylor let out a heavy breath. "Yeah, I'm sorry about that."

"We'll talk," Donny said and planted his brown eyes on Taylor before turning towards Cappy. "Cap, what do you have?"

Cappy reached into his pocket and pulled out a fat envelope. "The Gabapentin sold fast," he commented while handing Donny the money.

"Good," Donny stated and put the envelope in his top drawer. "Are you going down to Rhode Island for Easter?"

Cappy nodded. "Tomorrow."

"Nice. Enjoy the family time. Call me when you get back in town," Donny said and extended his hand to shake Cappy's. "Give Carol and Uncle Frank my best."

"Will do," Cappy responded and shook Donny's hand firmly. "T, take care," he said and patted Taylor's shoulder.

Taylor smiled. "Have a nice Easter," he remarked as Cappy turned to leave the room.

Although Taylor had known Donny and his men for over a year, he still found it strange that they were so warm and friendly. They were criminals, after all. It had been Donny's hospitality and congeniality, along with Taylor's lapse of reason, that had made Taylor comfortable enough to do business with him in the first place.

Last February, Taylor had gone to a party in Narragansett with his friend Rob Anuzelli to meet Rob's uncle Donny. At the time, the Percocet Taylor's doctor had prescribed him was no longer effective, so he had been buying stronger pills off Rob for about a month. Rob offered to connect Taylor with his uncle, thinking Taylor could get a better discount from him. Taylor knew Rob had meant well. He was not a drug dealer, just the kid in their group of friends who could get drugs if people wanted them. Moreover, Rob thought Taylor was in need of pain relief, not looking for a way to elevate his mood.

Taylor had never expected Donny to offer him OxyContin at cost if he agreed to sell drugs within his social circle. However, it turned out that Donny knew a lot about Taylor, including that he was Northeastern's "beloved QB" with an open invitation to every party, and he accurately sized up Taylor's money-making potential. Taylor could still vividly recall the moment he agreed to Donny's proposal. Standing near a cobble-stone fireplace with a fire blazing, surrounded by caterers in bowties with trays of prosecco, Taylor and Donny had struck their deal. At the time, Taylor did not know that Donny led an organized crime ring in Boston or that he was allegedly connected to the Italian mafia. Being high, Taylor had not put any thought into where the drugs might come from or what consequences he could face. He was sold on the idea of getting Oxy cheap and being able to sell coke to his friends at a discount. With a full scholarship to college, parents who paid for his car and apartment, and a weekly allowance, Taylor had not even factored the money he would make into his decision. All he had cared about was getting his hands on the drugs he needed to feel normal.

How did I not realize I had an addiction? Taylor wondered as he watched

Cappy walk out of the room. Turning around, he locked his blue eyes on Donny and took a deep breath.

"So, what do you have for me, T?" Donny asked and peered at Taylor expectantly.

Taylor reached into his jacket and pulled out an envelope with $5,000 in it. "Sorry this is so late," he said as he handed the money to Donny.

Donny took the envelope and opened it. "What are your plans for Easter?" he asked as he began counting the cash.

Taylor swallowed the large lump that had formed in his throat. "Just going home for the weekend," he replied.

"That's good. Did Rob tell you we're heading down to my brother's in Narragansett?" Donny asked nonchalantly while continuing to count the money.

Taylor cleared his throat. "No, I haven't seen him in a couple of weeks."

"He's busy with that co-op job. I've hardly seen him either. Well, five G's, man—looks like it's all here. You never disappoint," Donny remarked and slid the cash back into the envelope.

Taylor eyed Donny apprehensively, hoping he did not look as nervous as he felt. After Taylor agreed to sell drugs, Rob had warned him about his uncle's associates, including a few people who had mysteriously gone "missing" after crossing their family. Rob speculated that both of his mother's brothers were connected to the Rhode Island mafia, but because his parents were adamant that he have nothing to do with the Bilotti family business, he knew nothing for certain. At the time, Taylor had felt more intrigued by the news than worried, but Rob's warning had been at the forefront of Taylor's mind since Donny pressured him into selling one more stash.

After tucking the money into his top drawer, Donny locked eyes with Taylor. "So," he said and raised his eyebrows, "is this your last transaction?"

CHAPTER 8

***

Five Months Prior - October of 2017

CATHY KAGELLI STOOD BEFORE the calendar on her bedroom wall and drew a big X across the date—October 1st—the final day of her month-long groundation. She had never expected her first month of high school to be so lonely. Her only social outlet beyond school and her boyfriend Jason's visits on the weekends had been the Messenger app on her iPad. She was not allowed to use social media, so she had no idea what people were doing unless she heard about it at school. Her need to socialize had begun to negatively impact her teachers' opinions of her, despite her high grades, as she frequently got in trouble for talking during class.

Although Jason had not been grounded, Cathy thought he had an even lonelier month than her. He and his former best friend, Chris Dunkin, had not spoken since their argument on the second day of school, and to make matters worse, Chris had remained close with his other two best friends, Jon Anderson and Bryan Sartelli. It was clear that Chris believed Jason was a bad influence on him and a threat to his newly attained sobriety. While Cathy felt terrible for Jason, she thought Chris was right. However, she had not anticipated that Chris, his new girlfriend Marielle, Bryan, Bryan's girlfriend Courtney, Jon, and Jon's new girlfriend Julianna would form a clique exclusive of her and Jason. This made Jason, to his own detriment, spend a lot of time with his older brother Luke and Luke's friends.

As the month progressed, Cathy had noticed Jason growing more and more taunting—to the point that she suspected he was drinking during school. He claimed having straight A's was proof that he was sober in class, but Cathy knew MLH's curriculum was easy compared to what he had been accustomed to at St. Timothy's. It took her a few weeks, but she finally realized that without her or Chris around, Jason had been entertaining himself with drugs.

CHAPTER 9

As was typical of all Sundays during football season, Marc Dunkin had his blue eyes locked on the television screen in front of him. However, instead of watching the game with his friends, Marc had opted to spend the day in Boston at his oldest brother Taylor's apartment. Although Taylor was no longer a registered student, he was still a central part of Northeastern's social scene. Marc was surrounded by a handful of Northeastern's football players and their girlfriends. He enjoyed watching games with people who possessed a high sports acumen, and Taylor's friends certainly did. For everyone in the room, football season was their favorite time of the year.

Taylor's girlfriend Julie had prepared an array of food that covered the kitchen countertop. Marc was relieved to see that Julie was still a part of Taylor's life, despite his behavior of late. He wondered if Taylor had been honest with her about abusing his pain medication. The fact that she was still dating him pointed toward Taylor not being transparent with her. Marc felt bad if Julie was in the dark, but he feared if he told her the truth, she would break up with his brother. Knowing how against drugs Julie was, Marc believed she was the most positive influence in Taylor's life. She was younger than Taylor, so she still had over a year left in her five-year nursing program. Marc hoped their relationship would survive Taylor's addiction because Julie was his perfect match.

Sitting beside Taylor on the couch, Marc could not help but notice how frequently Taylor scratched his arms. *If he's like this all the time, how do people not realize he's high on opiates?* Moreover, Taylor's blue eyes made his pinned pupils stand out quite clearly. Anyone who knew the signs of opiate abuse should recognize what was taking place. Yet, Marc's own parents would not even believe Taylor was getting high. It was as though no one thought someone as "mature" and "successful" as Taylor could ever go down a dark path. This meant the only people trying to help Taylor were Marc and Jordan, because they were the only ones who realized Taylor had a problem.

Assuming that Jordan partied hard, Marc found it strange that he had taken such an interest in helping Taylor over the summer. Although Marc and Jordan had hardly spoken in two years because of their fight over Michelle Taylor, Marc could still vividly remember what his brother had been like in high school. Jordan had tried to turn every day into a party and every night into a hookup opportunity. He was the last person Marc had expected to worry about Taylor. In fact, over the summer when Jordan started visiting Taylor multiple times per week, Marc had assumed Jordan was buying weed off him. Only after Jordan asked Marc to team up with him and talk to their parents about Taylor's condition did Marc realize Jordan had been trying to help him. Now with Jordan back in Indiana, Marc was alone in his quest to save Taylor, and he felt helpless.

"Tough loss," Taylor said downheartedly after the Carolina Panthers beat the Patriots with a last-second field goal. "Good game, though."

"That hurts," Taylor's friend Josh Swanson said and shook his head. "Who needs a refill?" he asked as he picked up an empty pitcher of beer from the coffee table.

Ryan Blake, Matt McSweeney, Rob Anuzelli, and Brian Parker all raised their cups. Marc never ceased to be amazed by how much beer Taylor's friends could go through on any given Sunday. Taylor, however, no longer consumed alcohol because of how toxic it was to mix it with painkillers.

"I'll be right back," Taylor said before jumping off the couch and leaving the room.

Once Taylor was out of sight, Marc turned to Julie. "How's he doing?" he questioned her quietly.

The look of concern in Julie's eyes was apparent as she let out a heavy breath. "Drive me home later, and we'll talk," she replied.

"You're not staying over?"

Julie shook her head.

"Okay. Just let me know when you want to leave," Marc agreed.

When the 4:25 game was about to start and Taylor was yet to return, Marc became concerned. "Where did T go?" he asked everyone.

Josh glanced at Julie and then at Marc. "He might not be feeling well. Maybe he went to lie down between games?"

Marc lowered his eyebrows. "Has he not been feeling well?"

Josh gave Marc a strange look and then turned to Taylor's roommate Ryan. "Has he been sick, bro?"

Ryan let out a short laugh. "Taylor's been sick since he tore up his knee. That's why he needs Nurse Julie," he responded and playfully tossed a pillow at her.

"Right," Marc muttered. "I'll go check on him."

As Marc made his way towards Taylor's bedroom, he wondered if any of Taylor's friends were worried about him. The look Josh gave Marc made it clear he knew Taylor was on drugs. *Maybe they don't realize how dangerous snorting opiates can be? Maybe no one knows he's snorting them?*

A few seconds later, Marc knocked loudly on Taylor's bedroom door. After getting no response, he knocked again and called out, "Taylor! The game just started! Are you okay?"

"Come in," Taylor replied.

When Marc entered the room, he found his brother sitting on his bed, peering at an iPad. "What are you doing?" Marc asked and took a seat at the end of Taylor's bed.

"Watching highlights from the Pats game," Taylor responded without looking up at Marc.

"O-kay. You don't want to hang out with us?"

Taylor looked up at him. "I just need a few minutes by myself. Sometimes I get like this."

Marc lowered his eyebrows. He had expected to find Taylor nodding off, not being anti-social by choice. His brother was one of the most outgoing people he knew. "It's bothering you that you're not playing this season, huh?"

"More than you can imagine," Taylor replied and looked back down at his iPad. "I'll be back out there in a few minutes. Go keep Julie company for me."

"Does she know?" Marc asked.

"Know what?"

"That you get high."

"I don't think 'high' is the right word," Taylor remarked before taking a deep breath. "She knows I'm having a hard time dealing with things. I'm surprised she hasn't broken up with me yet."

"She loves you, dude. She thinks you're depressed."

"I don't know what she thinks anymore."

"Don't you want things to work out?"

Taylor shrugged. "I don't know."

"Well, she's great, so I would hang on to her as long as you can," Marc said before standing up to leave the room. "See you out there in a few."

"See ya."

Marc closed the door behind him, hating the apathetic person sitting in Taylor's bedroom. That person wasn't his brother but rather an imposter who had stolen Taylor from his family and friends. Sadly, Marc could not remember the last time he actually conversed with the brother he loved. He was curious to hear what Julie had to say because he was certain she felt robbed of her boyfriend the way he felt deprived of his brother.

When Taylor joined everyone in the living room before the end of the first quarter, his mood seemed elevated. He offered no explanation to Julie for his absence, even though she looked concerned. During the second quarter, Taylor's cell phone buzzed with a text that prompted him to jump up and say, "I'm going to run to 7-Eleven. Does anyone need anything?"

"Can you get me a sugar-free Red Bull?" Josh's girlfriend Jenn asked.

"Sure thing," Taylor replied and smiled at her. "What else?"

"Dunkin' Donuts is right next to 7-Eleven. Can you run in and grab me an iced coffee?" Matt's girlfriend Meghan asked. "I'll text you my order."

"Only because you're cute, Meghan," Taylor replied. "Actually, I could never say no to a Dunkin' run. I'd be betraying my name. If anyone else wants anything, just text me. I'll be back before halftime."

Marc assumed Taylor was meeting one of his customers in the 7-Eleven parking lot. No one seemed surprised by Taylor abruptly running out the door in the middle of the game, so Marc assumed it happened a lot.

"Can you drive me home at halftime?" Julie asked, turning toward Marc.

"Yeah. Absolutely," he replied, eyeing her sympathetically.

"Thanks," she said quietly.

Taylor returned to the apartment right as Marc and Julie were heading out the door. "Where are you guys going?" he asked while walking past them into the kitchen with a tray of iced coffees and a 7-Eleven bag.

"I have to study," Julie replied. "Marc's going to drive me home."

Taylor set the drinks down on the counter and then playfully tapped the visor of Marc's hat. "Thanks, buddy," he said. "Call me after you finish studying," he added and locked his blue eyes on Julie.

Julie looked downcast when she glanced up at Taylor. "Enjoy the rest of the game," she said halfheartedly.

Taylor hugged her goodbye and then gave Marc props before carrying the iced coffees out of the room.

"Are you sure you don't want to stay?" Marc questioned Julie as they neared the front door.

"Positive," Julie replied and led Marc outside.

"What do you think is wrong with him?" Marc asked as soon as he and Julie were situated inside his truck.

"I don't know if the ride to my apartment is long enough to answer that question," Julie remarked. "Do you know how to get to Newbury Street from here?"

Marc nodded.

"Great. Let's head that way. I live on Gloucester. Thank you for doing this, Marc."

"I'm happy to have a chance to talk to you."

Julie sighed. "You wouldn't have asked me how he's doing unless you could tell something's wrong with him."

"Right."

"I try, Marc. I try so hard. I can't reach him anymore. He's in complete despair."

"Well, his life is far from where he thought it would be. Taylor was told since the day he stepped onto a football field that he was a star destined for fame."

"He gave up on school. I mean, that is something I never expected. He never got anything below a B before his injury. He stopped going to class or studying. He became a hermit."

"I know you basically moved in with him and Ryan for the first few months after he got injured. You were a huge help."

"Taylor was appreciative back then. He didn't get lazy 'til after his second surgery. I thought it was just a side effect of his medication, but obviously that wasn't the problem."

"Why do you say that?"

"Well, he's still unmotivated, and he's been off his pain meds since the spring."

"Has he?" Marc questioned her.

Julie nodded. "I used to drop his prescriptions off for him at the pharmacy every month. The doctor stopped prescribing him Percocet in March."

"Percocet or OxyContin?"

"He was never prescribed OxyContin."

"Well, I'm sure he could get his hands on either one if he still wanted to," Marc stated-matter-of-factly, hoping to get Julie to consider the possibility.

"He could probably get anything he wants from Rob. Rumor has it, Rob's connected to the mafia and deals drugs."

"Yeah, I heard. He sold ecstasy to my friend. What do kids at Northeastern say about Taylor now that he's gone? Are there any rumors about him?"

"They all think it's sad that he blew out his knee," Julie replied. "Everyone hopes he comes back. People have nothing bad to say about your brother."

"Why do *you* think he's changed so much?"

Julie sighed. "I think it was a chain reaction. At first, he was depressed that he couldn't play but motivated to get better. He was in some pain, but I think he could have taken fewer meds. They made him too tired, and he had a hard time keeping up with his schoolwork. I still remember how upset he was when he got his first C on a test. After a while, he hoped for Cs and settled for even lower. He was convinced his teachers would give him the C+ minimum he needed to stay in his major. When two of them didn't, he was shocked."

"He should have just taken a medical leave of absence."

"After his second surgery? For sure. When he got his first trimester grades, he came over to my apartment and cried. It was the first time in a long time that he was open with me. He told me that he died on the football field. He said he didn't know who he was anymore and that he didn't deserve me. I had never heard him speak so dramatically, but I don't even think he was exaggerating. I think he really felt that way."

"He was every athlete from my town's idol," Marc said. "I grew up wanting to be him."

"It must be so hard for you to see him so lost."

Marc nodded.

"I promised I would see him through everything, but things didn't get any better. Even after being put on academic probation, he continued to blow off class. I stopped staying over on school nights because he would beg me to stay in bed with him all day."

"I know he gave up on school, and I think he gave up on football, but I'm curious if you feel like he's given up on you," Marc pressed.

Julie rested her head against the window and sighed. "I often wonder if he's cheating on me."

"Really?"

"He's secretive about things. He was never like that before. I think he's shutting me out, and people usually only do that if they're feeling guilty about something."

"I know Taylor's changed a lot, but I don't think he would ever cheat on you. He's always been a one-girl type of guy. Jordan's the womanizer in our family."

"I love Jordan," Julie said. "He tried to help Taylor a lot when he was home this summer, but Taylor pushed him away. I think it kills him that Jordan's playing for Notre Dame."

"It's surprising how well Jordan's doing. Everyone's money was on Taylor being the successful one."

"A long time ago, Taylor told me you and Jordan were more alike than either of you realized. After getting to know you both, I agree."

"You probably know Jordan better than I do."

"Despite how aloof Taylor has been, he still worries about both of you. He wants you and Jordan to mend things."

"Did he tell you why we're not close anymore?"

Julie nodded.

"Taylor believes Jordan, but he doesn't know Jordan pledged to take Michelle's virginity before graduation. If Jordan didn't tell me that, I wouldn't think he drugged her."

"It would mean a lot to Taylor if you gave Jordan the benefit of the doubt."

"It would mean a lot to me if Taylor would be honest with you."

"You think he's being dishonest?"

"Does he always disappear for a while when everyone's hanging out?"

"He loves watching football, but at the same time, it makes him sad. He doesn't like letting people see him depressed, so he disappears to recoup."

Marc rolled his eyes. Julie was far too innocent, pure hearted, and naïve to suspect that Taylor was disappearing to get high. "Do you think that's why he went to 7-Eleven in the middle of the game?"

"I'm sure he just wanted an energy drink or something," Julie replied.

"Why did he stop drinking?" Marc pressed. He was trying to bring up signs of Taylor's drug abuse in hopes something would register with her.

"He stopped drinking when he was put on pain meds because it's dangerous to drink on them."

"Yeah, but you said he stopped taking pain meds in March."

Julie eyed Marc thoughtfully before saying, "What do *you* think is going on?"

Marc took a deep breath and let it out slowly. He couldn't betray Taylor by telling Julie about his addiction, but he wanted her to figure it out. "I think you should tell Taylor that you're afraid he's cheating on you because he seems distant. See what he says. He might offer an explanation you've never considered."

"I want him to see a therapist. I think he needs to be put on an antidepressant."

"He's way too proud to go to therapy."

"Well, he has nothing to be proud of anymore," Julie muttered.

Marc glanced over at her. "Why are you still with him?"

"I love him," Julie replied immediately. "We've been together for a year and a half. He used to say he wanted to get married after I graduated. He said he'd take me wherever his football career led him."

"Well, what does he say now?"

"We haven't talked about the future lately. I want him to enroll in non-degree coursework at Northeastern or BC. I think he'll feel less depressed if he starts doing more with his time than working out, sleeping, and binge-watching TV shows."

"Julie, ask him to be honest with you about his problems," Marc said in a serious tone.

"You sound like you know something I don't."

"He's my brother, and I love him, but there's more going on with him than depression."

"I was afraid of that."

"What does your gut tell you?"

Julie shook her head and shrugged.

"Figure out why he doesn't drink anymore, and you'll be on the right track."

"Do you think he's still taking painkillers?" Julie asked.

Marc clenched the steering wheel tightly. "What do you think? I mean, you're going into the medical field. Does he seem like someone with an opiate addiction?"

Julie let out a heavy breath and rested the back of her head against the seat.

"Ask him to be honest with you," Marc insisted.

"I always ask him to be honest," Julie said.

"Then ask him if he still takes painkillers."

"But why would he do that? His knee is healed."

"Some people drink when they're depressed; others go to therapy; some turn to God; and some use drugs. T's depressed, and I wouldn't put anything past him at this point."

"He still comes to church sometimes."

"Well, good."

"When we started dating, he told me that your family was religious. He made it sound important to him. I'm Protestant, so we used to alternate going to Baptist and Catholic churches. He doesn't always get out of bed for church anymore, but if he's awake, he comes."

"Julie, if he depended on God the way my dad depends on God, he wouldn't be depressed like this," Marc said matter-of-factly. "Maybe he tries to turn to God? Sometimes? Maybe? I guess it's possible, but I think he's probably turning to something else more frequently."

"I'm not going to tell him we had this conversation," Julie pledged, "but I *am* going to figure out the problem. If he admits to taking pills, I can bring him to rehab or go with him to NA. I hate drugs, but I know they're addictive. I know his injury was brutal. I wouldn't leave him over it. I would help him."

Marc smiled. "Well, I really hope he lets you."

CHAPTER 10

ON MONDAY, JASON OPTED to stay after school for extra credit, so Cathy went over to her best friend Lisa's house. The girls spent the afternoon in one deep conversation after another, discussing everything from Chris's new relationship with Marielle to Jason's concerning behavior.

"The fact that Jay won't admit to drinking in school—when it's super obvious—proves that he's been lying to me," Cathy concluded after a half-hour discussion about her boyfriend.

"He's always lied to you," Lisa remarked. "How can you be surprised?"

"He hid things from me because he didn't want me to worry about him," Cathy said defensively. "He's not a liar; he just doesn't want to give me anxiety."

"I didn't say he was a jerk for lying. I just said he's lied to you throughout your entire relationship."

"He's lost without Chris."

"Well, I know what *that* feels like, but Chris is way better off without Jay in his life."

"I know," Cathy said downheartedly. "Maybe if I stop eating edibles, Jay will go straightedge with me?"

"What would that do to your anxiety?"

Cathy shrugged. "I don't know, but I'd do anything to get him to sober up."

"Anything?"

"Pretty much."

"Want me to help you come up with some ideas?" Lisa offered. "Jay's feeling how you felt after your fight with Chantal. He and Chris were like brothers. He's just trying to make the pain go away."

Cathy sighed. "I know, but using drugs is just going to put more space between him and Chris. I'm going to confront him about everything tonight. I know where he keeps his stuff, and I want to know what he's really been up to."

Lisa took a deep breath. "Well, be prepared for the worst."

***

Around seven o'clock, Jason and Luke picked Cathy up from Lisa's to bring her back to their home. Knowing she had to be home by nine, Cathy planned to keep her conversation with Jason short. He seemed excited to spend time with her, but she was dreading the argument she could foresee on the horizon.

When they entered Jason's house, his mother called him into the kitchen. "Meet me upstairs," Cathy said to him before following Luke up to the second floor. She was happy to have the chance to search Jason's room before he could stop her.

When she opened his desk drawer, her stomach dropped. She was staring at multiple prescription bottles, a rolled-up dollar bill, a half-full liter of vodka, a bag of weed, and an unopened pack of cigarettes. One by one, she put everything on top of his desk, reading the labels carefully: Adderall, Vicodin, and Xanax. She wondered if he had started dealing drugs or if he was actually using them all. Either possibility was frightening.

When Jason entered his bedroom a moment later, he halted at the sight of Cathy standing by his desk with her arms crossed. "I can explain," he said before shutting his bedroom door.

"Xanax, Jason?!" Cathy cried and held up the bottle. "What the heck are you doing with the drug you made me promise never to take?!"

Jason took a deep breath. "Sit down," he said and pointed to his bed.

Cathy glared at him. "I'll sit right here," she retorted and sat down at his desk.

"Okay. Okay."

"What are you doing with Xanax, Vicodin, and cigarettes?" she questioned him angrily.

"Those cigarettes obviously are not for me," Jason snapped. "Some of our friends asked me to get them from Missy."

"Who wanted them?" Cathy asked.

Jason shrugged. "Basically, everyone. You, me, and Jon are our only friends who've never smoked."

"None of our friends smoke."

Jason eyed her strangely. "Are you that naïve?"

Cathy lowered her eyebrows. She was a bit offended by his comment. Naïve was not a term she would ever use to describe herself.

"Okay, let me break this down for you," Jason said. "You, me, and Jon don't smoke; everyone else has at least tried it. If they don't smoke, they vape, which is just as bad."

"When did our friends start vaping?" Cathy asked, wondering if he was exaggerating. She had heard of upperclassmen getting caught Juuling in the bathrooms at school, but she did not think it had become a fad for the freshmen.

"People pass vapes around like joints," Jason informed her. "You'll see when we go out this weekend. Lisa, Leslie, and Bryan have all asked me if Luke can get cartridges."

"For weed oil?" Cathy asked.

"No. Nicotine, or, uh, 'nic' as the cool kids call it," Jason replied sarcastically. "I think it will just make everyone more apt to smoke in the future."

"Is Luke going to get them?"

"I haven't asked," Jason replied. "I don't want to condone it."

"But you got them cigarettes?"

"They knew Missy bought them last month, so I couldn't say no."

"Who are 'they'?" Cathy asked.

"Everyone," Jason responded. "You'll see what I mean."

Despite how perplexed she was, she knew she had to move on to the more pressing issue. "Why do you have Xanax?"

"I can't sleep without it," Jason replied matter-of-factly.

Cathy dropped her jaw. "You asked me to stop taking a drug that treated my anxiety and then started taking it?!"

"Adderall keeps me up," Jason responded defensively. "I can't smoke weed before bed when my parents are home. What do you expect me to do? Not sleep?"

"Eat an edible!"

"I don't have edibles. Luke gives every packet he gets to you."

Cathy crossed her arms. "You were petrified of Xanax, so you made me switch to edibles. Now, you take Xanax so I can eat the edibles?"

Jason nodded.

"Benzos don't scare you?"

Jason rolled his eyes. "I just take half a pill to help me sleep. It's not going to change my personality."

"What happened to weaning yourself off Adderall so you could sleep like a normal person?"

"That's not going to happen anytime soon," Jason muttered.

Cathy lifted the rolled-up dollar bill off the desk and held it in front of her. "Snorting it much?"

Jason dropped his eyes to the floor. "It helps me get through the day when I start to crash," he admitted.

Cathy felt fury rising up inside of her as she stared at him in disbelief.

"I'm sorry," he added. "I've just devised a system: Adderall to get me through the day; Xanax to help me shut down before bed."

"Do you know how bad it is to snort amphetamines?" she questioned him.

"You should try it. You'd probably like it."

Cathy groaned. "I hate you right now!" she exclaimed. "What is wrong with you?"

Jason laughed. "Nothing—I was kidding."

"If there was nothing wrong with you, then you wouldn't need uppers and downers to function."

"I've been lonely and bored."

"No kidding—me too—but I kept my promise to you," she retorted.

"If any of this was changing me, you would have noticed when I saw you on the weekends."

Cathy scoffed. "Changing you? I don't even know who you are anymore."

"Seriously?" Jason questioned her. "I think you're being a bit dramatic."

"Why do you have Vicodin?"

"When I take it, I only need one drink to feel buzzed."

Cathy rested her head in her hands. Without Chris in his life, Jason was a wreck. With that thought, she looked up at him. "A few months ago, you were worried sick about Chris. You wanted him to stay away from the pills you now take. How can you not see a problem with that?"

"Chris?" Jason questioned her with a disgusted look on his face. "My 'best friend' who begged me to try drugs with him and then ditched me because I did?"

Cathy scowled. "That's not what happened."

"I know better than anyone what happened," Jason snapped.

"I can't stand you right now!" Cathy stated with frustration. "Why can't I get through to you? *You are a smart person.* Why can't you see how ridiculous you are being?"

"I don't know. Maybe all the drugs are making me dumb?" he suggested sarcastically.

"You think staying after for extra credit is going to keep your teachers from noticing when you drink in class?"

Jason rolled his eyes. "I've never been drunk in school."

"This vodka," she said and held up the bottle, "you put it in a water bottle and drink it during school. I know this because you turn into a jerk. You become mean and annoying when you drink."

"Thanks. Love you too. So glad you're not grounded anymore."

Cathy took a deep breath before beginning to speak. "Your average day now consists of waking up, snorting Adderall, going to school, drinking in class, snorting more Adderall, smoking weed after school, and taking Xanax before bed?"

Jason eyed her thoughtfully. "I would describe it as waking up; taking medicine I'm prescribed; dominating in school; getting buzzed when I'm forced to be in the same room as Chris; taking more of my prescribed medicine; smoking weed to calm down from my prescribed medicine when I no longer need it; and then getting a healthy eight hours of shut-eye thanks to a sleeping pill."

Cathy covered her mouth and stared at him in disbelief. "You are so self-deceived," she remarked after dropping her hand to her side. As she took a deep breath and attempted to calm her heart rate, she wondered if she was on the verge of a panic attack. A few seconds later, she stood up and snatched the bottle of Xanax off Jason's desk. "I'm going to ask Luke for a ride home. Don't call me."

"I'm not going to call you until you stop being a bitch," Jason retorted.

Tears filled Cathy's eyes as she walked out of the room. She did everything in her power to prevent herself from crying before knocking on Luke's door. Nevertheless, she was certain she looked upset, and when Luke opened the door, his expression confirmed that notion. "What's wrong?" he immediately asked.

"Can you please drive me home?"

"Sure. Is Jay coming?"

Cathy shook her head.

"Are you guys in a fight?"

Cathy nodded.

"All right. Let's go," Luke said and nodded for her to follow him down the hallway.

Cathy remained silent as she followed Luke downstairs and outside to his car. Her mind was full of troubling thoughts. After she sat down in the front seat of his BMW, she found the courage to express herself. "Do you think Jay's been acting weird?" she asked once Luke began driving.

"He's a pain in the ass," Luke replied immediately.

"Well, maybe you shouldn't give him Xanax, alcohol, and Vicodin," she retorted in an accusatory tone.

"I gave him vodka; he took the Xanax and Vicodin out of my safe."

Cathy scowled. "Well, that's disturbing. I suggest you change the code."

"I did," Luke said. "Jay was bored out of his mind without you or Chris all month."

"Can you tell your parents?"

"If I do, he'll tell on me for giving him weed and alcohol," Luke replied. "My parents would kill me."

"Can Matt tell on him?"

"Matt hardly sees Jay because he's so busy with football. He doesn't know what Jay does."

"Why don't you tell him?"

Luke let out a heavy breath. "Matt would blame me for corrupting him. He loves Jason and hates me."

"You two hang out all the time. He doesn't hate you."

"Oh, he hates me for throwing a party that got him grounded for two weeks. Trust me; I am *not* Matt's favorite person right now."

"Well, if he loves Jason, he'll do more than just blame you. He'll try to talk some sense into him. Matt's always been able to get through to Jay."

"Truuuue...I guess I could mention it to him when we're in school, when he can't strangle me."

"I hate Jason right now," Cathy admitted. "I'm not just mad; I actually hate him."

"So, break up with him. That would wake him up."

Cathy gasped, surprised that Luke would ever suggest such a thing. "I don't like to act on my feelings," she remarked.

"Well, if there's one thing I know about Jay, it's that he loves you."

"He called me a bitch!"

"Was he drunk?"

"I don't think so."

"Well, he's usually only rude when he's drunk."

"I know, but he wasn't. Can mixing Adderall, Vicodin, weed, and Xanax make someone go psychotic?"

"I thought he weaned himself off Adderall?"

Cathy let out a short, unamused laugh. "Yeah, he weaned himself off taking it orally; now he strictly snorts it multiple times per day."

Luke quickly glanced at Cathy and then locked his hazel eyes back on the road. "So, he's a complete mess."

"He's bitter about Chris," Cathy said. "He's said a lot of bad things about him lately."

"Well, that's the pot calling the kettle black because Jay is doing just about everything Chris used to do."

"Thankfully not *everything*," Cathy muttered, "but Chris used things sporadically. Jason's binging."

Luke sighed. "He begged me not to give you Xanax. Why would he start taking it?"

"To sleep," Cathy replied.

"Well, if he stopped snorting Adderall, he'd be able to sleep."

"Right?"

Luke groaned. "I know I don't have a leg to stand on here, but Jason's been given everything he's ever wanted on a silver platter. No one ever says no to him. Everyone loves him. He's never had to overcome hardship—not until Chris stopped being his friend. He has no idea how to deal with rejection or pain. The mess he's made of himself is a product of being spoiled rotten."

Cathy laughed. "You drive a BMW convertible, and Matt has a Lexus SUV. You're all spoiled, but Jay's the only one with a drug problem. It's not your parents' fault."

"I don't think it's their fault either. What I'm saying is Jay's immature. When I transferred from St. Timothy's to Hamilton for middle school, I had a rough time. I hooked up with the wrong kid's ex-girlfriend, and before I knew it, a bunch of peeps were after me. I was used to fighting with Matt, so I had no trouble beating up anyone who picked a fight with me, but seventh grade was not fun. To this day, I'm hardly friends with anyone in my grade."

"The girls all like you," Cathy interjected.

"I'm flattered, but that's not my point."

"I get what you're saying. Jay's never had to deal with a letdown, so he has no idea how to cope."

"He's had the same best friends since elementary school; he's had his way with every girl he's liked; he's achieved every academic goal he's set for himself; he has never been let down by anyone—not even himself."

Cathy glanced at Luke thoughtfully, surprised that he had so much perspective. Clearly, Luke was intuitive, despite his party-boy reputation. She decided that Jason was wrong to consider Luke an idiot. "You're right! He's a big baby."

Luke laughed. "He is, and that's why I think you should break up with him. If he loses you, he'll realize he's being ridiculous. I know I'm partially to blame for this. I'm the one who brought the Vicodin and Xanax into my house. But when I gave him the code to my safe, it was to get weed. I never thought he'd take bottles of pills from me. I thought he was petrified of benzos and painkillers because of you and Chris!"

"I did too," Cathy said. "I took the bottle of Xanax when I left so he wouldn't take any more of it. You can have it back."

"Don't you want it?"

Cathy shrugged. "I haven't taken it in months. Jay thinks it makes me cold. I don't want to become an insensitive jerk."

"You might have to become an insensitive jerk to stay in a relationship with him," Luke joked.

"Touché," Cathy muttered.

CHAPTER 11

ON THE PHONE LATER that evening, Cathy filled Lisa in on her argument with Jason. "It makes no sense because he used to be against benzos and painkillers!" she cried after she finished explaining everything. "You know how worried he was about Chris."

"Well, watch out because Percocet, coke, and molly will probably come next if he's following Chris's footsteps," Lisa warned her.

Cathy sighed. "I fell in love with a rational person. How did I lose him? Where did he go?"

"I'd say it's been a slow fade."

"He's different; he's cynical; he was laughing at me for being concerned."

"So, break up with him," Lisa suggested.

"Why does everyone make that sound so easy? I can't give up on him! I have to help him!"

"How many times have we been through this with our friends? Sometimes losing someone is the best lesson of all."

"I'm not breaking up with him," Cathy stated flatly. "That's out of the question. He was patient with me when I was having anxiety attacks. He dealt with Xanax making me cold and stealing my drive to hook up with him; he dealt with me forgetting important things when I drank on Xanax; he put up with a lot."

"You're not wrong, but what's your plan?"

"I don't have one. I want you to help me come up with something. You're better at this than me."

"You don't give yourself enough credit," Lisa remarked. "What does Jay hate more than anything?"

"He hates me taking Xanax," Cathy replied. "He also hates cigarette smoking—even though he had a pack in his drawer to give to our friends. He tried to imply that everyone except me, him, and Jon smokes."

Lisa laughed. "Jay's so full of crap. Bryan and Chris are the only ones who ever smoked, and they both stopped."

"Well, the cigarettes must be for someone because Jay would never smoke."

"What if you tell him you'll start taking Xanax if he doesn't stop taking pills?" Lisa proposed.

"I don't want to take Xanax," Cathy stated.

"Well, good, but I'm suggesting you threaten Jason with it. You don't actually have to take it. Just start acting cold or careless, and he'll think you're back on it."

Cathy's stomach turned at the thought of lying to her boyfriend. "I don't want to be dishonest."

"What's more important? Being honest or getting him to stop taking pills?"

"I'm sure there's an honest way to make him stop."

"Okay, fine. What?"

"I don't know," Cathy muttered.

"You took the bottle home with you, right?"

"Yeah."

"Threaten him with it. If he doesn't take you seriously, pretend you're back on it. He'll start worrying about you and realize he's being a hypocrite. He's throwing himself a pity party, but once he starts to believe you need help, he'll take his eyes off himself and focus on you. Jay's at his best when he's helping other people."

"Cold and careless won't be easy for me to pull off, but I'd be fine with not hooking up with him."

"How far have you guys gone?"

Cathy's throat went dry. No one except Jason knew she had lost her virginity. "You know I don't like talking about that kind of stuff."

Lisa laughed. "Would you have something to say?"

"Stop," Cathy insisted. "I don't pry into your love life. I don't even know who you love anymore."

"I'm falling in love with Jeff," Lisa said, "but I still love Chris. I'm not *in love* with Chris—honestly, I don't think the boy I was in love with exists anymore. He's changed a lot since school started. Haven't you noticed? He even talks different."

"He speaks Christianese now," Cathy said with a short laugh. "That's what happens when you spend all your time in church."

Lisa laughed. "He does seem really into church. He messaged me a quote from the Bible the other day."

"So, he must still care about you," Cathy assumed. "Which one?"

"It was something about being a new creation. I figured he was trying to let me know he's in a better place."

"There is truth to the new creation thing," Cathy remarked. In fact, the change she saw in Chris gave 2nd Corinthians 5:17 new meaning.

"I guess time will tell. Anyone can go through a phase."

"I don't like church because the youth group kids are mean, but I believe the power of God is real. I just don't think many kids are aware of it unless their parents teach them."

"I always forget you're religious," Lisa said.

"Well, that's because you're not, so I don't talk to you about it."

"I'm not opposed to it. If it's helping Chris, then I'm all for it. I might not be in love with him anymore, but I want him to stay away from pills."

"I wish Jason would start going to church and stay away from pills!"

"Then pretend you're back on Xanax," Lisa pressed. "As soon as he thinks you need help, he'll forget about his own heartache and focus on you."

Cathy sighed. She knew she had plenty of legitimate reasons to give Jason the cold shoulder, but her natural instinct was to try to talk everything out with him. However, Jason was embittered, and Cathy knew his emotions were clouding his judgement.

***

On the following morning, Jason laughed in Cathy's face when she told him she would start taking Xanax if he didn't stop using Adderall, Vicodin, and Xanax. "You think it's that easy to come off Adderall?" he questioned her. "I always took you for a realist, babe."

Cathy scowled. "I'm serious, Jason! You're giving me anxiety!" She let out a heavy breath before angrily walking away from him. He left her with no choice but to take Lisa's advice.

Whenever Cathy set her mind to something, she typically got tunnel vision, so the risks of taking on a new persona did not concern her. Over the following two days, she discovered she was a far better actress than she ever imagined; acting cold and snobby was easy with the goal of helping Jason in mind.

CHAPTER 12

On Thursday afternoon, Cathy opened her locker and found a note written in her boyfriend's neat handwriting. She took a deep breath before unfolding it:

Cathy,

When Chantal broke away from you in eighth grade, I made comforting you my priority. I had never experienced the pain you were going through, but I hated seeing you gripped by depression and anxiety. I was patient with you when I could have gotten frustrated. I am asking you to show me the same courtesy.

When you took Xanax for anxiety, I did not make you feel bad for doing it. I just let you know when I got concerned. You're not just concerned about me. You're mad at me—really mad. It's not fair. I am now going through my first heartbreak ever. You are the only person I am closer with than Chris. I don't even feel like myself without him. We were best friends for ten years. No, he's not my identical twin, but it still hurts a lot.

I know Adderall is a problem. I have to cut my dose. I was planning to do that before my fight with Chris, but I've just been too sad to be motivated. Luke said today that he could get me a dab pen for weed that would help me sleep at night. I would rather do that than take Xanax. I beg you, please do not start taking Xanax again. Please don't let me be a bad influence on you.

September was the loneliest month of my life. I have never felt a burden like this before. You know what makes it worse? The fact that Chris still hangs out with Bryan and Jon. I'm pretty much the only person he ditched. I would never have done drugs if it weren't for him. Doing drugs was his idea of a bonding experience, but in the end, it tore us apart.

Please don't think I'm proud of my behavior lately. I'm just trying to learn how to cope with the emptiness I feel while keeping up my grades. I want to be a good student, a good friend, and a good boyfriend. I don't want to ruin any of that by partying. I just want to know how to take away the pain. Can you help me? The other day, you said you hated me, but what I really need is for you to love me. Please grant me some time to fix the mess I have made of myself.

– Jay

Cathy's eyes grew wider and wider as she read Jason's letter. She could not believe he had penned those words in school when a teacher could have found the note. It was so incriminating! She folded the note and stuck it in her pocket. Although she could not get past what he had written in school, his words brought her some comfort because he sounded like himself. Jason was gifted with words, and he also knew how to press Cathy's buttons. She assumed he was trying to invoke her sympathy. She was supposed to go over his house after school, but she wished she had time to process his letter beforehand.

"Hi," Jason greeted her as soon as he saw her coming toward him. She noticed that his eyes sparkled when he looked at her, which was something she had not seen in months.

"Hi," Cathy replied and dropped her eyes to the floor.

"Did you read my note?" Jason quietly asked once she reached his side.

Cathy looked up and saw a familiar look of concern in his eyes. "I did," she replied.

Jason raised his eyebrows at her. "And?"

"I just need some time to process everything."

"That's fair," Jason remarked and patted her shoulder. "I'm sorry."

Cathy could tell from the look in her boyfriend's eyes that he was sincere. Everything about his expression seemed reminiscent of the boy she had fallen in love with, and she wondered if her few days of role-playing were paying off. "I know," she muttered and looked away from him.

"Do you still want to come over my house?" Jason asked and turned her face toward his. "I know I dumped a lot on you in that letter," he added. "I get it if you want Luke to bring you home instead."

Why are you being so perfect right now? Where have you been all month? "I can think things over later," she said. "I'm fine with going to your house."

Jason smiled. "Great. Let's find Luke."

As Cathy continued to spend the afternoon with Jason, she observed that he no longer seemed angry, caustic, or bitter; he made no rude comments about Chris; and his mood was elevated. He seemed completely like the Jason of middle school.

"Why are you like this today?" she asked after he playfully tossed her down on his bed.

He hopped onto the bed beside her and wrapped his arms around her. "Like what?"

"Yourself," she replied and rolled over to face him.

"Who else have I been?" he asked before leaning in to kiss her.

"It doesn't matter," she said and pulled him on top of her.

He looked her directly in the eye and smiled widely before dropping down to kiss her neck. When he pulled her shirt over her head and began to unbutton her jeans, she realized they were about to have sex for the third time. Since August, she had been finding excuses not to sleep with him because doing so conflicted with her morals. However, the distance between them concerned her, and she thought sex could help bridge the gap.

"I love you, and I'm sorry for everything," Jason expressed and affectionately kissed her on the forehead.

"I love you too," she responded and pulled his body close to hers.

CHAPTER 13

On the following morning, Jason met Cathy at her locker before homeroom. She eyed him precariously, wondering if she had undermined all of her role-playing efforts by sleeping with him. She had no sex drive when she was on Xanax, and Jason knew that better than anyone. Therefore, chances were slim that he thought she was using benzos. This meant she would need to continue role-playing for a while to keep him fixated on her instead of his own heartbreak. Acting cold towards people made Cathy feel guilty, so she decided to focus on another side effect of Xanax.

"Did you think about my letter after you left my house?" Jason asked while peering at her expectantly. His tone and expression were reminiscent of his true self, and he appeared just as sober as he had on the previous afternoon.

Cathy took a deep breath before beginning to speak. "It was a great letter," she replied with a smile. "It's all good."

Jason looked perplexed. "All good?" he questioned her.

Cathy smiled again before saying, "Yes."

"You don't have anything else to say?"

Cathy shrugged.

"You're going to let me off the hook that easy?"

Cathy nodded.

Jason lowered his eyebrows. "Is this because I gave you an orgasm?" he whispered.

Cathy laughed and turned to grab a book out of her locker.

"Well, what can I do to make it up to you?" Jason asked and placed a hand on her shoulder.

She turned to him. "Forget it."

"O-kay," he sang gradually while staring at her skeptically.

"I have to get to homeroom," she said dismissively. "I'll see you in English, okay?"

"Let me walk you to class," Jason offered and draped his arm around her shoulders.

Cathy leaned into Jason and allowed him to lead her down the hallway. A moment later, she disappeared into her classroom, hoping her carefree attitude had rubbed her boyfriend the wrong way.

CHAPTER 14

TWO MINUTES LATER, JASON's heart sank as he spotted Chris Dunkin sitting in their homeroom. *How are you okay without me?* he wondered. Over the last five weeks, Chris had created a new identity for himself. As far as any of their teachers or peers were concerned, Chris was the star running back of MLH's JV football team, an attentive student, and a Christian. He had an innocent girlfriend who, just like him, had no interest in drugs or alcohol. He was completely sober and everything Jason had always believed Chris could be.

This made Jason begin to wonder if he had brought out the worst in Chris—or if he, in fact, brought out the worst in others. For Chris to achieve his goal of sobering up, all he had to do was remove himself from the party scene, cut Jason out of his life, and join a church. This hurt Jason deeply. He had never wanted anything but the best for his friend, yet he had somehow failed to be the type of friend Chris needed.

Deep down inside, Jason was proud of Chris, but he refused to admit that to anyone else. Instead, he tried to make himself feel better by making fun of Chris to their mutual friends. Bryan brushed everything off per usual, but Jon always defended Chris. Cathy also defended Chris, saying over and over again that Jason should not take Chris's actions personally and that Chris needed to remove himself from their social world to get a grip on his life.

After the bell rang, Jason left the room without taking another glance in Chris's direction. As he ventured towards his usual meeting spot with

Cathy, he thought about how strange her reaction had been to his letter. It was unlike her to neither express concern nor ask questions. The more he thought about it, the more he realized something was off about her behavior. Jason assumed that coming off of groundation only to discover that he had been abusing pills had increased her anxiety.

"Are you ready for our test?" he asked as soon as they met in front of her homeroom.

"I'm good," Cathy replied and began walking down the hallway. "It's only worth twenty points."

Jason raised his eyebrows. "That's as much as our term paper."

"I'll be fine," she insisted.

"Glad to see you're not stressed," Jason remarked.

Cathy smiled, and Jason wondered why she was acting so carefree. "What do you want to do this weekend?" he asked as they neared their classroom.

Cathy shrugged. "I'm up for whatever."

"Do you want to eat some 'shrooms?" he proposed, keeping his voice down to a mere whisper. He immediately turned to study her reaction: her facial expression, her breathing, the look in her eye—anything that pointed toward her being back on Xanax.

"Do whatever you want," she said in a tone that sounded neither pleased nor angry.

"Will you trip with me?" Jason pressed.

Cathy stopped short and turned toward him. Looking him straight in the eye, she shrugged and quietly said, "I think I'm done with weed."

Jason gazed at her in a perplexed manner. "What brought this on?"

Cathy smiled. "I'm not anxious anymore."

Jason eyed her skeptically, knowing she had avoided weed when she took Xanax. "Well, that's good. I guess," he said in an uneasy tone before leading her into their classroom.

CHAPTER 15

ON SATURDAY NIGHT, THERE was a bonfire in the woods behind the high school. Without Chris's house to convene at, more and more woods parties had been taking place. This particular gathering was comprised mainly of freshmen and sophomores. Matt and Luke had refused to bring Jason out with their friends, so he and Cathy were left to spend time with their own grade. Courtney had a family obligation, so Bryan was "allowed" to attend the party.

Jason, Cathy, Bryan, Alyssa, Lisa, Jeff, and Lisa's friends from student council—Leslie Lucus, Adam Case, Andy Rosetti, Bobby Ryan, and Katherine Rossi—all met at Lisa's house before the bonfire because she lived closest to the high school. Jason was surprised that Lisa's clique of preps was down for a woods party. Nevertheless, he was excited to have a large group of people he knew by his side.

"Are you going to get mad if I eat 'shrooms tonight?" he asked Cathy on the walk to the bonfire.

"No. If you eat them, I'll eat them," she replied.

"What?"

"I'll just do whatever you do from now on so we can be on the same page."

Jason's stomach dropped. "Why would you do that?"

"Well, you don't think you're being reckless, right?" Cathy questioned him.

"Is that a joke?"

Cathy laughed. "I'm serious. If you eat them, I'll eat them."

Jason's stomach turned. "You don't need to do that," he insisted.

"You seem fine and look at all the drugs you've been doing."

Jason's heart began to race; this was not his girlfriend speaking.

"I figure you won't steer me wrong," she added.

"I thought you were upset with me for being messed up all the time."

"I was," Cathy stated flatly. "Then I realized I wouldn't be upset if I did everything with you. I'm sick of being upset."

"You would take Adderall?" he asked.

"I'll try it," Cathy replied with a careless shrug.

Jason's throat went dry. "You don't have to do that," he stated flatly.

"I think it'll be for the best," Cathy insisted. "I don't want to fight with you anymore."

"Did Lisa put you up to this?"

Cathy scoffed. "No. She'd get upset if I tripped, took a painkiller, or snorted Adderall."

"So, you came up with this idea completely on your own?"

Cathy nodded.

"This is too big of a change for me to process," Jason expressed. "I thought you wanted me to get sober."

"I do," Cathy replied, "but you're not, and it's taking a toll on us."

"I'll keep trying to get there."

"Well, until then I'm going to follow your lead."

Jason wrapped his arm around Cathy's shoulders and pulled her closer toward him. "I'm only going to drink tonight," he decided.

"Are you going to take Vicodin? You've done that every weekend this month, right?"

"I've done it a lot," Jason admitted. "I don't need to do it tonight."

"If you've done it without having a problem, I'll be fine."

Jason widened his eyes, wondering what had gotten into her. "Let's just see what the scene is like at the party and decide from there," he suggested.

"Sounds good," she sang.

Jason held Cathy's hand tightly during the rest of the walk. When they reached the bonfire, he was surprised to see so many people from their grade. He honestly had no idea that many kids were interested in partying.

"Let's go over there," Andy called out while pointing across the fire. "I see Troy and Justin," he added, referring to other preppy kids in student council.

Jason rolled his eyes. The last thing he felt like doing was hanging out with a bunch of stuck-up goody-goodies. "We'll meet you guys over there in a bit," he said to Andy. "I want to see who else is here."

"All right," Andy replied and nodded for his friends to follow him.

"Jay, you brought alcohol, right?" Bryan asked.

"Oh, yeah. Anyone who wants to make a drink should do it now," Jason replied while taking off his backpack. "Luke gave me a handle of rum, so there's enough for everyone."

Cathy, Alyssa, Bryan, and Jeff stayed with Jason while Andy, Bobby, Adam, Leslie, Katherine, and Lisa headed around the bonfire to find their other friends. After pouring drinks for Alyssa, Bryan, and Jeff, Jason sent them off to find everyone else.

"What do you want to do?" he asked Cathy.

Cathy shrugged.

"You're sleeping at Alyssa's?"

Cathy nodded.

"You can't go there with dilated pupils."

"Right."

"Why don't we trip tomorrow and drink tonight?" Jason suggested.

"Whatever you want."

"If I take Vicodin, are you really going to take one?"

Cathy nodded.

"And you have no other drugs in your system?"

Cathy lowered her eyebrows. "Like what?"

"Like weed or Xanax?"

Cathy widened her eyes. "Jason!" she cried. "How many times are you going to ask me about Xanax?"

Jason sighed. "I just want to make sure because mixing Xanax, Vicodin, and alcohol landed Chris in the hospital."

"*I know*."

Jason gazed at her thoughtfully, deciding that offering her Vicodin would be a good test because he doubted she would take it if she were on Xanax. "Okay. If you take one Vicodin and have one drink, you'll be fine by the time you get to Alyssa's."

"Okay. It's your call."

A pit formed in Jason's stomach as he reached into his backpack to retrieve the Tylenol bottle that held his Vicodin. Although Cathy's willingness to take it placated his concerns about Xanax, he feared she would like Vicodin. "You really don't have to do this," he said before handing her a pill.

"You don't either."

"Well, now you're making me feel like I shouldn't."

"Of course, you shouldn't," Cathy snapped.

Jason eyed her precariously. "Are you going to resent me if you take that?"

"It's my decision," Cathy said. "I have a full stomach. I'll be fine," she added before popping the pill in her mouth and washing it down with rum and Coke.

Jason raised his eyebrows. "Okay, well, cheers," he said and clinked his cup with hers before swallowing two pills.

A large group of sophomores had shown up while Cathy and Jason were separated from their friends. There must have been at least seventy-five Montgomery Lake High underclassmen present at the bonfire. Usually, only twenty to thirty kids attended the pit parties. The chant of the crowd was growing louder and louder, and Jason feared the cops would find them if it became any rowdier.

"I didn't expect it to be this crazy," Jason admitted. "We'll have to leave if it gets too loud. You can't risk getting arrested again."

"No, I can't!" Cathy exclaimed. "How long does Vicodin take to kick in?"

"About a half hour," Jason replied. "You won't get high from one pill, but you'll feel extra buzzed from your drink."

When they joined their friends, Jason observed the scene. Leslie, Adam, and Andy were talking to a group of kids whom he did not know; Katherine and Bobby were sitting on a log near the fire; and Alyssa, Bryan, Lisa, and Jeff were standing near the trees, watching the party with amusement.

"I had no idea this many kids in our grade got after it," Jeff said to Jason as soon as he and Cathy approached them.

"Right?" Jason agreed with a short laugh.

"If I smoke weed, our whole grade will think I'm a pothead," Lisa stated in a frustrated tone.

"Why do you care what they think?" Jason asked.

"Because I could get kicked off cheerleading and student council," Lisa retorted.

"So, just go further into the woods where no one can see you," Jason suggested.

"Will you smoke with me?" Lisa asked.

"I guess," Jason shrugged.

"Cathy?" Lisa questioned her.

"No, I'm all set," Cathy replied.

Jason locked his eyes on Cathy. Had she meant she would do every drug he did except for weed? Weed seemed harmless compared to Vicodin.

"Anyone else?" Lisa offered.

"I'll smoke a cigarette," Alyssa said. "I don't want kids here seeing me and telling my brother."

"Since when do *you* smoke?" Bryan asked in a perplexed manner.

"Oh, I don't actually smoke," Alyssa responded and shook her head. "It just gives me something to do when everyone else smokes weed. I hate weed."

"I get that," Bryan said.

"You're welcome to join me," Alyssa offered. "Jeff, you are too."

"Nah, I'm good," Bryan replied.

"You guys can take your walk," Jeff said. "I'm going to talk to Andy."

Jason turned to Cathy. "Do you want to stay with Bryan and Jeff since you're not going to smoke?"

"Just come with us," Lisa urged Cathy before stepping further into the woods. "Why are you suddenly anti-weed?"

Cathy stepped in front of Jason and followed Lisa. "I just don't like it anymore," she replied. "It slows down my mind, and I can't socialize."

Jason caught up to Cathy and used his cell phone to illuminate the path before them.

"And you can't show up at my house high," Alyssa said while following after the girls. "My parents pick up on everything."

"Right," Cathy agreed.

"A couple of years ago, Day came over high, and my parents called her parents," Alyssa recounted as they walked deeper into the woods. "Then they forced my brother to take a drug test. They're paranoid. Day's been straightedge for over a year, and they still doubt her. John is planning to propose to her before they leave for college, and my parents are *not* happy about it—even though the girl is the mayor's daughter and basically a saint."

"It's so weird that your brother dates Courtney's sister," Jason remarked. "I remember seeing her at Chris's house during a few parties, but Bryan never told us she was related to Court."

"Bryan told us nothing about Courtney and told her nothing about us. That's why she was so eager to get to know everyone," Alyssa said. "I love Bryan, but it's weird that he isolated her."

Lisa scoffed. "Do you actually like that girl?"

"I was mad that she stayed friends with Jon after he broke up with me, but I'm over it," Alyssa replied.

"You're too nice," Lisa stated. "Courtney's shallow. Bryan deserves so much better. I wish you two would just date."

Jason laughed. "Sartelli would never do that to Anderson."

"I know, but I wish he would," Lisa retorted.

"You just hate Courtney because Chris dated her after you," Jason said and nudged Lisa playfully in the shoulder.

"Probably," Lisa admitted.

"How far into the woods do you guys want to go?" Cathy asked from the other side of Jason.

"This is good," Jason assessed, stopping in front of a large pine tree. "How do you feel, Cathy?"

"Fine," she replied flatly.

"Are you sure you don't want to smoke?" Lisa asked while pulling a joint out of her pocketbook.

"For the hundredth time—yes, I'm sure," Cathy stated firmly.

"You put so much pressure on people," Alyssa complained to Lisa. "I'm surprised you haven't gotten Andy to try weed yet."

Lisa laughed. "Oh, but I did!"

Alyssa, Cathy, and Jason widened their eyes.

"Does Chantal know?" Cathy asked.

"He said he would be honest with her," Lisa replied. "He's too honest."

"Did he like it?" Jason asked.

Lisa shook her head from side to side and passed Jason the joint. "Nope, and he doesn't want his other friends to know he tried it."

"You guys keep a lot of secrets from each other," Jason remarked before taking a hit off the joint. He was already starting to feel buzzed, so he did not want to get too high—especially since he knew the Vicodin would kick in shortly. "I'm out," he said and handed the joint back to Lisa.

Lisa lowered her eyebrows. "One hit?" she asked. "What else did you take?"

"Vicodin," Jason replied. "I shouldn't have smoked."

"Didn't mean to 'peer pressure' you," Lisa said facetiously.

Alyssa rolled her eyes and retrieved a cigarette and a lighter from her pocketbook. "Don't give me crap about smoking after you just smoked weed," she said to Jason.

Jason laughed and watched Alyssa light her cigarette. "I'm just wondering how long this phase is going to last because smoking doesn't suit you at all," he stated matter-of-factly.

"Relax. I've smoked, like, five times in my life," Alyssa retorted and playfully pushed Jason in the chest.

"Can I try that?" Cathy asked and gestured towards the cigarette.

At the sound of Cathy's words, Jason's heart began to race.

"Sure," Alyssa replied and passed Cathy her cigarette. "I'd rather you smoke with me than yell at me for doing it."

Lisa looked as though she was trying not to laugh. Then again, she was likely pretty high and finding things more humorous than usual. Jason, on the other hand, was not high enough to take Cathy holding a cigarette in her hand lightly, and he was not discrete enough to conceal his emotions.

"What are you doing?" he exclaimed as soon as he found his voice. He reached forward to rip the cigarette out of her hand, but she jumped backwards. "If you take a haul off that, I'm not going to speak to you for the rest of the night," he stated angrily.

Cathy's eyes sparkled. She appeared to be finding the situation extremely amusing for some reason. "You can't get mad at me if I try this," she said. "You just smoked weed."

Jason stared at her in awe. Even the look in her eye was different from usual. "Are you that messed up from *one* Vicodin?" he questioned her.

"I can't even feel the Vicodin," Cathy replied.

"Why am I the only one completely weirded out by this?" Jason questioned the other girls.

"You can't get mad if she would rather smoke a cigarette than weed," Lisa stated matter-of-factly.

Jason felt ambushed. However, Alyssa and Lisa's lack of surprise led him to believe they knew exactly what Cathy's motive was. The only thing apparent was that Cathy was trying to irritate him. He decided she would be less apt to smoke if he removed himself from the situation. "I'm out," he stated in a frustrated tone before hustling back to the bonfire.

CHAPTER 16

FIFTEEN MINUTES LATER, JASON was sitting on a log with Bryan and Jeff when he caught sight of Cathy, Lisa, and Alyssa. They looked as happy as could be, completely unfazed by Jason's outburst. Any buzz he had hoped to get from the alcohol, Vicodin, or weed had been completely squashed by his concern for his girlfriend. He was confused, worried, and angry all at once. Either she was trying to get under his skin, having a mental breakdown, or going through an identity crisis. Alyssa and Lisa's lack of concern was also puzzling. Even when he mentioned that Cathy took Vicodin, neither girl had looked alarmed.

"There are the girls," Jeff said. "Are they stoned?"

"Just your girlfriend," Jason replied.

Jeff sighed. "She shouldn't have smoked with so many people around. She has too much at stake to get caught."

"People give me crap for being a pothead, but Lisa smokes more than me," Jason said.

"I hate it," Jeff admitted. "I get that she's grieving her dad and that she doesn't like alcohol, but she used to be against drugs. She hasn't been herself since she dated Chris the second time."

"Chris was a mess, and he broke her heart," Jason stated bluntly.

"It's more than that," Jeff asserted. "She's different because of him."

"Aren't we all," Jason muttered, sounding more bitter than he had intended.

"Cathy convinced Lisa to try weed," Bryan spoke up. "Lisa might have hidden it from you, but she tried it before she ever got back together with Chris."

"I'm not surprised. She's full of secrets," Jeff said. "I'm not saying it's Chris's fault that Lisa smokes pot. I'm saying something happened between them that changed her."

"Speaking of secrets... she told me she got Andy high," Jason said, wondering if Jeff knew.

"Oh, yeah. I heard."

"I don't know why I'm surprised. She got *you* to try it," Jason stated with wide eyes.

"She hung a stupid comment I made over my head to make me do it," Jeff said. "I felt bad. Otherwise, I would never have given into her prodding."

"Lisa is, hands down, the most manipulative person I've ever met," Jason commented. "I love her to death, but she's vicious when she wants something."

Jeff nodded. "Thankfully, I've learned how to see through her."

"She has a lot of influence on Cathy," Jason stated and glanced at his girlfriend, "more than I do. Cathy's acting weird, and I bet Lisa knows exactly what's going through her head," he added, wondering if his friends had noticed the change in his girlfriend's attitude.

"Uh, Cathy's been having some *serious* mood swings this week," Jeff remarked.

Jason nodded. "I'm pretty freaked out."

"What drugs have you given her?" Jeff asked.

"I don't think she's on any drugs," Jason replied. "She doesn't even like weed anymore."

Jason locked his eyes on Cathy, who was chatting with Leslie, Katherine, Alyssa, and Lisa. Nothing about her seemed tense, and she clearly was not worried about Jason being angry with her. He looked down at his phone to check the time: 9:33 p.m. They would need to leave in an hour to walk back to Lisa's. He wondered if Cathy was going to ignore him for the remainder of the night.

"Are you and Cathy in a fight?" Bryan, who had been quietly observing the party, asked from the other side of Jeff.

"No," Jason replied. "I'm just trying to figure out why she's being weird." He knew in his gut that Cathy's behavior had something to do with him. "I better check on her. I'll leave my backpack with you guys. Feel free to make another drink. I'm done."

"You're a lightweight lately," Jeff teased him.

"Weed and alcohol don't mix well," Jason responded. "I need my legs to work for the walk back."

Jeff laughed. "Fair enough."

Bryan was eyeing Jason precariously, and Jason thought he looked worried. Although Bryan rarely spoke his mind, Jason knew he was astutely perceptive. There was a fair chance he could tell Jason had been using drugs more potent than weed.

As Jason approached Cathy, she gave him a mischievous smirk. Everything about her demeanor was peculiar. Cathy's kind eyes and sweet smile were two of the characteristics he loved the most about her. Those attributes had seemingly vanished, and he was dying to uncover the impetus. As he stepped into the girls' circle, he noticed that Cathy's drink was still full.

"Can I talk to you?" he asked.

She scoffed. "I knew you couldn't go the rest of the night without speaking to me."

Jason lowered his eyebrows. "Did you smoke?"

"Does it matter?" Cathy taunted him. "You were going to talk to me either way."

Jason rolled his eyes. "Can we talk alone?"

Cathy let out a dramatic sigh and then stepped past Jason toward the bonfire.

"What is this attitude?" Jason questioned her once anyone they knew was out of hearing distance.

"What attitude?" Cathy asked.

"I never thought you would take Vicodin or agree to trip with me. I don't even want to know if you smoked. I'm just trying to figure out what has happened to your morals."

"My morals? I'm following your lead."

"Don't," Jason stated flatly. "I'm trying to trace my steps backwards and climb out of the pit I dug myself into last month."

"Then why did you take Vicodin tonight? Why do you want to trip tomorrow?" Cathy asked and placed her hands on her hips. "I'm sorry, but it doesn't look like you're trying."

Jason scowled. "I didn't want to take Vicodin *or* eat mushrooms," he admitted. "I've been worried about you, so I mentioned mushrooms and painkillers to see your reaction."

"What?" Cathy asked and crossed her arms.

"Sometimes you're as easy going as Alyssa, and other times you're as caustic as Lisa. You are rarely yourself. You've been like this since our argument. I don't know what to think."

Cathy lowered her eyebrows. "So, tempting me with mushrooms and painkillers was your way of getting answers?"

Jason placed his hands on Cathy's shoulders and looked her directly in the eye. "I needed to make sure you weren't back on Xanax."

Cathy pushed his hands off of her in a frustrated manner.

"You took Vicodin, so I know you're not on Xanax, but that just raises more questions. If not Xanax, then what is going on with you?"

Cathy laughed. "This is priceless coming from you. You are the master chameleon. I've never met anyone who can wear so many faces."

Jason eyed her strangely.

"Don't look surprised," Cathy said. "I can read people like open books. You've taught me well."

"What are you talking about?"

"I want you to worry about me the way I've been worrying about you," Cathy explained.

Jason squinted at her. "You're worried? I would never have known by the way you've been acting."

"I'm a good actress," Cathy remarked. "I didn't know until I tried."

"Well, can you stop? Please?"

"Oh, no," Cathy said. "I meant what I said. Whatever you do, I do."

"That's not going to make getting sober any easier for me," Jason remarked.

"Yes, it will," Cathy sang. "You love me enough not to lead me down a dark path now that you know I'm following you. Luke and Lisa both told me to break up with you, but I love you enough to go wherever you take me."

Jason felt as though the wind had been knocked out of him. "This is your way of putting pressure on me to straighten out?"

Cathy smiled. "This is my way of pressing your buttons. You're at your best when you're trying to help other people. Few things bring you the satisfaction of someone else leaning on you."

At that moment, Jason wished he had never introduced Cathy to psychology. "I need to go home," he blurted out. "You can stay, or I can walk you back to Lisa's."

"I'm sleeping over Alyssa's. I have to do whatever she does."

"Right. Well, find out what her plan is," Jason said. "I'm going to say bye to the guys."

"I've risked getting a lot of people mad at me this week," Cathy remarked. "Don't make my efforts count for nothing. I don't enjoy acting like a bitch."

"You're too smart to put yourself through this," Jason stated before turning away from her.

As he walked over to Bryan and Jeff, he felt like a fool who had been played. Deciding it would be best to go home and sort out his thoughts alone, he quickly retrieved his backpack and said bye to his friends before walking back over to Cathy.

"Alyssa wants to stay," Cathy informed him.

"Then I'll stay, too," Jason responded.

"You said you wanted to leave," Cathy stated matter-of-factly. "You don't have to stay just because of me."

"I don't want to leave you when you're on Vicodin," Jason admitted.

Cathy rolled her eyes. "I'm not *on* Vicodin," she said and handed him her full drink.

"What?"

"If you dump that out, you'll find a half-dissolved pill at the bottom."

Jason lowered his eyebrows in confusion before slowly pouring the drink on the ground. Sure enough, remnants of a white pill were at the bottom. "I saw you swallow that," he said while eyeing her strangely.

"You saw me take a sip of my drink. You didn't notice me spit the pill into the cup."

"So, that's why Lisa and Alyssa didn't get upset when I said you took Vicodin? They knew you spit it out?"

Cathy nodded.

"You tricked me?"

Cathy nodded again.

"Why tell me? Doesn't that undermine the entire point?"

Cathy smiled. "Not when I want you to leave."

Jason's heart sank. "Why do you want me to leave?"

"Because I want you to think about what happened tonight," Cathy replied. "I don't want you to get drunk and forget. Tonight was a warning. I didn't do what you did, but from now on, I will."

At that moment, Jason did not know if he was mad at her for playing mind games with him or if he was relieved that she had not actually swallowed the pill. Either way, he was not used to being outsmarted by anyone, so his pride was hurt. "You're sober?"

Cathy nodded.

"And if I leave, you're not going to drink?" he asked.

"You're the only one I know with alcohol," Cathy replied.

Jason gazed at her thoughtfully. *She's not drinking; she didn't smoke weed; and she didn't take Vicodin. She could absolutely be on Xanax.* "I'll leave," he said, "but will you call me when you get to Alyssa's so I know you got there okay?"

"Sure," Cathy agreed. "Hopefully the Vicodin doesn't impair your ability to think about your destructive actions."

"I've taken it enough to know two pills won't impair my judgement," Jason replied, trying to disregard her patronizing tone.

Cathy looked him directly in the eye. "This is not who I thought you were," she said, "and this isn't how I pictured you acting when I agreed to be your girlfriend."

Jason glanced away from her. "I know I need to fix myself," he muttered.

"Well, do it fast because I'm going to lose myself trying to save you," Cathy stated before abruptly walking back over to the girls.

CHAPTER 17

After Jason left the party, Cathy sat by the fire with Lisa and Alyssa, observing the rest of the kids gathered around them. Jason was right; vaping was rampant. Cathy could not believe how many people were taking hits off vapes that were passed around the bonfire. The germ factor alone was enough to gross her out.

"I can't believe all these kids Juul," Cathy remarked. "Do you think any of them are dabbing?"

Lisa laughed. "I doubt it. Weed cartridges are hard to come by. Didn't you say Jay hasn't even gotten one?"

"Luke's working on it," Cathy replied. "So, you think everyone's just vaping flavored nicotine?"

"Most likely," Lisa assumed. "Lyss, you should vape instead of smoke. Your brother wouldn't kill you for vaping, and no one seems to think it's a turnoff."

"I don't 'smoke,' and if I started vaping, I would get addicted because it tastes good and it's easy to hide," Alyssa responded. "I won't get addicted if I only smoke every once in a while."

"Hopefully not," Lisa said, "but most guys think smoking is gross, so I wouldn't do it around them unless you want to stay single."

Alyssa rolled her eyes. "My boyfriend broke up with me over it, so I'm aware."

"Jon broke up with you because he only wants what he can't have,"

Cathy stated matter-of-factly.

"I guess we'll see how long he lasts with Julianna," Alyssa remarked.

"Did you ever find out how Jon and Julianna got together?" Lisa questioned Cathy.

"Julianna told me they randomly bumped into each other after Jason's party," Cathy replied. "I feel bad for her. She's super nice, and I think he's using her. Julianna's best friends with Courtney and Marielle, so it's convenient for Jon to date her."

Lisa rolled her eyes. "Everything changed once Courtney entered our social circle. I'm glad Bryan kept her away from us for so long."

"If she never dated Chris, you would like her," Alyssa asserted.

"I swear you wish you were still friends with her," Lisa stated dryly.

"Well, if my brother marries her sister, we'll be family, so odds are our paths will be crossing a lot in the future," Alyssa reasoned. "I have nothing against her."

"Can we just enjoy the fact that she's not here right now?" Lisa asked in a frustrated tone.

"Are you *ever* going to get over Chris?" Alyssa asked.

"I love Jeff," Lisa said defensively.

Alyssa raised her eyebrows. "You've hardly glanced at him all night."

Lisa rolled her eyes. "I'm mad that he's drinking. Jay's a horrible influence on him."

"We're at a party!" Alyssa exclaimed. "Lighten up!"

"Speaking of Jay... you guys should have seen his face when I showed him the Vicodin at the bottom of my cup," Cathy said. "He thought he was way too smart to get outsmarted by me!"

"Jay could use a few more bruises to his ego," Lisa remarked and rolled her eyes. "We should start walking back to my house if you guys are getting picked up at eleven," she added after glancing at her phone.

Cathy nodded and stood up. When she did, she noticed a group of freshmen girls were staring at her, Lisa, and Alyssa. They quickly looked away when Cathy glanced in their direction. A nearby group of boys also had their eyes locked on Cathy and her friends. Despite not talking to anyone outside of their group, the girls had somehow become focal points. Cathy still found it strange that people considered her "popular."

When Lisa told the rest of their crew that it was time to leave, Cathy observed that Jeff was drunk. She had seen him drink on a few occasions, but she had never seen him disorderly. He stumbled into Bryan when he stood up, and Cathy wondered if Jason had left his bottle of rum with the boys.

"Holy crap!" Lisa cried in dismay. "You better hope my brother's in bed when we get back to my house."

Jeff peered at her in a confused manner. "I only had one drink," he said defensively.

"You're an ass," Lisa rebuked him. "Andy, I'm walking with you!"

Andy laughed as Lisa pulled him away from the group. Jeff rolled his eyes before beginning to walk between Alyssa and Bryan. Cathy was on the other side of Alyssa; Bobby, Katherine, Adam, and Leslie were trailing behind them.

The woods that led to the bonfire were not thick, so it only took the group five minutes to find their way back to the high school. Worried that a cop might be parked in the lot, they ran around the back of the football field to the street alongside the school.

"Lyss, can I have that cigarette now?" Bryan asked.

"I thought you quit?" Alyssa questioned him.

Bryan laughed. "I quit all the time."

"You're drunk," Alyssa stated as she reached into her pocketbook. "You can have the rest of the pack because Jay gave me a new one, but you're going to regret smoking when you talk to Courtney."

Cathy glanced at Bryan, wondering if he was drunk enough to smoke. She had never seen him smoke in the two years they had been friends.

Bryan smiled as he took the cigarettes and lighter from Alyssa. "Courtney will forgive me more easily than I'll forgive myself," he said before lighting one. After taking one drag, he offered it to Jeff.

"No, guy. I'm good," Jeff responded and waved him off. "Ask Lisa. She might want to smoke—unless she's still hiding it from Andy."

"Seriously?" Bryan asked in a surprised tone.

"Oh, yeah. Sometimes, she smokes to spite me for making one dumb comment over the summer," Jeff replied while stumbling into Alyssa.

Alyssa put her arm around Jeff to steady him.

Bryan laughed. "She *would* do that."

"Andy saw cigarettes in her room, so she said they were mine. Now our friends think *I* smoke, and I'm a three-season athlete," Jeff rambled. He placed his arm around Alyssa's back for added support. "Lisa's the most vindictive person I've ever met," he added.

Cathy widened her eyes at the sound of Jeff's drunken rant.

Bryan laughed. "Lisa? Manipulative? I had no idea!" he joked.

"Andy's just as bad," Jeff remarked. "They're best friends for a reason."

Bryan chuckled. "Are you pissed that Lisa's walking with him?" he asked, likely wondering why Jeff was uncharacteristically running his mouth.

"No!" Jeff cried. "I'm just sick of all the secrets I'm forced to keep because I'm her boyfriend."

Bryan patted Jeff's back. "She's the hottest girl in our grade, dude. She's worth it," he assured him. "Rosetti? Lisa? Do either of you want this?" Bryan called out loudly to his friends who were walking about ten feet in front of them.

Andy and Lisa both stopped walking and turned toward Bryan.

"What?" Andy asked.

Bryan held up his hardly smoked cigarette. "Do you want the rest of this?"

"Nah, guy. I don't smoke," Andy replied when Bryan caught up to him. "My brother got me a Juul, and I haven't even used it."

"How did you get Robby to agree to that?" Bryan asked curiously.

"He heard a rumor that I smoked weed," Andy replied. "The next day he gave me the Juul and said he wouldn't tell our parents if I agreed to never smoke anything again."

"Isn't vaping just as bad for you?" Bryan asked.

Andy shrugged. "I have no idea. Like, all the seniors vape, so he thinks it's no big deal."

Lisa stared at Jeff with a look of disdain. "If you smoke, I'm using Andy's Juul," she threatened him.

"What the hell? You know I don't smoke!" Jeff exclaimed in an aggravated tone. "Stop implying that I do. People think that now, and it's pissing me off."

Lisa turned around abruptly, and Cathy wondered if she and Jeff were on the verge of having their first fight.

"Lisa, do you want this?" Bryan asked.

Lisa paused and turned around. "Why would I want *that*?" she asked and motioned towards the cigarette. "Smoking is my pet peeve."

"*This week*," Jeff taunted her.

Lisa scowled and stalked off ahead of the group.

"What is going on, dude?" Andy asked while turning toward Jeff. "Are you pissed at me?"

"No," Jeff replied immediately. "I'm pissed at her."

"Just keep walking," Alyssa said while tugging on the sleeve of Jeff's jacket.

Cathy glanced behind her to see how far away Bobby, Katherine, Leslie, and Adam were. They were one street back, so chances were low they had heard Lisa and Jeff's coarse exchange.

"How did you get so drunk?" Andy questioned Jeff once they resumed walking.

"I'm not drunk," Jeff replied.

Andy laughed. "Dude, you're shattered. That's why Lisa's pissed."

"I had one drink," Jeff stated earnestly.

A sickening thought occurred to Cathy. "Jay didn't give you any pills tonight, right?" she asked.

"I wouldn't take a pill from Jay if he paid me a thousand dollars," Jeff retorted.

"You took two Tylenol," Bryan recounted.

"So?" Jeff asked.

Cathy's stomach dropped.

"Guy, if you're this wasted from one drink, then I don't think you took Tylenol," Bryan stated matter-of-factly.

"I'm not wasted!" Jeff insisted.

Bryan glanced over at Cathy. "What does Jay keep in a Tylenol bottle?" he asked.

A giant lump formed in Cathy's throat.

"Jay said he took Vicodin tonight," Alyssa blurted out before Cathy could think of a response. "He might keep that in a Tylenol bottle."

"Vicodin?" Bryan questioned her. "Isn't that a painkiller?"

"I don't know," Alyssa replied.

"Why would Jay take a painkiller?" Bryan asked and turned toward Cathy.

Cathy let out a heavy breath. "No idea. Ask him," she muttered.

"You think I took *Vicodin*?" Jeff asked.

Cathy sighed. "Call Jay and tell him what happened," she said. "Let him explain it to you."

"That's really effed up," Andy remarked.

"What is Jay doing with painkillers?" Bryan asked.

"I don't know," Cathy responded defensively. "Call him."

While remaining arm-in-arm with Alyssa, Jeff used his free hand to pull his iPhone out of his pocket. "Call JD," he commanded Siri and then put the call on speaker.

"He's probably passed out," Alyssa assumed when Jason's voicemail picked up.

Jeff ended the call and put his phone back in his pocket. "Am I going to be okay?" he asked Cathy with wide eyes.

"Thankfully you only had one drink," Cathy said. "Just eat something when we get back to Lisa's and trust us when we say you're drunk and running your mouth."

"What I took looked like Tylenol," Jeff said defensively. "They were long white tablets."

"That's what Vicodin looks like," Cathy said. "I'm sure Jay never expected you to go in his bag."

"I went in there to make a drink and saw the Tylenol," Bryan explained. "Jeff had a headache, so I gave it to him."

"I'm going to explain what happened to Lisa," Andy said. "I think she'll redirect her anger towards Jay and away from you," he added and patted Jeff on the back before running off in Lisa's direction.

"What a mess," Cathy muttered.

"Is that why you two got in a fight?" Bryan questioned Cathy.

"He said we were in a fight?" Cathy asked.

"No, but I could tell something was wrong when he left," Bryan replied.

Cathy let out a heavy breath. "Just talk to Jay."

"Should I be worried about him?" Bryan asked.

Cathy glanced at Bryan. "Just talk to him," she repeated, hoping he was coherent enough to see the concern in her eyes.

CHAPTER 18

FIVE MINUTES LATER, CATHY noticed Lisa and Andy sitting on the front steps as she and her friends approached Lisa's home. As soon as Lisa made eye contact with Jeff, she jumped up and stalked towards him.

"How could you get like this, knowing Andy's brother was picking you up, knowing my brother could be awake when we got back here?!" Lisa cried out as soon as Jeff was within hearing distance.

Jeff looked stunned by her outburst.

"Lisa!" Andy called out as he ran up behind her. "Freaking out isn't going to make things any better. I told you it's not Jeff's fault."

"How do I know you didn't take Vicodin on purpose?" Lisa asked.

"Lisa," Alyssa spoke up in a disapproving tone, "chill out."

"I told him it was Tylenol," Bryan stated while eyeing Lisa sternly.

Lisa locked her piercing green eyes on Bryan. "You'd cover for him."

Bryan scoffed. "Now you're calling *me* a liar?"

"Lisa, just shut up before you say another offensive thing to any of us!" Alyssa exclaimed brashly.

Andy put his hand on Lisa's shoulder and attempted to pull her away from everyone else. "You need to calm down," he said in a low tone.

Lisa did the last thing Cathy ever expected; she burst into tears.

"Don't cry!" Jeff pleaded. "I'm sorry!" He reached out for her, but she pushed him away.

Cathy wracked her brain for a way to quell the tension in the air. She had never seen Lisa act so irrationally.

"Jeff, you didn't do anything wrong," Andy said. "Don't apologize to her."

"%$@# you, Andy!" Lisa cried and stormed into the house.

"Holy crap," Alyssa muttered. "What the heck is wrong with her?"

"I have no idea why she's being like this, dude," Andy said to Jeff. "Robby will be here soon, and we'll have to leave. Hopefully she'll come to her senses after she gets some sleep."

"She's *pissed*," Jeff said with a look of disbelief on his attractive face.

"I can go talk to her," Cathy offered and eyed Jeff sympathetically. "I'll get her to see it's not your fault. If Jason needs to explain things to her, I'll make sure he does. Follow me inside so you can eat something before Robby gets here."

"John and Day are picking us up in, like, five minutes," Alyssa said to Cathy as they began walking towards the front door. "Make it quick when you talk to her."

"I will," Cathy said. "I know what to say."

Cathy opened the front door and led her friends inside the Ankermans' split-entry home. "Just be quiet so you don't wake up JC," she warned them. "I'm going to find Lisa. Alyssa, stall your brother as long as you can when he gets here."

"Don't waste too much time on her," Alyssa said dryly. "She's being crazy."

"It has nothing to do with Jeff," Cathy whispered to Alyssa before hustling upstairs.

A moment later, she tiptoed down the hallway that led to Lisa's bedroom and knocked softly on the door. "Lis, it's Cathy," she said quietly, hoping she would not wake up JC, whose bedroom was across the hall.

A few seconds later, Lisa opened her door. Her face was glazed over with tears, and Cathy had never seen her look so despondent. Lisa stepped aside to let Cathy into her tidy bedroom and then quickly shut the door.

"I only have a few minutes before Alyssa's brother gets here," Cathy began, "but you need to hear me out."

Lisa sat down on her bed and buried her head in her hands.

"You weren't even like this after your breakup with Chris or when your dad passed away," Cathy said warily. "You are usually a pro at controlling your emotions. Something struck a nerve with you tonight, and you're taking it out on Jeff, but it's not his fault." Cathy took another step closer to Lisa before continuing to speak. "Jeff hates drugs. Bryan didn't know Jay kept Vicodin in a Tylenol bottle when he offered it to Jeff. Until tonight,

Bryan had no idea Jay is into pills. Can you imagine how scared Jeff must be right now? He has a drug in his system that he never intended to take. He's intoxicated from one drink, and he's about to face Andy's brother and parents. He's probably going to get in a lot of trouble! There's no way he did this intentionally, and you know it. You one hundred percent know it. You're upset because drinking on Vicodin is what ruined your relationship with Chris. You're crying because of what Chris did to you, not Jeff."

Lisa looked up at Cathy and lowered her eyebrows in a defensive manner. "I hate alcohol. Jeff knows it, and he drank anyway."

"It never usually bothers you when Jeff drinks."

Lisa searched Cathy's eyes before hesitantly saying, "I slept with him."

Cathy did a double take. "With who? What are you talking about?"

"With Jeff," Lisa clarified.

Cathy peered at her in a perplexed manner. "Um, okay. When did...never mind," she stammered, realizing she didn't have time to talk about Lisa's sex life. "What does that have to do with anything?"

Lisa fell back onto her bed. "I'm afraid he's going to lose interest in me like Jon lost interest in Alyssa after they had sex," she admitted. "When he got drunk, I thought he was disregarding my feelings, and I got scared."

Cathy raised her eyebrows. "You got mad because you were scared?"

Lisa let out a heavy breath. "I don't know. When I found out about the Vicodin, I got even more scared because that's how I lost Chris." When she said Chris's name, her voice cracked.

A knock on the door interrupted their conversation, followed by Alyssa's soft voice calling Cathy's name. "My brother and Day are outside in the driveway," Alyssa said after Cathy let her into the room. "I can't make them wait much longer."

"Lisa, do you want us to see if we can sleep here instead?" Cathy asked.

Lisa looked back and forth from Cathy to Alyssa. "You and I can talk more tomorrow," she replied. "I'll be fine."

"Are you sure?" Cathy asked.

Lisa nodded. "Don't make John wait. I'll be fine."

Cathy hugged Lisa and then followed Alyssa downstairs where the rest of their friends were gathered in the kitchen. After saying goodbye to everyone, Cathy and Alyssa hustled outside to Day's car. As Cathy climbed into the backseat, she struggled to process all that had just happened.

"What took you guys so long?" John asked as soon as Cathy and Alyssa shut their doors. John and Day were holding hands on the center console, and it only took Cathy a few seconds to notice a glimmering, princess-cut diamond ring on Day's left hand.

"Sorry," Alyssa said. "Lisa was having a meltdown over something."

As John began backing the car out of the driveway, Day turned around and waved her left hand before Cathy and Alyssa's faces. "It's official!" she exclaimed and spread a huge smile across her lips.

Alyssa shrieked and then covered her mouth. Her hazel eyes grew wide with excitement.

"Congratulations!" Cathy cried, wondering how John was able to afford such a large ring.

"I'm so excited!" Alyssa exclaimed. "Can I be a bridesmaid?"

Day laughed. "Of course," she replied and glanced at John.

Alyssa clapped excitedly. "I can't wait! How did you propose, John?"

"My friends helped me out a bit," John replied. "Matt, Marc, and I planned a scavenger hunt for everyone, and I worked the proposal into Day's clues. Her teammates were in on it, and when they reached the final location, I was waiting on one knee."

"Aww!" Alyssa sang. "You are so thoughtful. Day, were you shocked?"

"Yes!" Day cried. "Especially shocked that our friends were able to keep it a secret. John even arranged for my family to be there."

"Oh, so that's why Bryan wasn't with Courtney and why Matt and Luke refused to bring Jason out with them tonight," Cathy said. "Jay said they were being super shady about their plans."

John laughed. "Yeah, I wanted the smallest number of people possible to know about it."

"Do Mom and Dad know?" Alyssa asked curiously.

"Yeah. I told them my plan the other day. You know Mom and Dad," John said uneasily. "They think we're too young to know what we want out of life. They don't understand what it's like to pray and let God show you who you belong with. They don't put any stock in my beliefs."

Cathy knew it was common for Christian couples to marry young, especially since they often waited until marriage to have sex. Day and John were both active in Cathy's church, and for that reason, she did not find it surprising that they had gotten engaged.

"What did your parents say, Day?" Alyssa asked.

"My parents love John. They know he saved me from a world of darkness, and they hope we spend the rest of our lives together," Day replied. "My father gave John his blessing when he gave him my grandmother's diamond."

"It's beautiful," Cathy remarked.

"How soon do you want to get married?" Alyssa asked.

"We aren't going to think about setting a date until we see what colleges we get into," John replied. "Going to the same school would make things easier, but we have to wait and see what doors open for us."

"We're not in a rush," Day said. "John just wanted to solidify our commitment before going off to college."

"That's so nice," Alyssa remarked. "I think it's sweet. Don't let Mom and Dad's opinions taint anything. Those two are impossible to please."

Day laughed. "I haven't given them a ton of reasons to love me over the years," she admitted. "I'm lucky your brother is so forgiving. Two years ago, I was somewhat of a disaster."

"They'll come around," John said and squeezed Day's hand. "You're a completely different person now."

CHAPTER 19

LISA TOOK A DEEP breath before entering her kitchen, where Jeff and Andy were sitting at the breakfast nook. It appeared as though the rest of her friends had already been picked up by their rides, and Lisa was thankful she did not have to see them. She was incredibly embarrassed by her emotional outburst. Crying in public was not something she did. It left her feeling vulnerable and weak.

"I don't know what to do," Andy said as soon as Lisa entered the kitchen. "Robby's going to be here any minute. I can't take Jeff to my house like this."

Lisa planted her eyes on her boyfriend, who appeared to be passed out on the counter. "Did he get sick?" she asked.

"He tried to eat a sandwich and drink some tea, but he threw up within minutes," Andy replied. "After that, he passed out."

"His breathing is normal, right?" Lisa asked and moved closer to Jeff. When she reached his side, she ran her hand through his thick blonde hair. "Jeff, wake up," she said and gently shook him.

"I'm up," Jeff mumbled and slowly lifted his head.

"Do you want to spend the night on my couch?" Lisa asked.

"I just want the spins to stop," Jeff replied and slowly rose from his stool. He groaned and then stumbled toward the nearby half bathroom.

"If he goes home with you, he'll get in a lot of trouble," Lisa said matter-of-factly to Andy. "If he stays here, maybe he can keep his parents from finding out that he got drunk."

"If he doesn't stay at my house, my mom will tell his mom."

"Will your parents be awake when you get home?"

"I don't know."

Lisa sighed. "Will Robby tell on him?"

"Maybe," Andy replied. "If I tell Robby what happened, he might make a big deal out of it. He hates drugs."

"What a mess. I can't believe Jeff took Vicodin. Does Jay know what happened?"

Andy shook his head. "We couldn't get ahold of him. Does he do a bunch of drugs?"

Lisa eyed Andy warily. She did not want to betray Cathy's trust by talking about Jason, but she knew Andy's question was warranted. "I don't know how deep into drugs he is. Cathy doesn't even know. They've been having problems."

"Well, if he was drinking on painkillers tonight, then he's pretty far gone," Andy stated. "Where do you think he got the Vicodin?"

"There's so much you don't know about the Davids," Lisa remarked and shook her head, "and you're better off not knowing. I'm going to check on Jeff."

When Lisa knocked on the bathroom door, she heard Jeff dry heaving. She felt horrible for lashing out at him, and she wanted to do everything in her power to keep him from getting in trouble. However, it was risky to send him home with Andy and risky to let him stay at her house. She had no idea what to do. "Jeff? Are you okay?" she called.

"Make it stop," Jeff replied.

"Make what stop?"

"The room. It keeps spinning."

"Can you let me in? I'll try to stop the room from spinning."

As soon as Jeff unlocked the door, Lisa barged into the room. She found him on his knees in front of the toilet.

"I can't believe this happened to you," she said as she knelt down beside him and began rubbing his back.

"Are you mad?" he asked before beginning to heave.

"No!" Lisa cried. "I'm sorry. I got scared and overreacted."

"I didn't mean to scare you," Jeff said as beads of sweat began raining down his face. "I don't ever want to drink again."

"You can't go to Andy's like this."

"I don't think I can leave the bathroom."

"You can stay here, but your parents might find out."

"I'd rather them find out about that than *this*."

"Okay. I'll tell Andy you're going to stay."

Jeff resumed dry heaving as Lisa shut the door behind him. She hoped his stomach would settle down before JC woke up. Either way, her brother was going to be less than pleased about Jeff staying over.

"How is he?" Andy asked.

"Grossly sick," Lisa replied and sat down beside Andy. "He wants to stay here. He said he'd rather get in trouble for sleeping at my house than for being drunk."

"What am I supposed to tell my parents if they're up?"

Lisa shrugged.

"You always have good ideas. You can't think of anything?"

Lisa let out a heavy breath. "I'm not myself tonight. Jeff's behavior reminded me of Chris and stirred up a lot of bad memories."

"So, that's what happened?"

Lisa nodded.

"Jeff isn't anything like Chris. He's not going to go off the rails and break your heart."

"I know, but my emotions got the best of me."

"That's not like you."

Lisa shook her head. "I know...Chris just gets to me on a whole different level than anyone else ever has. I hate it."

Andy lowered his eyebrows. "Chris and I have become pretty good friends since he went straightedge. He's moved on to Marielle. I suggest you accept that and focus on Jeff."

"I do accept that," Lisa huffed. "I just have some scars."

"Jeff has scars too—from what you've done to him," Andy said. "You chose Chris over him twice—first in seventh grade and then in eighth. Don't do it again or you might lose him for good."

Lisa scoffed. "How could I do it again? Chris has a girlfriend."

"I mean in your thoughts," Andy clarified. "Love the one you're with."

"I love Jeff," Lisa asserted.

"You don't treat him right."

"Oh, like you're the perfect boyfriend?" Lisa retorted.

"I don't treat Chantal like she's disposable."

"Is that how you think I treat Jeff?"

"No. That's how *he* thinks you treat him."

Lisa lowered her eyebrows. "Well, that's awful."

Andy nodded and pulled his phone out of his pocket. "He ran his mouth tonight because he was bombed, but I wouldn't blow off anything he said," he warned her while reading a text message. "Robby's here. I better go."

Lisa cocked her head to the side. "Just tell Robby that Jeff wants to get in my pants. It will make him too uncomfortable to ask questions."

Andy laughed. "Okay, but I'll think of something else to tell my parents," he remarked as he leaned in to hug her goodbye.

"Good idea," she said and hugged him back tightly. "Text me so I know what you told them. Yours and Jeff's stories will have to match up."

"Will do. Good luck with him," Andy said before leaving the kitchen.

After Andy left, Lisa wanted to sort out her thoughts, but she knew tending to Jeff was more important. She felt bad about the way she had treated him all night. She assumed ignoring him the majority of the evening had been a defense mechanism. What she told Cathy was true—she was scared. She had hoped that sleeping with Jeff would loosen the grip Chris had on her heart; instead it just made her feel like she had less of a grip on Jeff's.

Standing up from her stool, she took a deep breath and braced herself before walking into the bathroom. She found her boyfriend passed out on the memory-foam bathmat in the fetal position. "Jeff, wake up. Let's go lie down in the living room," she said while kneeling down and shaking him.

Jeff groaned.

"Please? You can't sleep on my bathroom floor."

Jeff creased his eyes open. "You must be happy that I'm never going to drink again."

Lisa rolled her eyes and grabbed his hand to pull him upright. "I don't enjoy seeing you like this. Can you please stand up? I can't lift you."

Slowly Jeff rose from the floor. Cautiously, Lisa led him out of the bathroom, through the kitchen, and into the living room.

"Lie down," she directed him. "I'll go get you a puke bucket and some blankets."

Jeff flopped down on the couch and buried his head in his hands.

"I hope you're as mad at Jay as I am," Lisa muttered.

CHAPTER 20

At eleven-thirty, Jason was sitting in his formal living room when he heard Matt and Luke walk through the front door. He jumped off the couch and hustled into the foyer before either of his brothers could run upstairs. "What's up, guys?" he greeted them.

"Oh, hey, buddy," Matt said, after pausing at the bottom of the stairs. "How was your night?"

"I've had better," Jason replied and glanced at Luke. "Can I talk to you?"

Luke crossed his arms and eyed Jason skeptically. "What's up?"

"Can we go upstairs?" Jason asked.

"Yeah, whatever," Luke replied with a shrug. "I'll see you in my room. I just want to grab a snack," he added before walking toward the kitchen.

"Is everything okay?" Matt asked in a concerned tone.

"Yeah. I just have to ask Luke something about Cathy," Jason replied.

"Oh, okay. Well, I'll be in my room if there's anything you want to talk about," Matt offered.

"Thanks, but I'm good," Jason said before following Matt up to the second floor. He hoped Matt would not take offense to his interest in talking solely to Luke, but he was feeling a bit too dejected for an intense heart-to-heart.

After entering Luke's bedroom, Jason took a seat on his brother's unmade bed and locked his eyes on the framed collage hanging above the desk. As he glanced from picture to picture of Luke, Matt, and their large group of friends, Jason felt a bit envious that his brothers got to hang out with each other so often. He wondered if they realized how lucky they were to have such a large group of close friends.

"What's going on?" Luke asked as he entered his bedroom and shut the door.

"Will you shoot straight with me?"

"Yeah, always. What's up?"

"Is Cathy back on Xanax?"

Luke walked over to his bed and took a seat beside Jason while eyeing him strangely. "Wouldn't you know?" he asked.

Jason shook his head. "We're not in a good place. She's been weird ever since she found out I took it."

"How is she being weird?"

Jason shrugged. "She's all over the place. She's up; she's down; she's carefree; she's condescending. I don't know what to make of her mood swings. You would tell me if she got more Xanax from you, right?"

"She took your bottle, but she hasn't asked me for more."

"I thought she wanted me to go straightedge, but tonight she said she'll do whatever I do from now on. She said she'd even eat mushrooms and snort Adderall."

Luke eyed Jason thoughtfully. "I can't picture Cathy doing that," he stated flatly. "She's probably just trying to scare you."

"She pretended to take Vicodin tonight. She spit it out without me knowing. I think she's losing it."

"You two should break up. She has anxiety, dude. You need to take a break from her or a break from drugs."

"Not from her," Jason stated and shook his head. "How did I become someone who needs uppers to function and downers to sleep? I lost my best friend. I'm losing my girlfriend. How did this become my life?"

"You know how," Luke replied. "Actually, I think you know exactly what you need to do—you just don't want to do it. You can't have your cake and eat it too, little bro."

"How do you do it?" Jason asked. "How do you party so hard, keep all your friends, make your girlfriend happy, and stay out of trouble?"

Luke lowered his eyebrows in a perplexed manner. "I don't party *that* hard. Matt told you stuff that made you think I party way more than I do," he replied. "I get drugs for my friends when they ask me to, but I don't usually do them. Rolling once a month doesn't interfere with my everyday life."

Jason stared at Luke thoughtfully, trying to recall a time when he had seen his brother on drugs. He had seen Luke drink on a few occasions, but he could not think of one instance when Luke had been drunk or high.

"I don't think I've ever seen you sloppy," Jason admitted, somewhat reluctantly.

"Probably not."

"And you don't touch Adderall, painkillers, or benzos," Jason added. "You're dependent on nothing."

"Right."

"I've got to get off Adderall," Jason said and rested his forehead in his hands.

"Every day, you should make a list of the drugs you take," Luke suggested. "I bet seeing everything on paper will help you realize a few things."

"My habits are disgraceful," Jason muttered as he stood up from the bed. "I'm going to try to fall asleep. Maybe if I'm lucky, I'll sleep for more than an hour tonight."

"Tell Mom you can't sleep. See if she's okay with you coming off Adderall," Luke suggested as Jason walked toward the door.

Jason turned to face his brother. "Just let me know the next time you get edibles."

"Do you really think your grades will drop that much without Adderall?" Luke questioned him.

Jason shrugged. "I don't want to take that risk. The only way I'll get into Duke is by being Valedictorian."

Luke scoffed. "You can't be Valedictorian if you're dead."

Jason widened his eyes. "Dude, not cool."

Luke shook his head. "I'm only half joking."

Jason rolled his eyes and walked out the door without taking another glance in Luke's direction. When he reached his bedroom, he grabbed his cell phone off its charger and saw a missed call from Jeff. *Weird,* he thought. *Jeff usually only texts me. And no call from Cathy yet? She must be at Alyssa's house by now.*

After pressing Jeff's name on his missed-call log, he brought his phone to his ear. Jeff's voicemail picked up immediately. Because neither Cathy nor Alyssa had a cell phone and it was far too late to call Alyssa's house, he could not attempt to contact them. Jason let out a heavy breath and fell back onto his bed, feeling certain that a long, sleepless night was ahead of him.

CHAPTER 21

When Cathy, John, and Alyssa entered the Kellys' Victorian home, Mr. and Mrs. Kelly were sitting in the formal living room, located off the foyer. "Did she say 'yes'?" Mrs. Kelly asked, appearing a bit anxious.

"Of course," John replied.

Mr. Kelly shook his head. "That church has brainwashed you both," he stated.

"How can you say that?" John questioned his father. "You believe in the same God we believe in. We just make Him a priority. If I want to honor God by marrying the girl I love instead of just fornicating with her, how is that a bad thing?"

"Marriage is supposed to be for life," his father replied. "Unless a child or a disease comes from sex, it's not as permanent."

John widened his eyes. "What is wrong with you?"

"She was a drug addict, John," his mother stated matter-of-factly. "Do you want the mother of your children to be an addict?"

"She was never addicted to anything!" John exclaimed defensively. "Do you know how many kids experiment with drugs? The majority of my friends have tried what she tried, but you don't hate them. I should never have told you why we broke up in the first place."

"We just want the best for you," his mother said. "You are going to graduate in the top ten percent of your class. Day is not going to get into any of the colleges you like unless her father pulls a record amount of strings!

Are you going to sacrifice your future to go to the same subpar college as your fiancé?"

"Day has solid grades, and she's Class President. She has a lot to offer without her father's help," John replied. "Besides, we're not worried about college. We trust God to work out the details. I will end up exactly where I'm supposed to, as will Day."

Mr. Kelly scowled. "You can't leave everything up to fate."

"It's not fate; it's faith," John stated matter-of-factly. "You don't have to exercise your faith the same way I do, but you can at least respect my right to trust God with my future."

"Should we give you guys some privacy?" Alyssa asked in a timid manner.

"We need to talk to you, too," her mother replied.

"About what?" Alyssa asked.

"The school mailed us a letter about how rampant vaping has become," her mother replied. "It said they are going to be raiding lockers and bags to make sure kids don't have vape pens. Evidently, it is such a big problem that the school is planning to remove some doors from the bathrooms. The letter suggested all parents search their kids' rooms, backpacks, and pocketbooks for vaporizers called Juuls, which look like memory sticks."

Alyssa lowered her eyebrows in confusion. "What does that have to do with me?"

"Have you tried vaping?" her mother asked.

Alyssa shifted her weight uncomfortably before replying, "Once, but I know how bad it is for you, so I never did it again."

"Hopefully, that's true. We searched your room while you were gone and didn't find anything, but we want to search your bag," her mother said.

Alyssa stiffened. "I'm offended that you don't believe me."

Cathy also grew tense, knowing Alyssa had a pack of cigarettes in her pocketbook.

"Don't be offended," her mother said. "Just be happy that we care enough to check."

Alyssa scowled and bolted up the nearby stairs while yelling, "You are horrible! You don't trust your kids with anything!"

Mr. Kelly rushed out of the living room and ran up the stairs after Alyssa while Cathy stood frozen in the foyer, unsure of what to do.

"I've never seen Alyssa vape," John said to his mother. "A lot of kids do it, but I don't think her group of friends is into it. It's bigger with my grade and the juniors."

"The letter said it's even in the middle schools," his mother retorted.

"I'm just saying I think you hurt her feelings," John said.

"If we didn't have to pick her up at the police station a month ago, then maybe we would have more trust in her," his mother remarked.

John rolled his eyes. "You gave her permission to be at Matt and Luke's house that night."

"You were smart enough to avoid the party," his mother stated.

"I'm three years older than her," John responded. "She'll learn how to avoid trouble. You are suffocating both of us."

"Don't talk to me like that!" his mother shouted.

John shook his head and sighed. "I'm going to bed. Thanks for putting a damper on my special night."

When John ran upstairs, Cathy cringed. Being alone with Mrs. Kelly could easily trigger an anxiety attack.

"Cathy, maybe you should see if your parents are still awake and can come pick you up?" Mrs. Kelly suggested.

Cathy widened her eyes. "They usually go to bed at eleven. I can wake them if you want, but they are planning to get up early tomorrow to pick me up before church."

Mrs. Kelly looked startled when Cathy mentioned church. She cleared her throat and dropped her eyes to the floor. "What my husband said about your church was not meant as a blanket statement. We go to church. Day and John's situation is unique, and we don't think he is exercising sound judgement."

Cathy eyed Mrs. Kelly precariously, unsure of what to say.

"Sorry if anything we said offended you," she added.

"Um, thanks," Cathy stammered as her palms began to sweat. "I'm going to use the bathroom," she said before hustling across the foyer.

After shutting the bathroom door, she struggled to catch her breath. It had been a disaster of a night, and dealing with Alyssa's parents was the last thing she felt equipped to do. She ran her hands under cold water and splashed it on her face, hoping to thwart a panic attack. When Cathy exited the bathroom, she was relieved to see Alyssa sitting with her parents in the living room. Cathy wiped sweat off her forehead before taking a seat beside her.

"You both stink like smoke," Mr. Kelly said in a stern manner.

"I told you we were at a bonfire," Alyssa responded.

"We thought we had to worry about vaping. We never imagined we'd have to worry about smoking!" her father cried.

"We smell like smoke from the bonfire," Alyssa said defensively. "My clothes would not stink an hour later if it was from a cigarette."

"So, if we call Lisa's brother tomorrow, he'll confirm that you had a bonfire?" Mrs. Kelly asked.

"The bonfire was in the woods behind Lisa's house," Alyssa replied. "JC might know about it, but he wasn't there. It was for underclassmen."

"Even if the smell is from the bonfire, it doesn't explain the unopened pack of cigarettes in your pocketbook," her father stated matter-of-factly.

Cathy widened her eyes. This was surely not going to go over well.

"Unopened is the key word," Alyssa remarked, appearing unfazed.

"Why would someone give you a pack of cigarettes if you don't smoke?" Mr. Kelly asked.

"They were given to me to hold in my bag for the party… bonfire… whatever… but no one wanted them," Alyssa replied.

"Who gave them to you?" Mrs. Kelly asked.

"Jason," Alyssa responded.

Cathy winced.

"Does Jason smoke?" Mrs. Kelly pressed.

"No," Alyssa replied. "If he did, he wouldn't have given them away."

"Who did Jason want you to give the cigarettes to?" Mrs. Kelly asked.

Alyssa's parents were not dumb. Rude and strict—yes. Naïve—no. Therefore, Cathy knew Alyssa was going to have a very difficult time convincing them of her innocence.

"Anyone who wanted them," Alyssa responded.

"Alyssa, this is unacceptable," Mr. Kelly stated sternly. "You can't expect us to believe you were given the cigarettes to hold for other people."

"They're unopened," Alyssa retorted. "I could understand you being upset if cigarettes were missing from the pack."

"You admitted to vaping. Will you be honest with us about smoking?" Mrs. Kelly questioned her.

Alyssa rolled her eyes.

"Have you tried it?" Mrs. Kelly asked.

"The only kids I hang out with who haven't tried it are Cathy and Jason," Alyssa replied. "Everyone's tried it. I bet John's even tried it!"

"So, that's a yes," Mrs. Kelly said and looked at her husband.

"Alyssa, why would you try smoking?" Mr. Kelly asked. "I told you how hard it was for your grandparents to quit. Look at all the health problems they have because of it."

"Why did you try it?" Alyssa retorted. "You both admitted to trying it when you were teenagers. You are hypocrites if you get mad at me for doing it."

"We told you how disgusting it was so you wouldn't try it," Mrs. Kelly said. "Don't use our honesty against us."

"Don't use my honesty against me!" Alyssa exclaimed. "I know so many kids who smoke weed or vape every day. I do neither. If I occasionally smoke a cigarette, it is not the end of the world!"

"You've done it more than once?" Mrs. Kelly asked.

Cathy knew Alyssa was an honest person, but even so, she was surprised Alyssa was being so forthright.

"Yes, but I don't do it every day!" Alyssa cried.

"We have to ground you for this," Mrs. Kelly said crossly.

"I figured," Alyssa muttered.

"No," Mr. Kelly stated flatly. "You were honest. We'll ground you if we catch you with cigarettes again. Don't smoke."

Alyssa looked surprised by her father's words. "Um, okay," she stammered.

"Now, go up to bed before I change my mind," Mr. Kelly said and pointed toward the staircase. "Cathy, we're going to tell your parents about this when they pick you up tomorrow."

Cathy widened her eyes. "But I had nothing to do with it," she protested. "I've never smoked a cigarette in my life."

"We believe you, but your parents still need to know what happened," Mr. Kelly responded.

Cathy swallowed the lump in her throat. "I actually don't feel well," she said. "May I call a friend for a ride home?"

"Sure, but we're still going to tell your parents," Mr. Kelly warned her.

"That's fine," Cathy stated. "I just need to go home."

She scurried out of the room and into the kitchen to find the cordless phone. As she dialed Luke's cell phone number, her heart pounded heavily against her chest.

"What's up, guy?" Luke asked when he answered the phone, evidently assuming John was on the other end of the line.

"Luke, it's Cathy."

"Oh, sorry! Is everything all right?" Luke questioned her in an alarmed tone.

Cathy let out a sigh of relief. "I'm so glad you're still awake. Are you home?"

"Yeah. Why? What's up?"

"Things are super awkward at Alyssa's. Is there any way you could pick me up and drive me home? I don't want to wake up my parents."

"What happened?"

"Ugh, a bunch of stuff. I can't really explain right now."

"Let me see if my parents are still awake. I'll ask if I can come get you. If they're not, I'll just head out. Are you okay, though?"

"I will be once I leave here," Cathy replied.

"That stressful?"

"Tonight has been horrible from start to finish."

"I'm just walking downstairs now to see who's awake. I don't hear the TV. I think everyone's in bed."

"Oh, good. So, you can come?"

"Yeah. Just give me a second to change. I can be there in fifteen. Hang tight. Do you need me to bring you anything?"

"Like what?"

"Just say yes or no, and I'll use my imagination."

"Sure," Cathy replied, hoping he would bring something to calm her heart rate.

"Okay. You got it. Watch for my car."

"Thank you!" Cathy exclaimed, feeling immensely relieved. She hung up the phone and made her way back into the family room. "Luke is going to pick me up and bring me home," she informed Mr. and Mrs. Kelly.

"We'll call your parents tomorrow and explain everything," Mr. Kelly said. "Alyssa, wait with Cathy until Luke gets here. Then go to bed. We're heading upstairs."

Cathy took a seat beside Alyssa on the couch as soon as Mr. and Mrs. Kelly left the room.

"I'm so sorry about this!" Alyssa exclaimed. "I hope you don't get in trouble."

"I'll forewarn my parents. Hopefully they'll be reasonable. Sorry to bail on you. I'm just having some anxiety right now."

"It's okay!" Alyssa assured her.

"Jason's behavior earlier, what happened to Jeff, Lisa's outburst, your parents' reaction to John and Day's engagement, and the Juuling and smoking conversation—it's just way too much for one night," Cathy ranted.

"My parents suck," Alyssa stated flatly.

"I can't believe you were so honest with them."

"Well, I'd just rather be honest than have a lie on my conscience."

"I get that. I don't know how Lisa keeps so many secrets. Jeff sounded pretty fed up about it."

"I feel bad for him," Alyssa admitted. "Lisa walks all over him. He's one of the hottest guys in our grade. He could literally date *anyone!* It's unfortunate he only has eyes for her."

"Lyss!"

"Lisa's in love with someone else. You're crazy if you think she's over Chris."

"She and Chris have a special bond, but I think she loves Jeff, too."

"Her soul is tied to Chris," Alyssa remarked. "It's like she had sex with him or something."

"She never had sex with Chris."

"I only know that's true because Chris says he's still a virgin. I like Lisa, but I take everything she says with a grain of salt."

"She's just super private. You're an open book, so she seems shady to you."

"Speaking of shady... what are you going to do about Jay?"

Cathy put her head down. "I don't know."

"Who got him into painkillers? Chris was never into pills. Was he?"

Cathy swallowed deeply before responding. She did not feel right about disclosing Chris's drug history. "Jason started taking them *after* his fight with Chris, *after* I got grounded. I just found out the other day."

"You must have freaked out!" Alyssa cried.

"He's lost without his best friend. I told him to sober up and try to mend things with Chris. That's the obvious solution, but he said getting sober won't be easy."

"All he has to do is stop using drugs. That shouldn't be too hard if he isn't addicted to anything."

"Right, but he is."

"To what?" Alyssa asked curiously.

Cathy took a deep breath. "I shouldn't say anything. It's his business, and I feel bad talking about him."

"Well, everyone knows about the painkillers now. Jeff will probably keep his distance from Jay for a while."

"Jay doesn't need to lose any more friends. Hopefully Jeff won't hold it against him. Jay didn't give him the pills."

"Yeah, but hanging out with someone who's into drugs like that isn't a good idea. Look at what happened."

Cathy sighed. "I really don't even know what to say."

"I hope you're considering breaking up with him. Having a boyfriend who messes with pills is only going to increase your anxiety. Drugs make people selfish and immature."

"I miss the person he used to be," Cathy admitted. "It's surreal to me that this has become our reality. I never saw it coming."

CHAPTER 22

Luke arrived at the Kellys' house shortly after midnight. After quickly hugging Alyssa goodbye, Cathy dashed off toward Luke's car. He looked concerned when she climbed into the passenger seat, and she hoped his concern would translate into providing her with free anxiety meds.

"What happened?" Luke asked. "Were John's parents that upset about the engagement?"

Cathy scoffed. "Yes, and about kids at our school vaping, and about Alyssa smoking. I think they were even upset with John for going to church. They are the most uptight people I've ever met."

"That's crazy because John's so chill," Luke remarked.

"They started talking about church brainwashing John and Day. They know me and my family go to the same church. I couldn't believe they said something like that in front of me."

"Yikes. I'm sorry. I brought you some things that might help," Luke said and pulled a Juul, a bottle of pills, and a bag of weed out of his center console.

"What's in the bottle?" Cathy asked curiously.

"K-pins and Xanax."

"I promised Jay I would never take Xanax again, but he's making everything so much harder than it needs to be. Before Alyssa's parents freaked out, I was already on edge. One of our friends took Vicodin by mistake because Jay had it in a Tylenol bottle."

"That sucks."

"Yeah. Now everyone knows Jay's into painkillers."

"Well, Jay had a meltdown when he got home tonight. He said he's worried about you."

"Really? Good. I want him to worry about me so he'll stay out of his own head. Will Klonopin help me?" Cathy asked and held up the bottle.

"Probably. If you don't want to take Xanax, why don't you take a K-pin and hit my Juul a few times?"

Cathy eyed him apprehensively. "I've never vaped."

"All you do is this," he said and brought it to his lips to show her how to use it. He took a small draw off it and then offered it to her. "It tastes like fruit."

"Fine," she said and snatched it out of his hand. When she inhaled, she was surprised by how sweet it tasted. "How many puffs am I supposed to take?" she asked after exhaling.

"Just a couple," Luke replied. "Some people find it calming, and others find it stimulating. I don't know how it will affect you."

While Luke backed out of the driveway, Cathy took two more draws off it. She found it relaxing to exhale, and she could see why vaping had become so popular. It also gave her a bit of a head high, which she assumed was from the nicotine.

"What do you think?" Luke asked as he began driving down Alyssa's street.

"I actually like it more than I thought I would," Cathy admitted and put it back inside the center console. "I would just be afraid to try it more than a few times because it's so addictive. You can't be addicted to it, though. I've never seen you do it before."

"Me? No. I barely use it. Missy only got it for me so I could vape and not feel left out when our friends go outside to smoke."

"I didn't know any of your friends smoked weed," Cathy remarked.

"That's because most of them don't."

"I can't picture Matt or Marc smoking anything!"

"Oh, they don't," Luke stated with a short laugh. "Matt's still pissed that Missy got me a Juul. He thinks vaping is just as bad for you as smoking cigarettes."

"I heard John say vaping's a big problem with the upperclassmen."

"Yeah. A lot of kids do it."

"Who?" Cathy pressed, finding herself extremely curious about this new fad.

"Geez, you're a barrel of questions," Luke said. "Pretty much everyone—

not Matt, not Marc."

"A bunch of freshmen and sophomores were doing it at the bonfire."

"Yeah, they buy cartridges off seniors for, like, forty bucks."

"I thought vaping was for people who are trying to quit smoking?"

Luke scoffed. "None of my friends smoked before they started vaping."

"Geez. So, vaping is getting people addicted to nicotine who weren't addicted to it in the first place?"

"It's a bit backwards."

"Well, Jay's super against it, so you don't have to worry about him," she said. "Can I have a sip of your water?" she asked and reached for the VOSS bottle in Luke's cupholder.

"Sure."

After grabbing the water, Cathy poured a few pills into her hand and separated the blue Klonopin from the white Xanax. "Should I take one or two?"

"Just take one, but bring some home in case you need more."

Cathy popped a pill in her mouth and washed it down without a second thought. She hoped it would kick in as quickly as Xanax usually did. Her palms were still sweating, and her heart was racing. Her mind was juggling thoughts of Jason, Jeff, and Alyssa's parents. "I can't believe Alyssa's parents are crazy enough to give me an anxiety attack."

"They hate Day. That's what it boils down to."

"Why do they hate her so much? She's the mayor's daughter!"

"When I was a freshman and she was a sophomore, she used to hang out with the seniors. The guys made a big deal out of her being the mayor's daughter, so they all wanted to bang her."

"Did she cheat on John?"

"From what I've heard, she enjoyed herself an awful lot."

"So, yes?"

"It's assumed, but John has never said one way or other. He told me he broke up with her because all she wanted to do was party with the football team. They broke up and got back together a few times before she got religious. Now, we all joke and call her 'the new creation.'"

"Well, John's parents called her a drug addict."

"Her party phase was pretty hard on him. He freaked out when she started drinking. By the time she got into coke and Liquid G, he had a meltdown."

"Coke and Liquid G? Geez. She went all out."

"Oh, yeah."

"I remember seeing her at some of Chris's parties. She hung out with

Jordan?"

Luke nodded. "His grade was extra rowdy because he threw so many benders."

"Do you think Day slept with him? Jay told me he thinks Jordan's been with at least fifty girls."

Luke laughed. "Jordan will always be an MLH legend because he partied like a rockstar and kicked ass on the field, but I don't think he slayed fifty girls. He always had high standards."

"High standards? I saw him go to bed with two girls at once."

"Exactly. High standards."

Cathy playfully slapped Luke. "That's gross."

"Girls did some *crazy* stuff to get his attention, but he didn't take them seriously. He had his eyes set on the cream of the crop," Luke explained.

"Michelle Taylor?" Cathy assumed.

Luke nodded. "He was set on stealing her from Marc."

"Marc? When was he with *Michelle*?"

"A long time before Jordan ever tried to get with her. Michelle broke up with Marc in eighth grade because she felt tempted to hook up with him."

"Wow. That took some willpower," Cathy commended.

"She's a strong girl. They agreed to stay best friends and hopefully get back together when they're older."

"So, that's why Marc doesn't have a girlfriend? He's saving himself for Michelle?"

"I don't think 'saving himself' is the right term," Luke said with a short laugh, "but he's never committed to anyone but her."

"Were you at the party when Jordan tried to date-rape her?"

"That's *not* what happened," Luke stated and shook his head. "Jordan's a super nice kid. Michelle told me he was only trying to help her."

"Do you think someone else drugged her?"

Luke shrugged. "If anyone knows, they're not talking."

"Weird."

"So, not to change the subject, but... what's going on with you and Jay?" Luke asked.

Cathy let out a heavy breath. "I was trying to avoid talking about him," she admitted.

"Yeah, I could tell."

"I don't know who he is anymore," she muttered. "I don't think he knows either."

"Jay only knows who everyone wants him to be," Luke said. "I've never met anyone better at charming a crowd. He gets away with *everything*."

"Chris got fed up."

"Chris is another story, but I hope you'll reach that point, too, before Jay brings you down with him."

Cathy shook her head. "I want to help him."

"You need to break up with him. That's probably the only thing that will wake him up."

Cathy closed her eyes and rested her head against the seat.

"The K-pin didn't kick in already, did it?" Luke asked.

"No. I was just thinking," Cathy replied and opened her eyes to see that they were approaching her home.

"It takes longer to work than Xanax, but it lasts longer," Luke said. "I'm sure you'll sleep well. You can keep the bottle."

"Really?"

"I'd rather not have it in my house."

"Because of Jay?"

Luke nodded.

Cathy let out a sigh of relief. "Thank you, and thanks for the ride," she said while Luke steered the car into her driveway.

After hugging Luke goodbye and climbing out of the passenger seat, Cathy quietly entered her house and left a note for her parents, explaining why she had come home. Before getting into bed, she considered taking a second Klonopin because she desperately wanted a good night's sleep. She googled the code on the pill and found out that the strength was one milligram. Deciding that taking more than that could be dangerous, she poured the pills back into the bottle and sealed it tightly. Then she threw it inside the tissue box on her nightstand, where her parents would never see it.

CHAPTER 23

LISA AWOKE AROUND 9:00 a.m. to the sound of someone knocking on her bedroom door. Her oldest brother, JC, walked into the room before Lisa had a chance to respond.

"Why is Jeff passed out on our couch?" he asked as Lisa creased her eyelids open.

"What?"

"Why is Jeff here?" JC repeated, sounding more confused than upset.

Lisa stared at her brother blankly, hoping an excuse would enter her mind.

"What happened?" he pressed.

Lisa took a deep breath. "Sorry, I'm half asleep," she said and stretched her slender arms above her head. "We went to a bonfire last night, and Jeff took Tylenol from someone because he had a headache. When we got back here, he started throwing up. Andy talked to some people and found out Jeff took Vicodin by mistake. He took it on an empty stomach, so that's why he got sick."

JC widened his brown eyes. "Kids were taking *Vicodin* at the bonfire?"

Lisa yawned. "Evidently, and it was too dark for Jeff to see that it wasn't Tylenol."

"Holy crap. You guys are only fourteen!"

"Jeff was supposed to sleep at Andy's, but he was too sick to leave our bathroom."

"His parents won't be happy that he stayed here."

"He's prepared to get grounded."

"You should have woken me up. I could have called his parents and explained the situation. If he ever had an adverse reaction in our house, I could have been held liable."

Lisa winced. "I'm sorry. I didn't even think of that," she admitted. "I waited until he stopped puking to come to bed. I made sure he was okay."

"Stay away from whoever gave Jeff those pills," JC stated in a serious tone. "I saw painkillers ruin a few kids' lives in college. Two of them are heroin addicts now."

Lisa gasped. "That's terrible."

"If anything like this happens again, wake me up," JC said sternly. "Your boyfriend should not stay here without his parents' permission."

"It won't happen again," Lisa assured her brother.

"I'm just relieved you don't hang out at Chris's house anymore," JC admitted. "Even though Taylor was one of my best friends in high school, the idea of you being at parties with college kids always bothered me. If Dad knew what went on at that house, he never would have allowed you to spend so much time there."

At the sound of Chris's and her father's names, Lisa's facial expression fell. "I miss both of them every day," she admitted.

"I'm sorry you and Dad didn't get more time together," JC said. "He was a great man. I owe all my achievements in life to his guidance. I just hope I can be a fraction of the role model to you that he was to me."

Lisa smiled at her oldest brother, who never gave himself enough credit. He carried more responsibilities than any other twenty-three-year-old she knew—their father's business, their home and household bills, their brother Joe's law school tuition, and Lisa's guardianship—all while working as a paralegal and attending law school part time. In Lisa's eyes, JC was a superhero.

"You handle stress better than anyone I know," Lisa commended him. "You're a good role model. You've always been one. I don't have straight A's and a student council position by chance."

"Would you have let Jeff stay on our couch if Dad were alive?"

"Probably not."

"That says something."

"You're more understanding than Dad. That's not a bad thing."

"Maybe. Well, let me know if Jeff's parents call. I'll confirm that I was home and that he slept downstairs."

"Thanks," Lisa said and smiled appreciatively at her brother.

When JC left the room, Lisa felt like a load of bricks had been lifted off her shoulders. She had been more transparent with her brother than usual, and he seemed to appreciate her candor. At that thought, she began to wonder if being more open with Jeff would bring them closer. More than anything, she wanted her bond with Jeff to be as strong as her bond with Chris. She hated that Chris still owned so much of her heart.

CHAPTER 24

AT ELEVEN O'CLOCK, CATHY sat in church with her parents and younger sister Stephanie, gazing across the sanctuary at Chantal, Andy, Chris, and Courtney. Because of Chris and Jason's falling out, as well as her own distaste for Courtney, Cathy did not feel comfortable sitting anywhere near them. Church had become a very lonely place for her, and she envied Chantal for having a boyfriend and friends who shared her beliefs.

After the service concluded, Cathy's palms began to sweat when she noticed Chris walking toward her.

"Hi!" Chris exclaimed in a friendly manner as he approached her pew.

"Hey," Cathy greeted him nonchalantly while trying to gain her composure.

"Why don't you ever sit with us?" Chris asked curiously.

Cathy eyed him precariously. "I don't really fit in with you guys," she replied hesitantly.

"You're always welcome," Chris assured her. "How's Jay?"

Cathy took a deep breath and let it out slowly. "I don't even know what to say."

"He's so mad at me," Chris said with a sad expression on his face. "I thought he'd understand where I was coming from."

"He's not himself," Cathy muttered and dropped her eyes to the floor.

"I pray for him every day," Chris stated earnestly. "I've heard some of the things he's been saying behind my back."

Cathy looked up at Chris. "He doesn't mean it," she said sympathetically. "He's just hurt and bitter."

"Jay doesn't usually gossip."

Cathy sighed. "He's acting strange. There's no question about that."

Chris stepped closer to her. "Is he into pills now?" he asked quietly.

Although Cathy saw a tremendous amount of concern in Chris's blue eyes, she felt it would have been disloyal to tell him about Jason's drug use. "I know you're worried, but I can't say anything," she replied downheartedly. "If your gut is telling you something's wrong with him, then believe it."

"I know something's wrong. I would reach out to him, but I have to keep my distance from people who use drugs if I want to stay sober."

"I understand. Just keep praying for him."

Chris nodded and then hesitantly asked, "How's Lisa?"

"*Trying* to be happy with Jeff," Cathy responded. "How's Marielle?"

Chris appeared caught off guard by the question. "She's good. She's great. She's a nice girl," he replied.

Cathy squinted. "You and Lisa really did a number on each other," she remarked. "I've never seen her care more about anyone."

Chris hung his head. "I hurt her—and it bothers me every day—but I'm only, like, one month sober. I could easily relapse, and I don't ever want to hurt her again."

"You still love her?" Cathy asked.

"Too much to subject her to my instabilities."

Cathy cocked her head to the side in thought. "But you're not afraid to hurt Marielle?"

"I couldn't hurt Marielle the way I could hurt Lisa," Chris replied immediately. "Our relationship is brand new, our feelings aren't deep, and we're not physical with each other. It's totally different. We're basically friends who spend a lot of time together. If I slip up, her heart won't shatter the way Lisa's would."

Cathy nodded. "I guess you're right."

"Don't let Jay shatter *your* heart," Chris said in a serious tone. "Breaking up with Lisa killed me, but it was the right thing to do. If Jay's a mess, he should know better than to drag you through the mud."

Cathy let out a heavy breath.

"I'll be praying for you both," Chris pledged and touched her arm before walking away.

As Cathy watched him walk across the sanctuary, she wondered how Courtney had gotten him to begin attending church. Chris was one of the last people Cathy had ever expected to develop an interest in spiritual growth. The first time she ever heard of Chris was at the beginning of seventh grade when Jon asked her and Chantal to pray for his best friend who was "surrounded by darkness." After meeting Chris and seeing the way he partied, Cathy had doubted he would ever turn to God. Evidently, she had underestimated the power of prayer. Although it took two years of events to bring Chris to his knees, God had been working in his life all along. This gave her hope that God could also be working in Jason's life, despite how bleak things looked.

CHAPTER 25

JASON DOZED ON-AND-OFF BETWEEN ten o'clock and noon, failing to get into a deep sleep. Every time he awoke, he checked his phone, hoping to have a missed call from Cathy. He assumed she would not get home from church until twelve-thirty or later if her family went out for brunch. Picking up his phone, he decided to call Alyssa to find out why Cathy had never called him the night before.

Mrs. Kelly answered the phone and sounded less than pleased to hear Jason's voice. When Alyssa got on the phone, she filled him in on everything that had happened after he left the bonfire, including what happened to Jeff and what happened with her parents.

"$%#@!" Jason exclaimed once Alyssa let him get a word in. "That's why Jeff called me last night? $%#@! I feel so bad!"

"I'm pretty sure you just lost another friend," Alyssa remarked. "You also gave your girlfriend an anxiety attack. She called Luke for a ride home around midnight."

Jason swallowed deeply. "She must be so pissed at me. I'll find out the deal from Luke. That sucks your parents found the cigarettes. Maybe it's time to stop smoking?"

"I told them I got them from you, so don't be surprised if they call your parents."

Jason widened his eyes. "Why did you do that?!"

"Because they asked, and I was pissed at you. I said you gave them away because you don't smoke."

"Alyssa! My parents would kill me for giving those to you. I was doing you a favor."

"Well, hopefully my parents let it go. They didn't ground me."

"That's surprising."

"I think they're more upset about John and Day's engagement."

"They're young to get engaged."

"Don't worry about them; worry about Jeff and Cathy!"

Jason sighed. "If Cathy will even speak to me."

"Jay, cut the crap. You're a mess!" Alyssa exclaimed. "Stop doing drugs and try to work things out with Chris."

"Chris doesn't want to talk to me."

"I don't blame him. You say horrible things about him to people. Just because he doesn't want to party anymore doesn't make him a loser. You make fun of him for going to the same church your girlfriend goes to. Do you know how dumb you sound?"

"Whatever, Alyssa," Jason snapped.

"You're so irritable lately!" Alyssa cried.

Jason scoffed. "Sorry. I'm a little stressed."

"Good luck with Cathy. Don't be surprised if she breaks up with you. I'm sure every one of her friends is telling her to."

Alyssa's crass words made the cell phone fall out of Jason's hand. As it landed on the carpet, he struggled to breathe. Although he wanted to reach out to Jeff to explain himself, he had to make saving his relationship with Cathy his first priority.

CHAPTER 26

AROUND NOON, LISA WENT downstairs to wake up Jeff—after getting dressed, curling her long brown hair, and applying a light coat of makeup. JC had left the house to run errands, leaving Lisa home alone with her deeply sleeping boyfriend. She sat down at the edge of the couch and shook him until his blue eyes began to open.

"I can't believe I'm at your house right now," Jeff groaned, before pulling Lisa down beside him. "I'm going to be grounded for weeks."

Lisa eyed him sympathetically. "Maybe if you tell your parents the truth, they won't hold it against you?"

Jeff let out a short laugh. "The truth? That's not what I expected you to say."

Lisa smirked. "What happened wasn't your fault, and I don't think you should worry about getting Jay in trouble."

"I can't believe Jay's messing with pills."

Lisa rolled her eyes. "He's a wreck."

"He's so smart, though. Why would he do that?"

"I don't know, but he's losing it, and he's making Cathy lose it."

"I recall you losing it on me last night," Jeff remarked. "What was that about?"

Lisa eyed her boyfriend warily, wondering if she should confide in him. He deserved an honest explanation, but she feared the truth might hurt his feelings. "Do you really want to know?"

Jeff nodded.

Lisa hesitated before beginning to speak. "I don't think I'm ready for sex," she admitted. "It made me feel insecure."

Jeff affectionately brushed Lisa's face with the back of his hand. "I don't want to do anything that you're not ready for."

"I did it to bring us closer," Lisa explained.

"Well, it's not going to bring us closer if it makes you feel bad," Jeff reasoned.

Lisa took a deep breath. "I think being more open with you will bring us closer."

"About what?"

Lisa dropped her eyes to her fingernails. "Mainly about Chris."

"What about him?" Jeff asked hesitantly.

"About why we broke up."

"I thought he drank too much?"

Lisa took a deep breath and looked up at Jeff. "The truth is he almost overdosed from drinking on pills. He wasn't trying to hurt himself. That's just how he used to party."

Jeff widened his blue eyes. "Seriously? Like, Vicodin?"

Lisa nodded. "And some other stuff."

"I don't know why anyone would willingly drink on Vicodin," Jeff stated. "I thought I was going to die on your bathroom floor."

"When I found out you took Vicodin, it struck a nerve with me because it ruined my relationship with Chris."

"I would never purposely touch that stuff. You know that," Jeff said.

"I know, but my emotions got the best of me. I'm sorry. Things that have to do with Chris *really* affect me. I wish that weren't the case, but I'm not completely healed from our breakup."

Jeff dropped his hand to his side and looked away from her. "That's not what I wanted to hear, but I appreciate your honesty."

"I know I hurt you when I got back together with him out of nowhere."

Jeff let out a heavy breath. "We don't need to retrace the past."

"But I should tell you *why* I got back together with him."

"I'm not sure I want to know," Jeff admitted and eyed her questioningly.

"You deserve to know because you were everything I wanted. I even told Cathy I was ready to call you my boyfriend, but then I hung out with Chris and did something dumb." She took a deep breath and eyed him hesitantly.

"Lis, you can tell me anything."

"I know. It's just... I was really depressed about my dad, and Chris felt bad for me, so he offered me a drink with molly in it."

Jeff's eyes grew wide.

"I drank it, and it took away all my sadness," Lisa continued. "It was probably the happiest night of my life. It put me super in touch with my emotions—not the sad ones, just the good ones."

Jeff gave her a strange look. "I thought you hated drugs besides weed?"

"I do."

Jeff gazed at her questioningly.

"I never did it again," Lisa assured him, aware that he was stunned by her confession, "but just that one time ended up bringing me and Chris closer than I ever wanted. I bared my soul to him because the drug made me so expressive. I've had a hard time separating myself from my emotions ever since that night."

Jeff stared at Lisa for a few seconds before responding, "I don't really know what to say except I hope you can open up to me without taking drugs."

Lisa grabbed ahold of Jeff's hand and smiled. "I just did."

CHAPTER 27

WHEN CATHY ARRIVED HOME from church, Jason was sitting on her front steps. Her stomach immediately turned at the sight of him. His reputation was going to be smeared because of what had happened to Jeff, and people would likely judge her for continuing to date him. In her gut, she knew she should take her friends' advice and break up with him, but her heart would not let her entertain the idea for more than a split second.

A moment later, after Cathy, Jason, and Mrs. Kagelli entered the house, Mrs. Kagelli pointed to the blinking red light on the cordless phone in the kitchen.

"There's a message," Mrs. Kagelli said. "It may be from Alyssa's parents."

Cathy rolled her eyes. "Let me know what they say if you talk to them," she said before leading Jason down the hallway and into the family room.

"Last night was the worst," Jason said quietly once they were seated on the couch. "I talked to Alyssa this morning, and she told me about what happened to Jeff and what happened with her parents. I feel like the biggest A-hole in the world. How do I fix this?"

"I don't know if you can," Cathy replied. "Lisa might kill you. If Jeff's parents find out about what happened, you're going to get in a lot of trouble. Everybody was pretty upset when I left Lisa's last night."

"I never even thought of someone going into my bag, looking for Tylenol," Jason admitted.

"Hopefully Lisa thought of a way to keep Jeff from getting in trouble, but

I would be prepared for his parents to tell your parents."

"I don't know how to wiggle my way out of this. If everyone we went to the bonfire with knows I took Vicodin, that's going to spread around school quickly. Katherine and Bobby already hate me. This will just give them more of a reason to think I'm the devil. Bobby's friends with Chris now because of football, so I'm sure he'll tell Chris what happened."

"I think Chris already heard. He came up to me at church today and asked how you were doing," Cathy said. "He knows about the rumors you've been spreading about him, but he didn't seem mad. He just sounded worried."

Jason scowled. "I can't even think about that right now. I just need to know how to make things right with *you*."

"Isn't it obvious?" Cathy asked and held out her hands in a frustrated manner. "Wean yourself off Adderall. Even if you have to spend a week feeling exhausted, it will be worth it. You'll eventually be able to sleep. You won't need weed anymore, and then you'll be sober enough to hang out with Chris."

"It sounds so easy," Jason remarked, "and it makes so much sense. I mean, that's all I need to do, but for some reason, I can't break out of the cycle I'm in."

"Maybe you're trapped in bondage?"

"What does that mean?"

Cathy swallowed a lump in her throat. "The devil can grip people through drugs."

Jason raised his eyebrows at her. "What are you talking about?"

"It's just something I learned about at church. Maybe that's why you can't break free? Maybe you're gripped?"

Jason eyed her strangely. "Now you think I'm the devil, too?"

Cathy scoffed. "No. I just think you've let some darkness into your life, and maybe you could benefit from coming to church with me."

"You know I hate religion," Jason stated dismissively.

"It's just a suggestion," Cathy said defensively.

"You don't even like church," Jason added.

"That's just because the kids aren't nice to me. I would like it a lot better if you went with me."

Jason shook his head. "It's not going to happen if Chris is there. I can barely stomach seeing him in school Monday through Friday."

"Well, then, I'm out of suggestions."

"You scared me last night," Jason stated in a serious tone. "What was that act you put on?"

Cathy took a deep breath before responding. "I'm just trying to cope. When Luke drove me home last night, he gave me Klonopin. I took one, and it helped."

Jason scowled. "Oh, Cathy. Why?"

"Because I had an anxiety attack at Alyssa's," she replied.

Jason shook his head. "Don't you know anxiety meds can 'grip' people, too?"

Cathy glared at Jason.

"I find it bizarre that you think I'm horrible for taking Adderall and Vicodin, but you see nothing wrong with taking benzos," Jason stated.

"Keep your voice down," Cathy hushed. "My mom's right in the kitchen."

"I'm sorry, but I thought you were done with benzos," he whispered.

Despite his quiet tone, Cathy could tell he was livid. "I have to manage my anxiety somehow," she retorted. "Me taking one Klonopin didn't negatively impact anyone. You using Vicodin messed up more than one person's night."

Jason eyed her thoughtfully for a few seconds and then sighed. "I probably caused your anxiety attack. I'm really not good for you."

"So, what do we do?" Cathy asked, hoping he was not going to break up with her.

"You're not going to break up with me?" he questioned her in a surprised tone.

"No," she said in a confused manner.

"Alyssa made it sound that way."

"She wants me to break up with you," Cathy clarified, "so do Lisa and Luke."

"I don't blame them," he muttered.

"I want to stick this out with you," Cathy said. "I don't want to end up like Lisa and Chris—in love with each other but dating other people."

"What do you mean by 'stick this out' with me?" Jason questioned her.

"I'd rather take benzos to prevent anxiety attacks than break up with you," Cathy replied.

"Can't you just eat weed gummies?"

"They take over an hour to work, so they don't help me the way Klonopin or Xanax does."

"They worked fine over the summer," Jason argued.

"They keep me calm so I don't have panic attacks, but they make my brain foggy, and I find it hard to concentrate in school," Cathy explained.

"Seriously? Weed, like, helps me focus."

"Well, I don't have ADHD," Cathy stated matter-of-factly.

Jason sighed. "Do you have any gummies left that I could eat before bed?"

Cathy nodded. "I'll go get them," she said and jumped up from the couch. While she walked across the room, her mother appeared in the doorway.

"We need to talk," Mrs. Kagelli said in an abnormally stern manner.

Cathy stopped in her tracks. "Did you talk to Alyssa's parents?"

"I did," Mrs. Kagelli replied and walked over to Cathy.

"What happened?" Cathy asked curiously while eyeing her mother with concern.

Mrs. Kagelli darted her eyes at Jason and then back at Cathy. "Mr. and Mrs. Kelly are making Alyssa take a drug test, and they suggested I have you tested as well."

Cathy widened her eyes. "Why?!" she asked as her heart started pounding against her chest.

"Because Mrs. Kelly talked to Lisa's brother, and he said Vicodin was circulating around your bonfire last night."

Cathy did everything in her power to keep her composure, but she was certain all the color had drained from her face.

"I assume if Lisa is aware of this, then you are, too," her mother added.

Cathy swallowed deeply before beginning to speak. "Jeff took Vicodin by mistake. He thought it was Tylenol."

"Mrs. Kelly is going to call everyone's parents and suggest they have their kids drug tested."

"Alyssa will pass a drug test with flying colors," Cathy remarked, hoping she did not appear half as tense as she felt. "Mrs. Kelly made *John* get drug tested once. You know John from church. He's a saint!"

"I know Alyssa's parents are a bit over the top, but if painkillers are circulating around your parties, then you're hanging out with the wrong people," Mrs. Kagelli said matter-of-factly.

Cathy had never had a more awkward conversation with her mother. "My whole grade was there!" she cried, hoping to sway her mother's thoughts away from her friends. "No one realized Jeff took Vicodin until we left."

Mrs. Kagelli cocked her head to the side. "How did you figure out he took Vicodin?" she asked and stared directly into Cathy's eyes.

Cathy's stomach churned as she struggled to find words. "Mrs. Kelly didn't say?"

Mrs. Kagelli shook her head and peered at Cathy expectantly.

"Andy was with Jeff. Maybe he found out? Andy knows everybody."

"Andy was a part of this?"

Cathy nodded.

Mrs. Kagelli looked perplexed. "I didn't realize you were with Andy's friends. Chantal wasn't there."

"We were with Andy, Katherine Rossi, Bobby Ryan, Leslie Lucus, Adam Case, and some other kids they're friends with from student council," Cathy said, naming off everyone she could think of with stellar reputations.

"I went home early last night, so I didn't hear about what happened to Jeff until I talked to Alyssa this morning," Jason spoke up. "My brothers know everyone, so I'm sure they could find out who had Vicodin at the bonfire. Do you want me to ask them to look into it?"

Jason's words nearly took Cathy's breath away as she realized how misleading he could be without even telling a lie.

"Let me know if you hear anything," Mrs. Kagelli said. "It's probably someone you guys barely know, but you should stay away from whomever it is."

"Right. For sure," Cathy remarked and glanced quickly at her boyfriend.

"I also got a letter about kids vaping in school," Mrs. Kagelli stated. "Dad's on his way home with nicotine tests for you, Chantal, and Stephanie."

Cathy's stomach dropped. "What?! Why?"

"The letter said sixth-graders were caught vaping on the bus," Mrs. Kagelli added.

Cathy felt every part of her body clam up.

"That's crazy!" Jason cried. "Kids in sixth grade?" He sent Cathy a confused look, likely wondering why she appeared so tense.

"Vaping is easy to hide, so parents have no idea if their kids are doing it. The letter recommended parents buy a nicotine test at the pharmacy."

Cathy felt nauseous.

"Have you guys tried it?" Mrs. Kagelli asked and looked back and forth from Cathy to Jason.

"God, no!" Jason exclaimed. "I'll gladly take a test if there's an extra one. Kids are so stupid. They're ingesting a bunch of chemicals that don't even get you high. It makes no sense."

Mrs. Kagelli peered at Cathy. "Have you?"

Cathy's heart raced in her chest. "Once," she admitted and dropped her eyes to the floor.

"What? When?!" Jason asked, looking dumbfounded.

"Last night," she muttered, "after you left."

"Cathy!" Mrs. Kagelli shouted in a tone filled with shock and disappointment.

"I was stressed out about what happened to Jeff, and someone said it would help me relax," Cathy explained without making eye contact with Jason or her mother.

"Who?!" Mrs. Kagelli and Jason asked in unison.

Cathy stood in silence as they stared at her with heated expressions. "I can't say."

"If your friends are vaping, then I'm going to join Mrs. Kelly and suggest everyone's parents at least test them for nicotine," Mrs. Kagelli remarked crossly.

Cathy rolled her eyes. "It wasn't someone in my group of friends. Like, seventy-five percent of the kids at the bonfire were vaping."

"None of our friends vape," Jason said to Mrs. Kagelli. Then he peered angrily at Cathy. "Why would you do that?"

"I was upset, and someone tried to make me feel better—that's all," Cathy insisted.

"Who?" Jason asked again.

"It doesn't matter," Cathy stated flatly.

"Cathy, this is *not* okay!" Mrs. Kagelli cried and crossed her arms. "You should not be around kids who vape or take painkillers!"

"My entire grade was there!" Cathy hollered defensively.

"Chantal wasn't; Chris, Marielle, Julianna, and Jon weren't," Mrs. Kagelli retorted. "They were here, watching a movie."

Cathy rolled her eyes. "Okay, Mom. So, forget the fifty parties Chris threw at his house and focus on the one bonfire he skipped."

"Calm down," Mrs. Kagelli said. "Chris is not the one in question here. Dad will be home in a few minutes, and you're going to take that test with your sisters."

"Why?" Cathy whined. "I already told you I tried it. Save the test. Surprise me with it another time and then you'll know I don't usually do it."

"Oh, I'll surprise you with another test, but you're taking one today, too. I want your sisters to know what you did," Mrs. Kagelli said, "and I want them to see the consequences."

"Where would I even get a Juul?" Cathy questioned her mother in a frustrated manner.

"You know plenty of older kids who can buy e-cigarettes," Mrs. Kagelli replied matter-of-factly.

Cathy scowled. "Alyssa didn't get grounded when she told her parents that she tried smoking. Are you seriously going to ground me for vaping *once*?"

"If the test comes back positive," Mrs. Kagelli replied. "There are consequences for your actions, and you need to realize that. It will be good for Stephanie to see that."

"If you ground me for something I did once and never plan to do again, that's really unfair," Cathy argued.

"How do I know you've only done it once?" Mrs. Kagelli retorted.

"Were you even going to tell me?" Jason questioned Cathy in a disappointed tone.

Cathy turned and glared at him. "Yeah, of course. Just like you tell me everything." She turned to her mother wearing the same angry expression. "If you ground me for this, I'll make sure I vape every chance I get. I mean, I might as well... I will have already paid the penalty for it. Maybe I'll even smoke."

Mrs. Kagelli shook her head and turned out of the room. "They're your lungs," she called back. "I'm just trying to protect you."

"Who the hell told you to vape?!" Jason asked as soon as Mrs. Kagelli was out of sight.

"Luke," Cathy muttered.

Jason puckered his face. "Luke? He wasn't at the bonfire."

"No kidding! He drove me home from Alyssa's when I was mid-anxiety attack."

Jason looked furious. "I told him I was worried about you, and his response was to get you to vape and take a K-pin?"

"He was trying to help me. I was a wreck because of what *you* did to Jeff and what *you* did by giving Alyssa cigarettes."

Jason shook his head. "I hate that you're close with Luke," he stated bluntly and began walking toward the door. "Call me later if you're not grounded. I'm pissed, and I don't want to say anything I'll regret."

"Good idea," Cathy said flatly as Jason left the room. After she heard the front door slam shut, she ventured up to her bedroom in need of something to quell her anxiety. Her mother's disappointed reaction made her feel ashamed, and she dreaded the thought of facing her father and sisters. "Thank you, Luke," she sang beneath her breath as she popped open the bottle of Klonopin.

CHAPTER 28

On Monday, rumors about Jason began flying around Montgomery Lake High School just as Cathy had anticipated. Before lunch, Cathy had heard her boyfriend referred to as a drug dealer and a drug user, multiple times. People she did not know approached her in each class, inquiring about Jason taking Vicodin at the bonfire. The atmosphere at school was far more insufferable than Cathy's three-day punishment for vaping.

"People have been picking me apart for years," Jason said to Cathy on their walk to the cafeteria for lunch. "It doesn't faze me. Don't let it mess with your head. Their lives are just so boring that they have to live vicariously through us."

"It upsets me when people say bad things about you," Cathy expressed. "The things people were asking me were so disturbing that I almost ran out of homeroom. They said they heard I was on Vicodin, too. One person asked if I only date you to get free drugs. People think I do drugs, Jay. I am *not* okay with that."

Jason eyed her strangely. "You do use drugs, and I do give them to you for free," he stated matter-of-factly.

Cathy widened her eyes. "Are you kidding me?! I only take things to treat a medical condition. I hate drugs. I'm not a partier!"

Jason widened his eyes. "Who's the self-deceived one now?"

Cathy scowled. "Just because you're mad that I took Klonopin and vaped doesn't mean it's okay for people to badmouth me. People are only talking bad about me because I'm going out with *you*. I hope you plan on defending me."

Jason rolled his eyes. "Of course, I'll defend you. I'm sure Lisa will, too. No one's had the guts to ask me anything about Saturday night."

"That's because everyone's afraid of you," Cathy remarked. "They think you're as tough as your brothers."

"We're lovers not fighters," Jason retorted. "Luke hates fighting off the ice. He's good at it, but he'd rather everyone just get along."

"I know, but kids who don't know you guys think you're different. You're one of the nicest people I know, as long as you're not drunk. Luke probably *is* the nicest person I know, and Matt is basically perfect. But people assume Matt's a tough guy because he's captain of the football team; they think Luke is a rich brat; and now they think you're a drug dealer."

Jason rolled his eyes. "I'll believe that when someone asks me for drugs."

Cathy scowled. "How do you not care?"

Jason shrugged. "I just don't."

"Doesn't it bother you that people are making up lies about me?"

Jason draped his arm around Cathy's shoulders and pulled her through the doorway to the cafeteria. "If I hear anyone say anything bad about you, I'll set them straight. But in the meantime, the best thing you can do is act like you don't care."

Cathy let out a heavy breath. The only way the rumors were not going to bother her was if she upped her dose of Klonopin or started using Xanax again.

"You should just be glad that Jeff didn't blame me," Jason added. "The fact that we're still going to eat lunch with him will quench some of the rumors."

"Hopefully. Lisa wanted to kill you, so you're lucky Jeff convinced her it wasn't your fault."

"He's a reasonable guy," Jason said. "I didn't give him the pills."

"You get away with everything," Cathy muttered as they neared their lunch table.

"Don't be jealous," Jason joked before taking a seat beside Jeff.

"What's up, guy?" Jeff greeted him in a friendly tone.

"Cathy, come buy lunch with me," Lisa said before Cathy could take a seat.

By the look in Lisa's eyes, Cathy could tell she had something important to say.

"I can't believe you didn't break up with him!" Lisa exclaimed as soon as she and Cathy stepped away from the table. "Now your reputation is going to hell."

"He means more to me than my reputation," Cathy responded.

Lisa scoffed. "You're so blinded by your feelings that you can't see he's toxic—just like when Chantal couldn't see Jon was toxic."

"Jon was mistreating Chantal. Jason's not mistreating me," Cathy said defensively.

"He's bringing stress into your life," Lisa stated matter-of-factly. "You don't need that."

"Nothing would be more stressful than a breakup."

Lisa let out a heavy breath. "My brother told me that people who abuse painkillers usually end up becoming heroin addicts."

"Lisa!" Cathy exclaimed in disbelief. "Jason would never go down that road. Are you seriously worried about that? He's a straight-A student with a bright future. He's just in a rut."

"If he starts snorting painkillers to get high, he'll get addicted," Lisa said in a serious tone. "Promise me you'll break up with him if he ever does that."

"Why are you so worried about this?"

Lisa sighed. "The night before school started, Chris told me some stuff about Taylor. I don't think Chris told anyone else, so I feel bad mentioning it, but painkillers are ruining Taylor's life."

"Taylor Dunkin?"

Lisa nodded.

"Taylor's super smart and responsible," Cathy said in confusion. "Jordan's the one with the questionable reputation."

"Taylor *was* a straight-A student with a bright future, just like Jay," Lisa whispered while stepping into the lunch line. "He was prescribed painkillers by a doctor, but he started snorting them to get high because he was depressed. Now he's addicted to them, and his life is a mess."

"Are you serious?"

Lisa nodded.

"That's incredibly surprising."

"Chris is devastated about it, and he said Marc and Jordan are, too."

Cathy peered at Lisa skeptically. "Taylor hated it when Chris got drunk or smoked weed. He tried to keep Chris in line."

"I know, but drugs change people... and his injury messed with his head."

"That's horrible. I feel bad for him."

"Well, it was his dumb decision to snort the pills."

"He must have been feeling awfully low to do something like that,"

Cathy reasoned.

"Don't tell anyone what I just told you—not even Jason," Lisa commanded her. "Chris doesn't want anyone to know. I'm sure he only told me because he was tripping."

"I won't say anything," Cathy pledged. "But, geez. If it can happen to Taylor, it can happen to anyone. Doesn't he have a scholarship to college?"

"He did before he failed out of his major."

"Failed out?" Cathy questioned Lisa with wide eyes.

Lisa nodded.

Cathy's heart sank to her stomach, and she felt as though she might throw up. Although she did not know Taylor well, she could see similarities between him and her own boyfriend. If someone as highly respected as Taylor could turn into a drug addict, then so could Jason, and this realization jolted Cathy.

"Just promise me you'll break up with Jay if he ever starts snorting painkillers," Lisa urged her.

"I promise," Cathy responded immediately. She could feel her heart rate increasing, and she feared she was on the verge of an anxiety attack. She had taken one Klonopin three hours prior, but it clearly was not strong enough to calm her nerves. "Will you save my spot in line so I can run to the bathroom?" she asked Lisa in a frantic tone.

Lisa eyed her strangely. "Yeah, sure."

Cathy dashed off towards the Ladies Room located on the opposite side of the cafeteria, hoping a stall would be free so she could quickly take another Klonopin before succumbing to a panic attack. Thankfully the bathroom was empty, so she was able to toss a pill in her mouth and wash it down with water from the sink without anyone noticing. Just knowing the pill would eventually kick in brought her some comfort.

Before leaving the bathroom, she splashed water on her face, wiped sweat off the back of her neck with a paper towel, and pulled her long hair into a ponytail. She could not recall ever feeling more uncomfortable at school. How long would it be until her teachers heard the rumors and misjudged her? Would this get back to her parents? Hearing her and Jason's names rattle off the tongues of people she did not know was humiliating, and she wished she could hide in the bathroom for the rest of the day.

CHAPTER 29

***

ON FRIDAY, CATHY HAD never felt more relieved to hear the last bell of the day ring. She had just survived the longest and most stressful week of school in her life. By taking Klonopin each morning, she had been able to keep herself from having a panic attack, but the rumors were tearing her insides apart.

Mr. and Mrs. Davids were going to Newport for the weekend and leaving Matt in charge of the house. However, Matt forbade Luke from throwing a party—for obvious reasons. He told Luke and Jason they could each invite a few friends over but that *he* would call the cops if additional people showed up at their home.

"Are you inviting anyone over tonight?" Luke asked Jason on the drive home from school with Missy and Cathy.

"I told Bryan he could stop by after he hangs out with Courtney," Jason replied. "Cathy invited Alyssa."

"Missy and I are going to have a Sexy Party," Luke said with a short laugh.

Missy, who was sitting shotgun, also laughed and playfully slapped Luke on the arm.

"What the hell is a 'Sexy Party'?" Jason asked.

"Just a small get-together," Luke replied.

"Why don't I believe you?" Jason asked.

Luke chuckled. "I should have said an intimate gathering."

Jason widened his eyes. "Dude, are you planning an orgy or something?"

At the sound of Jason's words, Missy erupted into laughter.

"You have a wild imagination, Jay-dawg," Luke remarked.

"I don't put anything past you," Jason retorted. "Who did you invite?"

"Just Laurelle, Pat, and Marc," Luke replied. "But Marc said he might go to the movies with Matt and Ally if he doesn't go see Taylor."

"So, Matt won't be home to call the cops if your 'Sexy Party' gets out of hand?" Jason gathered.

"It won't get out of hand," Luke stated assuredly. "The smaller the better."

Missy again slapped Luke in the arm.

Jason rolled his eyes and glanced at Cathy, who was quite curious to uncover what a "Sexy Party" entailed.

***

"What do you think Luke meant by a 'Sexy Party'?" Cathy asked Jason as they sat down on his bed after Mr. and Mrs. Davids left for Newport.

Jason rolled his eyes. "They're probably just going to take molly and cuddle."

"As a group? That would be weird."

"Luke's weird," Jason said with a careless shrug. "I don't know. We'll find out soon enough. What time is Alyssa coming?"

"Around eight."

"Bryan's not coming until after nine, so we have some time before anyone gets here. Do you want to take a nap?" Jason proposed.

Cathy nodded. "I'm totally beat from this week of hell."

"I'm sorry," Jason said and leaned forward to hug her. "It will get easier."

"I hope so," Cathy muttered, wondering if she should take another Klonopin before lying down. She pulled free from Jason's embrace and lay back on the bed. "I'll probably take another K-pin before Alyssa gets here."

"How many of those have you been eating a day?" Jason asked.

"This week? A few."

Jason sighed. "If they help you deal with all the bullshit going on at school, then I guess it's good you have them," he remarked while stripping down to his boxers.

"Good," Cathy said and kicked off her gray UGG boots before crawling under Jason's down comforter. Wearing a Lululemon long-sleeved running shirt and leggings, she planned to stay fully clothed. Evidently, Klonopin took away her sex drive just as much as Xanax did. This actually brought her some relief because she could blame her lack of interest in sex on the medicine instead of having to defend her religious beliefs.

"Aren't you going to be hot in all those clothes?" Jason asked as he climbed beside her.

"I'll be fine," she replied and rolled onto her side so Jason could spoon with her.

"So, I guess we're back to abstinence?" he asked as he pulled Cathy's body close to his.

"I guess," Cathy mumbled, sounding more careless than she had meant. "Sorry," she added. "It's nothing personal."

"You had a rough week," Jason remarked before kissing the back of her head. "I'm not going to hold anything against you."

Cathy squeezed Jason's arm appreciatively before closing her eyes and drifting off to sleep. She awoke an hour later to Jason's alarm. Wishing she could sleep for the rest of the night, she rolled over to face her boyfriend. "Did you get any sleep?"

Jason nodded. "Not enough but some. I wish we didn't invite anyone over. I'm drained."

"Me too," Cathy admitted.

"Do you want to take Adderall?" Jason asked.

"Instead of Klonopin?"

Jason nodded.

Cathy shrugged. "That's probably a better idea. If I took a benzo right now, I would fall back to sleep."

Jason jumped out of bed. Cathy sat up but remained under the covers as she watched her boyfriend retrieve Adderall from his drawer. When he began crushing up pills with his library card, she wondered if he was expecting her to snort it. She had never snorted anything other than nasal spray, and she planned to keep it that way. "Jay, I don't want to snort it," she said.

"I figured. I'm just crushing it up so I'll have it on hand for later. I'm going to put it in a baggie and keep it on me."

"You're going to need *that much* to get through a movie?"

"I'm pretty sure we'll end up joining Luke's 'intimate gathering.'"

"Ugh, really? I'm way too beat to socialize with Luke's friends."

"You won't be after the Adderall kicks in," Jason assured her before leaning forward with a rolled-up dollar bill and snorting a thin line of blue powder. He sniffled twice and snorted a second line. After wiping his nose with a tissue, he turned to her. "I feel better already. Are you sure you don't want to snort a tiny bit just to help you get going?"

Cathy nodded. "I'm sure. Just give me one, and if we end up hanging out with Luke, I'll take another." Jason handed her a pill and a bottle of water. She washed down the Adderall without any hesitation, hoping it would improve her mood.

Twenty minutes later, when they went downstairs to greet Alyssa, Cathy noticed Luke's friends were yet to arrive. Luke and Missy were lying on the couch in the family room, watching TV. Missy was wearing light-pink pajama shorts and a Victoria's Secret tank top, and Luke was in sweatpants and a black wife beater. Cathy had never seen either one of them dressed so casually. On the contrary, Alyssa showed up dressed to the nines. Her long, dirty-blonde hair was curled; her makeup was perfect; and her outfit looked like it had come straight off a mannequin at Nordstrom's.

"You look nice," Cathy commented before giving Alyssa a hug.

"Thanks," Alyssa replied. "I wasn't sure if Luke was inviting people over. I figured a party could happen on a moment's notice with him."

Jason laughed. "I think it'll be pretty lowkey. Luke and Missy are falling asleep on the couch, and Matt took Ally to the movies."

"John and Day just dropped me off on their way to meet Matt and Ally. They said some of their friends were coming here," Alyssa explained.

"That's what Luke told us, but he and Missy don't look ready for company," Jason commented and nodded for Alyssa and Cathy to follow him upstairs. "Bryan's going to swing by after he hangs out with Courtney."

"Oh, good," Alyssa sang. "Then I won't feel like a third wheel."

"You're never a third wheel," Jason said. "I just like you enough to include you when Matt limits me to inviting a few people over."

Alyssa laughed. "Who else did you invite?"

"Jeff and Lisa, but they already had plans with Andy," Jason replied as he reached the top of the stairs. "I think Lisa's still pissed about last weekend," he added while walking down the long hallway that led to his bedroom.

"Our entire grade is mad at you," Alyssa remarked.

Jason rolled his eyes before opening his bedroom door. "They just have nothing better to talk about because they're lame. What do you guys want to do?"

"I don't think I have the energy to do more than watch a movie," Cathy replied and sat down on Jason's bed. "Adderall isn't doing much for me."

"You took Adderall?" Alyssa asked in a surprised tone.

Cathy nodded. "Yeah, in hopes it would wake me up. I took a nap before you got here, too."

"Why are you so tired?" Alyssa asked and sat down beside Cathy.

"Because I'm depressed that our whole grade thinks I drink on painkillers and date a drug dealer," Cathy replied.

"I doubt anyone actually thinks that," Jason interjected. "They just like to gossip. Everyone we're friends with knows Jeff and I were the only ones on Vicodin."

"Rumors suck," Alyssa stated flatly.

"Can I take more Adderall, Jay?" Cathy asked.

"Whatever you want," Jason replied and tossed her the bottle.

While twisting off the cap, she heard the doorbell ring. "Maybe Luke's friends are coming over, after all," she said before popping another five milligrams into her mouth. "Alyssa, do you want one of these?" she asked after washing the pill down with water.

Alyssa squinted in thought. "I better not in case my mother decides to drug test me again," she replied. "She's crazy enough to make it a weekly occurrence."

"Good point," Cathy said and handed the pills back to Jason.

"Let's scope out the scene downstairs," Jason suggested. "Then we can watch a movie in my parent's room. They have the best TV."

Upon entering the kitchen, they found Pat Ryan and Laurelle Mahoney, mixing drinks. Like Luke and Missy, they were dressed in sweats. It appeared they were having some sort of slumber party.

"What's up, JD?" Pat called out and gave Jason a high-five after setting his drink down on the counter. "Alyssa, what's John up to?"

"He went to the movies," Alyssa replied. "He's with Matt, so he'll stop by after."

Pat raised his eyebrows and smirked at Laurelle.

"Maybe if we're lucky, he'll bring Day," Laurelle said to Pat in a hard-to-read tone. "She always loved this type of gathering," she added with a short laugh.

Pat pushed Laurelle playfully in the shoulder before holding up a handle bottle of vodka. "You guys are welcome to make drinks if you want," he said to Jason.

"We're all set but thanks," Jason replied immediately.

Although alcohol sounded appealing to Cathy because she could not shake her melancholy mood, she was relieved to hear Jason turn it down. Thankfully, the Adderall was starting to give her some energy, and she hoped it would lift the cloud of depression that had been hanging over her head all week.

Suddenly, Missy and Luke came hustling into the kitchen with a Bluetooth speaker.

"Wait 'til you hear the playlist I made," Missy said to Laurelle. "Dance party. Called it!"

"Are you guys going to hang out down here?" Luke asked Jason.

Jason shrugged. "We're going to wait for Bryan and then watch a movie."

"Lau, come to the bathroom with me," Missy said and nodded toward the half bath located off the kitchen.

After the girls left the room, Luke walked over to the bottle of vodka and picked it up off the counter. "You guys made drinks?" he questioned Pat in a surprised tone.

Pat nodded. "Laurelle wants to go *that* route tonight."

Luke squinted at him in thought but said nothing. It appeared as though there was something he didn't want to say in front of Jason, Cathy, and Alyssa.

"What are you planning to do if you're not going to drink?" Jason asked his brother in a point-blank manner.

Luke smirked. "That depends on the council in the bathroom," he remarked facetiously.

"Let's go upstairs," Cathy whispered to Jason.

Jason gazed at Luke skeptically before nodding for Alyssa and Cathy to follow him up the backstairs. He said nothing until they reached the second floor. "I don't know what they're planning to do, but Matt's not going to be happy about it when he gets home," he said.

"Do you think 'Sexy Party' is code for some type of drug?" Cathy questioned him.

"What's a 'Sexy Party'?" Alyssa asked curiously.

"I guess we'll find out," Jason replied and motioned for the girls to follow him up to his parents' suite on the third floor.

CHAPTER 30

AN HOUR LATER, JASON, Cathy, and Alyssa were watching a movie when Jason received a text from Bryan: *Hey, I'm here. Luke let me in. You should come downstairs.*

What's going on? Jason replied.

Bryan: *Just come downstairs.*

Jason: *With Cathy and Alyssa?*

Bryan: *Maybe not.*

Jason jumped up from the couch. "I'm going downstairs to get Bryan," he announced before bolting out of the room. He hustled to the second floor and then ran down the backstairs into the kitchen. "Sartelli?" he called out, wondering where Bryan was inside his 12,000 square foot home.

"In the foyer," Bryan called back in a voice barely audible over the music blaring from the family room.

"What's wrong?" Jason asked once he and Bryan were face-to-face.

Bryan laughed. "You need to see what your brother has going on."

Jason eyed Bryan strangely.

"Luke showed me when I got here," Bryan added while trying to contain his laughter.

"Showed you what?" Jason asked curiously and hustled off toward the family room.

Jason's eyes grew wide when he reached the doorway. The lights were off, but the muted TV and a strobe light were illuminating the room. The loud dance music playing over the Bluetooth speaker was unfamiliar to Jason, but clearly familiar to Missy and Laurelle. Missy looked like a blonde goddess in the middle of the room, wearing nothing but a sports bra and pajama shorts. She was dancing with Laurelle, who was dressed the same as her.

"Luke, come here!" Missy cried and waved Luke over to her.

Missy's slender body was moving so perfectly in sync with the music that she looked like a professional dancer. When Luke reached her, she turned around and pulled him close. Then she leaned backwards and kissed Laurelle. Jason and Bryan stood in the doorway, watching the scene in awe. When Missy pulled away from Laurelle, she pushed Laurelle into Luke and told them to kiss. Then she danced over to Pat and pulled him up off the couch.

Jason turned around and tugged Bryan down the hallway. When they reached the kitchen, both boys stared at each other for a few seconds with wide eyes.

"Luke's the man," Bryan remarked. "Missy just let him make out with her best friend while she watched. What are we doing wrong?"

Jason laughed.

"What are you guys doing?" Cathy cried out as she and Alyssa entered the kitchen from the foyer.

Jason widened his eyes.

"Oh, hey, girls," Bryan greeted them in a clear attempt to sound nonchalant.

"You've been down here for, like, five minutes!" Cathy exclaimed.

"We were just checking out the scene in the family room," Jason replied.

"What's going on?" Cathy asked curiously.

"A dance party," Jason replied, "to weird music."

"Is it a 'Sexy' dance party?" Cathy questioned him.

Jason and Bryan both burst into laughter. Cathy and Alyssa peered at them expectantly.

"Uh, yeah," Jason responded between chuckles.

Cathy's green eyes sparkled. "What are they doing?"

Jason looked at Bryan and smirked.

"What?" Cathy pressed with an amused expression on her face.

Jason was debating over how to respond when Missy and Laurelle came running into the kitchen, laughing hysterically.

"Oh, hi, guys!" Missy exclaimed brightly.

"Hi!" Laurelle cried and quickly stopped to wave at everyone before chasing after Missy.

Jason peered over at the refrigerator, where Missy and Laurelle had begun to search for something.

Suddenly, Missy started jumping up and down with excitement. "Found it!" she cried and held a can of whipped cream up in the air.

"What are you girls doing?" Luke called over to Missy and Laurelle as he entered the kitchen from the back hallway. "Holy $#%@!" he cried once he noticed Jason, Bryan, Cathy, and Alyssa.

"We found the whipped cream!" Missy exclaimed.

Luke darted over to his girlfriend and pulled the bottle of whipped cream out of her hand. Then he placed it back inside the refrigerator and closed the door. "Missy," he said and put his hands on her shoulders, "my brother's girlfriend and John's little sister are standing right over there. Let's go back to the family room."

Missy pouted. "But you love it when—"

Luke placed his finger over her lips to interrupt her. Then, without warning, he scooped her up in his arms and carried her out of the kitchen, followed by Laurelle.

"Did that really just happen?" Alyssa asked.

"I need to see this," Cathy said before running out of the room.

"Cathy!" Jason called out while chasing after her.

He caught up to her in the doorway of the family room, followed by Alyssa and Bryan. Missy and Laurelle were dancing together, but not in a sexual way as before. They appeared to be doing some type of swing dance routine they both knew well.

"Wait!" Missy cried. "Do you remember our Super Bowl halftime routine to *One More Time*?"

"Yes!" Laurelle exclaimed with glee. "Is that on the playlist?"

"Of course!" Missy replied. "Luke, change the song!"

Without missing a single beat, Laurelle and Missy performed a halftime dance from two years prior. They were both incredible dancers with beautiful muscle tone. When the routine concluded, Missy ran across the room and jumped on Luke's lap. Laurelle flopped down on the couch that Pat was sitting on and stretched her long legs across his.

Jason was incredibly curious to find out what drugs Luke had given the girls to make them act so carefree. He would love to see his own girlfriend as cheerful as Missy or Laurelle.

"Cathy, come here for a second," he said and pulled on her arm.

"What's wrong?" Cathy asked while following Jason out of the family room and into a nearby bathroom.

After shutting the door, Jason took the bag of crushed-up Adderall out of his pocket and placed it on the vanity. "If we're going to hang out with them, I need more of this."

"So, why do you need me?"

"Do you want some?" Jason asked. "It will make you happy and give you a lot of energy."

"Do you think Missy and Laurelle snorted Adderall? They're off the wall."

Jason shrugged. "I have no idea."

"They're so crazy!" Cathy cried. "I would love to feel that happy."

"Do you want to?" Jason asked and motioned towards the blue powder.

Cathy hesitated.

"It's killing me to see you so torn up about the stupid rumors at school," Jason said. "I would do anything to cheer you up."

Cathy smiled slightly. "I feel a little better than I did earlier," she admitted. "Does it hurt to snort?"

"No. You can hardly feel it, honestly," Jason replied. "The drip afterwards might annoy you, but I think it's worth it."

Cathy eyed Jason apprehensively. "I took ten milligrams. How much is in that bag?"

Jason glanced at the blue powder. "I'm not really sure," he admitted while pouring some of it onto the vanity. "Just watch what I do," he directed her as he split the powder into three lines.

He brought a rolled-up dollar bill to his nose and blew one of the lines. When he handed her the dollar, she hesitated less than he expected before bending over and snorting the thinner of the two remaining lines. Afterwards, she stood up straight and widened her green eyes.

"Are you okay?" Jason asked.

Cathy nodded. "I barely felt it," she said in a surprised tone. "I see what you mean about the drip, though."

"It'll go away," Jason said and took the dollar from her. After blowing the remaining line, he wiped the vanity with a tissue. "How do you feel?" he asked.

"Awake!" Cathy replied and smiled widely.

Jason laughed. "Good," he said and then led her back to the family room.

The music was still blaring loudly, but the room was empty.

"Where is everyone?" Cathy asked.

"No idea. Let's check the kitchen," Jason replied and playfully tugged on Cathy's arm before pulling her down the hallway.

In the kitchen, they found Luke, pouring a glass of water. "Where did you guys disappear to?" he asked when Cathy and Jason dashed over to him.

"Nowhere," Jason replied and jumped up on the counter. "Where is everyone?"

"Outside," Luke replied and leaned against the center island.

"Why?" Jason asked.

"They wanted to smoke," Luke replied.

"Alyssa and Bryan don't smoke weed," Jason remarked.

Luke shrugged. "They went outside with everyone else. Maybe they're smoking butts or vaping. I have no idea."

"I'll go see," Cathy announced and ran over to the slider.

"What are Missy and Laurelle on?" Jason asked after Cathy disappeared outside.

Luke laughed. "That's how Missy and Laurelle get when they're drunk."

Jason widened his eyes. "Seriously?"

Luke nodded.

"Are they bi-sexual?" Jason asked.

Luke shook his head. "They say they're 'not B-I' they're 'B-F' and 'best friends can kiss each other.'"

Jason let out a short laugh. "You're lucky."

"Whatever they do is just to turn on me and Pat."

"That would never fly with my friends."

Luke shrugged. "To each his own. So, what were you and Cathy doing in the bathroom for five minutes? Really?"

"Just Adderall," Jason replied. "What did you take? You seem sober."

"Nothing."

"Why not?"

"I might roll later, and you can't mix molly with alcohol."

"Why not?"

"Because you could die."

"Seriously?"

Luke nodded.

"Well, why later?" Jason asked. "Isn't molly perfect for a 'Sexy Party'?"

Luke shook his head and laughed. "No. Molly's perfect for the after-party."

CHAPTER 31

I'll stop by Matt's on my way home from Boston if you'll be there, Marc typed into his cell phone and hit send. He placed his phone down on the table and glanced up at Taylor, who was chugging a glass of water. Because his football game had been cancelled, Marc had the rare opportunity to spend a Friday night in Boston with his oldest brother.

Taylor set his empty glass on the table and resumed eating.

"So, why isn't Julie here?" Marc asked as he watched Taylor twist long pieces of spaghetti around his fork.

"Why aren't you eating?" Taylor responded and nodded towards Marc's full plate of chicken parmigiana.

Marc put his head down and began cutting up his meal. The air felt thicker than usual, and the sense of awkwardness between him and his brother was foreign. "I'm not that hungry, I guess," he replied.

"She has a sorority thing," Taylor remarked after swallowing a piece of chicken.

"Oh. It seems really lowkey around here."

Taylor nodded and rose from his seat. He retrieved a pitcher of water from the refrigerator and set it down on the table. "Ryan and the guys are in NC. There are some parties going on, but I'm kind of over that scene," he said while pouring himself another glass of water.

Marc set his fork down and eyed his brother strangely. "*You* are sick of parties?"

Taylor took a sip of water and nodded. "It gets old, bro. Just a bunch of sloppy dudes and wasted girls hoping to hook up with each other."

"You're the king of beer pong, the master of the domain."

Taylor laughed. "Give it four or five years, and you'll know what I mean." He set down his fork to scratch his left arm for the fourth time in five minutes.

Marc cleared his throat. "I think I'm going to sign with BC."

Taylor smiled. "Glad you'll be close. It sucks only seeing Jordan on TV."

"I'm okay with that," Marc stated dryly before taking a large sip of Vitamin Water.

"There's no way J drugged Michelle," Taylor insisted. "You need to hear him out."

Marc set his drink on the table. "I've heard everything he has to say," he retorted. "There's no other way Michelle would have ended up topless in bed with him."

Taylor sighed. "She got sick from something and puked on her shirt. Jordan was trying to help her. For God's sake, Marc! He's our brother. He's a good kid."

Marc rolled his eyes. "He pledged to take her virginity before he graduated. You know how competitive he is. She was a conquest."

Taylor groaned. "Marc, he said that to bust your balls. Everyone knows you love Michelle. He was trying to get under your skin. Nothing more."

Marc swallowed a large lump in his throat. "He liked her."

"So, is that the real problem here?" Taylor asked. "That he dared to like your middle-school girlfriend?"

Marc could feel his face turning red. "Can we talk about something else?"

"You're missing out," Taylor remarked and scraped the last bit of food off his plate. "Jordan's a heck of a lot nicer than you or me. The kid probably smiles in his sleep."

Marc let out a heavy breath. "So, yeah, like I was saying... I think BC's the school for me."

Taylor brought his dirty plate over to the sink and turned on the faucet. "It's a great school," he said flatly. "Mom and Dad will go to your home games. You'll be happy there."

Marc pushed his nearly full plate aside. "What are you going to do?"

Taylor shut off the faucet and turned around. "I'm going to do whatever I need to do to get back on the field." He leaned against the sink and crossed his arms.

"At NU or somewhere else?"

Taylor shrugged. "I don't know."

"Can't you reapply or switch your major?"

"It's not that simple."

"What about going down south? You'd be able to get into some of the big schools down there."

Taylor let out a heavy breath and walked back over to the table. "I'm going to do what I need to do."

"Are you afraid to leave Julie?"

Taylor swallowed deeply and shook his head. "She'd be better off if I left."

Marc's phone vibrated on the table. "Don't say that," he said as he read Michelle's text, which said she would be at Matt's.

"Okay, but it's true. She deserves better than an ex-quarterback who failed out of college."

Marc abruptly looked up from his phone. "That's not you," he said sternly. "That's who pain meds turned you into."

Taylor scowled. "All the pain meds do is take away my migraines and relieve my depression. I did not fail out of my major because of Oxy."

Marc crossed his arms and eyed his brother disgustedly. "Then why did you fail, T?"

Taylor took a deep breath and let it out slowly. "Because I let myself get depressed and distracted."

"Distracted by what?"

Taylor put his head down. "Just bad stuff," he muttered.

Marc scoffed. "Oh, your new profession?"

Taylor swallowed deeply. "It wasn't even supposed to be like that. I was just going to get stuff for my friends at a discount, but it blew up into something I never intended."

"Was it worth it?"

"God no. I would never have gotten involved with these people if I had known who I was dealing with. I would have rather paid a hundred dollars a pill than be in this situation."

"So, get out."

"It's not like that."

Marc threw out his arms in a questioning manner. "What does that mean?"

"I can't get into it."

"If you weren't put on painkillers, you never would have become a drug dealer," Marc said matter-of-factly. "So, whether you realize it or not, your life is this way because of drugs."

"Drugs?" Taylor asked defensively. "I don't even drink. I don't touch coke, molly, weed—nothing."

Marc dropped his jaw and eyed his brother in disbelief.

"You don't believe me? Ask Julie."

"You take painkillers *every day*!" Marc exclaimed.

Taylor looked taken aback. "That's a prescription; it's different."

Marc scoffed. "It's not different. Oxy comes from the same plant as heroin."

Taylor widened his blue eyes. "Is that what you think of me? That I'm some kind of junkie because I take medicine that makes me feel better?"

Marc scowled. "I don't think you're a junkie. Of course, I don't. I just... I just think you'd feel more like yourself if you laid off the painkillers."

Taylor shook his head. "They help me."

"Help you what?"

"Feel normal. Feel like socializing. *Not* hate myself."

"Does Julie know?"

Taylor shrugged. "I don't know."

"She must see them in your room. She's not stupid."

"I don't know, Marc. Julie deserves a lot more than I can offer, and she would be wise to find a new boyfriend."

Marc held a steady gaze on Taylor. "You don't mean that."

Taylor nodded. "I do."

"You would just let her go?" Marc asked in disbelief.

"It's not safe to be with me," Taylor replied matter-of-factly, "and until I can find a way out of the mess I'm in, I don't deserve her."

CHAPTER 32

THE CRISP FALL AIR sent a chill through Jason's body as he stepped outside. His parents enjoyed entertaining, so their back deck was equipped with a lounge area, fire pit, grilling station, and built-in wet bar. Everyone was gathered on the plush, U-shaped couch in the lounge area. As Jason walked towards his guests, he noticed that Missy and Laurelle had put on sweatshirts. They were huddled together under a few cozy fleece blankets and laughing at something on a cell phone. Cathy, Bryan, and Alyssa were sitting together on one side of the couch across from Pat.

"Do you guys want me to light the fire pit?" Jason offered as he approached them. "It's freezing out here."

Missy looked up at Jason. "We have blankets! Do you want to come cuddle with me and Laurelle?"

Jason laughed. "Why did you guys come out here?" he asked and took a seat beside Pat. He looked down at the glass coffee table and saw a small bag of weed. "Oh, never mind. Whose weed is that?"

"Mine," Pat replied. "We already smoked, but you're welcome to."

Jason shook his head. "I'm good."

"Jay, do you hate weed like Matt and Luke?" Laurelle asked.

Jason shook his head. "No. I just don't feel like getting high. Did you smoke, Cathy?" he asked and turned towards his girlfriend.

"I smoked a cigarette with Alyssa, but I didn't touch the weed," she replied.

Jason lowered his eyebrows and eyed Cathy strangely. "Seriously?" he asked. He knew Adderall would make her more carefree, but he had never expected her smoke.

"Don't be mad," Missy sang.

"I'm just... surprised," Jason said, deciding that showing his disgust would only add to his girlfriend's stress level.

Missy stood up and stretched her arms above her head. "Oh, my, gosh, Pat," she said while yawning. "Your weed is knocking me on my ass. Did you get it from Luke?"

Pat nodded.

Missy yawned again. "I'm going inside," she said before wrapping a blanket around her slender body and stumbling her way into the house.

"Does she normally smoke?" Jason asked.

"No!" Laurelle cried with a short laugh. "Your brother's going to be mad. He prefers her up, not down."

Pat laughed. "I'm sure he'll fix the problem."

Laurelle widened her blue eyes with amusement. "Yeah, don't be shocked when Missy's ready for another dance party in five!"

Alyssa and Bryan both shot Jason confused looks. He assumed Laurelle and Pat were implying Luke would give Missy some type of upper.

"Are you guys ready to head in?" Jason asked, hoping to change the subject before Alyssa and Bryan caught on to what they had implied. "It's cold, and Luke's bored."

"Sure thing," Laurelle replied and stood up.

Jason glanced at Cathy, who appeared antsy. "Do you want to go inside?"

"Yeah," Cathy replied and hopped off her seat. "Are you mad at me?"

Jason sighed. "Don't worry about it," he responded and wrapped his arm around her shoulders to lead her inside.

"I'm just mad at my parents for grounding me," Cathy said as they walked toward the house.

"Right," Jason muttered.

"I can tell you're upset."

Jason let out a heavy breath and opened the sliding glass door to the kitchen. "You're high on Adderall. I should have expected something like that to happen."

"Can I go brush my teeth?" Cathy asked.

"Please do," Jason said dryly.

Cathy widened her green eyes. "I'm sorry!" she cried defensively.

"Just go. I'll be here."

Cathy turned away from him and hustled up the backstairs. Out of the corner of his eye, Jason noticed Luke enter the kitchen from the hallway.

"Where are you going?" Jason called out as Luke walked towards the stairs, carrying Missy like a bride.

"We'll be back," Luke replied and trudged up the staircase.

"Was she passed out?" Alyssa asked.

"I'd say," Jason replied. "She's all of ninety pounds. I doubt it takes much to mess her up."

"Is Luke putting her to bed?" Alyssa wondered.

"I bet she'll snap out of it," Jason replied. "I'm going to check on Cathy. You two hang tight," he added before jogging across the kitchen and up the staircase.

The bathroom across the hall from his bedroom was empty, but he found Cathy standing nearby in Luke's doorway. When Jason reached her side, he noticed Missy was asleep on Luke's bed. "Geez! She crashed hard," Jason stated and glanced at his brother.

"Yeah, I'd say so," Luke commented and locked his hazel eyes on Missy. "I don't know why she smoked. She has no tolerance for weed."

"Are you just going to let her sleep?" Jason asked curiously.

Luke shrugged.

"Good luck," Jason sang and grabbed Cathy's hand. "Let's go to my room for a second," he whispered before turning down the hallway. When they reached his bedroom, he shut the door. "I left Bryan and Alyssa downstairs, so we should be quick, but do you want more Adderall?"

Cathy raised her eyebrows. "I don't think so. I'm, like, shaking. Do we really have to be quick, though?" she asked and stepped closer to him. She widened her eyes in an excited manner and began unbuttoning his jeans.

Jason laughed. "What are you doing?"

She pulled his pants down to the floor and stood up to pull his shirt over his head. "You know what I'm doing," she replied with an unfamiliar mischievous sparkle in her eyes.

CHAPTER 33

Around ten o'clock, Matt Davids braced himself before entering his home. Despite the fact that Pat's black Highlander was the only extra vehicle in the driveway, Matt knew chances were high that Luke had smuggled extra bodies into their home. For some reason, Luke seemed set on befriending their entire school. Matt knew his brother feared having no friends left at MLH after the senior class graduated, but he thought Luke needed to use better judgement.

As Ally, Day, John, and Michelle followed Matt into the foyer, he let out a sigh of relief. "Maybe he actually listened to me," Matt said. "I thought we'd be walking into a party."

"My sister's here somewhere," John stated.

"Luke? Jay?" Matt called out loudly as he led everyone to the kitchen. "Oh, hey, guys," he greeted Alyssa and Bryan, surprised to see them sitting at the kitchen table. "Where's Jay?"

"Luke and Jay both disappeared upstairs," Alyssa replied.

"Are Laurelle and Missy still here?" Day asked.

"Yeah. Laurelle's in the family room with Pat," Alyssa responded. "Missy's upstairs with Luke."

"Let's go see what Pat and Laur are up to," Day suggested and nodded for Michelle and Ally to follow her.

"I'm sorry my brothers are horrible hosts," Matt apologized to Bryan and Alyssa.

"It looked like Luke was putting Missy to bed," Alyssa said. "I think she had a little too much to drink."

"It's pretty early for that," Matt remarked skeptically. "What about Jay?"

"He went upstairs to find Cathy," Alyssa replied.

"That's code for he went upstairs to get laid," Matt stated matter-of-factly and smirked at John.

Alyssa sent Matt a strange look. "Cathy's a virgin," she said assuredly.

Matt widened his eyes, wondering if Jason had kept his sex life a secret.

"You look like you don't believe that," Bryan commented and raised his eyebrows.

Matt laughed. "Jay lost his virginity an hour after he hit puberty. If you think he's gone the last two years without sex, you're extremely gullible."

Bryan and Alyssa looked at each other and shrugged.

"Cathy goes to my church," John said. "I wouldn't be surprised if she's waiting."

"Yeah, she is. She told me about her virginity pact," Alyssa insisted.

Matt was finding the conversation quite amusing. Clearly, he knew Jason better than anyone else did. "Go look for them," he suggested. "I guarantee you'll interrupt the sex you don't think happens." Hearing footsteps on the stairs, Matt turned to see who was entering the room.

"Oh, hey," Luke greeted him nonchalantly. "When did you get home?"

"Just now," Matt replied. "Do you know where Jay is?"

"If he's not down here, then he's in his room with Cathy," Luke replied and walked over to the table, where everyone was gathered.

"Where's Missy?" Matt asked, observing that his brother looked completely sober.

Luke rolled his eyes. "In a weed coma."

"Did Jay smoke?" Matt asked.

"I don't know. I wasn't outside," Luke replied.

Matt pointed to an empty bottle on the counter. "Who finished all that vodka? You didn't let Jay drink, did you?"

"Relax," Luke said and patted Matt on the arm. "That was Missy, Laurelle, and Pat."

Matt widened his eyes. "They must be lit!"

"Oh, yeah," Luke sang.

"Well, good job keeping it lowkey and not getting me arrested tonight," Matt joked and playfully swung his arm around Luke's neck.

Luke laughed. "I owed you *at least* that," he said and pulled free from Matt's grip. "I'm going to try to wake up Missy."

"All right," Matt said. "You guys can hang out with us until Jay turns up," he added and motioned for Alyssa and Bryan to follow him out of the room.

As Matt walked toward the family room, he overheard Alyssa ask Bryan, "Do you think they're really having sex?"

"I think they're doing something shady," Bryan replied.

"Do you think they're doing drugs?" Alyssa asked.

"Anything's possible with Jay," Bryan muttered.

"I thought he seemed more normal than her," Alyssa said. "She was fidgeting the whole time we were outside."

"Yeah, I noticed," Bryan responded.

"Why were you outside?" John questioned Alyssa suspiciously. "You didn't smoke weed with them, did you?"

"No!" Alyssa exclaimed. "I don't do that. If I did, it would have shown up on the drug test Mom made me take."

John laughed and wrapped his arm around Alyssa's shoulders. "It won't be the last time she does that."

"Why would your mother drug test *you*?" Matt asked and turned to face Alyssa. Although he had seen most of Jason's friends drunk or high, Alyssa always seemed as composed, well mannered, and in control as her straightedge older brother.

Alyssa rolled her eyes. "She heard there was Vicodin at a party."

Matt raised his eyebrows in surprise. "Vicodin?"

Alyssa nodded.

Matt sighed. He was fearful that whatever drugs were circulating around Montgomery had come from Luke. He hoped Luke had not been stupid enough to give painkillers to freshmen, but he could not ignore the possibility. The rumor was that Luke got everything from an acquaintance, but Matt had begun to wonder if his brother was actually a dealer. Luke was neither in need of extra money nor addicted to anything, so Matt could not fathom why he would ever deal. He had acquired a party-boy reputation due to his sociable nature, but truth be told, Luke rarely even drank. More often than not, he spent the weekends looking after Missy, who was typically the life of every party.

Nevertheless, what perplexed Matt the most was Jason's easy access to drugs. He feared that the person with the drug supply was not merely Luke's acquaintance but rather a part of their inner circle. Sadly, Luke being a dealer was beginning to seem more and more likely, and Matt was overwhelmed with haunting thoughts about both of his younger brothers.

CHAPTER 34

When Jason finally returned downstairs with Cathy, he was surprised to see Matt, Ally, Michelle, John, and Day in the family room with everyone else. Because most of Matt's female friends were cheerleaders, they saw every gathering as an excuse for a dance party; that night was no exception.

"Oh, look who it is!" Matt announced once Jason entered the room.

"When did you get home?" Jason asked.

"A little before ten," Matt replied. "Come talk to me for a second," he added and motioned for Jason to follow him into the hallway.

Jason's heart pounded heavily against his chest. It would take Matt one up-close gaze into his eyes to realize he was high.

"Holy $#@%!" Matt exclaimed when he locked eyes with Jason. "Your pupils are bugging. What the hell?"

"It's just from Adderall," Jason replied.

"You're twitching," Matt remarked and eyed Jason skeptically. "If you're only on Adderall, then you're on way too much."

"What did you want to talk about?" Jason asked impatiently.

"Is Cathy on Adderall, too?" Matt pressed.

Jason's stomach churned. "We took a nap after dinner, but she was still tired, so I told her to try it."

"Jason!" Matt cried. "That's your prescription. It's not meant for anyone else. Do you know how upset Mom and Dad would be if they found out?"

"I'm sure they'd be shocked," Jason replied. "In fact, I doubt they'd believe it."

Matt scowled. "Don't you realize you're betraying their trust?"

"I never looked at it that way."

Matt shook his head. "What is wrong with you?"

"What do you mean?" Jason asked and looked up at his brother curiously.

"You're apathetic," Matt replied. "I never thought I would use that word to describe *you*."

"What did you want to talk about?" Jason questioned his brother impatiently.

"Fine, dodge my question," Matt said and threw his arms up in the air.

"I'm not. I just don't have an answer," Jason replied.

Matt crossed his arms. "I don't believe you."

Jason let out a heavy breath. "Fine. I'm depressed."

"Why?"

"Probably because Chris joined a church and made a whole new life for himself. He wants nothing to do with me."

"Marc said Chris is in a good place. If he doesn't want to spend time with you, then you're probably not."

Jason scowled. "Can we talk about something else?"

Matt let out a heavy breath. "I heard there was Vicodin at a party, and I want to know if it came from Luke."

Jason widened his eyes as his heart pounded against his chest, faster and faster. "Why would you think that?"

"Because he gets pills for people sometimes," Matt replied matter-of-factly.

"Who?" Jason asked.

"Kids he's trying to become friends with," Matt stated and rolled his eyes. "He seems to think throwing parties and hooking people up with drugs will make him more popular with his grade."

Jason squinted in confusion. "That doesn't sound like Luke."

Matt shrugged. "Yeah, well, that's what he's doing."

"Why are you asking me about this? Ask him."

"He's not going to admit to giving Vicodin to freshmen. I would kick his ass. He told me he knows someone who deals and that he only gets stuff when people ask him for it."

Jason shifted his weight uncomfortably. He did not want Luke to get in trouble with Matt for his own blunder. "I don't think Luke had anything to do with it."

"Opiates are bad news," Matt said. "If they can mess up Taylor, they can mess up anyone."

Jason peered at Matt in confusion. "What are you talking about?"

"Chris didn't tell you?"

Jason shook his head. "He said Taylor wasn't ready to play this season, but he didn't elaborate."

"Taylor got addicted to painkillers after his surgery and failed out of Northeastern, so there are a lot of reasons why he's not playing football right now."

"What?!" Jason exclaimed and widened his eyes. "Who told you that?"

"Marc."

"I can't picture Taylor doing anything like that."

"Drugs mess people up," Matt stated matter-of-factly. "Stay away from opiates. If they can grip *Taylor*, they can grip you, me, Luke, Mom, Dad—anyone."

Jason was stunned. Although Taylor was known to party, he had always been a role model in the classroom and on the field.

"Just let me know if you find out where the Vicodin came from," Matt said, pulling Jason out of his thoughts. "I hope it wasn't Luke."

"Luke barely knows the kid who got sick from it."

"Your pupils are ridiculous right now," Matt said. "Don't take any more Adderall."

"I don't plan on it," Jason responded. "I better go make sure Cathy's okay," he added before turning away from his brother and hustling out of the library.

When Jason reached the family room, he saw that the dance party had continued. He was surprised to see his typically shy girlfriend right in the mix with everyone else. Unsurprisingly, Alyssa was singing and dancing while Bryan was shooting pool by himself on the other side of the room.

As Jason made his way over to Cathy, Luke and Missy entered the room. Jason was amazed to see Missy upright and smiling.

When she noticed Matt, she exclaimed, "Hi, Matty!" Then she bounced over to him, hugged him from behind, and swung around to kiss his cheek.

Matt laughed. "I heard you were in bed."

Missy giggled. "Luke got me up."

Jason glanced at Luke, who looked ready for bed, wearing a Patriots hooded sweatshirt and baggy sweatpants. Missy, on the other hand, seemed as vibrant as she had earlier in the night. She leaped over to where everyone was dancing in the center of the room and immediately joined the fun.

Laurelle threw her arms around Missy and cried, "I knew you'd bounce back!" Then she whispered something in Missy's ear.

Missy laughed and nodded for Laurelle to follow her over to Luke, who was still standing beside Matt in the doorway. "We have to get something upstairs," Missy informed him, before tugging on Laurelle's arm and pulling her out of the room.

Matt looked at Luke and raised his eyebrows.

Luke rolled his eyes. "I had to. She would have slept all night."

"Did you do it?" Matt asked.

Luke shook his head. "No."

Listening to his brothers' brief exchange, Jason wondered what Luke had given Missy to wake her up. Whatever it was had worked wonders.

CHAPTER 35

TEN MINUTES LATER, CATHY stared at her reflection in the bathroom mirror, wondering when her pupils would return to their normal size. "My mom is going to be here in less than a half hour. She'll freak out if she sees my eyes like this!"

Jason turned Cathy around to face him and then peered into her green eyes. "Pupils dilate when people are tired. You could just say you're exhausted."

"But I'm not. I'm shaking."

"Can you sleep over Alyssa's?"

"Alyssa's parents would drug test me if they saw me like this!"

"Alyssa's going home with John at midnight. You'll be fine by then."

Cathy eyed Jason thoughtfully. "I could ask to sleep at Alyssa's. If my mom says yes, I could stay here instead. I'm sure Luke could drive me to her house in the morning."

Jason widened his eyes. "That would be fun but risky."

"That's part of the reason why it would be so fun!" Cathy cried.

Jason laughed. "Make sure Luke can drive you before you make any calls. If Missy's staying over, Luke will probably be up all night long. I'm pretty sure she's on coke, and he said he might roll later."

"You think she's on *coke*?" Cathy asked with wide eyes.

Jason nodded.

"But not Luke?"

Jason shook his head.

"Well, if he's planning to roll, then I doubt he'll be able to drive me to Alyssa's in the morning," Cathy reasoned. "Would Matt drive me?"

Jason shrugged. "Your safest bet would be to just stay at Alyssa's."

"You don't want me to sleep over?" Cathy asked and eyed Jason sadly.

"I do," Jason replied. "I just don't want you to get grounded for another month."

"I know, but I'm having so much fun that I don't want the night to end!"

Jason smiled. "It's good to see you so happy, but I think you'll end up getting in trouble if you stay."

Cathy opened the bathroom door. "I'm going to find Luke," she announced and rushed out of the room. "Luke!" she cried as she ran down the hallway and into the family room. She found him standing with Matt, John, Pat, and Bryan near the pool table. Missy, Laurelle, Day, Alyssa, Ally, and Michelle were still dancing in the middle of the room.

"What's up?" Luke asked.

Cathy latched onto his muscular arm and pulled him away from the guys. "If I stay over, can you drive me to Alyssa's in the morning?"

"How early?"

"Sometime before ten. I'm going to ask if I can sleep over Alyssa's but stay here instead."

Luke raised his eyebrows. "Do Alyssa and John know that?"

"Not yet. Jay and I just came up with the idea."

"Ugh, CK, I don't know if I'll be up before ten," Luke said apologetically. "Now that Missy's awake, she's going to stay up all night. Laurelle, Pat, and Ally are all sleeping over. Marc is supposed to stop by on his way home from Boston. It's going to be a late night. I doubt Matt will even be awake before ten."

"Is Marc staying over?" Cathy asked.

Luke shrugged. "No idea."

"Well, if no one can drive me, I can just call my mom in the morning and tell her I came over for breakfast."

"What's with you?" Luke asked and searched her eyes. "I thought you were fed up with Jay. Now you want to spend the night here?"

"We're having fun," Cathy replied. "I want to keep it going."

Luke eyed her suspiciously. "Your pupils are dilated."

"Jay gave me Adderall."

Luke raised his eyebrows. "I thought you hated him taking Adderall?"

"Not when I'm on it!" Cathy cried.

"Were you serious about taking what he takes?"

Cathy shrugged. "If that's what I need to do to be happy."

Luke squinted at her. "Come here," he said and pulled her into the hallway. "I'm worried about you," he admitted and placed his hand on her shoulder. "I think Jay's too much for you to handle."

Cathy cocked her head to the side. "What do you mean?"

"He's stressing you out," Luke replied. "Jay's smart enough to get back on track. He just needs a reason to do it. If you start doing drugs with him, he'll have no reason to stop."

Cathy dropped her jaw. "You're the one who gives him drugs!" she protested. "Why are you being like this?"

"I did *not* give him the Xanax or Vicodin you found in his room," Luke snapped. "Those bottles were for kids in my grade. I don't touch that stuff, and Jay shouldn't either."

"But you're fine with *me* taking benzos?"

"You have anxiety," Luke replied. "I've never seen Jason look anxious in my life. He takes benzos and smokes weed to offset the Adderall he snorts; he drinks on painkillers to numb his depression; and he trips because he's bored. If he were sober, he wouldn't need weed or benzos to sleep. He also would still be friends with Chris, so he wouldn't be depressed or bored. Drugs are not fixing his problems."

"The only thing he took tonight was Adderall. He's trying to straighten out."

Luke looked genuinely disappointed in her. "I'm shocked you're letting him influence you."

"I just want to be happy," Cathy whined.

"That's my point!" Luke exclaimed. "If you break up with him, you'll be happy."

Cathy scoffed. "I don't want to break up with him. I want to spend the night with him. What time is it?"

Luke pulled his phone out of his pocket and turned on the screen. "Ten-fifty," he said flatly.

Cathy widened her eyes. "My mom is going to be here in ten minutes! It's too late for me to call her! She's going to notice my pupils. What do I do?"

Luke took off his hat and placed it on her head. "Wear that. The visor will make it hard to see your eyes."

Cathy smiled. "Thanks! I'm wide awake. If I sneak out of my house after my parents go to bed, will you pick me up?"

"Maybe," Luke replied. "But I'm not happy with you right now."

Cathy pouted. "Don't be mad at me."

Luke sighed. "Jay's messing you up."

"He's not trying to hurt me. He loves me."

"The Jason you are currently dating loves himself and his drugs. He's addicted to an amphetamine. If he wasn't, he would have already stopped taking it. I told him everything I just told you. He knows he's hurting you. He knows he's hurting himself. He can't stop without help, or he already would have."

Cathy crossed her arms and peered at Luke. He was making an awful lot of sense, but she hated thinking of Jason as an addict. Jason was her perfect match, her soulmate, her level-headed, rational, and witty boyfriend. He was the smartest and most loving person she had ever met. How could he be a drug addict? Drug addicts were losers; they didn't do well in school; they weren't teachers' favorite students; and they weren't well-kempt. Right? They certainly did not earn A's in classes with students three years older than them! Jason did not fit the description of a drug addict at all—except for the doing-drugs-every-day part.

"I'm not trying to put a damper on your night," Luke added, "but there's a thin line between having fun and forming an addiction. Jason crossed that line, and he's going to pull you to the other side if you let him."

Cathy crossed her arms. "This is really strange coming from *you*," she retorted. "You've done more drugs than Jay."

Luke raised his eyebrows. "Who have *you* been talking to?"

Cathy shrugged. "People."

Luke rolled his eyes. "People, CK? Well, 'people' are wrong. I don't do much of anything."

Cathy crossed her arms. "Don't lie."

Luke scoffed. "I'm not. I tried weed once when I was a freshman—hated it. I've rolled five times, and I've done coke twice. I've never taken acid, mushrooms, mescaline, amphetamines, painkillers, or benzos, so I would say my little bro has me beat by a landslide."

"You've never taken a painkiller or a benzo?" Cathy questioned him in disbelief.

"Nope," Luke replied and looked her directly in the eye.

Cathy eyed him skeptically. "Then how do you know so much about them?"

"The internet."

"Seriously?"

Luke nodded.

"I thought you tried everything you dealt."

"Dealt? You think I *deal*?"

"Um..." Cathy stammered, "yeah."

"I know *someone* who deals," Luke corrected her, "so I get stuff from him when my friends ask me to, but I don't make money off the sales, and I certainly don't try everything I get! You see me every day. Have you ever seen me on drugs?"

Cathy eyed him apprehensively. "I guess not," she admitted reluctantly. "Jason thinks you deal. I guess there's a 'fine line' between 'dealing' and 'hooking people up.'"

Luke scowled. "Great! My little brother thinks I'm a drug dealer, and you think I do a bunch of drugs?"

"Jay was afraid you tested out the pills you gave to Chris."

"Oh, you mean the pills Jay now takes?"

Cathy sighed.

Luke put his arms out in a questioning manner. "Do you hear yourself?"

"I need to say bye to everyone before my mom gets here," Cathy remarked dismissively and stepped past Luke towards the family room. "Thanks for the hat."

"Don't be mad at me for telling you the truth."

Cathy paused and turned around to face him. "I'm mad that I can't sleep over."

Luke rolled his eyes. "I'll talk to Marc and see if he can bring you home before your parents wake up. Call here after they go to bed."

Cathy smiled. "Thanks, buddy!"

"Just be careful so you don't get grounded again," he warned her.

Cathy gave Luke a thumbs-up sign and hustled off to find Jason. He was dancing with Missy in the middle of the girls' circle, clearly enjoying her attention. Cathy hesitated only slightly before pulling him aside. "I have to leave in a few minutes," she said, "but I'm going to try to come back."

"Nice hat," Jason commented sarcastically. "Where did you and Luke disappear to?"

"We were just trying to figure out a plan," Cathy replied. "Marc might be able to pick me up and bring me back home before my parents wake up."

"Cool. Just don't get caught. I'll go crazy without you for another month."

"I believe that," Cathy said as the doorbell rang.

"That's your mom," Jason assumed. "I can't answer the door with my eyes like this, so give me a hug and call me when you get home."

Cathy embraced Jason and then quickly said goodbye to her friends. As she made her way toward the front door, her stomach grew queasy. Considering Alyssa's parents' warning, Cathy was certain her mother would drug test her if she noticed her dilated pupils. When Cathy opened the front door, she was relieved to see Chantal. "Hi!" she exclaimed in an excited manner.

Chantal seemed startled by Cathy's perky greeting. "Um, hi," she stammered. "Dad's in the car. Mom's home with Steph. Are you... drunk?"

Cathy let out a short laugh and shut the door behind her. "No. I didn't drink anything. Why?"

"You seem... happy," Chantal commented as she began following Cathy down the cobblestone front steps.

"So, now I have to be drunk to be happy?"

Chantal scowled. "Forget it. It just sounded like there was a party going on."

"That's because Michelle Taylor, Ally Jordan, Missy Kent, Day Angeletti, and Laurelle Mahoney are having a dance party in the family room," Cathy replied, knowing Chantal would suspect nothing unruly after hearing Michelle, Day, and Ally's names.

"Oh! Were they practicing their halftime routine?" Chantal asked curiously.

"Yeah... and every cheer routine they've ever done."

"I wish I were on varsity," Chantal said. "I could learn so much from Ally."

"They're all really good dancers," Cathy remarked as she stepped up to her dad's white Ford Explorer. "You can have shotgun."

"Really?"

Cathy nodded.

"Thanks!" Chantal cried before opening the passenger-side door and hopping into the front seat.

Cathy was relieved to climb into the backseat. "Hi, Dad!" she greeted him, trying her best not to sound overly excited but finding it hard not to be cheerful.

"How was your night?" Mr. Kagelli asked as he turned around to back out of Jason's driveway.

Cathy hung her head so he would not catch a glimpse of her eyes. "It was fun," she replied. "We watched a movie and then hung out with Jay's brothers."

"New hat?" Mr. Kagelli asked.

"Luke gave it to me," Cathy replied and lowered the visor.

"You guys are pretty close," Mr. Kagelli commented in an uneasy tone. "I thought you were going to spend less time with the older kids to avoid getting in trouble again?"

"Luke and Matt *live* with Jason; it's hard not to spend time with *them*," Cathy retorted. "But Matt avoids trouble and Luke learned his lesson last month."

"Let's hope," Mr. Kagelli said in a skeptical manner.

"Luke's the nicest guy I know," Cathy assured her father. "He drives me home from school every day and treats me like a sister."

"Your mother and I love Jason, but we don't like the idea of you hanging out with juniors and seniors. There's a big difference between a fifteen-year-old and an eighteen-year-old."

"You know who was at Jason's house with Matt and Luke tonight? Michelle Taylor, Day Angeletti, and John Kelly," Cathy said, knowing her father's tune would change at the mention of their names.

"I didn't realize they were friends with Luke and Matt," Mr. Kagelli remarked.

"Oh, yeah. Great friends. Day is best friends with Luke's girlfriend, Missy, and Michelle is best friends with Matt's girlfriend, Ally," Cathy explained. "Matt and Luke are two of John's best friends. They helped him plan the scavenger hunt when he proposed to Day."

"Well, if you're going to spend time with older kids, I suppose you're hanging out with the right people," Mr. Kagelli stated, somewhat reluctantly.

"I think so," Cathy said. "Luke only threw that party last month because he wants to be friends with our entire school. He's not a bad kid; he's just really social. What did you do tonight, Chantal? You're extra quiet."

"Andy and I went to the movies with Chris and Marielle," Chantal replied.

"Were Lisa and Jeff with you?" Cathy asked.

"No. That would have been weird. Why?"

"Lisa told Jay she had plans with Andy," Cathy replied.

"Oh, maybe Andy invited her, but she decided not to go because Chris was coming?" Chantal speculated.

"I doubt it," Cathy remarked. "I think Lisa wants to come between Jay and Jeff's bromance."

Chantal turned around to face Cathy. "Can you blame her?" she asked and raised her eyebrows.

CHAPTER 36

MARC LEFT TAYLOR'S APARTMENT around eleven o'clock to drive back to Montgomery. To his dismay, he had learned that Taylor and Julie were in a fight, and he hoped his brother was not on the verge of losing her forever.

As Marc drove west down Route 9, he felt dejected. He had hoped that Julie would get through to Taylor, but when she pressed him about his shady behavior, it had only put more space between them. It pained Marc to see his brother's self-esteem so low, and he feared Taylor's depression could turn him suicidal. Marc sighed before picking up his cell phone and reluctantly telling Siri to call Jordan.

The emotion he heard in his brother's voice when he answered the call was alarming. "Is Taylor okay?" Jordan asked frantically, before Marc could even say hello.

"He's still alive if that's what you mean," Marc responded dryly. "Where are you?"

"In bed at a hotel in Michigan. I have a big game tomorrow. What's going on, though?"

"Sorry to wake you. I just didn't know who else to call."

"It's fine," Jordan assured him. "What's up?"

Marc let out a heavy breath. "I think Taylor and Julie are on the verge of breaking up, and if he loses her, I don't know what will happen. He's so depressed over not playing this season. If they break up, I'm scared he'll hurt himself."

"Do you want me to call her?"

"You have her number?"

"Yeah. We touch base here and there. I can find out what's going on. Unless he abused her in some way or cheated on her, I can't see her leaving him."

"He thinks she deserves more than he can offer."

Jordan sighed. "He's probably overloaded with guilt and pushing her away. You know that's what addicts do."

"Probably," Marc agreed. "I just left his place. He's extra low because his friends are in North Carolina for NU's game against Elon."

"He should move home. Hanging out with Northeastern's football team is not going to lift his spirits."

"He's too embarrassed to move home, and he doesn't want Mom or Dad to see him high. He hasn't returned any of their calls this week. I think he's shutting them out, just like Julie. They're finally starting to suspect there's more going on with him than depression."

"Good!" Jordan cried. "Dad can get him into a recovery program."

"Not if Taylor won't speak to him."

Jordan let out a heavy breath. "I wish I weren't so far away. How can I help?"

"Call Julie. Try to get her to be patient with him."

"Yeah, of course. Anything else?"

"Just let me know what she says. Good luck at your game tomorrow."

"Thanks," Jordan said in a surprised tone. "Who knows? We might be facing each other on the field soon. Are you going to sign with BC?"

"I think so. I briefly considered some other offers, but I need to stay close to Taylor."

"Good move. I hate being this far away from him, and every time I step on the field, I feel guilty."

"Why?"

"Because T shaped me into the athlete I am today," Jordan replied. "Without his training, I would never have gotten so heavily recruited. Notre Dame was his dream school, and I feel like I'm rubbing salt in his wounds."

"He's proud of you," Marc said, finding it odd that Jordan was being so compassionate and humble. "He tells me that all the time. If it bothered him, he wouldn't watch your games."

"Playing felt wrong last year because he was injured. This year, it feels even worse because he's so depressed."

"Mom and Dad are devastated over Taylor's injury. Your success gives them something to be excited about. Don't let Taylor's issues put a damper on your season. He wants you to succeed, and I do, too."

"Why are you being so nice, little bro?" Jordan asked, sounding slightly amused.

Marc let out a heavy breath. "Because Taylor's more important than the BS between us."

Jordan laughed. "Hopefully I can get ahold of Julie before my game tomorrow. I'll give you a call when I get back to school on Sunday and let you know what she says."

After Marc ended his call with Jordan, he reflected on his brother's words and tone. Although Marc hated to admit it, Jordan seemed to have matured since high school. He wondered if Jordan felt pressured to succeed because of Taylor's failure or if attending a Catholic university had inspired him to become a better person. Either way, Jordan no longer sounded like a cocky teenager who took nothing seriously.

"I really don't know who my brothers are anymore," Marc said out loud to himself. Sighing, he thought back to his sophomore year of high school when Taylor was NU's QB, and Jordan was MLH's varsity football captain and Homecoming King. At the time, both of his brothers had seemed invincible. Taylor was winning games against teams Northeastern hadn't beaten in a decade, and he was ranked by ESPN as an NFL top prospect. Jordan was receiving offers from every ranked team that interested him and leading MLH's football team to an undefeated season. Taylor and Jordan had left huge shoes for Marc to fill in their hometown, and he could recall feeling intimidated by their success. This had inspired him to prioritize fitness and academics over everything except for his family in hopes of getting a Division I scholarship. His hard work had paid off, and while he was excited by the possibility of becoming a BC Eagle, he hoped his success would not add to Taylor's pain. If Jordan felt guilty, Marc imagined he would, too.

Even though Marc was only thirteen when Taylor left for college, he owed his oldest brother a great deal of gratitude. Taylor taught Marc everything he knew about football while they were growing up. Although their age difference prevented them from ever playing on the same team, Taylor invested countless hours into helping Marc become a better running back. It brought tears to Marc's eyes whenever he thought about how motivated and disciplined his oldest brother had been prior to his injury.

CHAPTER 37

CHANTAL KNOCKED ON CATHY'S bedroom door about a half hour after the girls had returned home. Cathy glanced in the mirror. Her pupils were still slightly dilated but not to the point Chantal would suspect anything. She took a deep breath before opening the door.

"Hey," she greeted Chantal casually while stepping aside.

"Hi," Chantal responded uneasily. "I thought you would be in your pajamas," she added before sitting down on Cathy's neatly made bed.

"I'm not tired," Cathy replied and shut her door. "What's going on?"

"Are you okay?" Chantal asked in a tone filled with concern.

Cathy nodded and sat down beside Chantal. "Yeah. Why?"

Chantal cocked her head to the side and peered at Cathy. "Are the rumors true about Jay?"

Cathy winced. "Which ones?"

"Andy told me about what happened to Jeff, so I'm not talking about the bonfire."

"Then what do you mean?"

"Jay could have had painkillers on him for a bunch of different reasons. I know he didn't give them to Jeff, and I know Jeff isn't blaming Jay for what happened, yet the rumors going around are so bad. Why?"

Cathy shrugged. "I don't know."

"Does Jay deal drugs?"

"What?! No!" Cathy exclaimed defensively.

"Does Luke?"

Startled by the question, Cathy widened her eyes. "No. Why?"

"Last month when Andy went with Robby to Jay's party, Andy told me they only went because Katie asked Robby to pick her up."

"Okay... what does that have to do with Luke?"

Chantal sighed. "Katie was uncomfortable because Luke was giving out molly, and the friends she went to the party with took it."

Cathy lowered her eyebrows. "I didn't see anyone on ecstasy that night."

"Were you with the older kids?"

"No," Cathy replied, "but I've never seen Luke or Matt on drugs, and I'm around them a lot."

"So, if Jay and Luke aren't the ones giving out drugs, then where are all the rumors coming from?"

Cathy eyed her sister apprehensively. "A lot of people are jealous of the Davids because they're rich, smart, and good looking," she said. "That motivates people to gossip about them, but I think the latest rumors about Jay came from Jeff's friends who were upset about the Vicodin—probably Leslie, Katherine, Bobby, Adam, and Andy."

"Andy's not mad at Jay; he's worried about him."

"Well, that's nice."

"Andy likes Jay," Chantal added. "Why was he on Vicodin, though?"

Cathy peered at her sister, trying to decide how much information to divulge. She wanted to confide in Chantal like she used to, but she needed to respect her boyfriend's privacy. "I can't say. I'm sorry. He just has some pain to treat."

"Is he okay?"

"He's been better. At least he doesn't let the rumors get to him. He's so confident in himself that it doesn't bother him when people misjudge him."

"That's because if our grade turns against him, he can just hang out with his brothers."

"I think he's just arrogant enough to think he's smarter than everyone else, so their opinions don't faze him."

Chantal laughed. "You might be right."

Cathy nodded. "I know my boyfriend."

"But, are *you* okay?"

"I hate being the center of attention. Hopefully something scandalous will happen to someone else this weekend so everyone will move on to talking about that."

"Has Jay tripped since Chris's party?"

"No," Cathy replied and shook her head, "and tonight he turned down weed *and* alcohol."'

"Good!" Chantal cried.

Cathy's iPad beeped, drawing her and Chantal's attention toward the device on her nightstand. Cathy leaned over to read the alert from a number she did not recognize. *Hey it's Marc. Luke said you wanted a ride. I can come get you if you want. LMK!*

"Oh, it's Marc!" Cathy exclaimed after reading the message.

Chantal cocked her head to the side in a perplexed manner. "Dunkin?"

Cathy nodded.

"Do you guys talk?"

"Sometimes. He's at Jay's, and they want me to go back over."

"Now?"

Cathy nodded.

Chantal widened her green eyes. "You'll get grounded for another month if you get caught sneaking out."

Cathy took a deep breath and picked up her iPad. "I know. That's why I have to make sure Marc can bring me home before Mom or Dad wakes up."

Cathy read Marc's message one more time before replying, *Hey Marc! Thanks so much! I'd love to come hang out for a bit but I have to be home before 5.* When she sent the message, butterflies immediately began fluttering around in her stomach.

"Do you like him?" Chantal asked.

"Marc?"

Chantal nodded.

Cathy lowered her eyebrows and peered at her sister in a confused manner. "Why would you ask that? I love Jay."

"Because Marc's gorgeous and you can like more than one person," Chantal stated flatly and raised her eyebrows.

"Do *you* like more than one person?" Cathy asked.

Chantal dropped her eyes to her hands. "Not at the moment."

"Good," Cathy said. "For a second I thought you were going to say you still like Jon."

Before Chantal could respond, Cathy's iPad dinged with another message from Marc: *I can drive you home around 3.*

Cathy's eyes lit up. "Awesome! He can bring me home. Do you want to come?" she asked and glanced up at Chantal.

Chantal widened her eyes. "I could *never* sneak out!" she cried. "I would feel too guilty. I'd end up telling Mom."

"I'm sure Mom and Dad did the same thing in high school," Cathy remarked.

Chantal shrugged. "Maybe, but I have no reason to go there."

"You could get to know the varsity cheerleaders. Ally, Laurelle, and Missy are staying over because Mr. and Mrs. Davids went to Newport."

Chantal shook her head. "I can't, but thanks for the invite."

"If I tell Marc to pick me up in twenty, will that give us enough time to talk?" Cathy asked before responding to his text.

"Yeah. I just want to make sure you're okay because I have a bad feeling."

"A bad feeling?"

Chantal nodded.

"Hold that thought," Cathy stated before texting Marc to meet her at the corner of High Street and Pico Ave. After sending the message, she locked her eyes on Chantal. "A bad feeling about what?"

"You," Chantal replied. "You seem weird."

Cathy lowered her eyebrows and eyed Chantal questioningly. "What do you mean?"

"Well, even the fact that you're going back to Jay's is surprising. After a month on house arrest, I thought you'd be afraid to get grounded again."

"It was really fun over there tonight. You'd understand if you were there."

"Are you *that* worried about Jay?"

Chantal's words caught Cathy off guard. "What do you mean?"

"Are you going there to keep an eye on him?"

"I don't need to keep an eye on him. I just want to spend time with him."

Chantal eyed her skeptically. "You've seemed off all week."

Cathy was surprised her sister had taken notice of her strange behavior. It pleased her to see that Chantal still cared about her, but it also made her fearful that Chantal suspected she had taken drugs. "This week was stressful," Cathy replied. "I spent most of the time trying to convince people that my boyfriend is not a drug dealer. His reputation is terrible now, and that bothers me because he's a really good person."

"You didn't seem stressed. I heard you defend Jay a few times, and you never got emotional about it. You were quite stoic. It was weird."

Cathy's heart pounded against her chest. "Why are you surprised?" she asked. "You know I don't show my feelings to people I don't know well," she added as her palms began to sweat.

Chantal shook her head. "This was beyond that. Anyone would show emotion if they were taunted the way you were all week."

"What are you getting at?"

Chantal let out a heavy breath. "I don't know... I guess... I guess I'm afraid you're internalizing everything or slipping into denial."

Cathy's heart rate slowed. "Jay taught me ways to deal with stress," she responded. "I don't concern myself with other people's opinions anymore."

"That's not true. You defend Jay every time someone says something bad about him," Chantal retorted.

Cathy scoffed. "So, I seem concerned *and* unconcerned?"

"No. You seem unemotional—kind of like Lisa," Chantal clarified.

"I seem cold?"

Chantal nodded.

"Oh, don't worry about that," Cathy said and waved off her sister. "It's just a defense mechanism. Lisa taught me a few things, too. She comes off cold, but she's really not."

"We're not as close as we used to be, but I still know you well enough to notice when something's wrong. I'm worried that you're growing a hardened heart."

"Towards who?"

"Everyone," Chantal replied flatly. "Andy and Jeff both think you've been acting strange. I assume it's because you're stressed out about Jay."

"I *am*."

"We're talking in circles," Chantal said and shook her head. "Something isn't right, but I can't put my finger on it."

Cathy shrugged. "I don't know what to tell you. My boyfriend messed with some drugs, and it bothered me."

"Chris is worried about him, too," Chantal added.

Cathy rolled her eyes. "Chris used to beg Jay to do drugs," she said dryly.

Chantal looked surprised by Cathy's statement. "Are you mad at Chris?"

"I'm not mad. I just hate seeing Jay so hurt."

"Chris didn't mean to hurt him," Chantal insisted. "Ask Marc. Chris said Marc's helped him a lot."

"I should go," Cathy said and abruptly stood up from her bed.

Chantal slowly rose beside her. "Are you sure you're okay?" she asked in an uneasy tone.

"Yes," Cathy stated firmly while stepping into her boots. "I'm fine, really."

Chantal crossed her arms and eyed Cathy apprehensively. "I wish I believed you," she muttered before walking over to the door.

CHAPTER 38

After ending his call with Marc, Jordan restlessly tossed and turned in bed for a half hour. As wonderful as it had been to speak with his younger brother, he knew that for Marc to resort to calling him, Taylor had to be in desperate need of help. Sitting up straight, Jordan snatched his cell phone off the nightstand and began composing a text message to Julie. *Hey Jules if you're still up call me. If not try to catch me before my game tomorrow.*

After sending the text, Jordan scrolled through his messages until he found his thread with Taylor. He carefully read over his and Taylor's conversations from the past month, trying to decipher if his brother sounded more depressed than usual. Taylor's messages had all been very typical, wishing Jordan good luck on the field and sending him tips about opposing teams' defenses. Despite being clinically depressed, Taylor never allowed Jordan to see that side of him. He seemed to only let his guard down around Marc.

During his childhood, Jordan had strong relationships with both of his brothers, but high school tore apart him and Marc. Looking back, Jordan regretted not being more supportive of Marc when they were at MLH together. It had never dawned on him to help Marc on the field the way Taylor had once helped Jordan. Perhaps they would have stayed close if he had pulled Marc onto varsity as a freshman. At the time, Jordan thought Marc was good enough to forge his own path, and although he had been right, he missed out on being the friend to Marc that Taylor had been to him. Now, a thousand miles away from home, Jordan wanted nothing more than the chance to toss a football around his backyard with his brothers.

Jordan's phone began vibrating in his hand as Julie's name appeared across the screen. He let out a sigh of relief before answering. "What's up, girl?" he greeted her in a playful tone.

"Hey, Jordan," Julie replied, sounding disheartened. "Why're you up this late the night before a game?"

"Taylor's killing me," Jordan replied. "I'm all in my head, thinking about us as kids, us this summer, you and him. I can't sleep."

"What's going on?" Julie questioned him in a perplexed manner.

"Oh, Jules. C'mon. You gotta know by now."

"Know what?"

Jordan sighed. "Taylor told Marc you two are in a fight. T sounded upset enough for Marc to call *me*. I don't know if you realize how much Marc hates me, but to put it into perspective, tonight was the first time he's called me since I left for college."

"That's funny because Taylor didn't seem upset to me at all," Julie remarked.

"Okay, I'll rephrase that. Taylor's reaction to your fight upset *Marc* enough to make him call me."

"That makes more sense."

"What's going on? Are you guys done?"

"I'm in love with a person who no longer exists. I doubt he's losing any sleep over our fight. He wants me to forget about him."

"No. No way. You seriously think that?"

"I know that," Julie replied. "He told me I would be better off without him and that I should move on while I'm still in college and around a bunch of guys."

"Seriously? What the heck?"

"He doesn't want to be with me," Julie continued. "I think he's cheating on me. He denied it but offered no explanation for why he never wants to go out anymore or why he sometimes disappears for hours on end."

Jordan's stomach turned. Julie was one of the sweetest girls he had ever met. "He's not cheating on you," he assured her. "He's just effed up on a bunch of crap."

"What?" Julie asked, sounding caught off guard. "What do you mean?" she questioned him in a hesitant manner.

"He didn't tell you?"

"Tell me what?"

Jordan widened his eyes. "All this time, he's let you think he's just depressed?"

"Marc implied there was more going on, but when I asked Taylor about it, he picked a fight with me."

Jordan sighed. "If it makes you feel any better, he won't tell me the truth either. I don't know why, but for some reason he'll only talk to Marc about it."

"What's wrong with him?"

"I can't believe I have to dump this on you," Jordan stated apologetically and then groaned. "Taylor's messed up on pills."

"What pills?"

"It used to be Percocet, but it's something stronger now. I don't really know. He can get his hands on anything he wants."

"He's still taking painkillers even though his knee is healed?"

"Unfortunately," Jordan replied. "I don't know how he hid it from you, but he's been high every time I've seen him in the last six months. That's why I made a point to spend so much time with him this summer. I was trying to get him to go to rehab, but I couldn't even get him to admit he has a problem."

"He admitted it to Marc?"

"For some reason he caved when Marc confronted him."

"Is he addicted to something?"

"Marc said it's OxyContin. People usually crush it up and snort it."

"But OCs break up into gel now. You can't snort them anymore."

"He gets the old tablets, somehow," Jordan stated matter-of-factly. "He's basically one step away from snorting heroin."

There was a thud on the other end of the line, followed by the sound of Julie gagging or, perhaps, vomiting. Jordan groaned and wondered if he had just precluded Julie and Taylor's relationship.

"I'm literally sick," Julie said in an exasperated tone a moment later. "I know what painkiller addictions do to people, and I'm not ready to... lose him."

"None of us are," Jordan said. "I'm sorry I didn't tell you sooner. I assumed you knew. I thought if Taylor hadn't told you, then Marc would have by now."

"Marc hinted at it. I just didn't want to believe it."

"Well, at least you know why T's pushing you away. There's no other girl."

"I'd rather there be another girl," Julie muttered.

Jordan sighed. "I want to do everything I can to help. It sucks I'm so far away. When Marc called me tonight, I thought he was going to tell me Taylor had OD'd. I live with that fear day and night."

"If you thought I already knew about the pills, then what did you want to talk to me about?"

Jordan sighed. "I heard you and Taylor were in a fight, and I wanted to ask you to be patient with him. Marc and I are both afraid of what will happen if he loses you."

Julie was quiet for a few seconds before saying, "But he doesn't want me."

Jordan winced. "I'm sure he feels guilty, and that's probably why he doesn't want you around. Taylor's filled with shame."

"Do you know where he gets the pills?"

Jordan took a deep breath. That was a whole different story. He had no idea how Julie would react if she found out Taylor had become a drug dealer. "I can get back to you about that," he replied.

"I don't know what to do. How can I help him if he won't admit he has a problem?"

"Just tell him I told you," Jordan said. "I don't care if he gets mad at me. He knows I know. He denies it to my face, but he knows I don't believe him."

"Your parents must be devastated. Now I know why Taylor hasn't gone home in months."

Jordan scowled. "My parents are part of the problem. Taylor's their golden boy. I told them this summer that he was still using painkillers. They asked him about it, and he fed them some BS story about only using them after tough workouts."

"Taylor was always really honest. I'm not surprised they believed him."

"Right, but it's a problem because he's full of crap now. It's unfortunate my parents don't take me more seriously."

"Should I call your mom?"

Jordan took a deep breath before responding. "I would hate for Taylor to get mad at you for it. You're probably the only one who can help him. He still loves you. He's just out of touch with himself."

Julie sighed. "I should go over to his place. There's no way I'll be able to sleep tonight."

"I'm sorry I ruined your night," Jordan said apologetically.

"A football game thirteen months ago ruined my night," Julie remarked, "not you."

CHAPTER 39

CATHY'S STOMACH FLUTTERED AS she watched Marc's red truck approach their meeting spot. Did she like Marc? Maybe. He certainly was capable of stirring up her emotions. Nevertheless, crushing on him was pointless. He was in love with Michelle, and Cathy was in love with Jason. The likelihood of a senior as highly sought after as Marc having an interest in a freshman was slim, but she liked entertaining the idea.

Cathy waved as Marc pulled over to the side of the road. "Thank you so much for doing this!" she cried as she climbed into his truck a few seconds later.

Marc smiled back at her. "Anytime," he said. "Good to see you."

His cheerful tone did not correspond with the sad look in his eyes. "Is everything okay?" Cathy asked as Marc began driving.

"It's just been a long night," Marc replied.

"What was it like at Jay's?" Cathy asked.

"Oh, fine. Matt lit the fire pit, so everyone went outside—except Pat, who passed out before I showed up."

"Missy and Laurelle weren't passed out?"

"They were as hyped up as usual."

"That's amazing, considering how much vodka they drank."

"Yeah, well, not much slows those two down," he remarked and then cleared his throat. "Sorry if I seem distracted. I have some family stuff going on."

"Don't apologize!" Cathy exclaimed. "I appreciate the ride."

Marc anxiously tapped his fingers on the steering wheel. "My game got cancelled, so I went into Boston to see my brother. Do you remember meeting Taylor at Chris's?"

"Yeah, of course. Everyone knows who Taylor is," Cathy replied.

"Well, he's a lot different now."

"Is his knee better?"

Marc nodded. "Thankfully. He's just not where he needs to be mentally, so playing this season was out of the question."

"Oh, I'm sorry... well... that's good you got to hang out with him tonight. I'm sure he's sad about missing another year."

Marc let out a heavy breath. "Devastated is the right word. He has no idea who he is apart from football. It's the pinnacle of his identity, and without it, he feels like a complete failure. I never thought someone so bright and talented could go down such a dark road."

Cathy winced. "I'm sorry. It must be hard to see him like that. I'm sure you thought he'd be in the NFL by now."

Marc nodded. "I put him on a pedestal just like everyone else."

"Maybe his injury will make him stronger in the long run?"

Marc quickly glanced at Cathy and smirked before locking his eyes back on the dimly lit, empty road. "Someone's an optimist."

"I try to be," Cathy said and glanced out the window. In the few minutes they had been driving, they had not passed a single car. Nearly every home they drove past was dark, which reminded Cathy of the risk she was taking by going out past her curfew.

"How's Jay?" Marc asked. His eyes were staring blankly ahead, and Cathy could tell he was trying to make light conversation, but his mind was elsewhere.

"Jay's a lot to handle," Cathy admitted. "You must have heard some stuff from Chris, Matt, or Luke."

Marc shrugged and continued to stare straight ahead. "All Chris said was he's trying to avoid temptation and Jay surrounds himself with tempting things, but Matt's as worried about Jay as I used to be about Chris."

Cathy swallowed a lump in her throat and fidgeted uncomfortably. "You must be happy about Chris getting sober. I'm sure the night he almost overdosed was one of the scariest nights of your life," she said, trying to shift the conversation away from her boyfriend.

"Jay told you about that?"

"Yeah. He was pretty horrified."

"That night was, by far, the worst."

"Some good came out of it, though, right?"

"Like?"

"It made Chris realize how dangerous drugs can be," Cathy replied. "I know he didn't sober up right away, but I think it put him on a better path."

"True," Marc said reluctantly. "I wish it didn't happen at all, but at least there was a silver lining."

"So, maybe Taylor's injury will put him on a better path, too," Cathy suggested, hoping her words would lighten Marc's sullen mood.

"You sound like your sister," Marc stated in an amused manner.

"Do you know Chantal?" Cathy asked, wanting to gauge Marc's impression of her.

"I met her once at Chris's," Marc replied. "I called her a few times after that, but she never called me back."

Cathy's heart sank. Was he interested in Chantal? "Oh, well, she's pretty hung up on Andy Rosetti," she said quickly and glanced out the window.

"I wasn't trying to date her," Marc clarified. "I just found her interesting to talk to. She's different."

Cathy looked back over at him. "What do you mean?"

"I don't know," Marc said thoughtfully. "There's just something about her that intrigues me."

Cathy eyed Marc apprehensively. "Chantal was always my best friend, but we drifted apart last year. I don't think she likes me with Jay."

"That's because she cares about you, and Jay's the type of kid who trips on acid the night before school starts," Marc stated in a point-blank manner.

Cathy sighed and rested her head against the window. "I wish he would become friends with Chris again. All these years they dreamed of going to high school together, and they stopped being friends on the second day."

"Chris never meant to end their friendship."

Cathy nodded. "I know. Jay took it personally, which was weird because he usually has thick skin."

"I've known Jason since he was, like, five. Even as a little kid, he was obsessed with following all the rules and being perfect. Matt and Luke used to tease him for spending more time studying than playing sports. They thought he was so weird."

Cathy laughed. "Aside from skiing and playing baseball, Jay's not much of an athlete."

"I always found it strange that he and Chris were best friends," Marc admitted. "Jay was, like, OCD, and Chris was laidback to a fault."

"Jay's still like that with school, but other than being totally anal about his physical appearance, I don't see much of the kid you just described."

"He's the last person I expected to become a pothead. It's really bothering Matt, and as carefree as Luke is, he's worried, too."

"Jay only likes weed because it calms him down from Adderall. If he didn't need Adderall, he would hate weed as much as Matt and Luke do."

Marc sighed. "I just can't figure out how Chris and Jay got their hands on so many drugs."

Cathy's stomach dropped.

"I used to think Jordan was Chris's hookup until Chris started dabbling with benzos, painkillers, and acid," Marc admitted. "As irresponsible as Jordan can be, I don't think he'd ever touch that kind of stuff."

"Chris won't say who he bought from?"

"No. Weird, right?"

"Well, Chris is good at keeping secrets," Cathy remarked.

"Yeah, but it's weird that he would protect a drug dealer's identity now that he's anti-drug."

Cathy felt her palms begin to sweat. She shifted in her seat and cleared her throat. "Jay claims he never would have tried weed, 'shrooms, or acid if Chris hadn't talked him into it, so—"

"—I know," Marc interrupted her. "Chris is the one who got the stuff."

Cathy nodded. "When I met Jay, he was so against drugs that he didn't even take the Adderall he was prescribed. He got straight A's without it."

"Then what happened?"

Cathy took a deep breath and let it out slowly. She missed Jason—the real Jason—so much that outing Luke to Marc had crossed her mind a few times. But how could she do that to Luke? His heart was in the right place—his goal was to help people relax and have fun—but she knew Marc would not see it that way.

Cathy turned towards Marc and shook her head. "I don't know... I don't think people realize they're abusing drugs until their relationships start to crumble."

"Maybe," Marc muttered.

"I know Luke hates weed, but he's not against drugs," Cathy said casually. "He told me he's rolled a few times. Does that bother you?"

Marc cocked his head from side to side in thought. "Eh, not really," he admitted gradually. "Luke doesn't roll a lot, and molly's not addictive. I just worry about Missy getting him into coke."

"She does coke?"

Marc nodded. "A lot of kids in Montgomery do, especially in my grade. I love Missy, but... well... I probably shouldn't say this—"

"—No, it's okay. I won't say anything," Cathy assured him.

"Well, sometimes I wonder if she's dating Luke just because he..."

"Just because he what?" Cathy asked, wondering why Marc's voice had trailed off.

"Just because he gets her coke."

Cathy did a double take. "Wait. What? Why would *Luke* have coke?"

Marc groaned. "I shouldn't have said anything."

"Too late now!" Cathy cried. She had always assumed Marc was in the dark about Luke's dealings, so she was incredibly curious to uncover what he knew.

Marc sighed. "I brought Luke to visit Taylor at college, and he bought molly off one of T's friends. Luke kept the connection open, so now he's the person my friends go to when they want stuff."

"Luke's a drug dealer?!" Cathy asked.

Marc scoffed. "No! God, no. He's just a middleman, but he gets coke and molly for people all the time."

"Do you think Missy's using him?"

"No. She's a nice girl, and they have a lot of fun together, but it *is* convenient for her to date him. He has plenty of money to burn, and that's another reason why I worry about him getting into coke."

"I don't think Luke would do that," Cathy said. "He's pretty lowkey. Earlier tonight, he wasn't even drinking."

"I know, but Missy's not the best influence," Marc said in an uneasy tone.

"Well, if Luke's the one getting drugs for people, it sounds like he's not the best influence either," Cathy stated matter-of-factly.

Marc nodded. "Fair enough."

"Do you think Luke's the one who gave drugs to Chris?" Cathy asked as her heart pounded heavily against her chest. She peered over at Marc expectantly, wondering why he had not yet put two and two together.

Marc widened his blue eyes. "No way. I would kill him. Taylor and Jordan would kill him, too."

"So, he would die three times?" Cathy joked.

Marc laughed. "At least."

Cathy smirked.

"Kidding aside, though, there's a possibility that Luke got drugs for someone in my grade who then went and sold them to Chris. Matt and I have talked about that, but we can't think of anyone stupid enough to cross us."

Cathy's stomach was churning. She knew way too much information, and she felt terrible withholding it from Marc. It was rather miraculous that Luke, Chris, and Jason had kept Matt and Marc from finding out about their arrangement.

"Do Jordan and Taylor have any ideas?" Cathy asked. "They must know Chris almost overdosed."

"Jordan's in Indiana, and Taylor's... not really... around," Marc replied hesitantly. "They know I've been helping Chris stay clean, but they don't know anything about Montgomery's drug supply. I used to think Jordan hooked Chris up with weed, but when he left for college, Chris still had access to it."

"Is Jordan really a pothead?" Cathy asked. She had heard plenty of rumors about Jordan, but Chris, Luke, and Jason only had good things to say about him.

Marc shrugged. "Honestly, I don't know much about him. We're not close, but he seems to be doing well at ND. I don't think he would be that productive if he was a stoner."

"I've seen him on TV. He's good."

Marc nodded. "Yeah, he is."

"Why aren't you guys close?" Cathy inquired, wondering if Marc would tell her about the love triangle between him, Michelle, and Jordan.

Marc sighed. "We got in a fight two years ago over a girl... actually my ex-girlfriend. I thought he was trying to take advantage of her, so I got between them."

"Oh, I heard about that," Cathy said. "Michelle's your ex?"

"Yeah, but I think of her more as a best friend," Marc replied as his phone began ringing in his cupholder. "Do you mind if I answer this? It's actually my brother."

"No, of course not," Cathy replied, wondering if he meant Taylor or Jordan.

"Hey, what's up?" Marc asked after accepting the call with a button on his steering wheel.

"So, I talked to Julie," a deep voice replied over the Bluetooth radio.

"Wow, that was quick. What did she say?" Marc asked.

"Dude, she had no idea T was snorting Oxy?!"

Marc widened his eyes and glanced at Cathy before responding. "I hinted at him having a problem with painkillers. She said she would ask him about it. I assumed that was what they've been arguing about lately."

"He denied it. He denied everything. He told her to move on while she's still in college and around a bunch of guys. What an idiot!"

Marc sighed. "He doesn't think he deserves her, and he's right, but I hope he doesn't lose her for his sake."

"She's heading to his place now. I asked her to be patient with him. I feel so bad. She's heartbroken. I mean, she's been watching him downward spiral for a year. He was on top of the world when they got together."

"What is she planning to say?"

"I don't know. I told her to tell him what I told her so he couldn't deny it."

"He's going to get mad at you," Marc gathered.

"I don't care. She can't help him if she doesn't know what's wrong with him. She can do more for him than I can, a thousand miles away."

"True."

"All right, I need to try to pass out. Don't watch my game tomorrow. I'm going to be junk."

"Not watch the Notre Dame/Michigan game?" Marc asked with a short laugh. "Dream on, bro. Everyone will be watching."

"Yeah, yeah. I know," Jordan admitted reluctantly. "If you hear anything from T tonight, text me."

"Will do. Good luck tomorrow."

"Thanks. Good night."

"Later," Marc said and ended the call. He let out a heavy breath and turned toward Cathy. "Sorry you had to hear that. I should have shut off my Bluetooth."

"It's okay. I won't say anything," Cathy promised while he steered the truck into Jason's driveway.

Marc sighed and parked his vehicle behind Matt's SUV. "Thanks. I appreciate it. Taylor's depressed as it is. He doesn't need people finding out about his issues."

"I can imagine," Cathy said and peered at Marc, wondering if he wanted to continue their conversation or if she should get out of the truck.

"I still can't believe he got addicted to his painkillers," Marc huffed and rested his head against his seat. "Of all people, I thought *Taylor* was smart enough to *never* let something like that happen. He would be gearing up for a game tomorrow if he never snorted a painkiller."

Cathy cringed. "I'm sorry. I can't imagine how hard this must be on your family."

Marc scoffed. "My parents don't get it. I told them. Jordan told them.

They asked Taylor about it, and he lied to them. In the end, they believed him."

"Why?"

"Because he's their idol," Marc replied and shook his head. "It's sad because he needs help and the only people who realize it are me and Jordan."

"Do you think his girlfriend will be able to help?"

Marc sighed. "I hope." He reached for the door handle and then glanced back at Cathy. "Sorry to dump this on you."

She smiled slightly. "It's okay. I'm a good listener. If you ever need someone to talk to, you have my number."

"What do you mean?" Marc asked in a perplexed manner.

"I don't have a cell phone yet, but Chantal and I have the same landline... or you can just message me on my iPad."

Marc smirked. "So, maybe I called the wrong twin?"

Cathy laughed and reached for the door handle. While climbing out of the truck, she felt Marc tap her shoulder. "What?" she asked and repositioned herself in the passenger seat.

"Don't you think Jay would get mad if I called you?"

Cathy shrugged. "I'm not worried about it."

Marc smiled and climbed out of the vehicle. Seconds later, Cathy walked behind him up Jason's walkway, feeling a mixture of emotion. She was happy to have connected with Marc on a deeper level and to have swayed his attention away from Chantal, but at the same time, she was troubled by Marc and Jordan's conversation. The more she heard about Taylor's problem, the more frightened she became over Jason's use of Vicodin. Clearly, Lisa had not been exaggerating when she said Taylor's life was in turmoil. Cathy realized that could be her own boyfriend's future if he did not sober up. The idea of breaking up with Jason turned her stomach, and even though Luke was probably right—Jason would most likely sober up to win her back—she couldn't bear the thought of a breakup sending him further into despair.

CHAPTER 40

Julie lightly knocked on her roommate Meghan's bedroom door. She wiped black mascara from beneath her eyes as she waited in the dimly lit hallway. She was failing miserably at gaining her composure. She would not feel better until she saw Taylor.

"What's going on?" Meghan asked as soon as her brown eyes met Julie's. With a concerned look coating her face, she stepped aside to let Julie into her room. Julie, Meghan, and four of their sorority sisters lived in a three-story brownstone off of Newbury Street. Due to the apartment's close proximity to Copley Square and the green line, the girls' boyfriends usually stayed over. Scattered throughout Meghan's bedroom were plenty of her boyfriend Matt McSweeney's belongings. Matt was Taylor's very best friend, and Julie desperately wanted a chance to talk to Matt about everything Jordan had shared with her. Matt, however, was out of state with the football team, so talking to Meghan was second best.

As Julie walked over to Meghan's bed, she locked her eyes on a framed picture of her, Meghan, Matt, and Taylor that was hanging above Meghan's desk. It had been taken over a year ago at their sorority's formal. Taylor's smile lit up the photo, and the joy he felt could be seen in his eyes. Julie had fallen in love with a beautiful person. More than anything, she wanted to believe he still existed, somewhere, inside the shell that Taylor had become. Tearing her eyes off the photo, she sat down on Meghan's bed and brought her knees to her chest.

"What's wrong, girl?" Meghan asked while closing the door.

Julie felt despondent as she glanced up at her best friend. "Taylor's..." She took a deep breath as her voice trailed off. "He's..."

Meghan took a seat beside Julie and glanced at her warily. "He's what?" she asked and placed a supportive hand on Julie's arm.

Julie took another deep breath. "Jordan just told me that Taylor... ugh... that he's still taking his... that he... that he has a drug problem," she admitted reluctantly, finding it almost unbearable to hear the words come out of her mouth. Tears once again filled her light blue eyes.

Meghan lowered her eyebrows in confusion and peered at Julie skeptically. "What do you mean? Taylor doesn't even drink."

Julie shook her head. "He doesn't drink because he's still on painkillers."

"Still?" Meghan asked and cocked her head to the side. "I thought the second surgery fixed everything."

Julie nodded. "Everything with his ACL, not his depression."

"Jordan who? His brother?"

Julie nodded.

"How would he know? He's in Indiana. Don't you think you or Matt would know better?"

Julie sighed. "It's true, Meg. I didn't want to believe it either, but it explains so much. The kid in that picture on your wall," she said and pointed to the framed photo, "when was the last time you saw him?"

Meghan looked at the picture. Then she turned back to Julie. "He was happy then. He's kind of lost now. I don't blame him. I mean... he doesn't have football or college anymore." She looked at Julie sympathetically. "Why does Jordan think he's on drugs?"

"Ugh, Meg. More than anything, I wish it wasn't true, but it is. Deep down, I've known something was wrong for months. I just didn't want to admit it. When Marc drove me home a couple of weeks ago, he basically told me the same thing. I asked Taylor about it... and he lost it on me."

"He yelled at you?" Meghan questioned her in surprise.

Julie shook her head. "No, he didn't yell. He just got so offended by me asking if he ever needed pain meds anymore that he told me to leave. Then I didn't hear from him for, like, two days."

"That seems overly dramatic."

Julie nodded. "And the next time I saw him, he told me I should move on while I'm still in college, while I'm around a bunch of guys."

Meghan looked completely baffled. "When did this happen? Why didn't you tell me?"

Julie shrugged. "The other day. I didn't want to involve you and Matt. I was afraid Matt would say something to Taylor and that Taylor would get mad at me for telling you."

"Well, Matt's at Elon, so he's not going to hear about this unless you want me to call him."

Julie shook her head. "No. I'll talk to him when he gets back, but I want you to come with me to Taylor's. I want to go over there and confront him, but I don't want to go alone."

"Okay," Meghan agreed. "Now?"

"If we can? If that's okay? I won't be able to sleep until I see him."

Meghan hugged Julie tightly. "Of course. Just give me two minutes to get ready."

"Thanks, girl," Julie said as tears once again began streaming down her face.

CHAPTER 41

When Jason led Cathy and Marc outside to the fire pit, only Matt, Ally, and Michelle were on the deck. They were huddled around the coffee table, playing Phase 10.

Cathy took a seat beside Jason and watched as Marc sat down next to Michelle. Michelle quickly smiled at Marc before planting her brown eyes back on the cards in her hand.

Marc glanced over Michelle's shoulder at the game. "Who's winning?" he asked.

"Who else but Jay," Ally replied dryly but then laughed.

Jason picked up his cards and leaned back with a confident smile.

"Where's Luke and everyone else?" Cathy asked curiously.

"Luke disappeared with Missy and Laurelle," Jason replied distractedly, while scanning the cards in his hand.

"When did Bryan leave?" Cathy pressed, wanting some of her boyfriend's attention.

"With John, Day, and Lyss around midnight," Jason said while reaching for a card on the table. "Oh, you better believe I'm phasing up!" he exclaimed triumphantly.

Michelle and Ally rolled their eyes as Matt scowled—but in good humor.

"Jay, why don't you go get Cathy something to eat or drink and give the rest of us a chance to win a round," Matt suggested facetiously.

Jason smirked. "413 to 72," he stated in a cocky manner.

"What is that?" Ally asked.

Jason laughed. "My game-winning record against my family members since I was ten."

Ally dropped her jaw. "You keep track of that?"

"Of course, he does," Matt muttered.

Jason nodded. "Oh, yeah. It's all right here," he said and tapped the side of his forehead.

Cathy shook her head and rolled her eyes. "What's *our* record?"

Jason quickly turned to her. "Oh, me versus you?"

Cathy nodded.

"I conveniently lost track of that the last time you beat me at Rummy 500," Jason replied with a smirk.

"Figures," Cathy sang and playfully nudged him.

"I don't think Cathy came all the way back here to watch you play Phase 10," Matt stated matter-of-factly. "We should start a new game."

"Dude, c'mon. I'm two phases away from 414!" Jason protested.

"Take the win, JD," Matt remarked carelessly. "None of us are going to catch up to you."

"If you say so," Jason agreed and tossed his cards onto the table.

"Can we get something to drink before we start?" Cathy asked.

"Yeah, sure," Jason replied and stood up from the couch. "Does anyone need anything in the kitchen?"

"Do you love me enough to make me another hot chocolate?" Ally asked and held up an empty mug. She smiled at Jason with a childlike grin.

"Love you enough to wait thirty seconds for it to pour from the Keurig?" Jason questioned her while grabbing the mug out of her hand. "I don't know; we'll see."

"Thank you, Jason," Ally sang.

Jason smiled and then grabbed Cathy's hand to help her off the couch. "Let's go," he said and nodded towards the slider.

"Bring me a Gatorade," Matt called as Jason and Cathy made their way towards the door.

"And a water!" Marc yelled.

Jason pretended not to hear them and opened the sliding glass door. "I'm glad you came back," he said quietly.

"Things really simmered down without Missy and Laurelle, huh?" Cathy gathered as they stepped into the kitchen.

"They always do," Jason replied. He walked over to the counter where the Keurig was stationed and selected a K-cup. "How'd you sneak out?" he asked while placing Ally's mug on the machine.

"Through the basement," Cathy replied and leaned against the center island. She watched the hot chocolate begin to dispense into the cup. "I should be okay as long as Marc brings me home in an hour or two."

"Play it extra safe," Jason warned her and hoisted his body onto the island.

"You seem less jittery," Cathy observed.

"I can't be like that around Matt," Jason stated matter-of-factly. "I feel guilty."

"Why?"

Jason shrugged. "I don't know."

"So then maybe you should spend more time with Matt?"

Jason looked puzzled. "I thought you had fun earlier," he stated and jumped down from the counter to tend to Ally's hot chocolate.

"I did but...I feel kind of crappy now," Cathy admitted. "Like, worn out."

"That's normal," Jason remarked. He walked over to the industrial-sized refrigerator and swung open one of the doors. He set bottles of water and Gatorade on the granite countertop. "I grabbed you a water. Do you want a snack or anything?"

What she wanted was to talk to Jason about Taylor. Although she could not betray Marc or Lisa's trust by telling him about Taylor's drug problem, she wanted to touch on the subject, somehow, to find out if he knew anything.

Jason walked over to her and eyed her expectantly. "What?" he asked. "You look like you have something on your mind."

"Marc knows Luke gets drugs for people," Cathy blurted out.

Jason looked less surprised than she expected. "I figured. Matt knows, too."

"What?! Then why don't they realize Luke's the one who sold to Chris?" Cathy asked, keeping her voice to a whisper.

"Because they overestimate Luke's intelligence," Jason replied matter-of-factly. "I've been telling you forever that Luke's an effing idiot."

"Luke doesn't make money off the sales."

"Who told you that?"

"Luke."

Jason shrugged. "That could be true; he gives me everything for free."

"He doesn't think of himself as a dealer. He said he just gets stuff for his friends when they ask for it. Marc told me Luke's hookup is one of Taylor's friends in Boston."

Jason widened his eyes. "I've been trying to figure that out forever! I thought Taylor might have something to do with it."

"Why?"

"He bought alcohol for Luke, and I found it weird they were in touch. If Luke buys drugs off Taylor's friend, then that makes more sense."

"Do you think Taylor does drugs?" Cathy asked.

Jason appeared taken aback by her question. "Why would you ask that?"

Cathy shrugged. "I heard Luke rolled for the first time at Taylor's. It made me curious."

Jason eyed her precariously. It looked like he was contemplating something. "I actually heard some stuff about Taylor from Matt. Let's bring everyone their drinks. We can talk later." He handed Cathy the bottles of water, picked up the Gatorade and hot chocolate, and then nodded for her to follow him outside.

"Was it about him not playing football?" Cathy asked curiously while following Jason across the kitchen.

"Yeah, but I don't want to talk about it in front of Marc," Jason replied and opened the slider with his elbow.

"Can we talk instead of play the game?" Cathy whispered as she followed him through the door.

"Is that hot chocolate?" Ally called out. "Aww, Jay! You're the best!"

"Here ya go," Jason said once he reached Ally. He set the mug before her on the table. "Matt," he added while handing his brother a Gatorade.

Cathy walked over to Marc and gave him a bottle of water. He smiled widely when she handed it to him, and again, his smile gave her butterflies.

"Cathy and I are going to sit this game out, but we'll be back in a bit," Jason announced.

"Didn't you already get laid once tonight?" Matt teased him.

Cathy immediately felt her cheeks start to burn.

"Matt!" Ally cried and slapped him in the stomach.

Matt laughed as Jason hooked his arm around Cathy's neck.

"You shouldn't say such derogatory things in front of all these virgin ears," Jason retorted facetiously and then pulled Cathy toward the house.

Cathy could hear Matt, Marc, Ally, and Michelle laughing as Jason led her back inside the house. "Does Matt know I lost my virginity?" she asked anxiously after Jason closed the slider.

"He assumes that much," Jason replied, "but I've told him nothing."

"We've only had sex four times," Cathy said defensively.

"I'm well aware," Jason remarked dryly.

"Well, it's not like we do it all the time! I don't want people to know.

It's against my morals. If Chantal ever found out and told my parents, they would kill both of us."

Jason rolled his eyes and put his arm around Cathy. "Will you relax? Matt was just kidding. We tease each other all the time. We're brothers. Can you imagine the crap he gave Luke when Luke went upstairs with Missy *and* Laurelle?"

Cathy pulled free from Jason's embrace and looked at him curiously. "What do you think they're doing?"

"*Not* having sex," Jason replied.

"Do you think they're rolling?"

Jason shrugged. "Luke might be. The girls are drunk. I guarantee they're awake, if you want to go find out."

Cathy shook her head. "It doesn't matter. I'd rather hear about Taylor."

"Okay. Let's go in the living room. That way, no one will think we're having sex."

"Good!" Cathy exclaimed and started walking towards the foyer.

Jason caught up to her and led the way. "I'm surprised you came onto me earlier," he admitted. "If sex is still against your morals, then I feel kind of weird about it."

Cathy's heart began to race. Would he be okay with them not sleeping together? Was this the out she had been praying for? She swallowed deeply. "I didn't mean that I don't want you," she clarified. "I just..." her voice trailed off as they entered the foyer.

"What?"

Cathy took a deep breath as her palms began to sweat. Despite how large the two-story foyer was, with its monumental twin bridal staircase, Cathy felt as though the walls were closing in on her.

"Let's just sit down," she blurted out and dashed off towards the living room. She sat on the couch and pulled her knees tightly to her chest.

Jason sat down beside her and eyed her curiously. "So, what were you saying?" he asked.

Cathy took a deep breath. For her own peace of mind, she had to tell him the truth. Withholding information from him would only put space between them, and they were already drifting apart. "I don't want you to think I'm not attracted to you or that I don't love you," she began, "but when I came onto you, I wasn't myself. I know it was only a couple of hours ago, but I feel like a completely different person now, and that kind of scares me."

"Are you scared of how you feel now or how you felt earlier?"

"Earlier," Cathy clarified and put her head down. "Don't get me wrong. I had fun, but I feel guilty."

"Guilty about having sex or taking Adderall?"

Cathy looked up at him and released her legs from her chest. "Both... and guilty about being here now... I don't know who I am anymore," she admitted in a quiet tone.

Jason rolled his eyes and looked away, but when he turned back to her a few seconds later, he looked more concerned than annoyed. "What do you mean? What's wrong?"

She gazed at him hesitantly. Why *was* she being like this? Was it her conversation with Marc? Was it what she had learned about Taylor? Or could it just be the comedown from the Adderall? "Just tell me what Matt said about Taylor, and I'll gather my thoughts."

"Are you sure?" Jason asked.

Cathy nodded.

"All right, but we're talking about the sex-thing before you leave."

"Fine," she agreed and took a deep breath. "So, what's going on with Taylor?"

"He's addicted to painkillers," Jason stated bluntly. "That's why he's not playing football this year. He got addicted to Oxy after his injury and failed out of school."

Cathy needed to act surprised. "Taylor?!" she cried.

Jason nodded. "And now Matt's trying to figure out who had Vicodin at the bonfire. He's afraid it came from Luke. I don't know what to do."

"Wait, back up. Taylor's addicted to painkillers?"

"Yeah. I mean, it's shocking. I always looked up to him," Jason said, "but the bigger problem is that Matt's going to find out I took Vicodin. All he has to do is ask any freshman or sophomore who was there that night."

Cathy swallowed deeply. "How did Matt hear about that?"

"I don't know. He asked me tonight if I thought the pills came from Luke."

"It may be time to have an honest talk with Matt," Cathy suggested. "If you think he's going to find out, then it's better if he hears it from you."

Jason let out a heavy breath. "I dread that conversation."

"If a smart kid like Taylor got addicted to painkillers, then you need to be really careful, Jay," Cathy warned him in a serious tone.

"I am," Jason said assuredly. "Taylor probably crushed them up and snorted them. Plus, Percocet's stronger than Vicodin."

"Jay, c'mon," Cathy said matter-of-factly. "I doubt he started out snorting Percocet. One thing leads to another."

Jason leaned back and folded his hands behind his head. "I bet that's why Chris did a 180. What happened to Taylor probably scared him straight."

Cathy stared at Jason intently. "Doesn't it scare you?"

Jason leaned forward and gently brushed his thumb against Cathy's cheek. "Babe, don't worry about me. I'm never going to snort an opiate. It's like snorting heroin. It's a death sentence that can lead nowhere good. Hopefully, Taylor will recover, but most people don't."

"You say that now, but when you're upset or messed up, you might think it's no big deal and do it."

Jason searched her eyes. "You're really worried about this, huh?"

"*Yes*. Jordan called Marc on the way over here, and I overhead some things about Taylor. I promised Marc I wouldn't tell anyone."

"I feel bad for Mr. and Mrs. Dunkin. They're super nice people, and Taylor had a lot of potential."

Cathy eyed her boyfriend strangely. "How can you feel bad for them but not your own parents? You're abusing your prescription just like Taylor!"

Jason widened his blue eyes. "Wow, babe. You suck after an Adderall comedown," he said with a laugh.

Cathy dropped her jaw. "Jay, I'm serious. You're scaring me."

Jason scoffed. "You felt differently earlier."

"I told you I wasn't myself."

"Which must be why you had sex with me," he retorted.

Cathy scowled. "I don't want to have that conversation when you're like this."

"Like what?"

"Argumentative."

"I'm not arguing with you."

Cathy rolled her eyes. "You know so much about psychology, but you have no idea how you come off to people."

Jason laughed.

"It's not funny! You have no idea who you are."

Jason smiled. "Is that supposed to be an insult? Because you said the same thing about yourself five minutes ago."

"I don't want to fight with you!" Cathy exclaimed. "We had a good night."

Jason held his hands out in front of him in a questioning manner. "Who's fighting?"

Cathy scoffed and leaned back against the couch. She crossed her arms and shook her head.

"Babe, chill," Jason pleaded. "It sucks about Taylor. Trust me. The news shook me up, too. And it sucks Matt found out about the Vicodin, mainly because I don't want Luke getting in trouble for it. But none of this has anything to do with our relationship."

Cathy sat with her arms crossed, staring straight ahead.

"Just tell me what's on your mind," Jason pressed.

Cathy took a deep breath and let it out slowly. Reluctantly, she glanced over at him. "I need to get back in touch with myself. It's like what you said last weekend. I'm all over the place."

"I can see that. The Cathy I met *never* would have—" Jason paused for dramatic effect. "—passed up a chance to beat me at Phase 10!"

Cathy rolled her eyes. "Stop making light of this. I'm upset."

Jason put his arm around her. "You'll be fine if you stop worrying about me."

"I can't. I love you, and you're playing with fire."

"Well, then don't join me," Jason stated matter-of-factly. "This whole 'whatever you do, I do' thing isn't good for you. Look at how guilty you feel."

Stop making so much sense. "I had sex with you the second time because I wanted to know what it felt like. The third time, it was because I felt disconnected from you and thought it would fix something. Earlier tonight, I felt, almost, daring. Usually, I feel a 'check' in my spirit before I'm about to do something that doesn't align with my beliefs. I felt nothing like that. It was like I *wanted* to rebel."

"You had a really stressful week," Jason said in a sympathetic tone. "When people get stressed, they slip into the grip of their inferior cognitive function. When you're stressed, you're going to be drawn towards risky behavior."

Cathy glared at him. "Thanks for making me feel like I'm in a counseling session," she remarked sarcastically.

Jason put his head down. "Sorry. I just feel bad because I'm the one stressing you out. This year hasn't started out the way either of us thought it would."

Cathy sighed. "So, what do we do?"

"I don't know," Jason admitted and looked up at her. "I hate watching you suffer with anxiety and depression, but the only way I know how to help makes you feel guilty. That just compounds everything."

Cathy nodded. "Right."

"Maybe Luke's right… maybe we should break up for a little while," Jason suggested.

Cathy's stomach immediately dropped at the sound of his words. "No!" she cried and widened her eyes. "I love you!"

Jason placed his hand on her shoulder and eyed her with compassion. "I love you, too, and I don't want to be with anyone but you. I just don't want to hurt you any more than I already have."

"Nothing would hurt worse than breaking up!" Cathy insisted. "Please don't even think that way."

"I just need some time to get over my fight with Chris," Jason said. "I know I've been a whiny little bitch about the whole thing. I've been handling everything horribly since school started... actually, since the night *before* school started." Jason sighed. "The most important thing to me right now is making things right with you and Chris. I love you guys more than my own family."

At the sound of Jason's words, Cathy felt everything inside of her relax. She had just caught a glimpse of the boy she had fallen in love with.

"I'm going to talk to Matt soon," Jason continued. "He'll help me think straight."

"So, we don't need to break up, right?" Cathy asked, eyeing him intently.

Jason let out a heavy breath. "What if we pretend to break up?" he proposed.

Cathy lowered her eyebrows. "What do you mean?"

"Like, what if to protect your reputation and get people to leave you alone at school, we tell everyone that you broke up with me over what happened at the bonfire?" Jason suggested.

"Lying is *not* going to make me feel better," Cathy stated matter-of-factly.

"Well, I don't want you to lie. I just want people to disassociate us for your peace of mind. I'm not going to date or hook up with anyone else. I would still be one hundred percent committed to you. I just think you'd have an easier time at school if no one knew that."

"I'm confused," Cathy admitted.

"I'm just trying to figure out how to make things better for you. I know I'm the problem."

"I don't want to hide my feelings for you."

"I know, but I can't in good conscience keep doing things with you that make you feel guilty or like you've lost yourself. I love you too much to do that."

Cathy smiled slightly. "I'll feel a lot better if I know you're okay with us not having sex."

"I've been okay with that from the start," Jason said. "Just because some girls were easy and let me in their pants, doesn't mean I think that's normal. I don't even think Ally has slept with Matt yet."

"Really?"

Jason nodded. "I assume Matt slept with at least one of the hot cheerleaders he dated, but I honestly don't even know. He might still be a virgin. Marc might be, too. I mean, we're really young to have already had sex."

I'm such a slut. "Are you saying this to make me feel better or worse?" Cathy asked.

"I'm just being honest. I don't want you to feel like we're supposed to have sex just because we're dating."

"If I never drank on Xanax, I'd still be a virgin," Cathy said. "That bothers me every day."

Jason winced. "I'm sorry about that... I should have realized you were acting weird that night, but I was buzzed and horny and... I just didn't catch on."

Cathy shook her head. "Not your fault."

"So, if we take sex out of the equation, you'll feel better?"

Cathy nodded. "Much better."

"No more Adderall for you either," Jason said and shook his head.

"No," Cathy agreed. "No more of that. It made me want to sin against my conscience. I'm glad it doesn't have that effect on you."

"I don't have a conscience," Jason remarked facetiously.

"Stop," Cathy laughed.

"It does help me focus, but I haven't been taking it for that reason. I don't need forty-five milligrams of it a day. If I need any, it's, like, five."

"Forty-five?" Cathy asked and widened her eyes. "Jay!"

Jason nodded and closed his eyes. "I know. Terrible."

"Holy crap."

Jason opened his eyes and sheepishly gazed at her. "I don't know how, but somehow, I am going to get a handle on this."

Cathy eyed him apprehensively. *Forty-five?!* As her stomach churned, Luke's words from earlier rang through her mind: *He's addicted to an amphetamine. If he wasn't, he would have already stopped taking it... He can't stop without help, or he already would have.*

CHAPTER 42

JULIE'S HEART POUNDED HEAVILY against her chest as she turned the brass key in her trembling hand—first the deadbolt, then the doorknob. She had done it hundreds of times before but never with such hesitation. Taylor's Jamaica Plain apartment had been her second home for the better part of a year, but that night she felt like a trespasser.

Taking a deep breath, she slowly pushed open the front door and stepped inside the pitch-black hallway. With Meghan close behind her, she felt the wall to her right for the light switch. A second later, the hallway and the living room ahead illuminated with incandescent lighting. Despite the warm golden hue flowing from the wall sconces, the apartment felt cold and unwelcoming.

Meghan touched Julie's arm. "I'll wait on the couch. Yell for me if you need anything," she said quietly.

Julie looked Meghan in the eye. "Thank you for coming."

Meghan's brown eyes were full of concern. "Of course. You can do this, Jul. Make him be honest with you."

Julie swallowed deeply. "Pray for us, okay?" she asked.

"Done," Meghan replied and hugged Julie.

"Thank you," Julie said and released Meghan from her embrace.

She took a deep breath, wiped the wet mascara from beneath her eyes, and walked directly to Taylor's bedroom. Dull light from the hallway illuminated the room enough for her to see that Taylor was alone in bed. She flicked on the light switch, but Taylor did not stir. His room was messier than usual; a laundry basket of unfolded clothes sat on top of his desk; a pile of presumably dirty clothes were on the floor beside his overflowing hamper; a towel hung over the top of his open closet door; and multiple dishes and glasses sat upon his bureau and nightstand. For a neat freak like Taylor, the condition of his bedroom screamed "depression."

The dried food on the plates looked days old, and his down-comforter lay in a heap at the end of the bed. Taylor was wrapped in a single sheet, lying on his right side and hugging a pillow. *You used to hug me all night long,* she thought, remembering how loved she used to feel in his arms. Before sitting down on the bed, she glimpsed at a framed photo on the bureau of Taylor, Jordan, Marc, and their parents—one happy family, many years ago. Taylor's eyes were filled with hope. Surely everyone believed bright things were in his future. At the time, he had been committed to attend his dream school, where he never would have met Julie. She could recall Taylor once saying that he believed things happened for a reason and that falling in love with her took away the sting of not attending Notre Dame.

Julie swallowed deeply and peered at another framed photo in which Taylor's eyes shined brightly. The picture had been taken two summers prior, when Taylor visited her in South Carolina. *My whole family fell in love with you just as quickly as I did.* Taylor's charisma was unmatched. How could someone so filled with personality, drive, and love turn into the apathetic being lying two feet away from her?

She kicked off her shoes and sat Indian style on the bed. With her eyes locked on Taylor, she prayed for God to guide her next move. Taylor looked like his true self while asleep, which allowed Julie to pretend, momentarily, that all was right in their world. She would climb into bed beside him, and he would hug her tightly because they were in love and going to get married.

Closing her eyes, she turned away from Taylor and told herself to face their current reality. When she opened her eyes, she noticed another framed photo of her and Taylor sitting on his nightstand. It would have been heartbreaking to find that Taylor had put away their pictures. Glancing around the room, she noticed that all of their photos were in place, which gave her some hope that he did still love her.

As she set her eyes upon the nightstand, a prescription bottle next to the lamp caught her attention. After picking it up, she noticed that the label was old and faded. Inside, she found a handful of green pills marked OC.

"How did you even get these?" she wondered beneath her breath while flipping a pill over to see its dosage.

To her dismay, the number read eighty. All hope within her that Jordan might have been mistaken immediately dissolved. Her chest tightened, and her throat went dry. *Eighty.* No doctor would ever prescribe OC-80s after a knee surgery. Eighty was the number embossed on the pills that people snorted to get high.

Julie counted six pills as she put them one-by-one back into the bottle. She wanted to flush them, but she knew that could send Taylor into withdrawal. A painkiller addict going through withdrawal was a dangerous and desperate being—one that often turned to heroin. Heroin was significantly cheaper, readily available, and much dirtier than Oxycodone. It was the last thing she ever wanted Taylor to go near. Flushing his pills simply was not an option.

After placing the bottle back onto the nightstand, she lay down facing Taylor and began to run her hand through his thick blonde hair. Tears filled her eyes, and within ten seconds, she was fully sobbing into the pillow. She felt a hand touch her hip and slide past her waist. When she lifted her head, her eyes met Taylor's. He looked concerned.

"What's wrong, Jul?" he asked quietly and gently wiped a tear from her cheek.

"You're awake," she said softly and took a deep breath.

Every part of her body was shaking. Taylor wrapped his muscular arms around her and pulled her tightly to his chest. Julie felt like she was "home" for the first time in months.

"I'm so glad you're here," Taylor said faintly before kissing the top of her head. "But why are you shaking? Why are you crying?"

She squeezed him tightly and struggled to catch her breath.

"Jul, you're scaring me," Taylor said as he continued to comfort her.

She didn't want him to let go of her; she didn't want that moment to end. Instead of pushing her away, he was pulling her close again. She knew everything would change once she told him why she had come over, and she didn't want it to change. She wanted to cherish the feeling of his arms around her; she wanted to pretend for a couple more minutes that the boy lying beside her was the person she had fallen in love with.

CHAPTER 43

TAYLOR HELD JULIE TIGHTLY in his arms as she continued to sob quietly. Glancing past her shoulder, he noticed his bottle of OxyContin was on the edge of the nightstand. He swallowed deeply as his heart began to race.

"Jul," he said quietly and caressed her in a soothing manner, "just tell me what's wrong."

Slowly, Julie pulled back so that she was lying face to face with him. She looked anguished. "I'm losing you," she said in a faint voice.

The pain in Julie's eyes pierced Taylor's heart. "I'm losing me," he remarked and gazed up at the ceiling.

Julie sat up, and Taylor heard the sound of pills rattling. Glancing over, he saw her holding the bottle of OxyContin in her hand.

After clearing her throat and wiping tears beneath her eyes, she asked, "Why do you have these?"

Taylor took a deep breath and let it out slowly. He widened his eyes, sighed, and then sat up with his back against the headboard. He let out another heavy breath before turning to face her. Deep feelings of fear, regret, shame, and anxiety washed over him.

"You were right about me still taking pain meds," Taylor admitted sorrowfully. "I was too ashamed to tell you, and I took it out on you... and I'm sorry." He turned to Julie, hoping she could see in his eyes how truly sorry he was. He took the bottle of pills out of her hand and held them in front of her face. "This is why I said you should move on to someone else." He put the bottle of pills down on the bed. "You deserve so much better than the version of me sitting here right now," he added in a defeated tone.

Julie eyed him apprehensively. "Are you still in pain? I... I don't understand."

Taylor swallowed deeply and nodded. "I don't know how else to deal with it."

"To deal with what?"

Taylor shook his head. "Losing it all."

Julie placed her hand on his shoulder. "Everything is still there for the taking. You just have to go get it."

Taylor put his head down. "I don't have it in me anymore. I don't have... *me*... in me anymore."

"Will you please go for counseling? We could go together."

Taylor sighed. "Jul, I've got to be the one to get myself out of this rut if I'm ever going to find myself again."

Julie nodded. "I understand, but maybe an antidepressant could help more than these?" she suggested and picked up the bottle of pills.

Taylor groaned. "All those do is get rid of my headaches and give me the energy I need to socialize and work out. It's not what you think. It's not what Marc thinks. I don't sit around snorting lines of Oxy to feel euphoric. I don't take them to get high. The idea of sitting in bed all day, nodding in and out of consciousness, doesn't appeal to me."

Julie stared him directly in the eye. "Okay," she said. "Then why do you have OC-80s?"

Taylor sighed. "Remember how I told you I sometimes did coke before we met? Just to sober up after long nights of drinking?"

Julie nodded.

"I shouldn't have done that," Taylor said and shook his head. "I should have just drank less."

"Right," Julie agreed. "What are you getting at?" she asked hesitantly.

"Coke would, like, snap me back into sobriety—well, a feeling of sobriety—and suddenly the drunken haze I was in would lift. I'd have perfect vision, perfect balance, perfect focus. It was like an 'edit undo' button for drinking."

Julie peered at him in a confused manner.

Taylor took a deep breath. "What I'm trying to say is that Oxy is like an 'edit undo' button, too—not for drinking but for..." Taylor allowed his voice to trail off. He swallowed deeply and dropped his eyes to his hands. "... self-loathing."

"You hate yourself?" Julie asked in an alarmed tone.

Taylor shook his head. "No," he replied. "I miss myself. I hate the person I've been for the past year... I hate what my life has become and that I can't tap into the drive I used to have to pull myself out of this rut." He groaned. "The only time I feel even close to normal is when I take those pills."

Julie winced. "Are you addicted to Oxycodone?" she asked.

"No," Taylor replied immediately. "I told you it's not like that."

"I think when people are addicted to opiates, they don't feel normal unless they take them," Julie said in a hesitant manner, as though she were afraid to speak candidly with him.

Taylor took Julie's hand. "Don't be afraid to say anything to me."

Julie swallowed. "I just want to understand what you're going through."

Taylor sighed. "I do, too."

"Will you consider seeing a therapist? Even just once? Maybe this type of thing happens to a lot of people and there's an easy solution."

Taylor let out a heavy breath. "I'll think about it."

"Thank you."

Taylor turned to Julie with eyes full of sorrow. "I hate that you're being impacted by my issues. The guilt gnaws at me, every day. I want to be so much better for you. I want to be better for my parents... for Jordan and Marc... for my team. I mean, they're not even technically my team because I'm not even technically in college, but it still feels like they're my team... and I carry every loss on my shoulders, knowing if I were back on the field, I could make a difference."

Julie eyed him sympathetically. "Babe, you need to be better for *you*. Worrying about the rest of us is just going to weigh you down even more."

Taylor nodded. "I know, but I can't help it."

"Don't you think you would feel better if you enrolled part-time in classes? You know, just take a small step toward getting back to where you were?"

Taylor shook his head. "I don't trust myself not to fail."

"You never actually got an F," Julie said matter-of-factly.

"I'm not a C- student," Taylor stated flatly, "but that's who I was last year. I can't go back to school until I feel like myself."

Julie sighed. "I just think..." Her voice trailed off, and she let out a heavy breath. "... that maybe... maybe you won't feel like yourself until you start doing things you used to do."

"That's the problem," Taylor said; "I have no drive left in me to do what I used to do."

"That's because you're depressed," Julie insisted. "That's why I think a therapist could help. If you weren't depressed, you could reapply to school for a different major, walk onto the football team, and win back the starting job."

Everything Julie was saying made sense, but Taylor was having a hard time conveying how apathetic, purposeless, and empty he truly felt. Every day, he became more and more of a failure because every day he failed to take the appropriate steps to get his life back on track.

"You deserve so much better than this," Taylor stated with frustration. "I mean, it's three o'clock in the morning. Look at you. Look at what I've done to you. You came here in tears." He rested his head in his hands and tensely pulled on his hair.

"Can I tell you something?" Julie asked.

Taylor nodded without lifting his head out of his hands.

"You're the only person who can give me what I deserve because you are the only one who can revive the Taylor Dunkin I fell in love with," Julie said and rubbed his back.

Taylor began to sob. Julie wrapped her arms around him and kissed the top of his head.

"I want to," Taylor said in a faint voice.

"If you keep relying on Oxy to feel normal, you're only going to lose more of yourself," Julie warned him. "I know that's not what you want to hear, babe, but it's the truth."

Taylor lifted his head out of his hands and glanced at her.

"I learned about it in school. Opiates mess up the way your mind functions," Julie said. "They can even rewire your brain, and if that happens, the chance of ever feeling 'normal' again is slim."

Taylor cleared his throat and sat up straight. "I don't want that to happen," he stated flatly.

"No, you don't."

Taylor took a deep breath. How in the world could he ever tell Julie that he had become a drug dealer? Or how about the fact that he wasn't sure he could stop dealing without putting his life in danger? He was grateful that Julie was willing to stand by him in full knowledge of his continued opiate use, but he could never expect her to knowingly stand alongside a criminal. He believed the guilt he felt over dealing drugs was largely contributing to his depression. He needed to figure out how to keep Julie and his family safe while maneuvering a way out of the Bilotti crime circle. He feared that distancing himself from the people he loved the most would be the only solution.

CHAPTER 44

March 2018 - Present Day

INSIDE THE RAUCOUS NIGHTCLUB, Michelle, Katie, and Robby completed a lap around the tightly packed dancefloor without one sight of Missy. After climbing the stairs up to the slightly-less-packed mezzanine level, Michelle tucked herself into a corner so she could have a moment to check her phone.

"She could be anywhere in this place," Katie sighed. "It must be filled to capacity by now."

"Did she text you back?" Michelle asked as she retrieved her phone from her pocketbook. Her home screen had text notifications from Marc, Jordan, and Ally, but nothing from Missy or Laurelle. Sliding open the text from Jordan, Michelle was relieved to see the words, *Landed safely! Call me later.*

"Nothing from Missy or Laurelle," Michelle reported to Katie and Robby. "Robby, can you text Pat?"

"I already did," Robby replied. "Nothing."

Yay! Glad you had a safe flight. I'm not sure how late we're staying. Evidently our Seaport dinner turned into a high-end rave thanks to Luke Davids. I'm a bit out of my element! Call you when I can talk, Michelle wrote back to Jordan.

Michelle looked up at Katie and Robby, who were gazing at her expectantly. "Sorry," she said and slipped her phone back into her bag. "Katie and I should check the bathroom."

"If you don't see her in there, we should tell Luke what's going on," Robby suggested. "I mean, he's out of it but not so much that he won't try to find her."

Katie nodded. "Let's go check Missy's favorite room," she joked and tugged on Michelle's arm.

◐ ◐ ◐

While waiting for his luggage inside Logan Airport, Jordan pulled his phone out of his pocket. He widened his eyes as his noticed multiple alerts had come through after he got off the plane. He had a voicemail from his father, a few texts from Taylor, a text from Michelle, sixty-four notifications from his friends' group chat, and multiple NHL notifications about the Bruins game.

After sliding open Michelle's text, he laughed as he imagined her in the midst of Kandi-covered ravers. He began to write back, *PLUR*, but deleted it, assuming the reference would only confuse her. The baggage carousel buzzed, prompting Jordan to tuck his phone into his pocket and move closer to the conveyor belt. His blue and gold duffel bag came into view a moment later, which he quickly grabbed before heading outside to the pickup area. Once he stepped outside, he could see his breath. He shuddered and rubbed his hands together before playing his father's voicemail.

"Hi, Jordan. T's going to pick you up tonight because he's coming home for the weekend. I'll see you guys soon. Text me so I know you landed safely. Love you. Bye," Mr. Dunkin's voicemail rang into Jordan's ear.

Jordan's stomach fluttered as soon as he heard that Taylor was going to join their family for Easter. This gave Jordan hope that Taylor was truly in recovery. As far as he knew, Taylor had not been home in months.

Navigating to his text messages, Jordan grinned as he read the heartfelt message Taylor had sent him while he had been mid-flight. However, his smile faded when he saw Taylor's last text. "Why did you send me your location?" he muttered.

Jordan looked at the time on the message, which read 9:37 p.m., and then at the current time, 10:15 p.m. Baffled that Taylor would stop for pizza on his way to the airport, Jordan wondered if their father had asked him to bring home food.

"Weird," Jordan said aloud and then brought his phone to his ear to call Taylor.

The call immediately went to Taylor's voicemail, so Jordan left a message:

"Hey, T. So glad you're picking me up, dawg. I'm standing outside by the one... two... the third JetBlue sign—a little past the taxi area. It's flippin' freezing out here, so I'm going to wait inside. Call me when you're pulling up, and I'll be out STAT. Thanks, bro."

Assuming that Taylor was driving through the Callahan Tunnel without service, Jordan thought nothing of getting his voicemail. He found a vacant bench to sit on inside the baggage claim area and called his father.

"Hey, J," Mr. Dunkin greeted him warmly after answering the call. "Safely in Boston?"

"Hi, Dad. Yup. I got my luggage. I'm ready to go, just waiting for T."

"How were your flights?"

"They were both fine. I got a lot of reading done."

"Look at you, the academic."

Jordan laughed.

"All that studying's been paying off," Mr. Dunkin remarked. "I saw your mid-term grades online—pristine."

"Just tryin' to make you proud."

Mr. Dunkin laughed. "Have you heard from Taylor yet?"

"He sent me a text that he was running late. Did you ask him to pick up pizza?"

"What? No. Your mother has wings in the oven."

"Oh, weird. He texted me that he was heading to the airport from some pizza shop."

"Oh, I don't know. I told him your mother and I would have food ready for you guys."

"Hmm. Well, I'm sure he'll be here soon."

"Call me if he's not there by ten-thirty."

"Will do."

After ending the call, Jordan attempted to reach Taylor, but the call went straight to his voicemail again. Wondering if there was a backup heading into the airport, Jordan googled the local traffic; the roads were clear. Baffled, Jordan sent a text to Taylor: *Hey, bro. Not sure if you got my voicemail??? But I'm waiting inside for you to get here. Are you close?*

When Jordan hit send, it took a few extra seconds for the message to go through. When it did, it showed up green instead of blue, meaning that it had not been sent through iMessage.

"Why the heck is your phone off, T?" Jordan asked beneath his breath.

Jordan re-read Taylor's texts from earlier in the night. He thought his brother sounded genuinely excited to see him and a bit sentimental. Jordan could understand that; they had not seen each other since the summer. Jordan had only been home for a few days during Christmas break, and at the time, Taylor had still been detoxing.

Navigating to his messages with Michelle, Jordan composed a text to her: *I'm still at the airport. Taylor's picking me up but running late. Maybe I should take an Uber to the Seaport after all. Ha!*

Less than a minute later, Michelle replied: *You're welcome to do that. I actually ran into some kids who know Taylor.*

Michelle's offer sounded tempting, but Jordan wanted to see Taylor as soon as possible. He replied: *Thanks. I'm hopeful he'll show up soon. I bet everyone at that club knows T.*

Michelle responded: *That's funny. That's what the kid said. I can tell you the rest later. Right now I'm trying to find my friend who's MIA.*

Jordan: *Who?*

Michelle: *Missy. She's dating Luke but he has no idea where she is either. They're not thinking straight.*

Jordan: *I doubt many people around you are.*

Michelle: *Thankfully most of my friends are fine but I'm worried about Missy.*

Jordan: *I remember Missy. Check all the platforms and the stage. She's not one to hide!*

Michelle: *Good point. Although earlier she wanted to stay in the bathroom, talk, and cuddle - so you can imagine where her mind is!!*

Jordan: *I wish I could say I have no idea what that's like! If she was like that earlier then she's probably full of energy by now.*

Michelle: *I'm going to do another lap around the dancefloor. Let me know if Taylor shows up. Katie and I can pick you up if you're stranded.*

Jordan: *I would love to see you but I wouldn't make you do that. I'll let you know when I get picked up. Keep me posted about Missy.*

Michelle: *Will do!!*

Jordan locked his phone and sighed. It had been almost an hour since Taylor last texted him. *Why would he stop to eat pizza on the way to pick me up if he knew he would be late?* Jordan wondered. *And why send me his location?* Deciding to wait a few more minutes before calling his dad, Jordan ventured to Dunkin' Donuts and ordered a coffee. He didn't want to make Taylor's tardiness a "thing" unless it was absolutely necessary.

◐ ◐ ◐

Marc followed Cathy through the sea of Bruins fans inside the Pro Shop. Everyone was excited over the victory. Although Marc was a bigger fan of football than hockey, he appreciated any solid athletic performance. The Bruins had not disappointed. The line inside the Pro Shop snaked through the store, as people dressed in black and gold purchased celebratory mementos.

Marc tapped Cathy's shoulder when his phone began to vibrate in his pocket. "Hold on a sec," he said to Cathy once she turned around.

Checking his phone, he saw that his father was calling him. "Hey, Dad. Can you hear me? I'm still at the Garden," he shouted into his phone.

"Hi. Can you pick up Jordan at the airport on your way home?" Mr. Dunkin asked.

"I thought Taylor was grabbing him."

"Did you talk to him?"

"No. Taylor sent me a text, saying he was picking up Jordan around ten."

"What time was that?"

"I don't know. Let me check." Marc pulled his phone away from his ear and checked his messages. "8:50," he informed his father. "Why?"

"Jordan can't get ahold him. It's strange. T texted him around 9:30, saying he was getting pizza and running late."

"A half hour late? That's not like T."

"I know. I'm getting worried. I can't get ahold of him either."

"So, Jordan's just sitting at the airport?"

"Yeah. Do you mind grabbing him?"

"Uh, no. I'm just supposed to have Cathy home by eleven-thirty. Can you, um, call her parents and tell them what happened? I don't want her to get in trouble."

"Yeah, that's fine. Do me a favor and head there now. Jordan's been waiting a while. I'll keep trying to get ahold of Taylor."

"Okay. I'll let you know if I hear anything."

When Marc ended the call, he had a pit in his stomach. Had the police taken Taylor in for questioning? Or worse, had his supplier? Marc cringed. Had he put his brother's life in danger by giving him the burner phone?

Cathy peered at Marc. "What's wrong?" she asked.

"Uh, we have to pick up Jordan at the airport."

"Now?"

Marc nodded. "Taylor was supposed to get him around ten, but he hasn't shown up yet."

"That's weird."

"Yeah. My dad's going to call your parents to let them know you might be late."

"Okay. Let's leave now then," Cathy said while nodding towards the exit.

Marc put his arm around Cathy and led her through the crowd. "Hopefully we can get out of the parking garage fast. The traffic's usually pretty brutal," he said as they left the store.

"I know, and you won't have service in the garage either," Cathy said.

"Ugh, that's right. Well, maybe by the time we get out of the garage, Taylor will have shown up and we won't have to go."

"I bet you're just dying to see Jordan," Cathy teased him.

Marc rolled his eyes. "There are worse things, I suppose."

Cathy laughed. "Did you text him that you're coming?"

"No, but I should," Marc replied and pulled his phone out of his pocket.

As Marc and Cathy navigated towards the garage elevators, he began writing a text to Jordan: *Hey. Dad asked me to pick you up at the airport. I'm leaving the Bruins game now. I parked in the garage so traffic's going to be a problem. I'll get there as soon as I can. Hopefully within a half hour.*

While Marc waited with Cathy for the elevator, Jordan wrote back: *Thank you so much! I have no idea what happened to T. Have you heard from him?*

Marc sighed as the elevator dinged, announcing its arrival. He quickly replied: *Stepping into an elevator. Won't have service in a minute. Text me where I'm supposed to get you. I'll call you when I'm out of the garage.*

Marc put his phone away and rode the elevator to P4. The line of traffic could be seen as soon as he and Cathy stepped off the elevator.

"Yeah...we're not getting out of here in less than a half hour," he remarked dryly as they walked towards his truck.

"Well, I'll have plenty of time to tell you about my afternoon with Luke," Cathy stated in a hard to read tone.

CHAPTER 45

SITTING INSIDE HIS TRUCK moments later, Marc drummed his fingers on the steering wheel as he peered impatiently at the long line of traffic inside the parking garage. He glanced at the clock on his dashboard: 10:43 p.m. Reaching ground level to find out if anyone had heard from Taylor could easily take another half hour.

The sickening feeling in Marc's stomach intensified with each moment that passed. Neither his father nor Jordan knew about the police investigation, so they had no idea Taylor was in a significant amount of danger. Marc dreaded breaking that news to them and hoped he would never have to. Marc sighed and glanced at Cathy; she appeared more anxious than she had during the game. She did not know about the police case, so Marc doubted she was worried about Taylor being in any trouble.

"Are you okay?" Marc asked.

Cathy nodded and peered straight ahead with a distant look in her green eyes.

"What did you want to tell me?" Marc asked nonchalantly.

Cathy began tapping her right foot and then glanced out the window. She took a deep breath and adjusted herself in the seat so that she was facing Marc. "I don't really know where to start," she admitted.

Marc glanced away from Cathy to drive forward. "Did Luke get in trouble today?"

"Not exactly," Cathy replied.

Marc rolled his truck to a stop about a foot behind a black Chevy Tahoe. "Then, what happened?" he asked and turned back to her.

Cathy looked down at her hands and fidgeted uncomfortably. "Before lunch, we went to Taylor's," she replied in such a faint voice that Marc was not sure he had heard her correctly.

"To Taylor's?"

Cathy looked up at him and nodded.

"So, that's why Taylor recognized you?"

"Yeah," Cathy hesitantly admitted.

Marc felt his heart rate increase.

"I'm really glad that you guys talked, and I'm so afraid that what I'm going to tell you will make you mad at him again," Cathy said.

Marc sighed. "Just say it. You shouldn't have the burden of keeping anything about Luke and my brother on your chest."

Cathy cocked her head to the side. "Do you already know about Luke and Taylor's arrangement?"

Marc scoffed. "The arrangement in which my brother sells Luke illegal drugs?"

Cathy widened her eyes and stared at him expectantly.

"Yeah," Marc continued. "I've known for a while."

A look of relief washed over Cathy's face. "Oh my gosh. I had no idea, and I was so afraid to tell you, but I had to. I couldn't keep it from you."

"So, that's what's been eating at you?"

Cathy nodded.

"I'm sorry Luke put you in that situation," Marc said while inching his truck forward.

"Luke doesn't think things through," Cathy remarked and leaned against the window.

Marc sighed. "That's what mine and Taylor's fight was over. That's why I stopped talking to him."

"Because he sold to Luke?"

Marc nodded.

"Luke doesn't know that you know."

"Right."

"Why didn't you confront him?"

"If we argued over it, the rest of our friends would find out, and I don't want anyone to know Taylor deals drugs."

"Oh, that makes sense. How did you even find out that he sold to Luke?" Cathy asked curiously.

Marc smirked. "Your friend told me Luke gave Jason pills."

Cathy shot him a puzzled look. "What friend?"

Marc tapped his fingers on the steering wheel. *I guess it's time to finally have this conversation.* "You came to a party at Samson's house when you were dating Jay. You brought that girl who used to date Jon Anderson."

"My friend Julianna who you hooked up with?" Cathy questioned him, sounding slightly resentful.

"We only kissed," Marc replied defensively.

"She said Luke gave Jason pills?"

Marc nodded. "And when Jay got sick that night, you told Matt that Jay got painkillers from Luke."

"I did?" Cathy asked, sounding genuinely surprised.

Marc eyed her strangely. "Uh, yeah. That's why Matt got so pissed."

Cathy put her head down. "I don't remember any of that."

"When I found out Luke was buying painkillers and not just club drugs, I assumed Taylor was his dealer," Marc explained while shaking his head sadly. "At that time, Taylor was deep into Oxy. I thought he might have even turned to snorting heroin. Thankfully, that wasn't the case, but I was done giving him the benefit of the doubt."

"You knew back then that Taylor was dealing?"

Marc nodded. "I found a box of drugs in his room."

Cathy widened her eyes. "And he admitted to it?"

"He had to," Marc replied. "I caught him, red-handed, with hundreds of pills and pounds of weed."

"No pun intended, but that must have been a hard pill to swallow," Cathy remarked dryly.

Marc nodded. "My hero fell from his pedestal that day." He paused and sighed. "Finding out that T was Luke's dealer answered a lot of questions for me. I finally understood how Chris and Jason had access to so much stuff. I had assumed Luke would never sell to his little brother or to my cousin. I don't know what he was thinking. They hid it from me—Luke and Chris. Even after Chris got sober, he protected Luke's identity."

Cathy put her head down. "I've known for over a year that Luke was Chris and Jay's hookup. I wanted to tell you, but I felt like I would be betraying all three of them."

Marc swallowed a lump in his throat and looked Cathy directly in the eye. "What did Luke give to *you*?"

Cathy peered at him uneasily.

"I probably already know, but I want to hear it from you," Marc said and placed his hand on top of hers. "Be honest."

Cathy put her head down and played with her fingernails. "Just tell me what you heard," she responded quietly.

"You won't tell me?"

Cathy looked up at him. "I will if you want me to, but it's tough to talk about."

"You protected Luke's identity because he gave you pills, too. Right?"

Cathy shook her head. "It wasn't like that. Luke was trying to help me deal with a medical condition—a problem I've had for a couple of years."

Marc eyed Cathy expectantly. "What kind of problem?"

Cathy hesitated. "I don't want you to look at me differently."

"I won't," Marc pledged and again rubbed her hand.

Cathy took a deep breath and looked away from Marc for a couple of seconds. When she turned back toward him, she looked like she was on the verge of tears. "I have an anxiety disorder," she admitted. "Luke used to give me weed gummies to treat it, but I hated being high, so he gave me benzos to take if I felt a panic attack coming on."

Marc eyed Cathy thoughtfully. He knew that Luke cared deeply about her, so he assumed Luke's intention had only been to help her, but he could not fathom how Luke remained so ignorant about the consequences of benzo addiction. People could not only die from benzo withdrawal, but also go through withdrawal for over ten years.

Marc took a deep breath before asking Cathy the question that had been burning in his mind for three months: "When was the last time Luke gave you benzos?"

Cathy fidgeted uncomfortably and glanced down at her hands. "I don't remember," she replied. "The entire month of November is a blur." She swallowed. "I'm not trying to hide anything... I really just don't know."

Marc gazed at Cathy sympathetically. "I know you went through a lot with Jason."

Cathy nodded. "He blamed me for Andy's accident."

Marc's stomach dropped. "What?"

Cathy let out a heavy breath. "He felt it was *our* fault, and he accused me of not feeling bad about it. I felt responsible for what happened, but I didn't feel any emotion because the Xanax made me numb. So, Jay was right about me not responding appropriately to what happened. I wasn't there for Chantal or Lisa; I was... just... horrible."

"Is that why you and Jay broke up?" Marc asked.

Cathy sat up straight. "I don't know," she muttered. "I don't remember."

Marc widened his eyes. "What do you mean?"

Cathy fidgeted uncomfortably. "I mean exactly what I just said."

CHAPTER 46

JORDAN TAPPED HIS PHONE screen over and over again, navigating from one Instagram story to the next, as he sat on a bench inside the airport, hoping to hear from one of his brothers. His flight had landed over an hour ago, and he was growing more and more worried about Taylor as each moment passed.

After seeing the fifth video clip of his friends in Punta Cana, Jordan closed out of Instagram and began composing a text to Michelle: *Any luck finding Missy?*

Still looking but Katie and Robby want to leave soon. I don't know what to do, Michelle replied.

Jordan: *Who did Missy go to the club with?*

Michelle: *My friends Laurelle and Pat. Missy and Luke are supposed to ride home with them but all four of them are on molly. Even if we find Missy, I don't think any of them should drive.*

Jordan sighed. Michelle had previously admitted that she often felt like the "mom" in her group of girlfriends. Jordan remembered thinking in high school that it was strange she was close with girls as wild as Missy, Day, and Laurelle. According to rumors, Day had matured into a role model after becoming a born-again Christian, but Missy and Laurelle had continued in their rowdy ways. *Are you going to drive them home? Who else are you with?* Jordan typed into his phone.

Michelle: *I think so. Robby is going to leave with Katie. John and Day already left. Matt and Ally will stay with me until we find Missy.*

Jordan: *Matt Davids?*

Michelle: *Yeah.*

Jordan felt relieved; Matt was someone whom he held in high regard. In fact, Jordan had chosen Matt as a co-captain of the varsity football team when he was only a sophomore because he was more mature than the majority of the seniors. Jordan responded: *Good. You'll be safe with Matt. I would come and help you look for Missy but Marc is on his way to pick me up. We still can't get ahold of Taylor.*

Michelle: *What do you think happened to him?*

Jordan had plenty of ideas about what might have happened but none that he wanted to discuss over text. He replied: *The last thing he texted me was his location. I'm afraid he's in trouble. I can explain more to you in person.*

Michelle: *I hope he's okay!! He looked really good today. Totally sober and healthy. He seemed exactly like the Taylor I remember.*

Michelle's words brought Jordan some comfort. He doubted his brother would relapse on his way to the airport, and the fact that he sent Jordan his location proved he wasn't nodding off in bed.

Jordan: *He sent me his location around 9:30. It looks like he was in Mission Hill for some reason. He didn't explain why he sent it. I want to check it out on the way home if Marc's up for it.*

Michelle: *That's weird. Maybe he sent it by mistake?*

Jordan: *I don't think so because he made a point to say he was at a pizza shop in the area. He wanted me to know where he was for a reason. I just wish he told me the reason.*

Michelle: *Is he involved with shady people?*

Jordan's heart skipped a beat. He replied: *Why would you think that?*

Michelle: *Because some of the kids here who said they knew him seemed pretty sketchy.*

Jordan wondered if that was Michelle's way of saying she found out Taylor was a drug dealer—another thing he did not want to say over text. His thoughts were interrupted as his phone began to ring, and Marc's name appeared across the screen.

"Hello?" Jordan answered after bringing the phone to his ear.

"Hi. We just got out of the garage. Traffic was bad. I'm heading towards 1-A and should be there in ten minutes as long as there's no more traffic."

"Nice. I'm ready."

"I'm sure you are."

"Who's 'we'?"

"I'm with Cathy."

Jordan assumed Marc meant the girl who had recently tagged him in a few Instagram posts. Jordan recognized her from his time spent at Chris's. "The Cathy who's a twin?"

"Good memory," Marc replied.

Michelle had casually mentioned that Marc was seeing someone new; evidently Marc had a thing for a freshman. "I remember her getting stuck staying over Chris's house one night because Chris wanted to hook up with his girlfriend—when he was, like, ten."

Marc laughed. "So, where do I pick you up?"

"Follow the signs for Jet Blue and call me when you're pulling into the pick-up zone. I'll be standing by the third sign."

"Will do. Later," Marc said and abruptly ended the call.

Jordan assumed Marc was less than excited to see him. He hoped Michelle would be able to help him and Marc work out their issues while he was in Montgomery. However, Jordan was not sure how Marc would respond to their relationship. Although Michelle was not Jordan's girlfriend, he wanted her to be. In fact, he was praying she would get into Notre Dame and choose it over her other offers. She had already been accepted to Villanova, Fordham, BU, Holy Cross, Liberty, Providence, and UMASS; however, she was waiting to hear back from Northeastern, Notre Dame, Georgetown, BC, and Wake Forest. Although Jordan was partial to ND, he knew getting in without recruitment was extremely difficult. Even with recruitment, he had to maintain a 3.8 GPA and score above a 30 on the ACT. Michelle had above a 4.0 and a 34 ACT, which Jordan hoped would be enough for the Irish to open the door to her. He believed having Michelle by his side in South Bend would help him continue along the straight and narrow path he had been walking for the past seven months.

◑ ◑ ◑

Michelle stood inside the nightclub beside Ally, listening to Matt berate Luke for losing sight of Missy. Katie, Robby, Day, and John had helped Michelle diligently search for Missy before they left. Neither Laurelle nor Pat had texted anyone back, and no one else knew where Pat had parked.

"You walk your girlfriend to the bathroom, and you wait for her," Matt said sternly to Luke.

"I didn't even know she went to the bathroom," Luke insisted. "We were all standing by the coat check, and the girls just took off."

Matt scoffed. "If that's what you think happened."

"That is what happened," Michelle spoke up, finding herself in the odd position of defending Luke. "Missy didn't tell him she was going anywhere. She just grabbed Laurelle's arm and pulled her into the crowd. Katie, Day, and I bumped into them in the bathroom line a minute later."

"She ditched me the second we checked our coats," Luke said with a shrug. "I love that you're all, like, worried about her, but I doubt she's worried about any of us."

Matt sighed.

"Pat and I assumed she and Laurelle were on the dance floor," Luke explained, "so we headed that way."

"And she hasn't texted you?" Matt asked.

Luke shook his head. "Not once."

"Do you think she saw you outside talking to that blonde girl?" Michelle asked.

Luke smirked. "Even if she was completely sober, she wouldn't care about that. I mean, I kind of wish she would, but she doesn't have a jealous bone in her body."

"Do you think she's with Pat and Laurelle?" Ally asked.

"I don't know," Luke replied. "I don't know any more than you."

Luke's mood was far different from earlier when Michelle had conversed with him outside. Whatever drug he had taken had most likely worn off because he looked as ready to leave the club as her.

Luke let out a heavy breath. "I'm sorry, guys. I don't know what to tell you. I mean, I'll stay. You guys can go. Missy and I can take an Uber home if we can't find Pat and Laurelle."

"But what if you can't find Missy?" Ally asked. "She's, like, really hot, and I doubt she's sober enough to make smart decisions, so if you don't find her—"

"—I know," Luke interrupted Ally. "Another guy will try to take her home."

Ally nodded.

"Whatever the hell you guys took earlier is going to start wearing off, right?" Matt gathered. "Won't she come looking for more?"

Luke eyed Matt apprehensively.

"What?" Matt asked.

"Do you see me right now?" Luke asked and circled his face with his hand.

Matt peered at Luke in confusion.

"This," Luke stated and pointed at himself. "Sober Luke."

"I guess...I guess you're sober," Matt replied, eyeing his brother strangely.

Luke nodded. "Yeah, because I'm not the one holding the drugs."

Matt scowled.

"You trusted *Missy* with them?" Ally asked with wide eyes.

Luke rolled his eyes. "She said if she hid them in her bra, no one would find them if we got patted down at the door."

"They didn't pat us down," Ally stated matter-of-factly.

"I know, but they could have," Luke said. "So, wherever Missy is, she's probably less sober than me."

"She's always less sober than you," Ally remarked in a frustrated manner. "What do you want to do?" she asked and turned to Matt.

Matt glanced from Ally to Luke to Michelle and then back to Ally. "Let's go outside where it's quieter and see if we can get ahold of Missy, Pat, or Laurelle. Maybe one of them will finally answer."

◑ ◑ ◑

Jordan stood up and grabbed his duffle bag off the bench as soon as his phone rang. "Hey," he said into his phone as he began walking towards the exit. "Are you here?"

"Pulling into the pick-up area now," Marc replied. "I'm in my truck. I'll pull over with my hazards on."

"All right. See you in a sec," Jordan said and hustled out the door.

The frigid March air felt like a slap across the face when Jordan stepped outside. Thankful he would be hopping into a warm vehicle, he smiled when he saw Marc's red truck in the distance. Walking towards the curb, he waved Marc in his direction.

After Marc parked in front of Jordan, Cathy hopped out of the passenger seat.

"Hi," Cathy greeted Jordan. "You can have shotgun."

Jordan smiled. "I don't mind the back. Just push the seat forward."

Cathy smirked. "You're over six feet tall. There's hardly any legroom back there. Take the front."

"If you insist," Jordan sang and pulled the seat forward for Cathy to climb in back. "Hi, little brother," he greeted Marc.

"Nothing from Taylor?" Marc replied.

"No," Jordan said and pushed the seat back. He tossed his duffle bag on the floor and then climbed inside the truck. "I think he might be in trouble."

Instead of driving forward, Marc turned to Jordan with a perplexed expression on his face. "What did you hear?"

"Look at these texts," Jordan said and pulled his phone out of his pocket. He navigated to his messages with Taylor and handed the phone to Marc.

Marc read over Taylor's texts to Jordan and then squinted in thought. "He sent something similar to me around the exact same time," Marc said and picked his phone up from the cupholder. A few seconds later, he handed it to Jordan. "He sounded more emotional than usual, but I assumed it was because we had just talked for the first time in four months. He didn't send me his location, though."

Jordan read Taylor's message to Marc and then set the phone in the cupholder. "How did Taylor seem when you saw him?" he asked. "Did he seem stressed or like he was in danger at all?"

Marc let out a heavy breath. "He's being investigated by the police," he said in a somber tone.

"What?!" Cathy exclaimed from the backseat.

"Today at BC, a detective interrupted my meeting and gave me a burner phone to deliver to Taylor. He told me that Taylor was in danger and that the BPD wants to help him break out of his crime ring."

"Crime ring?" Jordan asked. "What crime ring?"

Marc sighed. "Evidently Taylor's supplier isn't just his friend's uncle; he's connected to organized crime."

Jordan scoffed. "Taylor got involved with the mafia?"

"I don't know if it's the mafia. It might just be a gang. The detective said the less I know, the safer I'll be. But what he said scared me, and when I relayed the message to Taylor, he didn't exactly say anything that put me to ease."

"Holy crap," Jordan huffed. "So, the cops want T to become an informant?"

"It sounds like it," Marc replied and gripped his steering wheel tightly.

Jordan widened his eyes. "Is Taylor going to do it?"

"I don't know," Marc said. "He was kind of shocked when I gave him the phone. He had no idea the cops knew who he was, let alone that they had investigated him."

"So, he finally gets clean, and then this gets dumped on him?!" Jordan exclaimed. "I hope the stress doesn't cause him to relapse."

"He said something about hiring a lawyer," Marc recounted. "If he doesn't show up at home tonight, I don't know how I'm going to break this news to Mom and Dad."

"Taylor sent me his location for a reason," Jordan stated. "We need to go there and look for him."

"That was almost two hours ago," Marc retorted.

"Just do it. Let's look for his Jeep or some clue as to where he went. Let's check out the scene at Brigham Pizza and ask if anyone saw him," Jordan stated in a serious tone. "He wouldn't have sent me his location if he didn't want me to know where to look for him."

Marc sighed. "You're probably right." He glanced at Cathy in the rearview mirror. "This is going to make you even later for your curfew."

"It's fine," Cathy assured him. "Your dad explained things, and my parents know that traffic after a Bruins game is brutal. Go to his location. I agree with Jordan. He sent it for a reason."

◑ ◑ ◑

Michelle followed Matt, Ally, and Luke over to an unoccupied couch near one of the outside fire pits. Despite the frigid temperature, the nearby heaters made the area feel quite warm and cozy.

"Who's calling who?" Matt asked and pulled out his phone.

"Missy's more apt to answer a call from Ally or Michelle than me," Luke said. "After being MIA for this long, she's probably going to assume I'm mad at her and try to avoid me."

"I'll call her," Ally offered. "You should call Pat," she said to Luke.

"I guess I'll try Laurelle," Michelle stated and began searching through her bag for her phone. When she turned it on, she hoped to see a text from Jordan, but he had not written back to her yet. Although she wondered what had happened to Taylor, she fought off all temptation to text Jordan. Instead, she pulled up Laurelle's contact information.

"Are you going to call Pat, or do you want me to?" Matt asked Luke.

"Why don't you try him," Luke replied. "I've already called him three times. Maybe if you call, he'll realize something's wrong."

"Why? Because I never call people?" Matt gathered.

"Exactly," Luke said before burying his head in his hands and groaning.

Michelle waited patiently for Laurelle, or her voicemail, to pick up. It seemed strange that Laurelle would leave Missy by herself in the club. Despite how carefree Laurelle was, she was actually quite intelligent. It had always amazed Michelle that Laurelle could party so hard and still maintain a high GPA in all Honors and AP classes. While Laurelle certainly egged on Missy's craziness, she kept her love for partying from affecting most areas of her life. The fact that Laurelle and Pat were notorious for disappearing together, led Michelle to believe Laurelle and Missy enjoyed parties for different reasons. Missy basked in the glory of the limelight; Laurelle wanted to win Pat's undivided attention by being the most attractive girl at every event. She enjoyed the challenge, and she had perfected how to look sexy, cute, and classy at the same time—never slutty, always stylish, never flashy, but still alluring. She had the ability to act silly when it suited her audience but, at the drop of a hat, come out with a quick-witted comeback that made everyone else in the room feel dumb. Laurelle was committed to attend Bowdoin as a pre-med student in the fall. She was *that* smart, so Michelle knew there was no way she had left Missy alone.

"I got Laurelle's voicemail," Michelle said to Luke after ending the call. "I'm starting to think Missy might have left with her and Pat."

"Why would she do that without texting me?" Luke asked. "Why would she want to be with them and not me?"

Michelle eyed Luke warily. "I don't really understand her," she admitted. "I'm sorry."

Luke sighed. "Maybe Marc was right."

"About what?" Michelle asked.

Luke shook his head. "Nothing. Forget it."

Michelle glanced over at Ally and Matt. It sounded as though Matt was leaving Pat a voicemail; Ally was typing a text message.

"Any luck?" Michelle asked.

"Missy's voicemail was full, so I'm texting her now," Ally replied. "I told her to meet us outside by the fire pit if she's still here. I said we're leaving soon. Hopefully that will get her attention."

"I left Pat a voicemail," Matt said. "If they went back to the car, they might not have service. The garage we parked in is underground. They probably have no idea we're trying to reach them."

"Do you have any idea where Pat parked?" Michelle asked Luke.

"There are so many garages," Luke said and shook his head. "Your guess is as good as mine."

"I doubt Missy wanted to walk far in heels," Ally remarked. "It's got to be close by."

"Good point," Michelle agreed. "I really don't think Laurelle would ditch Missy. I also don't think Missy would let her. Chances are high she's with them somewhere."

"So, do we leave and start looking in garages?" Luke asked.

"I guess we could, but that's like looking for a needle in a haystack," Matt replied. "Every garage has a few floors, and I saw five on this street alone."

"Could we go eat somewhere and wait for them to call us back?" Ally suggested. "I'd rather get breakfast than spend any more time here."

"I like that," Matt stated with a nod. "I'm down."

Luke sighed. "I hate leaving without her, but after searching this place five times over, I doubt she's even here."

"I'm sure we'll hear from one of them soon," Michelle assumed and stood up from the couch. "Let's take a Lyft to a place that's still serving food. It's too cold to walk around looking for an open restaurant."

"Agreed," Luke said and stood up beside Michelle. He patted Michelle's shoulders before draping his arm around her. "I'll be your escort," he joked, "so no guys try to sweep you off your feet between here and the exit."

Michelle smiled. "Thanks," she said appreciatively and allowed Luke to lead her back inside the club.

CHAPTER 47

JORDAN PEERED ANXIOUSLY OUT the windshield as Marc drove slowly down Huntington Avenue, first past Northeastern, then Wentworth and Mass Art. Brigham Circle was straight ahead. "The location Taylor sent me is 0.1 miles away from here. It's slightly before Brigham Pizza on the map," Jordan informed Marc while peering down at his phone.

"On the left or right?" Marc asked.

"No idea. Let's park somewhere and walk," Jordan suggested. "Wherever you can find a meter."

"I don't know this area too well," Marc admitted.

"Just stay on Huntington Ave., and we'll be fine," Jordan said. "It's the back of the hill you have to worry about. This part is fine."

"A Boston expert now, J?" Marc questioned him.

Jordan laughed. "I spent the majority of my senior year at Northeastern with T. Not much has changed in two years." Jordan glanced to his left and right, hoping to spot a free meter. "Is that a hydrant up ahead on the left or a spot?"

"I can't tell," Marc replied. "I'll make a U-turn."

"If that's not open, we can always park in the lot behind CVS," Jordan said. "It's heading up the hill, but it's not a bad area."

Marc turned left at the light to drive over the Green Line trolley tracks before steering his truck eastbound down Huntington Ave. Jordan peered out the window at the bars, restaurants, and convenience stores lining the block. His blue eyes locked on a neon sign about ten yards ahead that read "Brigham Pizza."

"There it is!" Jordan exclaimed as his heart pounded. "Let me out here and go park. You guys can meet me inside."

"You want me to just pull over *here*?" Marc questioned him.

"Yeah, just double park and let me out," Jordan replied anxiously. "Throw on your hazards."

As soon as Jordan felt the truck come to a halt, he swung open his door and leaped out of the vehicle. Nearly launching into a full sprint, he reached the pizza shop in seconds. He whipped open the thick glass door and stepped inside the small restaurant, which was filled with kids who looked close to his age. Brigham Pizza was evidently a college hot spot, which gave Jordan hope someone might know Taylor.

Jordan darted his blue eyes around the room, looking for either Taylor or any of his friends. He recognized none of the faces surrounding him but, even so, did not hesitate to approach the first table, where two guys and a girl were sitting. "Hey, sorry to interrupt but do you guys know Taylor Dunkin?" Jordan asked.

The group stopped talking and gazed up at Jordan with confused expressions on their faces.

"He's my brother, and I can't find him anywhere," Jordan added.

One of the boys widened his eyes. "You're Jordan?" he cried. "Holy $#@%, dude. You're sick on the field." He turned to the girl and said, "He plays for Notre Dame."

"You're Taylor's brother?" the girl asked.

Jordan nodded. "It's really important that I find him. Have you guys seen him in here tonight?"

"No, man," the other boy replied. "But we just got here five minutes ago. Check with the guys behind the counter."

"All right. Thanks," Jordan said and turned to walk away.

"Can we snap a pic with you before you leave?" the first boy asked.

"Uh, yeah, sure," Jordan replied and patted the kid on the shoulder. "I'll circle back before I head out."

"Thanks!" the boy exclaimed, as Jordan pushed through the crowd towards the line.

As good as it felt to be recognized as an elite football talent, Jordan didn't want his ego to get in the way of finding Taylor. He reached the end of the line and counted six people in front of him. Turning to his right, he called out to a nearby table, "Hey, have any of you guys seen Taylor Dunkin pass through here tonight?"

"The QB?" one kid asked.

Jordan nodded.

"I heard he wasn't really around anymore," the boy replied with a shrug. "I haven't seen him."

"Nah, me either," another guy at the table added.

"Okay, thanks," Jordan said and peered around the room again. As he did, he noticed a well-dressed, middle-aged man standing in the back corner of the restaurant, talking to an extremely buff, burly-looking guy with tattooed arms. They appeared to be engaged in light-hearted, casual conversation. The well-dressed man, who was leaning against the wall with his arm crossed, had an at-ease disposition and a loud laugh. Jordan assumed the man was the owner or manager of the restaurant, but the burly looking guy seemed out of place in the establishment.

"Hey, any luck?" Marc's voice rang out as Jordan felt someone tap him on the shoulder.

Jordan whipped around to see Marc and Cathy, peering at him anxiously. He shook his head. "People here know T, but no one, so far, has seen him tonight," he replied. "I'm going to ask the kids behind the counter."

"This placed is packed," Marc commented while glancing around the room. "Someone must have seen him if he was actually here."

"Why don't you go ask around?" Jordan suggested.

"And say what?" Marc retorted.

"Just ask people if they've seen Taylor," Jordan replied matter-of-factly.

"What if they have no idea who I'm talking about?" Marc asked.

Jordan moved forward in the line and turned back to Marc. "Bro, unless they're freshmen, they'll know who Taylor is."

"I feel weird interrupting people," Marc admitted.

Jordan sighed. "Fine. Hold my spot in line. I'll ask around." Before walking away, Jordan added, "But, hey, keep your eye on those guys back there." He inconspicuously nodded toward the men in the back corner.

"Why?" Marc asked while sliding into Jordan's spot.

"I'll explain later," Jordan replied and pulled out his cell phone. He navigated to his photos and scrolled until he found a picture of him and Taylor. Then he walked over to a table of kids who looked like they were getting ready to leave.

"Hey, guys," Jordan interrupted them without any hesitation. "Have you seen this kid anywhere?" he asked while pointing to Taylor's picture.

The three girls and two boys glanced from the photo to Jordan and then back at the photo.

"You're Taylor's brother who plays for the Irish," one of the boys said and glanced back up at Jordan.

Jordan sighed. This was exactly what he had wanted to avoid by having Marc do the questioning. However, he still could not fathom why anyone in Boston knew who he was.

Two of the girls started laughing.

"Yeah, I'm Jordan. I'm looking for Taylor. Have you seen him tonight?" Jordan asked, wondering why the girls were so amused.

"What's so funny?" one of the boys asked.

"Kelly has his picture from the article hanging up," one of the girls replied.

Jordan felt his cheeks flush.

"Ohhh, yeah!" the third girl cried.

"I guess you're almost as popular as your brother around here," one of the boys said to Jordan.

"What article?" Jordan asked in a confused manner.

"Our school newspaper ran a spread on Taylor after his injury, and there was a paragraph in there about how his younger brother was playing for Notre Dame. There was a photo, too, and... well, one of the girls in our sorority cut it out and taped it to the fridge," the girl explained. "It's still there."

Jordan widened his eyes. "Taylor got hurt in 2016," he said in bewilderment. "I've been on your fridge for a year and a half?"

The girl nodded.

Jordan laughed. "I'm flattered, but I really need to find my brother. I just flew in from Indiana tonight. He said he was here, but I can't find him."

"Would Julie know?" one girl asked the other two.

"I don't think they're talking right now," one of the girls replied.

"Julie? You guys know Julie?" Jordan asked.

"Yeah," the three girls said in unison.

"She's the president of our sorority," one of the girls added.

"Aww, I love Julie!" Jordan exclaimed with a wide smile. "Tell her you saw me. Wait, so my picture is on Julie's fridge?"

"No, she lives next door with the other officers," the girl replied.

"She must have gotten a kick out of seeing my picture on your fridge," Jordan said in an amused manner.

The girl laughed. "Taylor did, too."

"Well, now that you guys have made me feel like a local celeb, I better keep searching for my MIA big brother," Jordan remarked playfully. "Any idea where to look?"

"You should call Julie," one of the girls suggested.

Jordan nodded. "Yeah, I could do that. But either way, tell her I said hi. Okay?"

"Sure," the girl replied and smiled brightly, "if you'll tell your little brother that Samantha said hi."

Jordan did a double take. "Are you Samantha?"

The girl nodded.

Jordan smirked. "You can tell him yourself. He's right over there," he said and pointed at Marc.

Samantha widened her eyes and laughed. "Oh, $@%#! Yeah, he is."

"How do you know Marc?" Jordan asked curiously.

Samantha giggled. "We made out once," she replied.

"Made out?" Jordan questioned her, realizing she was most likely the sorority girl Marc had once brought home to Taylor's, prompting Taylor to claim that Marc was following Jordan's footsteps.

Samantha nodded.

"In that case, he may get a *little* distracted if he sees you," Jordan gathered. "We really need to find Taylor, so maybe you shouldn't say anything."

Samantha smirked. "Is that his girlfriend?"

"I think so," Jordan replied, "but I don't really know. I just want to find Taylor."

"Jack, why don't you text Matty?" Samantha suggested to one of the boys at the table.

The kid named Jack pulled out his phone. "I can see if, uh, Matt McSweeney knows where he is. They're tight."

"Aww, Matt. I know Matt," Jordan said. "Tell him I said what's up. I gotta go ask the guys who work here if they've seen T, but someone take down my number so you can get ahold of me if you hear anything."

"What is it?" Samantha asked.

"617-555-1355," Jordan replied. "Thanks, guys," he added and headed back over to Marc and Cathy.

"Any word?" Marc asked.

"No, but, uh, I met someone who knows you," Jordan informed him.

Marc looked confused. "Me? Who?"

Jordan nodded in the direction of Samantha's table. "Recognize anyone over there?"

Marc glanced over Jordan's shoulder. Jordan watched with amusement as Marc's blue eyes grew wide.

"Oh," Marc said and swallowed deeply.

Cathy glanced over at the table and then looked up at Marc. "Are those Taylor's friends?"

"They're Julie's friends," Marc replied.

"Oh. Cool," Cathy said nonchalantly and turned back around.

Marc gave Jordan a look that made it clear he did not want to talk to Samantha in front of Cathy. At that point, Jordan was confident that Marc and Samantha had done more than "make out."

Jordan smirked. "Samantha's going to text me if she hears from Taylor."

"Great," Marc said awkwardly. "How lucky we are that you ran into Julie's friends."

"They suggested I call Julie, but I don't think they've talked in a few months," Jordan said while stepping forward in line.

"According to Taylor, she's not happy with him," Marc stated. "She found out about some stuff he was doing behind her back."

"Oh, shoot. Yeah, that's a problem," Jordan remarked.

Marc nodded. "Speaking of that, two guys walked into a room with those men you wanted me to watch. See that door? They went in there," he explained and nodded toward the door. "Do you think this place is a front?"

Jordan raised his eyebrows. "It's a darn good one if it is. A pizza joint in the middle of a college town? That would explain the need for a tatted-up bodyguard."

"Then be careful with what you say when you ask for T," Marc warned him. "Seriously."

Jordan swallowed a lump in his throat.

"In fact, maybe we should leave," Marc suggested. "Like, now."

Jordan lowered his eyebrows, feeling alarmed by the fear he detected in Marc's tone. "Why?"

Marc cleared his throat. "Because Taylor said his supplier could come after our family," he whispered so faintly that Jordan struggled to understand him.

Jordan darted his eyes from Marc to Cathy and then back to Marc. "Let's go," he stated seriously and nodded towards the door.

"Can I help you?" a worker behind the counter called out to Jordan.

Hesitantly, Jordan turned around. The person who had spoken looked like a college student, not a criminal. Still, the idea of Taylor's supplier possibly finding out that Jordan and Marc were in Boston was unnerving enough for Jordan to reply, "Actually, I'm just looking for a takeout menu. Do you have one?"

The kid reached under the counter and handed a trifold menu to Jordan.

Jordan smiled. "Thanks," he said and quickly turned to leave the restaurant.

As Jordan, Marc, and Cathy were heading to the door, the group of kids at the front table called out Jordan's name.

Crap, Jordan thought, *the picture*. Normally, he would have loved to enhance his social media presence and talk football with fans, but that night, all he wanted to do was uncover his brother's whereabouts.

"Oh, sorry, guys," Jordan apologized and walked over to the table. "I totally forgot you wanted a photo."

"It's all good," one of the kids said and pulled out his phone.

Marc and Cathy stared at Jordan strangely as he squeezed into a selfie with two guys and a girl.

"What's your Insta?" the kid with the phone asked.

"Uh, @jordan_dunkout," Jordan replied distractedly. "Tag me or whatever. I gotta jet, but nice to meet you guys."

"Yeah, man. Good luck finding Taylor," the kid replied.

Jordan waved goodbye and then hustled to the door where Cathy and Marc were waiting for him.

"What was that about?" Marc asked, while holding open the door.

"Nothing," Jordan replied. "Let's just get out of here."

"How do those kids know you?" Marc pressed as they stepped onto the slushy sidewalk.

"They don't. They know Taylor," Jordan stated flatly.

"They seemed pretty hyped up to see you," Marc commented and eyed Jordan skeptically.

Jordan sighed. "I guess they follow ND football or something. I don't know. It doesn't matter, Marc."

"You're just so used to being a star that it doesn't even faze you anymore, does it?" Marc asked.

Although his brother's words were complimentary, Jordan perceived frustration in Marc's voice and disdain in his blue eyes. Jordan eyed Marc precariously before asserting, "I really just want to find T."

"C'mon, let's look for his car," Cathy suggested, breaking up some of the tension between the brothers. "What does he drive?"

"A Jeep," Marc replied and turned away from Jordan to walk beside Cathy.

"What kind?" Cathy asked.

"A black Grand Cherokee," Marc said.

Jordan started walking behind them and pulled out his phone to find the text with Taylor's location. "I want to walk to the exact spot he sent as his location. It's up ahead, about a tenth of a mile from here—on this side of the street."

"Then lead the way," Marc said and paused so Jordan could step in front of him and Cathy.

CHAPTER 48

Michelle walked arm-in-arm with Luke out the door of the nightclub onto the slush-covered sidewalk parallel to Seaport Boulevard. As frustrated as she had been with Luke earlier for bringing them blindly to an EDM festival, she felt nothing but pity for him. Whatever Missy did that night instead of hanging out with Luke was wrong, and he deserved to be treated with more respect than that. Considering Missy an unbridled free spirit, Michelle was surprised that she had committed to Luke in the first place. Moreover, Michelle thought they were completely mismatched.

At first glance, it was easy to write off Luke as a party-boy, who would gleefully dance with Missy along the highway to hell. In fact, some of their friends—Day, Laurelle, and Ally, specifically—thought they were a perfect match. Michelle, however, shared Matt and Marc's opinion: Luke was a pushover who loved to please people, and Missy was a bad influence on him.

While Matt stood by the curb with Ally, waiting for their Lyft to arrive, Michelle sat down with Luke on a nearby bench. She leaned in close to him, hoping to steal some of his body heat.

"Do you want my jacket?" Luke offered and pulled her in close to his chest.

Michelle shivered. "No, I have my own jacket. I'm okay."

"Are you sure?" Luke asked. "I practically live outside in the winter, between ice skating and skiing. The cold really doesn't bother me."

"Okay," Michelle acquiesced. "Thank you," she added, as Luke draped his coat around her shoulders like a blanket. "You know you are the nicest Davids, right?"

Luke laughed. "Nicer than Matty? I don't think anyone would agree with you."

"I love Matt, but you're a warmer person."

"Thanks, Shells," Luke said, sounding genuinely flattered.

"Missy's been my friend since fourth grade, but I think you deserve to be treated better than the way she treated you tonight."

Luke sighed. "Who knows what she did tonight..."

"Wherever she is, I'm sure she's with Laurelle. Laurelle's the only person I've ever seen Missy attach herself to."

"Marc thinks Missy's secretly in love with her," Luke stated jokingly.

Michelle laughed. "Well, we all know Laurelle's in love with Pat and only Pat."

"Do you think Missy uses me?" Luke asked in a serious tone. "Like, for my money and my drug connection?"

Michelle sighed. "I don't know. She's not open with me about her drug use."

"I know someone who can get me coke and ecstasy whenever I want," Luke admitted, "but it's never me who wants it. I mean, I enjoy rolling—don't get me wrong—but what I mean is it's usually Missy prodding me to take a trip into the city for stuff."

"More often than not, you're completely sober," Michelle said matter-of-factly. "I don't think it's a secret that she's the one in your relationship who likes to get messed up."

"So, then you think it's possible that she's using me?" Luke asked.

Michelle shrugged. "If she is, she doesn't see it that way. Missy's not malicious. Selfish, maybe. Unreliable, definitely—but she's not mean. I think she's just oblivious to how her actions affect other people."

"I agree with that."

"Stop giving her stuff. If she stays with you, then you'll know she isn't using you."

"Can I be really honest?" Luke asked hesitantly.

"Of course," Michelle replied and put her head on his shoulder.

"There are a few people who expect me to get them stuff whenever they ask, Missy being one. Earlier today, I felt relieved when my dealer told me he was out of what some kids in my grade asked for. I have seen drugs mess people up, bad. *Real bad.* And I'm talking about drugs that were supposed to help them with legit problems. It's scary, and... I don't want to get drugs for anyone anymore."

"Are you talking about Taylor?" Michelle asked.

"What do you mean?"

"Did it scare you to see how painkillers messed up his life?"

"Oh, yeah. Of course, it did," Luke replied. "But I don't even mean just him. I'm talking about my own little brother and Marc's cousin... and some of their friends."

"Marc told me about Chris," Michelle said, "but thankfully he's doing great now."

"Yeah, Chris got a second chance."

"I think Chris will become everything his family thought Taylor would be," Michelle remarked.

"He found something to believe in and ran with it, and he's doing great. Jay's right there with him, but it could have turned out really bad for both of them."

"I didn't know Jay ever had a drug problem."

"Ally and Matt didn't tell you?"

"No."

"Hmm. Matt has no problem talking about me behind my back. I have no idea why he always protects Jason."

"Matt never talks bad about you,"' Michelle said. "He just worries about Missy being a bad influence on you."

"If you say so."

"What was Jay's problem?" Michelle asked curiously.

"Mainly Adderall, which my parents forced him to take. It made him wired, so he got into weed to calm himself down. Then it became a vicious cycle, and honestly, it ruined his relationship with Cathy."

"Cathy seems happy with Marc," Michelle commented nonchalantly, hoping Luke would shed some light on their relationship.

"Yeah, he's good for her," Luke said. "He's had a thing for her since the summer, but now that Jay's thinking straight, I foresee some drama on the horizon."

"A fight?"

"Between Marc and Jay? No. Jay's not a fighter, and Marc would never touch him," Luke replied. "But I can't get Cathy to talk about Jay at all, which makes me think she's not over him yet."

"Are you worried about Marc getting hurt?" Michelle asked.

Luke shrugged. "He's leaving for college soon, so I don't think he's taking what's between them too seriously," he replied. "But I expect Jay to try to win her back, sooner or later. He still loves her."

"Do you think Cathy's good for Marc?"

"I don't think she's bad for him," Luke responded vaguely.

"You can be honest," Michelle insisted. "It won't hurt my feelings."

"Shelly, I think you and Marc were the perfect couple back in the day, and I think deep down, you'll both always love each other because you kept everything so innocent. But you guys have been best friends for so long that I can't see you as anything else. You're like siblings."

"But Marc hates his siblings," Michelle joked.

Luke laughed. "Touché."

Ally and Matt began waving Michelle and Luke over to them as a silver Toyota Camry pulled up to the curb.

"Oh, the Lyft's here," Michelle announced and sat up straight. She handed Luke his jacket and rose from the bench.

Luke put on his peacoat and stood up beside her. "Shall we?" he asked and extended his arm to her.

Michelle took hold of him and asked, "When you hear from Missy, what are you going to say?"

Luke sighed. "I have no idea. She clearly didn't want to hang out with me tonight. I doubt I'll get much of an explanation from her. I just hope she's with Laurelle and Pat."

"She is. I'm sure of it," Michelle insisted as they approached the car.

"I hope," Luke muttered.

"You deserve better," Michelle said before climbing into the backseat of the Camry beside Ally.

"Maybe I don't," Luke remarked as he slid beside Michelle and closed the door.

Michelle glanced over at Luke in surprise. "Why would you say that?" she asked as Matt and Ally began making light conversation with the Lyft driver.

Luke shrugged. "Maybe I'm just reaping what I've sowed."

Michelle rested her head on Luke's shoulder and took his hand. "It's never too late to plant good seeds."

Luke rested his head against Michelle's and let out a heavy breath. "Yes, but is it possible to dig up ones you've already planted? Ones you've been watering for over a year?"

"I'm not quite sure," Michelle replied thoughtfully, wondering what Luke was referring to, "but there's no harm in trying."

"Missy just texted me!" Ally exclaimed loudly while waving her phone in the air.

"What?!" Luke cried and leaned across Michelle to grab Ally's cell phone.

"What did she say?" Michelle asked, peering at Ally with wide eyes.

"He took my phone. I have no idea!" Ally exclaimed and locked her brown eyes on Luke, who was intently reading Missy's message with a perplexed expression on his face.

"Where is she?" Michelle asked.

Luke finished reading and locked the screen. "I think she's still in the club," he said.

"What?!" Ally cried and grabbed her phone out of Luke's hand. She turned on the screen and read Missy's message out loud: "Owner's lounge w/ DJ and VIPs. Come!!! Everything's free. Tell them you know Taylor Dunkin."

At the sound of Taylor's name, Michelle's stomach dropped.

"Really?! She's still there?" Matt asked from the front seat.

"I don't know what she means by 'owner's lounge,'" Ally replied and began typing a response.

"What are you saying to her?" Luke asked.

"I'm asking who she's with," Ally replied.

Seconds later, Ally's phone dinged loudly, prompting her to quickly read Missy's response. "She's with Laurelle and Pat. They're going to stay for after-hours. She asked if I'm with you, Luke."

Michelle looked at Luke to gauge his reaction; he appeared more hurt than angry. Turning back to Ally, Michelle asked, "What does Taylor have to do with anything?"

"No clue," Ally replied carelessly. "I'm going to tell her we're heading to a diner. I don't want to go back there tonight. Do you?"

Matt let out a short laugh. "No."

"Can you find out if Taylor's there?" Michelle pressed. "Jordan and Marc have been trying to get in touch with him for hours."

"You talked to Marc?" Matt asked.

Michelle's stomach squirmed. She had purposely kept Marc's closest friends from finding out she had been in touch with Jordan so Jordan could break the news to Marc in person. "No," Michelle replied quietly.

Matt gave her a strange look but said nothing.

"Missy must have seen your missed calls," Ally said to Luke. "That's sketchy of her to text me instead of you."

"That's also low of Pat not to call you back," Matt remarked.

Luke sighed. "None of them are thinking straight. Pat and Laurelle are probably deep in conversation, oblivious to Missy's existence. This isn't on them." He paused for a few seconds before asking, "Do you think she's with another guy?"

"Anything's possible with Missy," Ally replied dryly.

"Sadly, I think you're right," Michelle admitted.

"I wonder what she meant by 'everything's free.' I hope she isn't drinking," Luke stated in an alarmed tone.

"Stop worrying about a girl who doesn't give a $#@% about you," Matt warned his brother.

"That's a little harsh, Matt," Ally said disapprovingly.

Matt scowled. "I'm just sick of worrying about you dating her."

"Matt. Stop," Ally insisted. "Luke already feels crappy enough." She tapped the female Lyft driver on the shoulder and said, "Sorry that you have to listen to us right now."

"Oh, it's fine," the woman responded with a chuckle. "I've heard worse. The diner's only another block away."

"We are *not* going back to that club," Matt said sternly to Luke. "I don't care if Missy calls and begs to see you. After we eat, we're getting my car and heading straight home."

"That's fine," Luke agreed and waved his hand submissively.

"This is why I didn't want you to date her," Matt muttered.

"We don't even know her side of the story yet," Luke retorted defensively.

"Do you not see that she walks all over you?" Matt questioned his brother.

"Matt!" Ally exclaimed.

"I can see it," Michelle admitted.

"Thank you," Matt said triumphantly.

Luke let out a heavy breath and peered out the window. Michelle eyed him with compassion, praying he would find it within himself to stand up to Missy. Michelle could not recall a time when she had ever seen Luke get upset with one of their friends. It was clear that Luke preferred to keep things light and agreeable, but Michelle believed a sensitive soul existed beneath his happy-go-lucky demeanor.

CHAPTER 49

JORDAN PLANTED HIS FEET firmly on the slush-covered sidewalk from the spot where Taylor had texted his location. Facing the street, he stared directly at Taylor's Jeep, which could never be mistaken for another black Grand Cherokee; a Northeastern Huskies and a Notre Dame Fighting Irish decal were adhered to the small rear window.

"He never left for the airport," Jordan remarked and swallowed a large lump in his throat. He stepped into the mound of snow between him and the vehicle and leaned forward to peer into the window. A backpack that appeared fairly stuffed was sitting on the front seat; otherwise the interior of the SUV looked bare.

"My friend keeps calling me, and every time I think it's going to be T," Marc complained.

"Everything looks normal in the Jeep," Jordan reported and stepped out of the snowbank and back onto the sidewalk. He learned over and brushed snow off his boots and jeans before glancing up at Marc.

"Who just called you?" Cathy asked curiously.

"Pat," Marc replied and rolled his eyes. "I guarantee you whatever drugs Luke got earlier were for him, Pat, Laurelle, and Missy. I'm in no mood to talk to someone messed up right now."

Jordan wondered if Pat was calling to tell Marc that no one could find Missy. He hoped nothing bad had happened to her. Michelle had said they were having a hard time getting ahold of Pat as well, so Jordan wanted Marc to take the call. Considering their present circumstances, however, he knew it was not the right time to tell Marc he had spoken with Michelle. "Does Pat usually call you?" he questioned Marc.

"What?" Marc responded and sent Jordan a strange look.

"My friends usually just text me unless something's wrong," Jordan said with a shrug. "Maybe you should answer."

Marc waved off Jordan and put his phone back in his pocket. "There's a ninety-nine percent chance Pat's on molly," he said in a disapproving tone. "People don't shut up when they're rolling. Laurelle probably went to the bathroom for, like, one minute, so he called me."

Jordan sighed. He reached into his pocket for his phone to see if he had any new texts from Michelle. To his dismay, there were no alerts on his lock screen. "I wonder if Dad has heard anything," he stated as he unlocked his phone.

"If T's Jeep is still here, then he must be in the area," Marc gathered. "Do you think he's still at Brigham Pizza? Maybe in that backroom where I saw those other guys go?"

"He could be anywhere," Jordan reasoned. "I'm going to call Dad and tell him we found the Jeep." As Jordan brought his phone to his ear, he heard Marc's cell phone begin ringing. "You should answer that," he insisted.

Marc shook his head. "I can't deal with my idiotic friends right now."

"Jordan, where are you guys?" Mr. Dunkin's voice rang into his ear, pulling his attention away from Marc.

"Dad, we found Taylor's Jeep parked near that pizza place I told you about," Jordan replied.

"You're not on your way home from Boston yet?" Mr. Dunkin asked.

"I wanted to check out the location Taylor sent to me, and his Jeep is parked in that exact spot," Jordan explained.

"I need you guys to come home right now," Mr. Dunkin stated in an urgent tone.

"Did you hear something?" Jordan asked, finding his father's tone alarming.

"Just come home and we'll talk," Mr. Dunkin replied. "Okay?"

At the sound of his father's words, Jordan's heart began beating loudly and heavily against his chest. "Yeah. Yeah. Okay, Dad," he said and ended the call.

Marc and Cathy were both peering at Jordan with concerned expressions on their faces.

"What did he say?" Marc asked.

Jordan swallowed deeply. "He wants us to come right home," he replied. "He knows something. He didn't say what, but he has something to tell us."

Marc lowered his eyebrows in confusion. "He didn't say anything about the Jeep?"

Jordan shook his head. "He didn't even sound surprised. It was like he already knew."

GRIPPED PART 5 PREVIEW

March 2018

A lump formed in Taylor Dunkin's throat as he wracked his brain for the best way to respond to Donny Bilotti's question. Thoughts raced through Taylor's mind. *Is this my last transaction? Would Donny really let me get out? Or would my body turn up in a ditch?*

Taylor cleared his throat. "Have you found another college kid to take my place?"

Donny shook his head. "My nephew came by in the fall and begged me to stop giving you OCs. I never ran out of them. That's just what I told you so you could get clean."

Taylor did a double take. He gazed blankly at Donny, trying to make sense of his words. "Wh-wh-what?" he stammered. "Rob did *what*?"

Donny sighed and leaned back in his chair. "He said your life was falling apart because of oxy. You broke up with your girlfriend, failed out of your major, and were no longer on the football team. He said if I didn't stop giving you pills, you would end up overdosing."

Taylor swallowed deeply.

"He begged me to cut you out of the crew, too," Donny added. e sd

"Why didn't he tell me about this?" Taylor asked in confusion.

Donny shrugged. "I don't know, but I would do anything for my nephew."

Taylor wondered if Donny was implying that he was free to leave the crime ring or if he was merely trying to gauge Taylor's commitment to the job. Considering Donny's connections, he could easily know about the police investigation and even their desire to make Taylor an informant.

"Why doesn't Rob want me to work for you?" Taylor asked.

"C'mon, T," Donny said with a smirk. "You know why."

Taylor raised his eyebrows and peered expectantly at him.

Donny sighed. "He says you're not cut out for this, and you never would have gotten into it if you hadn't been injured. I told him I'd give it a few months to see if you could get clean and stay that way."

Taylor's palms began sweating profusely as he agonized over his next words. Getting out of the crime ring without a target on his back would be a dream to come true. But would Donny actually allow that? Would he do that for Rob's sake? Or would Taylor end up "missing" in a few short days? Taylor cleared his throat. "I've been clean since November."

Donny nodded. "I heard."

"I'm trying to get back on the field," Taylor added.

Donny crossed his arms. "What will that entail?" he asked.

Taylor let out a heavy breath. "I need to take some classes to bring up my GPA and then try to transfer wherever my former coach lands. I'm sure Rob told you NU cut the program."

Donny nodded.

"I don't have a scholarship anymore, so I'm going to have to pay tuition," Taylor explained. "I would like to sell another batch for you if possible. I could really use the money right now." Taylor decided the safest play was to convince Donny he did not want out of the ring because if he admitted he did, then he would be considered a liability. He would have to look over his shoulder everywhere he went. That much stress could easily trigger a relapse, especially within his first year of sobriety.

Donny eyed him strangely. "I told Rob you were done."

Done. That sounds so good. "I can be," Taylor said uneasily, "but one more batch would help me out."

"How much money do you need for tuition?" Donny asked curiously.

"It depends on how many classes I take," Taylor replied. "Each one is around two-thousand dollars."

Donny sighed. "My nephew's gonna be *real* mad if I keep you."

Maybe this isn't a trap...maybe Donny really wants to let me out. Regardless, Taylor knew he needed to seem committed to the job. "He won't know if you don't tell him," Taylor remarked.

Donny groaned. "Kid, you're not offering to do this because you're scared, are you?"

Taylor's heart sank to his stomach. His throat went dry. "Scared of what?" he asked, trying to appear unfazed.

"Rob was afraid my guys would come after you for leaving," Donny explained. "I told him he's seen too many movies and that's not the way I do business."

Taylor's heart pounded as he pondered his options. He wished he could verify everything with Rob before giving Donny an answer. Getting out of the crime ring meant he would not have to use his savings to pay for the drugs he pretended to sell or become an informant for the police. He could start rebuilding his life, completely free of negative influences. Knowing a bit about organized crime, Taylor thought it sounded too good to be true. "Rob thought that?" he questioned Donny in a surprised tone. "I had no idea he was so worried about me."

Donny flipped his hands in the air. "He says you're one of his best friends. He wants you to get back on track. A recovering addict shouldn't be dealing drugs. I mean, that's common sense."

Taylor sighed. "I know. I just need money so I can go back to school."

Donny squinted in thought. "How 'bout this," he said a few seconds later. "Jimmy's swinging by on his way to the club. Why don't you go with him? You always did well there. You can make some quick cash and then be on your way."

Jordan, Taylor thought as he glanced at the clock on the wall. *I am so late. Crap. But how can I turn down Donny's offer? I've convinced him that I need money. If I don't go, he'll question my sincerity.* Taylor swallowed deeply. "Is that something I could do more than once?" he asked.

"Yeah, if need be, fine. But as far as Rob is concerned, you're no longer a part of my crew," Donny stated. "Everyone at that club knows you, loves you, etc., so if you want to push some product there from time to time, it would be good for business. I'm not going to say no."

Either Donny was an A-list actor in disguise, or he was genuinely concerned with pleasing Rob. *If I go to the club, what am I going to do about Jordan? And my parents? They're waiting up for us. This could be the difference between life or death for me. I have to go.* Taylor hoped he didn't look as conflicted as he felt.

A heavy knock on the back door pulled Taylor out of his thoughts. Seconds later, Jimmy, one of Donny's higher ups, entered the room and handed Donny a manila envelope.

"All set?" Donny questioned him.

"Yeah, it's all good," Jimmy replied.

"T's gonna go with you and move some product," Donny said and nodded toward Taylor.

"Oh, you're back, man?" Jimmy asked in a surprised tone. "It's been a while."

Taylor nodded.

"Just for tonight. Just for the club," Donny clarified. "Anyone looking for coke or molly will run right up to him. That'll be his role."

Jimmy glanced from Donny to Taylor and smiled. "All right."

"Is Marty out there?" Donny asked and motioned toward the back door.

"Yeah, in the Escalade," Jimmy replied.

"All right. You guys should head out. The club's packed by now," Donny said. "T, Marty will drop you guys off. His guy's working the door."

Taylor's heart pounded. Getting a ride to the club in a luxury vehicle was business as usual for Donny's crew. He hated the idea of not taking his Jeep, but he was too nervous to ask Donny if he could drive himself. "Sounds good," Taylor said before following Jimmy outside.

CHAPTER 2

AFTER PARKING HIS CAR in his mother's driveway, twenty-three-year-old Rob Anuzelli carefully picked up the bouquet of roses lying on his passenger's seat before making his way to the front porch. The drive from Boston to Jamestown, Rhode Island provided him with a lot of time to ponder the possible reasons why his mother had asked him to visit her that night. He already had planned to spend the weekend with his family in Rhode Island for Easter, so the urgency in his mother's tone both baffled and concerned him.

After entering the home he grew up in, he found his mother sitting at the kitchen table with piles of paperwork in front of her. Although she appeared overworked and drained, her face lit up at the sight of her only child and the flowers he bore. Rob's father had passed away from cancer five years prior, and every holiday since had accentuated the pain of his absence. One tradition Mr. Anuzelli had maintained throughout the lifetime of their marriage was bringing Mrs. Anuzelli red roses every week. So, for the past five years, Rob had continued his father's tradition by bringing his mother flowers every time he visited her. It was a small piece of his father he was able to help live on, despite the huge shoes he left for Rob to fill.

"You're so sweet," Mrs. Anuzelli said affectionately and stood up from the table to hug her son. Then she bent down to smell the flowers and placed them on the quartz countertop. "Lately, I see so much of your father in you."

Rob smiled slightly and took a seat at the round, cherry table. He eyed his mother curiously when she sat down beside him. "What's going on, Ma?"

Mrs. Anuzelli took a deep breath and let it out slowly. "Rob, there's something I have been keeping from you for the past few years in order to protect you, but unfortunately the time has come to involve you in what I always hoped could be avoided."

Rob squinted in confusion. "What does this have to do with?"

"Uncle Donny, Uncle Paul, and your great uncle, Frank," Mrs. Anuzelli replied.

Rob widened his eyes. "Ma, if you're going to tell me that they're connected, I already know. I've known for a while."

Mrs. Anuzelli shook her head. "No, that's not it," she said and placed her hand on top of his. "You know I love you more than anything in the world, right?"

Rob nodded as his level of concern heightened.

"Your grandfather never wanted Donny or Paul involved in Uncle Frank's business," Mrs. Anuzelli began. "But when Grandpa passed away, Uncle Frank became a father-figure to them. He put Donny and Paul to work for him, knowing that they needed to help Grandma with the bills. They were grateful for the work and, at the time, did not understand why our father never wanted them to work at Uncle Frank's shop. Grandma said very little. She needed the financial help, and she wanted to stay ignorant to Uncle Frank's business."

Rob eyed his mother warily, wondering what was prompting the family history lesson.

"You know how close I've always been with Uncle Donny," she continued. "He was sixteen when he started working for Uncle Frank, and he made the mistake of telling me some things that went on. He was my kid brother, and he wanted me to know what was happening in his life. But it horrified me, and there was nothing I could do about it. I tried to tell your grandma, but she told me never to speak of such things. I was twenty at the time, and I kept everything I knew to myself until three years ago."

"What happened three years ago?" Rob asked in confusion.

"Three years ago, Uncle Donny decided to move to Boston so he could go to all your football games and keep an eye on you. As your godfather, he felt responsible for you, and he felt bad that you lost your dad. Donny's always had a kind heart and put our family first."

"What does that have to do with what you were just talking about?"

Mrs. Anuzelli took a deep breath. "More so than Donny, Uncle Paul is who I've wanted you to keep your distance from. He's Uncle Frank's righthand man. He's basically Frank's son, at this point. He will be the one to take over… everything… when Uncle Frank retires."

Rob continued to eye his mother precariously. She had never talked openly about her brothers' connection to organized crime. In fact, even when Rob had inquired about the rumors that they were in the mafia, she had told him not to ask questions.

"Once Donny got to Boston, I saw how close you two became, and Paul saw it, too," Mrs. Anuzelli continued. "I know about Donny's main source of income, and it has little to do with his pizza shop. When I found out that Donny had involved you in some of his affairs, I saw history starting to repeat itself."

Rob dropped his eyes to the table and turned slightly away from his mother. Shame and guilt washed over him. Before his best friend Taylor became one of Donny's drug dealers, Rob had been the one to get his friends drugs whenever they would go out to parties, raves, and clubs. Donny had sold plenty of coke, molly, Liquid G, and painkillers to Rob, saying that he wanted to be Rob's friends' supplier because he knew his products were clean. Even though Rob had not touched an illegal drug in well over a year, he felt ashamed of his past use of them. Watching Taylor's life fall to pieces because of a pain-killer addiction had given Rob a very bad taste in his mouth about narcotics. No matter how often he reminded himself that he thought he was helping Taylor treat knee pain, Rob still felt responsible for Taylor's addiction. Begging his uncle to stop selling Taylor oxy had been his first attempt to fix the mess he had created.

"Rob, what is it?" Mrs. Anuzelli asked and turned her son's face so he had to look her in the eye.

"I just know that I never should have gotten involved with anything my uncles were doing," Rob replied and let out a heavy breath. "I'm sorry. I think I just missed dad and gravitated towards both of them."

"I know, honey," Mrs. Anuzelli said and squeezed his hand.

"I don't do *any* of that stuff anymore," Rob insisted, looking his mother directly in the eye.

"I know. Jimmy told me," Mrs. Anuzelli said, referring to her boyfriend of a few of years.

"How are you okay with him working for Uncle Donny?" Rob asked. "I mean, I know he didn't start until after you guys had been together for a while, but it must kill you to know he's involved in what you hate most about our family."

"Rob, this is all connected to what I need to talk to you about," Mrs.

Anuzelli said and stiffened slightly. She took a deep breath. "When I saw you getting involved in your uncles' dealings a few years ago, I couldn't even sleep at night. I dreaded you becoming like them. I dreaded losing my son to their dark world of drugs, gambling, and... ugh... I don't even have to say what else. I was beside myself."

Rob winced. "I'm sorry, Ma," he apologized and hung his head.

"I asked Paul and Donny to keep you out of things, and... I'm sure they both thought they did... but the truth was, just being around them and their associates was damaging enough," Mrs. Anuzelli explained.

"Uncle Donny's always been good to me," Rob said. "I've never felt uncomfortable around him or anyone who works for him. I love being the nephew of the guy who owns the pizza place all my friends go to."

"I know, sweetie. And your uncle loves you like a son," Mrs. Anuzelli said, "and that means he is going to do everything he can to help you and protect you."

"Protect me from what?" Rob asked, surprised by his mother's choice of words.

She swallowed deeply and eyed him warily. "What's to come."

CHECK OUT THE REST OF THE GRIPPED SERIES

Gripped Part 1: The Truth We Never Told

In high school, Taylor Dunkin broke more records than any other athlete to step foot in Montgomery, Massachusetts. As a sophomore in college, he was ranked by ESPN as one of the NFL's top 100 prospects. However, his aspirations came to a jarring halt when a knee injury and two surgeries left him sidelined.

One year later, Taylor is a person of interest in a highly confidential investigation headed by the Boston Police Department. He has entangled himself in a crime ring notorious for pushing opiates, cocaine, and benzodiazepines on local college campuses. When Taylor's younger brother Marc discovers that Taylor is behind the copious drug supply circulating around Montgomery Lake High School, he sets off to not only reverse the damage Taylor has caused, but also save his lifelong role model from becoming a casualty of America's deadly opioid epidemic.

Gripped Part 2: Blindsided

Fourteen-year-old Chris Dunkin is known for being the life of the party and everyone's favorite friend. Despite his amicable nature, he carries around deep-seated pain from his childhood that he frequently numbs with alcohol and drugs.

After hosting a party, Chris awakes with a strange vibe running through his body and no recollection of the previous night. When he learns the horrifying truth of what his night entailed, the trajectory of his life is changed forever.

Gripped Part 3: The Fallout

After a near-death experience, Chris Dunkin begins

surrounding himself with positive influences and putting his efforts towards living a clean lifestyle. However, the night before school starts, his best friend Jason convinces him to host a party that shows Chris more about himself than he actually wants to know.

Meanwhile, Marc Dunkin has received word from a detective that his oldest brother Taylor is a person of interest in a highly confidential case headed by the Boston Police Department. They know Taylor's clean; they know he wants out of the game; and they want to help make that happen. However, their "help" will come at a cost—one that may put Taylor and his entire family in grave danger.

Taylor is trying to get his life back in order after an opiate addiction wreaked havoc on his once promising athletic future. Getting clean was a difficult feat, but breaking free from the Bilotti crime ring will present an even greater challenge.

Gripped Part 5: Taylor's Story

Taylor Dunkin is missing.

The last message Jordan Dunkin receives from Taylor leads him to Taylor's abandoned Jeep. Each of Taylor's family members holds a piece of the puzzle, and as the Dunkins begin putting the details together, they are awakened to the possibility they may never see Taylor again.

No one can find Missy Kent.

Missy's boyfriend Luke Davids last saw her dancing with their friends at a nightclub, but she hasn't responded to anyone's texts or calls for hours.

Everything is connected.

Taylor and Missy's friends are dangerously close to learning the truth, but their ignorance might be the only thing keeping them safe. Every clue is leading them closer to peril.

The fifth book in the Gripped series moves through details at a thrilling pace. Secrets are revealed and lives are at stake. Taylor, Missy, their friends, and their families must figure out who they can trust before it's too late.

IF YOU ENJOYED *GRIPPED*, CHECK OUT MONTGOMERY LAKE HIGH

Montgomery Lake High #1: The Right Person

Growing up in the shadow of two NFL-destined cousins, Chris Dunkin has high hopes for his own future in football. However, a drug addiction threatens to destroy everything he has worked hard to attain. When Chris meets Courtney Angeletti—the mayor's straightedge Christian daughter—he believes she could be the source of inspiration he needs to overcome his destructive lifestyle. Courtney, however, has other ideas.

The desire to rebel has been tugging on Courtney's heartstrings for some time, and Chris's "bad-boy" reputation draws her to him like a moth to a flame. After all, he is a central part of the most popular clique in her high school. Will Chris pull Courtney away from her faith or will Courtney inspire him to overcome his rebellious lifestyle?

Montgomery Lake High #2: When Darkness Tries to Hide

A powerful supercell is spawning above Montgomery Lake High School, while a separate storm is brewing in its halls. The question is which one should Cathy Kagelli, Jason Davids, and their friends fear the most?

Montgomery Lake High #3: The Aftermath

At age fifteen, Jason Davids appears to have it all: high grades, popular friends, a beautiful girlfriend, and nearly any worldly thing that promises enjoyment at his disposal. Despite this, there is a persistent emptiness inside his heart. After failing to fill the void with achievements, relationships, and illicit substances, Jason finds himself intrigued by Jessie: a rather quiet girl, who is the daughter of a local pastor. How is it possible that she stands for everything his lifestyle opposes yet possesses the one thing he has been searching for all along?

Montgomery Lake High #4: The Battle for Innocence

Jon Anderson and Chantal Kagelli are trying to live moral lives, but temptations are plaguing them in and out of school. Will they continue to be lights in their best friends' lives or will they get pulled into the darkness?

Montgomery Lake High #5: The Forces Within

After being trapped inside his own body, unable to communicate with anyone but his own thoughts, Andy Rosetti finally wakes up from the coma that controlled his life for one month. But upon awakening, Andy finds himself and his friends in an unfamiliar setting: a mansion riddled with secret passages and supernatural forces. As his friends fall prey to the entities surrounding them, Andy must figure out if the darkness lies within the mansion's walls or within the people surrounding him.

ABOUT THE AUTHOR

College counselor, award-winning author, and entrepreneur Stacy Padula of Plymouth, Massachusetts has accrued years of experience working with adolescents as an educational consultant, as well as a mentor, life coach, and youth group leader. She is the author of eleven Young Adult novels. Her first novel, "The Right Person," was published in 2010. In 2011, "When Darkness Tries to Hide" was published, and it was followed by "The Aftermath" in 2013. In 2014, both "The Battle for Innocence" and "The Forces Within" were released, and in 2015, all five books hit the shelves of Barnes & Noble. For Stacy, it was a dream come true to see her books for sale in the popular, mainstream bookstore! In 2016, Barnes & Noble chose Stacy to be a featured author for its teen book festival. In 2019, she released a new book series titled "Gripped," that takes place in the same "world" as Montgomery Lake High but focuses on different main characters. "Gripped Part 1: The Truth We Never Told" was released in February 2019, and "Gripped Part 2: Blindsided" was released in July 2019. "Gripped Part 3: The Fallout" was released in November 2019, and "Gripped Part 4: Smoke & Mirrors" was released in May 2020. In 2019, Stacy Padula also wrote her first screenplay, an adaptation of her novel "The Aftermath" and worked on writing a pilot for "Gripped" which caught the attention of Hollywood producers. The "Gripped" series is currently being adapted for TV by Emmy-winning producer Mark Blutman. In 2020, Stacy began writing a third book series with NBA Coach Brett Gunning. Geared towards children ages three through eight, Stacy and Brett's soon-to-be-released "On The Right Path" book series has been endorsed by Joel Osteen, Mike D'Antoni, and Kevin McHale as a series that belongs in every school, library, and household.

Stacy was featured in Marquis Who's Who in America (2018, 2019, & 2020) for excellence in literature and education, Marquis Who's Who in the World (2018, 2019, & 2020), and Cambridge Who's Who for Young Professionals (2009). In 2018, she was awarded the Albert Nelson Lifetime

Achievement Award, and in 2019, the International Association of Top Professionals (IAOTP of New York, NY) chose Stacy Padula as its "Top Educational Consultant of the Year." Then in 2020, she was named "Empowered Woman of the Year" by IAOTP. Each of her novels have risen to best seller status in a variety of categories on Amazon from 2010-Present. From February through March of 2019, "Gripped Part 1" was the #1 New Release on Amazon Kindle in its category. In November of 2019, "Gripped Part 3" was the #1 New Release on Amazon in Paperback and on Kindle in 3 different genres. In May and June of 2020, "Gripped Part 4" became the #1 New Release on Amazon in multiple genres as well. In November of 2020, Stacy was named a "Social Impact Hero" by Authority Magazine for her support of animal rescues through her publishing company. That month, she was also chosen to be featured on the cover of T.I.P. Magazine, an international business publication. In April of 2021, "On The Right Path" because the #1 New Release on Amazon in its genre. In June of 2021, Stacy was featured on the famous Reuters Building in Times Square as Empowered Woman of the Year.

Background: Stacy grew up in Pembroke, Massachusetts and graduated from Silver Lake Regional High School. She was a Presidential Scholar and on the Dean's List at Wentworth, where she studied Architectural Engineering and Interior Design. After graduation, she worked at an architecture firm in Boston from 2006-2008. Although she enjoyed her work, she felt something was missing-she wanted to spend more time helping people grow academically, personally, and spiritually. For close to a year, she split her time between tutoring, writing, and working at a design firm in Plymouth. When she fell in love with tutoring, she left the A&D industry completely and took a full-time position with a private education company in Dover, Massachusetts. She attained tutoring certification in 2009 through The International Tutor Association. Her career took off, and within one year, she was promoted to Director. Stacy knew she had found her niche! During her eight years with that company, she received multiple promotions and held a variety of titles, including Manager of Curriculum & Instruction and Director of Operations. In 2016, Stacy founded South Shore College Consulting & Tutoring. Then in 2019, she founded

Briley & Baxter Publications—a publishing company that uses part of its monthly proceeds to support animal rescues. Stacy is currently enrolled in the University of Pennsylvania Wharton School's online Entrepreneurship Specialization to pursue her passion for business. In her spare time, she enjoys skiing, taking online classes, following the stock market, attending Bruins games, playing fantasy sports, reading about psychology, hosting Bible studies, taking her dogs to the beach, and spending time with her family, husband Tim, and friends.

CONNECT WITH US!

Stacy's Instagram @author_stacypadula
Stacy's Twitter @MLHBookSeries
Cathy's Instagram @ckagelli99
Chantal's Instagram @chantal_kagelli
Jason's Instagram @jds_on
Lisa's Instagram @lisa_ankerman99
Chris's Instagram @dunkin_85
Luke's Instagram @lukedavids97
Alyssa's Instagram @alyssa_kelly02
www.stacyapadula.com
www.brileybaxterbooks.com
www.highambition.org

Did You Enjoy Gripped Part 4?

If you loved this book, would you please leave a review on Amazon?

www.ingramcontent.com/pod-product-compliance
Lightning Source LLC
Chambersburg PA
CBHW030356310726
48979CB00001B/324

* 9 7 8 1 7 3 5 0 1 6 8 2 5 *